Green Fields #12

ANNIHILATION

Adrienne Lecter

Annihilation

Green Fields #12

ISBN: 9781707598595

Editing by Marti Lynch
Interior design & cover by Adrienne Lecter

www.adriennelecter.com

Give feedback on the book at:
adrienne@adriennelecter.com

Twitter: @AdrienneLecter

First Edition November 2019
Second Print Edition November 2021
Produced and published by Barbara Klein, Vienna, Austria

To M

for being along on this craziest of crazy rides.

Chapter 1

The cars were still waiting for us where we'd left them days ago. A few shamblers had taken an interest in them but mostly to find a place to hide from the sun mercilessly beating down on all of us. I remained in the car, my fingers tight around the M4 I'd scavenged from one of the guards in the underground lab below Dallas as I watched Nate and the few others who were more or less uninjured clean up the squatters. My mind was singing with the need for violence, but I was in too much pain to risk it. Nate wasn't exactly unscathed himself, but at least it had been a full day since he'd last bled through the thick bandages covering half of his torso. I was, at best, two more days away from that.

I'd managed to stay behind the wheel of our car for the first two hours of our journey out of Dallas, doing my very best to concentrate on the lights of the vehicle ahead of me and not crash into the obstacles around the abandoned train tracks we were following. We had to stop then, both to give the drivers some rest to be able to stay focused, and to take care of the injured. It had only taken a single sharp look from Nate for me to lumber over to the passenger side instead, teeth clenched against the whimpers and groans trying to escape my compressed lips. Nobody needed to tell me it would have been best to wait another day to give my body enough time to heal, but there wasn't a single one of us who didn't constantly hear the ticking clock breathing down our necks, so we'd left as soon as possible. My injuries were the most acute, and since I managed to remain on my feet—or sitting on my ass—we left.

When we'd entered the abandoned train tunnels, we'd done so through a heavy iron sliding door. It didn't come as a surprise that our exit was barred in a similar way, although the door was a gate large enough to allow the vehicles to pass through—which made sense since the route had been used repeatedly before. Burns, Hill, and Cole had checked the door cautiously and also made sure there were no booby traps left for us on the other side. The same process had repeated itself twice more until the last section of the tunnel spilled us out into the much wider, debris-strewn drainage tunnel that eventually led us back to the surface—miles outside of the Dallas city limits. There were some zombies around but not enough to be alarming to us, and it had taken us less than an hour to backtrack to the highway and the cars we'd used to get to the city. I couldn't have been the only one who was angry at the fact that, had we known where to look, we wouldn't have lost a good portion of our people in the infested labyrinth of the city and could have pretty much strolled right up to the lab. That we likely would never have made it from the tunnel to the garage and on into the lab since it had all been set up like the perfect kill chute was of no consequence, but it made me wonder why they hadn't secured the other side of their complex better. Realistically speaking, they must have relied on us all biting it long before being able to knock on their front door. That still didn't make up for everyone we'd lost.

As much as I hated the car for where it had come from, it still had working AC, and I was reluctant to lose that small measure of comfort, electricity demands be damned. I fully expected Nate to chase me out of it and into one of ours, but after they'd made sure the site was as cleared as it would get, he came sauntering right back to me and got behind the wheel. I watched in silence as packs were redistributed and people switched places. With only a few more people than vehicles, we were presented with a peculiar problem of not having enough drivers for all the cars available since several— me included—couldn't be trusted to do more than, at best, keep a car on the road. Evasive driving was definitely out of the question.

We ended up only having to leave a single car: the beat-up heap of scrap metal that the scavengers had been using. Amos, himself forced to ride in the backseat because of his injuries, didn't seem heartbroken about leaving it behind. The loss of his three friends must have overridden that.

We didn't go far, just far enough away from the highway so as not to attract any attention, unwanted or otherwise. This time I followed Nate out of the car, to the vehicle he'd been driving on the way over that Burns had commandeered. Sonia was already waiting next to him, apparently glad for a quick respite from driving the largest of our new vehicles—our makeshift ambulance, carrying those that couldn't quite sit up yet.

Reaching in to grab the mic, Nate remained leaning against the passenger door, heavily favoring his bad side. It took Burns a good ten minutes to make contact, but once he had the right frequency, we heard the voice on the other side as clear as the radio would make it.

Nate was quick to go through the code phrases we'd agreed on, and then demanded to talk to whoever was in charge. It took a few more minutes—presumably for cars to stop and people to gather—until a different voice responded. I was surprised that it was Martinez, but probably shouldn't have been.

"Thank fuck you're still alive," he said rather emphatically. Under different circumstances I would have smirked, but I was too tired and drained.

Nate didn't comment on that and instead asked, "Romanoff and Zilinsky aren't with you?"

"No. They went ahead, trying to make it as fast as possible." Back to the California coast, as we'd agreed. Our destination was likely not a stretch of the imagination, but we didn't have to make it too simple for anyone who might be listening in. We'd ditched the radios from our three new cars back where we'd left the others, but we had no clue if that was enough, or if anyone had in the meantime bugged the cars left behind. After the most recent events, I wasn't going to bet my life on anything I couldn't be one hundred percent sure about. "We have a check-in coming up with them in a few hours from now. We'll relay the news that you made it."

Nate grimaced. "Get them on the line as soon as we're done coordinating. Tell them that we're on high alert and not to trust anyone they're not completely certain is on our side. We need to err on the side of extreme caution."

Stunned silence followed before Martinez acknowledged. "What happened?"

If it had been me, I would have gone for some wisecrack or other, but Nate left it at a simple, "I'll explain when we rendezvous with you. We're just outside of Dallas, roughly northeast. Tell us where you'll be relative to our position at what time." It took some coordinating, but a few minutes and hastily scrawled lines on maps later, we had two possible spots where the others could be waiting for us. I had no clue how, but I was certain that neither of our groups would get anywhere near those places, and Nate's finger rested on a part of the map that was a good fifty miles south of any town mentioned. I tried to commit it to memory but gave up when my eyes wouldn't focus. I was sure that someone else would do a better job acting as our pathfinder.

As soon as that was done, Nate killed the connection, not even bothering with saying goodbye—not that unusual, but it still rubbed me the wrong way. In short order, we scrambled back into our respective vehicles, but rather than form our usual column, the cars broke up into small clusters of two or three vehicles each, taking different turns wherever possible. Soon we were spread out like a very loose net over a good mile or two, even the clusters breaking up to leave several hundred yards' distance between the cars. It made sense—we'd send up way less dust this way, and even a well-aimed RPG wouldn't take out more than a single vehicle at a time. I didn't expect that to happen, but I was very much on board with going into paranoia mode. Literally getting knifed in the back will do that to the best of us, and it had been a long time since I'd been the exception to that.

I did my best to keep munching on our provisions as Nate drove, but between the heat, exhaustion, and pain, even my stomach was too upset to make it easy to fill myself up. Nate tried munching on what high-protein snacks I fed him, but even well-salted jerky came back up after the fifth piece, forcing him to stop so he could retch out the door. He hadn't exactly been able to take a snack pack on the road, although if he'd told me sooner about how he'd gone about acquiring his last meal, I would have badgered him into trying. I didn't quite understand why he couldn't hold down something as close to meat as the preserved variant—we'd seen enough chewed-up boxes everywhere that shamblers had gotten into, not bothering to do away with the packaging first. If they could smell something moderately edible, they ate it. My suspicion was that he needed fresh meat, the source less important than the lack of cooking or preservatives. Studying him from the side, I didn't like how sharp the lines of his jaw looked—not exactly gaunt but all extra subcutaneous fat used up. He was still stronger than Hamilton—a little more than a week of regular nutrition hadn't been enough for either of them to fatten up again, and Hamilton had months of a more severe starvation diet behind him than Nate—but I could have done without that worry on top of everything else. This close to Dallas, no way would we be able to find fresh game to hunt, but maybe I could try feeding him some kibble next. That had worked well enough last winter when our stocks had run dry—but that had been before those hellish nine weeks in the camp with its arena, questionable food sources, and assholes shooting him up with all kinds of chemicals. That we'd happened to find the lab where those had come from—and I was sure, if I'd paid more attention and had more time, I could have honed in on exactly what had screwed in what way with him after finding the documentation—didn't matter now. The main takeaway for me still was that nothing good would have come of anything there since they hadn't been working on the original serum project anymore, but instead had done their best to somehow subvert the effects of it. To what end was still anyone's guess. I didn't trust what Stone had told us in the hot lab, and since Walter Greene—illustrious senior scientist and asshole extraordinaire—had been dead on our arrival, there was no way to get answers.

It didn't really matter. We were all doomed to die, the serum's protection against the zombie virus that all of us had gotten infected with sooner or later too shoddy to hold out indefinitely.

In a sense, that was a relief, however horrifying. It cut my list of priorities down to two things only: One, to make sure we got to Decker and killed him before he could make things even worse for the few people who had managed to survive this far. And two, to make sure that when I inevitably turned into a mindless killing machine, it would happen somewhere that I couldn't come after any of my friends, or anyone else, preferably. In the days after getting up from my deathbed—the first time, after the factory—I had sometimes joked, to myself inside my head, that wouldn't it be tragically romantic if one final day Nate and I would have to kill each other with perfectly timed headshots to make sure the other couldn't turn into our worst, shared nightmare? That scenario had lost all sarcastic appeal now since it was way too close to home. Before Marleen had pulled a number on me, I'd have said it was much more likely that I'd have to shoot Nate first, but the injuries must have set me back some. Since we had no way of knowing—or even guessing—it was just as well. Decker first. After that, I wasn't required to have much of a care for pretty much anything, and I could appreciate the simplicity of that.

Pain and exhaustion were a great way to keep the latent panic at bay.

Our rendezvous was planned for tomorrow, but when we didn't stop for longer than absolutely necessary to keep from killing ourselves on the road, I figured that had been a ruse as well. Driving spread out like this, it was hard to tell, but everyone seemed to be keeping up for now. We only had to wait once when one of the older vehicles blew a tire, but that was only a twenty-minute hitch in the plan. After the insane mobs of zombies in the city, seeing a few shamblers pop out of ditches didn't do much more than get my pulse up slightly.

On and on we went, the day stretching endlessly. Doing nothing but staring out at the passing landscape shouldn't have been enough to wear me down, but it did. I could tell that I wasn't fooling anybody by pretending I was doing okay, catching Nate's cautious glances every once in a while. There wasn't much I could do about that except to keep hanging on, so that's what I did. It left me too much time to mull over Marleen's betrayal and the bad aftertaste it had left. I couldn't quite believe that Richards had been in on it, even though Nate seemed more than ready to. Sure, that Marleen had waited until now to spring her trap was suspicious, but Richards had had so many better chances to kill me or make sure I'd never become a bother for anyone ever again. Without him, I'd never have made it to California to mobilize the others, and he could have easily made me disappear when we'd infiltrated the camp and blamed it on Cortez and his men. That would have sent Nate over the edge just the same as thinking Hamilton had killed me. Speaking of Cortez, it made no sense that Richards, full to the gills with drugs, had managed to hold up the pretense. Marleen had seldom been anywhere alone with me and never with my life depending on her, and she'd also been conveniently ready to help us escape from the prison cell. Why she hadn't killed Nate and me right there, I didn't understand, but considering how long she must have been working as a mole, it was hard to gauge any part of her behavior. I was tempted to ask Nate what annoyed him more— that she'd managed to make him trust her, or fuck her—but refrained. It may have been amusing for a moment to drag a growl out of him, but probably not worth the reminder in the long run.

Afternoon turned to evening, and still we were going on. The batteries of all cars should have been fully charged when we set out, and we could always take a longer break once we met up with the others. I didn't think that likely to happen, but the idea of it made it just a little easier to get through the next five minutes, and the five after that. The sun disappeared in the distance, and Nate called for the other cars to close in once more, making staying on the roads easier for those who weren't gifted with supernatural low-light vision. I'd always considered that as kind of a fair trade, a nice bonus to keep in turn for almost dying and getting infected with the virus. That had continued to lose its appeal as I'd come to accept what the infection was doing to my body, but I'd tried to hold on to it even when I'd lost most of my toes and more fingers than I could afford. Realizing that ultimately the virus would kill me and make me convert should have been just an afterthought, but it made it all the harder to see the benefits. Watching the landscape spread out in front of me lose the last orange tints and actually become sharper, cast in blacks and grays, made me downright miserable.

It also made me see the light of a single flashlight a good two miles ahead minutes before that should have been possible, my brain drawn toward it like a moth to the flame. Nate gave the order to course-correct for those who hadn't caught it yet, and at the next intersection where little more than a trail ran off into the hills, we all turned from the small road we'd been following. The two Humvees went first, their extra plating giving them a better chance to make it should this turn out to be yet another trap.

It wasn't, which was just as well as I wasn't convinced we could have defended ourselves against well-rested, uninjured, organized people. As it was, I recognized a few marines and people from California before we eased the cars to a stop right where Santos was switching off the flashlight he'd been waving as soon as the last car came to a halt. Through the trees, I could see that they had set up a small camp around two fires, those kept well shielded from the plains and only visible because we were in shouting distance of the people milling around them.

Pushing the car door open, I sighed when the cool evening air hit my face. AC or no AC, the interior of the car stank of bleach, sweat, and a multitude of organic scents that I didn't want to further analyze. Nate was already up and moving, asking for a status update now that we had caught up with our people—or at least some of them, as it turned out. What I saw were the volunteers from five cars that had veered off the track the much larger caravan was taking to come meet us. Already they were swarming toward our cars to redistribute gear and resources, making sure that if we had to abandon the site quickly, the cars would be ready for it.

I waited for the world to stop spinning before I trusted my legs and took a step forward, but that was enough for the constant pain in my lower right torso to flame up into blinding agony, hours of stiffness from moving too little not helping. I managed to drag myself around the car door and leaned against the side of the hood, fighting for breath more than trying not to whimper—that fight I'd already lost. My guess was that I'd bled through the bandages, which had turned them and my clothes into one congealed mess, and twisting my torso now had torn all that free. From the direction of the fires, I could just make out the worry etched onto Martinez's features as he came trotting over to us, two bags with what I presumed were medical supplies slung over his shoulders. He needn't have bothered—we'd taken everything we could find from the lab, and although it had been raided before and never gotten restocked, that was a lot more than we'd had on the road since just after hitting Sioux Falls what felt like a million years ago. I gave him my best reassuring grin as I partially hunched over, trying to ease up the stress on all injured parts. Cut muscles and ligaments weren't anything I'd wish on my worst enemy—

Who just so happened to come heaving himself out of another car, way too close for comfort. Then again, Hamilton could have been standing three states away from me and it would still have been too close. He watched me with a grim look of satisfaction on his face, which I decided was worse than his usual condescending sneer. That made an appearance a few moments later when he saw Martinez come to a halt between us, his expression etched with worry. "What the fuck happened?" Martinez asked as he dropped the bags, already snapping on gloves. He knew better than to get close to either of us without that flimsy latex layer of protection.

Grimacing, I got ready to offer up my new favorite sentence, but Hamilton beat me to it. "Nothing much," he jeered. "She's just annoyed that I got to plug one of her holes that she probably didn't want to get plugged by me."

Martinez gave him a "what the fuck is wrong with you" look before stepping up to me.

I couldn't very well let that go, so I straightened, hand uselessly pressed against the thickest wad of the bandage as I sneered at Hamilton. "I swear I will make sure that you survive this entire fucking mess so I can then bash your head in with a boulder!"

As expected, Hamilton was less than impressed by my threat, grinning brightly. "I thought you wanted to castrate me. Toned down your list of what you think you can accomplish, eh?"

I glared right back. "Don't worry. I have an entire laundry list of things I will do to you, and if it's the last thing I do—"

"Enough!" Both Hamilton and I jumped at Nate's roar that was loud enough to make the many critters hidden in the grass and trees around us pause for a moment. We both drew up short as he came stalking around one of the cars to join us, his eyes narrowed in anger. "You"—he pointed at me—"get fixed up. I've been smelling the blood leaking out of your wound for the past two hours so it won't do to just slap on a new bandage. And you"—he rounded on Hamilton—"come with me." Neither of us protested, and the two of them were gone within moments, like two shadows gliding into the night. I stared after them, silently gnashing my teeth, before I turned to Martinez. His worry had shot up a notch at Nate's words but irritation was still lurking in his eyes, making me guess that his tolerance for Hamilton's bullshit was all used up. For mine possibly as well, I reminded myself. I hadn't forgotten Sonia's talk, and finding myself face to face with one of the people she'd specifically mentioned didn't make it easier to ignore her accusations.

"Let's put it this way," I said, trying my hand at levity—and finally getting to that precious line. "As it turns out, my new friend Marleen wasn't my friend after all. She knifed me in the back, thinking she'd kill me if she hit my remaining kidney, and set things up to make Nate think Hamilton did it. Turns out I'm a tougher nut to crack."

Martinez was still staring at me, a different kind of horrified now, but dutifully reached over to help me peel myself out of my layers. I wasn't yet down to my tank top when Burns joined us, giving Martinez a bump with his shoulder in greeting. Sonia was nowhere to be found, so I figured she must have been helping Blake out of the car to be reunited with his people. "Yeah, that was quite something," Burns chimed in, apparently having heard the beginning of our conversation. "You really missed out on a shitload of fun!"

Martinez grimaced as if he was taking Burns seriously, but his concentration was on peeling away the bandages that, just as I'd expected, were sticking to my skin and the fabric of my clothes alike, or had been. "Tell me all about it," he muttered as he started wiping away blood with the part of the bandages that was just grimy with a day of sweat to get a better look at the damage. "You pulled a few stitches, and there's likely a little pus underneath that's draining out now with the lymph, but could be worse." He briefly paused to look at my face where I was trying to crane my neck to see, which was, of course, impossible. "Sonia sewed you up?" I nodded. "She did a good job, but looks like you got up to move too soon."

"Tell me about it," I echoed his words, if not the sentiment. When he eyed me askance, I explained. "Nobody saw Marleen's betrayal coming. Apparently, she's been Decker's mole for fucking forever. If she managed to embed herself like that in Nate's trust, it stands to reason that she's not the only one. We need to make sure to close ranks and get our weakest links to safety." Meaning Sadie and her kid, but also other dependents who might not be able to go toe-to-toe with a psychotic assassin or the likes.

All Martinez had for me was a cut-off grunt before he got out some fresh gauze and alcohol, and set to work. While all I could do to keep from screaming at the top of my lungs was to clench my hands into fists and lean against the car, Burns quite conversationally brought Martinez up to speed, making sure to stress between the lines just how impossible survival would have been for our medic with his healed but not fully repaired spine injury. Martinez kept offering the token protest but when I caught a look at his face, I could see relief there.

Damn, but it was good to see him again.

It was late enough in the evening that all anyone wanted to do was to eat and sleep. Since most of us hadn't had a chance for any breaks during the day, the caravan group got guard duty. Hearing our recounts from Dallas, they seemed more than happy with their lot. I spent most of the time chewing meditatively while listening to the others talk, which got me more than the odd concerned look from Martinez, but after sewing me back up he could likely guess why I wasn't quite up to chatting. Nate spent the entire time on the radio or sifting through maps, plotting and asking for updates. I was aware that I should have been more engaged in that myself, but tonight I simply wasn't up to it. As soon as Blake stretched and asked one of his people to help him up so he could limp back to the cars to catch some sleep, I got up and excused myself for the night. Thanks to the others coming at full strength, we were once more too many people for everyone to sleep in the cars, but since nobody had evicted me from our commandeered vehicle, I stretched out in the back, molding myself against packs and provisions. The pain kept me wide awake and uncomfortable for the first ten minutes, but eventually, that dulled to manageable levels, letting me doze off…

Until, maybe half an hour later when the back door on the passenger side opened, admitting Nate. He was moving slowly so as not to wake me, halting briefly when he saw me turn my head to look up at him. We stared at each other for a few seconds before he climbed in and pulled the door shut behind him, nudging stuff away until he could stretch out next to me. Part of me wanted to just close my eyes and sleep, but there was no telling when we'd get the next chance to have an uninterrupted night together in a safe place. I wasn't exactly feeling up to working my way through five positions of the Kama Sutra, but deep down, underneath the pain and exhaustion and dread of what was waiting to come for us next, churned that unbridled joy of survival and the need to—physically and mentally—flip the apocalypse off. Too bad, fuckers—today is another day you didn't get me.

Some of that must have been mirrored in my expression, drawing a wry smile from Nate. "Some things never change, huh?" he whispered as he leaned closer, but rather than follow up words with actions, all he did was stroke my cheek in a strangely tender way. Why that made me uncomfortable, I didn't want to analyze, but he stopped with a snort when I turned my face into his palm—and bit into the fleshy part below his thumb, not hard enough to draw blood, but there were fading marks left when I moved back. He flashed me a grin at the challenge in my gaze, and—moving faster than his own injuries and the space available in the car should have made possible—the next moment he was perched above me, his grip on my arms gentle yet his weight pinning me down. There was clear intent in the way he kissed me as he pushed my thighs apart with his body, and I was only too happy to wrap my legs around his hips— until I arched my back and twisted slightly, which sent bright agony through my body, making me gasp in a quite different way than Nate had intended. He froze immediately and let up, his eyes narrowed in concern.

I did my best to smile, but it must have been closer to a grimace. "Yeah, not sure that's working for me right now."

He smirked, ever the asshole—but I didn't miss him absently pushing a hand against his own wound as he moved off me. "That makes two of us," he confessed, chuckling under his breath.

I rolled my eyes at him—both of us, really—and waited until he stopped wincing. Critically eyeing what most comfortable positions we'd both assumed, I couldn't help but laugh. "Not sure that'll work. Side by side?" I suggested.

He considered but then shook his head. "My hip's too stiff right now. I don't think I can get enough motion going."

Pursing my lips, I grinned. "Do we really need a technical manual now to get it on?"

"The side effects of old age," he suggested, smiling himself.

"You'd think that not getting shot and stabbed might help, too," I grumbled back.

Someone else might have shown pity for my plight now. Nate's smirk didn't bode well, so mostly to shut him up, I pushed myself up and climbed over him. My back protested, but once he scrambled up into a sitting position, his hands conveniently cupped around my ass cheeks to push me against him, it wasn't so bad. As long as

I didn't twist my torso, that would work—and contrary to his hip issue, mine were doing just great. A few seconds of experimental dry humping had him nod his affirmation, which made me chuckle in turn—until the unmistakable sounds of someone overstraining a car's suspension, overshadowed by a woman's very enthusiastic utterance that she didn't give a shit about the vehicular damage, cut through the night. My face almost hurt from my resulting grin, Nate mirroring it if with a somewhat critical frown on his forehead. Others didn't seem to take it with the same amount of amusement, though, as about ten seconds after the moan had cut off with a fit of giggles, Martinez called across the clearing—a little too loud for the middle of nowhere with who knew what lurking out there, but very understandably, "I just put you two back together! Can you at least let others sleep even if you absolutely need to tear your stitches—again!"

Nate and I shared another amused look before I leaned toward the door—careful not to twist—so I could open it a crack and shout back. "Sorry to disappoint you, chico, but we haven't quite made it there yet. I'll make sure not to leave you with more work this once. Promise!"

Someone else laughed, and I could hear a few more chuffs and chuckles coming from all around. After a pregnant pause, Martinez answered, his voice pitched lower now. "Sorry, my bad." More amusement followed, particularly when he added, "Please resume."

Rather than deign to answer, I pulled the door shut again, the sound itself raising another round of what now sounded tantalizingly close to cheers. Nate was grinning at me, and before he could say something to ruin the mood—and the wonderful, bright feeling of levity that flared in my chest—I silenced him with my lips and tongue, and soon hands and other parts. There was some grunting and wincing involved on both sides that didn't exactly belong to these activities, but it wasn't the first time that we somehow had to make it work outside of perfect conditions. I couldn't deny that once my heart rate was up enough to shut my brain up, there was also desperation twisting into the mix, fueled both from the sheer joy of survival, and also fear that the very thing we were celebrating—being alive—was a resource that was dwindling too fast. And it wasn't just me—I could tell from the way Nate tensed underneath me, how his hands turned from teasing and supporting to holding on to me for dear life—

I hadn't expected to come—circumstances aside, my body was trashed and every single motion brought spikes of pain zinging away from the stab wound—but my mind clearly had other priorities than comfort and being reasonable, allowing me a few seconds of losing myself in the endorphin rush that, for once, didn't have anything to do with fighting for my life. Not exactly having been passive before, Nate took over, letting me ride out the waves of my pleasure as he succumbed to his own. We stopped moving, joined together not just physically. He stared at me, wide-eyed, just as I must have been staring at him, breathing heavily. His hands let go of my ass—carefully skipping the middle of my back—and stroked up my arms before he wrapped them around my head and pulled me down into a tender kiss. I felt a twinge in my heart, but for once it wasn't guilt or misery but something soft and positive, something I felt I needed to close my own hands around to protect and keep alive for as long as possible. We stayed like that for several minutes when, usually, that was my cue to scramble away and clean up. It felt good to just be there, with him, stealing seconds that turned into minutes that, for whatever reason, we'd always felt we didn't have.

And then the moment was over, my back complaining about the same time Nate winced, muttering something about a cramp in his thigh as I pushed off him. I plunked down on my ass, momentarily not quite sure what to do with myself. In true Nate fashion, he had to make the moment perfect—or perfectly destroy it—as he scrutinized me, still rubbing his hip. "Do you need to lie down with your legs raised, or some shit like that?"

Irritation zipped up my spine, even though it made me realize I'd ended up sitting there weirdly with my pelvis tilted up and forward, as if to prevent… leakage. I couldn't help but snort, even as I reached for what was left of my discarded shirt, using the side that wasn't caked with blood and other fluids to wipe myself clean before dumping it in a trash bag—that was already half full of other blood-soiled clothes ready to be burned. "What, don't trust your swimmers to go in the right direction? Maybe you should have drawn up a map for them, too."

Nate looked vexed—probably because I hadn't handed him the shirt to use before dumping it, as usual—but set to dressing himself, leaving my barb uncommented on. I followed suit, but couldn't shake off that pervasive feeling of something I couldn't make sense of clinging to me.

"Is this weird?" I mused. "Why is this weird? I don't want this to be weird."

Nate paused, giving me a—well, weird—long look before he moved over, reaching for my shoulder to make me halt. "Nothing's weird," he assured me. A rueful smile replaced the slight frown on his expression. "Neither of us is dying just yet. Stop overthinking this. It is what it is—nothing more, nothing less."

I wished it was that easy. Throughout the day, I'd had light cramps and spotting after Sonia had removed the IUD, and even now there'd been some smears on the tank top. "I don't even know if I can get pregnant," I muttered, more to myself than Nate. "And I don't know if I even want to, with everything that's going on. I hate that it's suddenly something I can't ignore anymore, like a cancer growing in my brain—always there, impossible to ignore."

Nate's mouth took on an amusing twist as he leaned back, looking at me as if I were some peculiar specimen. "If your reason to make it through this alive is so you can kill Hamilton in more ways than even you can imagine, mine is so I can tell the world that you equated our possible future child to cancer."

I stared at him, hard-pressed to keep scowling rather than break out in laughter. "You're such an asshole."

He flashed me a bright grin. "And your verbal diarrhea has reached peak performance."

"Yeah? If you keep going like that, you won't have anything to tell anyone because the only action you'll be getting is your right hand."

With the way he grinned back at me, I was waiting for him to correct me that since he was left-dominant, I'd chosen the wrong limb, but instead he leaned closer, kissing me—under quickly dwindling protest from yours truly. "Considering that for fucking forever I wasn't sure I'd ever hear those outbursts again, you won't get any protest from me," he whispered against my lips, then kept me from responding for a while longer. Which was a good thing, because how exactly was I supposed to respond to that? The need to touch him—to physically make sure that he was really here, and here to stay—got overwhelming, and with no reason whatsoever not to follow up on it, I did. Nate's arms came around me, still careful not to hurt me where possible, taking me down with him as he stretched out on his back. There were a million things I could have said, but my mind was quiet for once, and it took me a while to realize why: I was content. Not happy; not without fear or dread. But right here, right now, I had everything I needed—and that was enough. And I didn't care whether it was the exhaustion, or latent trauma from our mission to Dallas, or acceptance of our limited future, or plain old post-orgasmic bliss—the need to rail against my fate was gone. Oh, I was sure that it would rear its ugly head soon enough, likely as soon as I saw Hamilton lurking around somewhere, my constant reminder of all the things that were wrong with my world. But for one night only, it felt good to just let go and simply exist. In the end, there was nothing I could do against the mountain of misgivings and grievances that I kept dragging around with me, and having a moment to just be together and not give a shit was a luxury to be cherished.

I had the distinct feeling that it would be a close to singular circumstance to get to enjoy it.

Chapter 2

I woke up when Nate did his best to extricate himself from me without jostling me awake. I got a pained grimace for his failure—and whatever his hip was getting up to—and a peck on the nose before he slid out the door, leaving me feeling bewildered and quite drowsy. I hadn't expected to get much rest but had actually slept well for a few hours, even with the occasional painful wake-up call when I moved in my sleep. I tried to doze off again but my bladder was full and my torso and old scars needed some movement before I inflicted another day of sitting on my body, so I forced myself to get up as well.

It was early still, maybe thirty minutes to sunrise, the quiet of the morning settling like a comfortable blanket around my shoulders. Coffee was already brewing and the omnipresent rice and beans was cooking over a low fire, thanks to the last guard shift having gotten hungry—or bored. Someone had dumped canned soup from our laboratory raid in there as well, adding flavor that I was kind of glad I couldn't taste. Nate was nowhere to be seen so I got some coffee, and after staring off into the quiet Texas landscape for a bit, I joined Amos and two scavengers I didn't know by the fire. He hadn't mentioned Eden since we found her—also killed by Marleen—or the other two of his people who hadn't survived. The three of them were chatting quietly about some mall raiding they had done before joining the assault on the camp. I got a few curious glances from the two men, but since Amos had greeted me with a nod, I was apparently to be treated as one of their own. The marines on the other side of the fire were also quite chatty for the early hour but kept eyeing us as if they couldn't quite believe nobody was coming for them. I still hadn't found out whether it was all prejudice, or caution based on a rough three years of bad experiences.

Maybe it was about time that I changed that.

"Amos, can I ask you a question?" I interjected when the other two shut up for a moment.

The tall scavenger smirked. "I think you just did."

I playfully scowled at him as I took a sip of coffee. "I feel like I'm still missing some details about what happened while we were gone. I have three different versions—why not add another? Why did the scavengers blow up the docks of New Angeles?"

The other conversations didn't exactly screech to a halt, but I could tell that I wasn't the only one curious for his reply. Santos and Martinez meanwhile joined us, sitting down on my other side—not exactly apart from the scavengers, but with me as a convenient go-between.

Amos watched them, still amused, before he focused on me. "What if I told you that we didn't?"

One of the marines spat into the dirt in front of the log he was sitting on, but Amos ignored him. Martinez and Santos were both quiet as they tried to decide whether the food was edible—nothing out of the ordinary, but very inconspicuous at the same time. The other two scavengers held their tongues, but they looked defiant—a reaction I'd seen from a lot of them recently, when they weren't loud, boastful, and probably playing up the effects of whatever drugs they liked to consume recreationally.

"Everyone else says different," I pointed out, but tried not to make it an accusation.

Amos grinned, but it was on the nasty side. "And everyone's calling you a vengeful cunt."

I shrugged. "They might not be wrong about that," I pointed out, not really feeling guilty about it.

"True," Amos admitted, still grinning. "But it completely ignores context, and the fact that people are lining up to give you plenty of reasons to come after them."

He wasn't wrong there. "So what motive did you have for blowing up the docks?"

For whatever reason, he hesitated, giving one of the marines the opportunity to inject himself into our conversation. "Because they're a bunch of violent assholes who think the rest of us owes them shit."

Amos definitely had some "here we go again" going on in his expression, and for once, it was easy for me to agree with him. "You did ostracize us," I pointed out. "We were convenient for all the settlements that didn't dare leave their cozy little barricades, and even the Silo was happy to send us out on little fetch quests that ended up killing scores of us—even without the involvement of other parties. You went as far as not just telling us to our faces that we were dispensable, you wrote it right into your statutes how long we were allowed to stay. How anyone expected that not to bite everyone in the ass is beyond me."

The marine looked ready to swear up a storm, but Blake limping over to us and, sitting down between his people and Amos—and exchanging a quick nod in greeting with the scavenger—put a swift end to it. I couldn't help but smirk, and didn't miss how in tune with the scavengers that put me. Martinez and Santos were still pretending to be neutral, but I was sure that they, too, were remembering how our mission at the factory had ended—and the Silo had been passingly involved in getting us headed there.

Damn, but sometimes it was really hard not to be paranoid about every single little thing that had happened.

"So what did happen with the docks?" I asked Amos while everyone was watching Blake turn into the next one to be suspicious of breakfast. "All personal animosity aside, New Angeles always treated us fairly, and they were actively helping with establishing more towns where we could bug down—for the winter or much longer. Why bite the hand that literally fed us?"

I fully expected Amos to slap me in the face with new information I'd missed so far—like that Greene had changed the terms of the deal and I was, again, being too naive. Instead, he pursed his lips, as if he were trying to decide how much to tell me, present company considered.

"What if I told you that it was all an accident?" he finally offered, not without a sidelong glance at the marines—whose disbelief was out in full force. Even Blake scowled, and neither Santos nor Martinez looked happy—but they weren't protesting.

I couldn't exactly keep my own bewilderment out of my voice. "So you accidentally found yourself with enough explosives right there, and then someone lit a cigarette, and, oops?"

Amos nodded, as if he was agreeing with me on how ridiculous that sounded. "Of course not. Our people had spent a good month dragging sacks of fertilizer from abandoned farms and factories across the country to load three ships, and Greene had sent half of the scientists he had in the city there to make sure that nothing could go wrong. I was with one of the parties involved in the gathering, but we remained behind because there wasn't enough room for all of our vehicles, and we figured we might better keep looking and catch a head start for ship number four. That's why Eden and I got away—we weren't there. Of course, no one directly involved survived, so it's hard to guess at what actually went down."

"That's a load of bullshit," said a gruff voice behind us—Hill, it turned out, with Cole on his heels. The two of them looked a little lost with none of their buddies a part of the group, but at Martinez's gesturing ended up sitting down next to him and Santos.

The younger scavenger next to Amos snorted. "Sure. The army would say that."

Hill gave him a condescending look that I was all too familiar with, but his answer was surprisingly sensible. "No. I'm saying that as someone who has a clue about explosives. You can ask Miller or Burns, too, if you trust them more. Fertilizer on its own is incredibly explosive, and three ships of that shit is more than enough to blow up the docks and maybe even some buildings close by. Nobody who's ever had anything to do with agriculture would be stupid enough to allow those ships to dock at the same time."

I wasn't the only one frowning at that statement, but when I turned to Amos, I realized he was still riding the usual animosity train. I wasn't just trying to distract him when I asked, "What scientists?" When he glanced from Hill to me, I clarified. "You said New Angeles scientists. Last time I dropped in there before we left the stage for the rest of you, there were no scientists in New Angeles, or none who declared themselves as such. I'm sure that they had their share of survivors with PhDs and other titles, but no science division I was aware of."

At first, Amos seemed irritated by my question, but unlike with someone else posing it, he gave me the benefit of the doubt. "That was two years ago," he reminded me. "And I'd never been to the city before. Neither had Eden, or our leader. We got the call to go fetch, so we went to fetch. At the ships, the people in charge sure behaved like scientists. Very uppity, wouldn't answer questions, just told us what to do—you know the drill."

Silence fell, mostly because I didn't respond and, suddenly everyone seemed to be hanging on my lips. I couldn't help but feel unease creeping up my spine. I wondered who else to ask about this, but both Blake and my people just gave me blank stares. Pia or Sadie might have known better since I was sure they had quickly established strong ties to Greene, or whoever handled the day-to-day shit in New Angeles. And none of them seemed to think that what Amos had just shared was out of the ordinary, except that he was obviously lying and downplaying the scavengers' role in this…

I really didn't like the conclusions my mind was jumping to, but part of me absolutely hoped that I was seeing nails everywhere because my only tool was a hammer.

"Has anyone seen my husband?" I asked. "Or his asshole lapdog?"

Hill frowned at my question—or, more likely, at that last part—while Cole smirked, but both shook their heads. Some muttering went on between the others until one of the marines got up and went into the trees, only to return with Nate and Hamilton in tow a few moments later. I would have much rather not talked to him directly, but since Nate was even more unlikely than me to know, Hamilton was my best option.

"Hey, dipshit," I addressed him, earning myself a glare back. "Winter when we left for France—how many people were in the New Angeles science division? Don't even deny that you have moles there. I was standing next to Richards when he pulled a few of them out just weeks ago."

Hamilton wasted a few seconds thinking—that felt like hours to me. I was surprised when he didn't even use the occasion to bad-mouth me. "They don't have a science division. At least then they didn't have one, and that didn't change until command sent me to the camp. You'd have to ask your buddy Greene, but I think they sent all shit they wanted analyzed up to the Silo."

Amos gave a twitch but didn't speak up. Nate noticed me glance at the scavenger leader, his brow furrowed when he looked back to me. "Just a thought," I mused, mostly speaking to him. "Is it completely paranoid of me to say that either Decker got his moles into the New Angeles supply line, or otherwise orchestrated it so that the scavengers were to blame for blowing up three ships full of fertilizer that arrived at the New Angeles docks?"

Nate's frown deepened. "Who'd be stupid enough to send even one ship, let alone three of them at the same time? You don't have to be a conspiracy nut to know that fertilizer has a penchant for horrific explosions. History is full of accidents and home-grown terrorists getting ambitious."

My first impulse was to ask if he'd just made the worst pun ever—home-grown... fertilizer—but that he pretty much echoed Hill's statement firmed my conviction.

"Amos said they got told to bring the fertilizer to the ships. By scientists, behaving very scientist-y." Hamilton smirked, ready to unleash a volley in my direction, I was sure, but I talked right over him. "What if someone else set this up? It couldn't have been hard to get the scavengers to do something after a long, hard winter where half of them starved. And I saw myself that, even now, it wouldn't take too many people to kill the guards on one of those supply ships. Everyone on the ships and at the docks died that day, so there are no witnesses, except for people like Amos who are, at best, being blamed for this, and likely never spoke up because they knew squat. Is this something Decker would do, to further heat up the conflicts that were already coming to a boil the summer before that? Because that sounds like a much better explanation to me than the scavengers suddenly turning into a faction of well-organized terrorists when I could barely get enough of them organized for a single raid on a base, and that was before we fractured into small groups with a million different purposes."

Nobody answered at first. The marines took their cues from Blake, who did his best to remain neutral. My guys equally so, although Martinez looked like he was going to be sick. Cole had his poker face on but Hill was nodding slowly, as if what I'd just said went well with his statement about the fertilizer. Surprisingly, it wasn't Nate but Hamilton who spoke up.

"I'm not saying it makes sense, but if someone asked me how I would have retaliated for having to swallow a god-awful truce forced on me, I would have looked for a way to utterly discredit my antagonists first, and make their own support turn on them. Killing hundreds, damaging their supply lines, annihilating their trust and willingness to continue cooperating with them—sounds like a jackpot to me." He paused before adding, "And I probably shouldn't admit to this, but since we're already best buds, who cares? Two of my people died that day, and I doubt they would have been anywhere near the docks had they known this was going to happen. They were both good plants since they'd been part of your rabble when you attacked the base in Colorado, but saw reason during the winter when half of their group starved to death because they were too proud to come to us and accept help. I know nobody suspected them because their families—also working with us—remained and kept reporting in when the coast was clear once more. Since their so-called leaders claimed responsibility for it, we never thought to investigate. Even Greene kicked them out for a year and massively increased security after that." His smirk let me know that my actions the year before that had paved the way for that kind of thinking. As much as I hated to admit it, he wasn't wrong there.

One of the marines finally broke his silence, ignoring Blake's stoic take on things. "This makes no fucking sense! You said everyone on those ships died? That must have included those scientists, fake or not. Who'd be insane enough to do that?"

This I had an answer for. "Days ago, we busted down the doors to the lab where the last of the serum project scientists were holed up. They committed communal suicide so we couldn't beat the answers out of them. Any answers, really. I'd say that's exactly the same kind of person who'd willingly turn themselves into a suicide bomber."

The guy just kept staring at me, blinking furiously. "No shit?"

"No shit," I insisted.

"Those were the people you were working with, right?" he went on asking.

If he'd slapped me in the face, it would have stung less. "Never," I growled, more emphatically than I'd intended.

The guy looked from me to Nate, then back again, but before he could choke on the metaphorical foot he'd rammed down his own throat, Blake cut in. "It's true what she says about the scientists at the lab. I've never thought about what happened at the docks like this, but after the shit that went down in Dallas, I'm not categorically discounting it, either." His eyes briefly flitted over to Amos, and I couldn't help but feel like he and the scavenger had formed at least an easy bond of friendship, if not actual trust. "Even a week ago, I would have said you're all drugged-up, trigger-happy assholes. Not saying you're not, but what I've seen from you and your people was a lot closer to how Miller and Lewis run their gang than the wild tales that have been circulating. Could you have destroyed the docks? Yes, but theoretically, so could a team of my people, or the army's. And Hamilton's not wrong—when we heard the declaration that this was an act of retaliation, nobody thought twice about it. A lot of us felt like we hadn't treated the scavengers right that first year, but that alleviated our guilt as it confirmed the worst of the prejudice any of us were harboring—ignoring that a lot of our own people had been part of their ranks." The way he shot me a sidelong glance made me guess that the three guys we'd left at the Silo—my Idiot Brigade, as I'd not-so-lovingly called them—had long since been uncovered as what they were, and the fact that they'd come with Blake and Buehler made it easy to believe that they had found some new allegiance.

Amos let out a harsh peal of laughter, only shutting up when he realized that we were all staring at him. "I wish Eden was still around to see this," he muttered before he sobered up. "How would we have profited from turning New Angeles against us? They were the only ones who always had an open door for us. They were also our best takers for pretty much any shit we dragged out of houses and stores. Why else do you think we even went searching across three states to get enough fertilizer to their ships? We trusted them, and they trusted us. Until the docks blew up, that is."

This kept getting weirder and weirder. "Why did none of you speak up?"

More laughter answered me, even harsher now. "Do you think anyone would have listened?"

The other two scavengers agreed, the so-far silent one adding, "Besides, it wasn't like we've ever been a united front except for when we followed your call. We didn't know for sure that it wasn't us, you know? Harris is one of our most successful leaders, and he has maybe two hundred people who are willing to listen to him, if not follow him into war. Just because we hadn't done it and didn't know anyone personally who'd been that insane didn't mean there wasn't anyone else that crazy. And yes, we did feel betrayed by you and what they told us you did. A lot of us starved to death or otherwise didn't make it, and nobody was doing anything about it. That suddenly stopped after the docks, and some kind of leadership started cropping up in our ranks. That's also why we kept coming back to that damn camp with the arena. At least they let us in and fed us. That was more than a lot of the settlements were willing to give us." He glanced at the marines then. "No offense, but the deal the Silo offered wasn't interesting for a lot of us. We went out on the road to be free to do whatever we wanted. What you offered was indentured servitude with maybe a sliver of hope to rise into the ranks of foot soldiers. Even the army's deal was better; at least they promised us gear and weapons from the day we signed on. More people than we care to admit took that deal, and nobody's heard from them since. Shows you what trusting anyone has gotten us."

Hamilton let out a nasty little chuckle. "You haven't heard from them because they're feasting like maggots while they sit securely in their bases or play guards for the settlements. Why go out on the road and get slaughtered by you maniacs when there was lots of other work to be done elsewhere? Even so, we lost a good third of the people we had and those that we managed to recruit. We've been bleeding just as heavily as you have, idiot."

I knew it was about time to stop playing the blame game, and I absolutely hated having to speak up after Hamilton, pretty much agreeing with him. "It doesn't really matter," I pointed out, immediately drawing everyone's ire on me. "Seriously, it doesn't. We can't undo the damage, and we can't raise the dead. What we can do is try to uproot the cause of all this, and hope that will help. That's our mission, anyway, so let's get to it. Believe whatever you want, but to me it sounds more likely that someone has actively been working on sending our country into chaos, and what Amos brought up fits perfectly into that."

Hamilton smiled sweetly at me. "Spoken like a true scavenger whore."

I waited for Nate to say something, but he didn't. Anger flared up inside of me but I did my best to put a lid on it before it could get out of hand, choosing to instead ignore them both. "It does explain why Greene has opened their gates to the scavengers again. He must have realized that they did not order any fertilizer, or not in this way, and that the ships had been turned into bombs by someone else."

Amos didn't look happy at that assessment. "Then why not exonerate us?"

I shrugged. "Who would have believed him? And what would it have mattered since the incident united your ranks, in a sense? He must have figured this was best for his people." I turned to Martinez. "Did their sanctions fall back on you, too?"

Martinez shook his head. "Heightened security, yes, but that was about it. They also didn't keep anyone from getting into the city who went through us first. I'm not sure, but I think he had a deal with Zilinsky about vetting people. But most of it wasn't necessary since a lot of people lost faith in New Angeles after that. Add the fires, and a year later there were fewer people on the coast than when you were still around and when we started building the new towns. The impact on New Angeles may have been the most direct, but it affected us, too. I know at least twenty people who gave up and turned either to the Silo, took the army's offer, or headed to New Vegas to join Harris and his people—and that's considering that Zilinsky has always been running a tight ship and we've had a lot of people who were way more loyal than the average settlers. I know that farther up the coast, only one in three new settlements tried to make it through the next winter. The others were all abandoned before the end of summer, and people went elsewhere."

Silence fell as everyone was contemplating the ramifications of this—or maybe that was just me. Blake was the first to speak up. "Does it really matter? The damage is done. And from what you shared about the serum, it's a problem that will inevitably take care of itself."

I wasn't the only one who grimaced at his statement but did my best to remain diplomatic. "The thing is, I'm much more inclined to work with and trust the scavengers than anyone else since they have virtually no skin in the game, and they are the faction that hasn't betrayed me yet and never stood by idly when I needed help." Blake opened his mouth as if to object, but I silenced him with a raised hand. "I know that a lot of people had very good reasons for why they did what they did. I'm not looking for blame here. I'm looking for allies. I trust my people, but that's also the faction most likely to still harbor moles directly planted by Decker—like that bitch that tried to kill me. While I don't think Richards was involved, his disappearance doesn't cast a better light on the army. Scott and all his men bit it so I doubt we'll get support from their half of the marines. We still have the marines from the Silo, but you keep reminding me that your cooperation with us has been conditional and limited for a variety of reasons. That leaves the scavengers. At the very least, they have no reason to be in cahoots with Decker since he was the one to sign their death warrant. I'll take that as motivation to help us as we gun for him any day."

I wondered what Hill and Cole were making of this, but since they didn't speak up, I figured that was a discussion that could wait for another day. I was surprised when none of the marines objected, either, although Blake eventually downed his coffee and got up laboriously. "I'll have to talk to Buehler when we catch up to the rest of the convoy," he offered. "But when we left, Wilkes made it plain to us that we were to act at our own discretion. If you want us, we're along for the rest of the ride. I wouldn't have committed people to the Dallas suicide mission otherwise."

I accepted that with a nod, but then thought better of it and offered him my hand to shake. His grip was firm, not that wishy-washy thing most people went for who knew what was hiding underneath my leather gloves—or missing, rather. Neither Hamilton nor Nate said anything, leaving this up to me. It was just as well, as a moment later one of the perimeter guards dropped in, letting us know that we had a call on the radio. Nate was gone as soon as the marine stopped speaking, leaving us to enjoy our breakfast. I sat back down and braved the rice-bean-soup concoction, ignoring how Amos kept watching me.

I had a feeling that things wouldn't get much better than this.

Chapter 3

By the end of the day, we finally caught up to the convoy thanks to them having bugged down for the night early. Sitting in the passenger seat for hours on end hadn't been much more pleasant than the day before, although I hadn't torn my stitches again. Martinez still insisted on checking my wound, muttering to himself the entire time when he was forced to lance it once more to drain what felt like an unhealthy amount of pus. When I remarked on that—and how the serum was letting my body get so much of an infection going—he snorted. "You can still run a fever, too," he muttered as he went about sewing me back up. "In fact, what's going on right now is your immune system hurling everything it has into that part of your body—think three weeks' worth of healing in less than twenty-four hours. That's where all the pressure and pus is coming from. Give it a day or two, and you're good." He said that with a latent note of wonder, and when I eyed him askance, he shrugged. "That's about as bad as what Miller had when he got speared by that rebar. Remember how he had to sit on the sidelines for pretty much everything except walking and running for weeks? If you can work through the pain, you'll be cleared for duty by tomorrow, the day after at the latest. Not sure what this does to the general degradation of your body by the virus, but for your fitness, it's a godsend. I'm pretty sure that Miller and Hamilton are green with envy considering their much minor wounds haven't healed that well yet. And it's not a stretch to say that, deadly ramifications aside, I think Blake would opt for the shot in a pinch if it meant he could run, unhindered, by tomorrow."

That sounded about right, although Hamilton wasn't being all that stealthy with his misgivings toward me—but what else was new?

"Still don't regret that you never got inoculated, huh?" I hazarded a guess.

Martinez gave me a pained smile in return. "You know that I objected long before I knew it would kill me faster than any of you are comfortable with," he remarked. "But my choices are my own just as yours are yours. This wound would have killed you if you hadn't gotten it. And you'd never have made it out of the Canada base without it, either. I can't say what I'd have done in your position. Probably the same. It's always easy to be high and mighty when you don't have a knife pressed against your throat." He paused, his gaze fastened on my face. "I almost hesitate to ask, but why the sudden need to reflect? From the very day we met, you've always been pretty straightforward about your drive to survive. And you don't exactly look like you're filled with regret."

"No, just pus and lymph," I joked, stretching experimentally to see if the two new stitches he'd just put in would hold. They hurt like hell, but unlike last night I could now twist my torso at least half of the range that was normal. "And no real reason. I'm just a little out of it."

Martinez grimaced. "Losing half of your people and getting stabbed in the back will do that to the best of us—and that's ignoring the stress of the months before that." Just then, Sonia and Burns walked by us, and although she ignored me, I must have made a face since Martinez frowned after them before turning back to me. "What's going on between the two of you? Don't tell me she's still jealous of you because you and Burns are friends. He has other female friends as well. He's even friendly with the army folks, although that's true for you, too. So what's up? And don't bother denying it. She's behaving around you almost as bad as you do with Hamilton."

I gave him my best fake smile. "Why don't you ask her that?" I almost added, "since I'm being so unreasonable," but thankfully managed to suppress that part. I absolutely didn't have to give anyone even more ammunition against me than they already had.

Martinez narrowed his eyes. "Just one problem: I care a lot more about you than her. And considering only one of you is married to a manipulative asshole who's right now coming apart at the seams, I won't let you push me away, too."

I didn't like his assessment of Nate but couldn't exactly protest there. I still hesitated but then spilled the beans on the most recent update on my reproductive status. He was grinning brightly before I even got to finish my last sentence, hugging me tightly enough that the fresh bandages felt loose in comparison. "That's fantastic news!"

I stared at him for several seconds flat. "Did you miss the part where both of us are dying?"

Martinez didn't even have the grace to look taken aback. "Yes, eventually, but not right now!" He seemed to be waiting for his enthusiasm to catch on. When all I had for him was a flat stare, a light frown appeared on his forehead. "Why aren't you happy? I get that it's a shock, and I understand if you're foaming-at-the-mouth livid that they did this to you without telling you, but why the sour look?"

I hadn't realized that my expression was mirroring my feelings that accurately. "There's the small detail that just because nothing is keeping me from getting knocked up doesn't mean it's possible. And we are heading into war, which makes this absolutely the last priority on a very long list." Martinez regarded me as if I was stupid but had the sense not to tell me that. At his insistent patience I finally brought up the part that actually rubbed me the wrong way. "And Sonia and I had a little heart-to-heart where she told me how much Nate and me deciding to hide from the world screwed you all over and that I have no right to expect you all to just forgive us like that, and, yeah, she's not wrong."

Part of me was satisfied to watch the angry twist come to Martinez's lips, and I wondered what his internal monologue must have looked like in the few seconds he took to calm down and search for the right words. "Well, she's not," he finally settled on saying. "Right, I mean. No kidding, you both up and disappearing threw us for a loop, but not because you were gone. It was because we didn't know what contingency to plan for. Burns didn't tell us a thing, which turned into quite the rift for a while—which I think she caught on to when he brought her to live with us. I admit, I may have said a few unflattering things about you both, but nothing worse than you've called me to my face. She must have gotten a very wrong idea about the dynamics of how our group works."

"She said you were floundering because you didn't know what to do, and also because Zilinsky wouldn't assume leadership since she was holding the place open for someone else."

Martinez blinked, clearly irritated. "That's because she never wanted to be a leader. A few of the imbeciles that didn't get it begged her to become mayor, and she threatened to kick them out if they ever brought it up again. She never wanted to be responsible for anyone, and that hasn't changed."

That confused me. "But she's been Nate's XO for fucking forever."

"Yes, exactly," Martinez insisted. "His executive officer. The one who makes sure everything is running smoothly and everyone knows what their tasks are. But she doesn't like giving the overarching orders. Miller left her with little more than to make sure our civvies were taken care of, and not to—accidentally or deliberately—start a new war. She did exactly that. That Burns brought nothing for us back made it obvious that we were to be kept in oblivion. Did that suck? You bet. But I think both Zilinsky and Romanoff agreed that Miller must have had a very good, non-selfish reason for that, and going on what I know now, there couldn't have been that many possibilities they considered. Venting was the only thing we could do, so that's what we did. It also played well into the narrative of him abandoning us."

That made sense, even if it didn't do much to alleviate my guilt. "She also pretty much called me a self-centered cunt."

Martinez seemed to be waiting for more, giving me a shrewd look when I kept my trap shut. "And?"

"And what?"

His smile was dazzling, and not entirely nice. "Are you contending that point? Because I thought that, by now, you'd know better than to lie to yourself."

"Very funny," I harped.

He was still smiling, but now toned it down to a more amicable expression. "Bree, I've watched you become the woman you are now—although I'm still playing catch-up with the last legs of that journey. You turned into who you are because you had to. Miller made you into this—"

I tried to protest but he talked right over me.

"—and you actively helped him. I get it. Sometimes you hate it—all of it. That it was necessary. How many people ended up left dead because of it. What it did to you. War sucks, if you haven't learned that lesson yet, and what else is the apocalypse, really? I bet you didn't bargain for everything you agreed to when you threw in your lot with Miller, but you've always been an all-or-nothing kind of woman. That's what people admire about you, and that's why we trust and follow you. You can't please everyone, and I honestly didn't think you'd try. What do you care whether Sonia likes you? Just so you know, she doesn't like me much, either. Probably because I've always defended you. We, who know you well, are allowed to bad-mouth you. She hasn't earned that benefit yet."

"She did put me back together," I admitted grudgingly. "That should count for something."

Martinez uttered an exasperated sigh. "If you want to be difficult, sure. But, seriously, who cares? There's a good chance she only meant half of what she flung in your face. She had less than a month to really get to know you, but years of stories that were, at best, wildly exaggerated. I'd like to think that you're more than a trigger-happy bitch with a penchant for convenient disappearances."

I couldn't help but grin. "But I am that, too."

He gave me a deadpan stare before making sure that his work here was done—physically, but also psychologically. "Anything else on your mind? We can keep up this one-issue-each-evening thing if you like, but it would be much easier if you dumped it all on me at once so I can deal with it and get back to my life."

"Why, am I turning into a nuisance?" I teased.

He grimaced. "I can't make fun of you when you get all depressed and serious on me. I miss making fun of you. I need it to feel complete and cozy."

I gave him a critical look for that. "I think you need to get laid."

Martinez laughed, although he seemed slightly scandalized. "Yeah, that, too. Speaking of which—"

I quickly raised both hands between us to forestall him. "I'm so not against you dishing the dirty on what's going on between your sheets, but I need booze before you start."

His mouth twisted into a disapproving line, but laughter was still sparkling in his eyes. "Maybe for external disinfection, but I'm not letting you put your body under any more stress than it already is in! But this is serious."

I made a face, but when I realized he wasn't having it, I gave him a grave nod. "Sure. What's up?"

He hesitated—which usually wasn't a good sign—but the slightly uneasy feeling in my stomach quickly disappeared when he explained what was on his mind in turn. "If you actually get pregnant, I want to be the baby's godfather."

Still, I couldn't help but frown slightly. "Not that I'm protesting—and I really am not. If I'd given a second's consideration to the topic beyond panic, you'd have been right at the top of my list of candidates. But this sounds more serious to you than just a token nod of appreciation." And as much as I was happy to ignore the fact that he was scores more religious than me, this also didn't sound like he felt it was his obligation to combat our heathendom.

Martinez looked exceptionally nervous all of a sudden, stopping his bona fide hand-wringing when he saw me frown. "Once this shitstorm that's going on has blown over, I'm going to propose to Charlie. And, well, neither of us is ever going to have any biological children, and since you're hell-bent on expecting not to live much past your kid's birth, I might just as well point out that I fully intend to step up to the challenge." He softened the impact of that with a slight smile. "Plus, someone has to teach that poor thing manners, and how to be a good human being. No offense, but you take pride in being the poster child for the opposite. I've long since given up on saving your soul, but the kid deserves at least a fighting chance."

I didn't know how to react to that—too many emotions at once—so I decided to take it one offense at a time, starting with the most bone-crushing hug I could manage. "I'm so happy for you both," I whispered before letting go, hard-pressed not to give him a shit-eating grin. "But I'm not quite sure if I can inflict that on any offspring of mine. It sounds like a terrible fate—growing up with two loving surrogate parents who will try their best to turn my hell spawn into a decent human being? I feel like I need to set some ground rules up ahead of time for that." His squint made me laugh. "Oh, come on! Next you'll tell me you'll get ready to stop me from eating the baby as soon as it comes splashing out of my uterus. I mean, maybe the placenta, but I'd give the little critter time to fatten up some." And my, didn't that stupid sentence do a number on me, considering Nate's dietary changes. For a morbid moment only I asked myself, would I feed him my placenta? Probably, if it kept him from losing it and eating our child instead. All that screaming and blood involved could throw off the best of fathers…

It was real concern shining on Martinez's expression when he muttered, "Normally, I'd say 'penny for your thoughts' but considering how dark they often run, I don't think I want to know." He paused, his frown increasing when I didn't protest. "You know you can tell me absolutely everything. It's bad enough that you feel you need to physically keep me away from some things—and you are absolutely right with that. At least for Dallas you were right. But I'm your friend. Trust me, I can take it."

"I know," I was quick to assure him—which earned me a scowl I totally deserved. Pressing my lips together, I tried to weigh my options, but when my eyes fell on the camp around us, full of people I was kind of in command of but barely knew except for a handful, I realized my need to keep my thoughts to myself was overrated. Leaning my ass back against the car, I sighed, briefly rubbing my eyes with the back of my glove. "It's easy to ignore some things with everything that's going on, you know? Things I'd much rather ignore than deal with, even though I'm well aware that they might eventually come to bite me in the ass if I ignore them for too long."

Martinez relaxed a little, and I could tell that it was a deliberate show for me. Inside, he must have been steeling himself. "Knowing your track record, they will bite you in the ass, and harder and maybe more literally than you'd expect."

I was snorting loudly before I could turn it into a fake laugh. "That's one way of putting it."

There was so much I needed to say—and should have, really, but when I remained silent, thinking, Martinez took it upon himself to start prodding. "You two talked about what happened in those, what was it? Nine weeks while you were apart?" I nodded, still not elaborating. "Talked about everything? Even the painful parts that are likely to tear open old wounds you've become so very good at pretending don't exist?"

I had a certain feeling I knew exactly what he was talking about— as did he—and realized I couldn't leave it at just another nod. "Yes, we did. Once. I think that's all he's willing to give himself. And no, I'm not completely torn up over it, or that he's as closed-mouthed as ever, and no, I'm also not wallowing in the agony of my own past. What happened, happened. That's it. Nothing changes that. We have much more pressing issues that we can actually do something about. I'd much rather concentrate on those."

Martinez took that with a frown but eventually inclined his head. "Like what?" he asked, his tone still casually neutral.

"You heard Hamilton's speech in the arena, right?" He nodded. "He's right, and I don't see it getting any better going forward."

Real anger flashed in his eyes, and it was quite bemusing for me to realize that Martinez was livid at Bucky—for once, someone was ready to fully take my side without compromise. "You can't really believe the bullshit he keeps spewing in your direction? Yeah, you may not be a bleeding heart, but you weren't that way before you got infected, either."

I almost laughed when I realized where he'd gone wrong. "Ugh, yeah. Not about that. Am I a little disconcerted about how downright easy it has become for me to play judge, jury, and executioner? But, yes, I fully realize all that was necessary to survive. And somebody has to do the job. No, I'm talking about Nate's… feeding habits."

Martinez gave me a weird look—full of misunderstanding— likely at my weird phrasing. "So he's gone full carnivore. Hate to break it to you, but most of the guys in the field I've been serving with much preferred steak over salad. From a nutritional standpoint, going for fat and protein over carbs when you're forced to go through long stretches without reliable food sources isn't the worst idea. I'm sure you're familiar with the principle of ketosis—"

He broke off when he realized why I was scowling. "He's eating people, chico," I pressed out, trying to keep my voice from carrying. "Not jerky. Not steak. Not even fresh game. People. Hamilton wasn't wrong about that. I don't think that's particularly good for his sanity, and I'm not quite sure how much it's even working."

Martinez didn't like hearing that but he didn't look as scandalized as I'd expected; more like he was fighting hard to clamp down on any number of morbidly curious questions. "Okay. Like, how isn't it working?" He grimaced. "I didn't miss the part where we realized that they'd been feeding the dead prisoners to the alive ones. That's why Hamilton almost starved to death—he refused to eat any of that. Miller was a lot smarter about it. I thought Hamilton was trying to rub the emotional impact of that in. You sure were barfing more than either of them, so I chalked it up to the drugs that he couldn't keep much food down."

I shook my head. "I wish it was that easy. He hasn't eaten anything since we left Dallas." I couldn't keep a low, sarcastic laugh from escaping. "I'll spare you the details of the crispy chicken incident, although, if you ask me, it couldn't have been actually crispy since UV light burns skin, but it doesn't braise and baste it." I got a weird—and concerned—look for that comment but Martinez didn't ask me to elaborate. "Honestly, I'm taking the switch in food sources in stride. I'd be lying if some part of me wasn't deeply concerned, but it helps being a scientist. I worry more about prions and mad cow disease than the emotional impact—for me. I can ignore all that shit, although it must be weighing on his mind. But how do I keep him fed, huh? I can't very well make the rounds and ask if someone feels like they can do without the fleshy part of their left ass cheek. I hate to say this, but while it was up and running, the arena was working relatively well for that. And there were plenty of fresh kills in the lab underneath Dallas. But what do we do now?"

I could see Martinez's underlying horror slowly morph to real concern as he followed my explanation, choosing to act in sync with me and to concentrate on the practical rather than the moral side of things. "I presume you've already given him the talk about the human body having however many thousands of calories as a food source?"

I narrowed my eyes at him. "What do you think I am? An amateur? That's where I started. But that's exactly the problem. Considering our lifestyle, he needs somewhere between three and five thousand calories a day for maintenance, and he doesn't exactly have full stores right now."

Martinez nodded absently. "My guess is he's around five percent body fat right now, considering how cut his abs look."

Despite the grim topic, that made he laugh. "Chico, have you been checking out my husband?"

I got a truly exasperated look for that, well-deserved as it was. "It's my job to keep tabs on everyone's general status of health. You're way too skinny yourself for a woman who intends to have a child. When I checked on you back home, you were down to maybe ten percent, and you haven't exactly bulked up since then. And, for the record, Miller is not my type."

I couldn't help it; I just had to keep teasing him. "What, too tall? Too straight? No, wait—too bossy?"

I got the smirk I deserved. "We can't all go for the psychopathic killers, you know?"

I fended that off with a grin, followed by a "whew" gesture. "You'd better not change your mind," I warned him. "Else I know a way to have his meal plan covered for the next…" I gave his body an appraising look. "Two weeks? Maybe three if we don't move much. You're lucky Charlie clearly has a preference for short and sweet with a pert ass." Coming from anyone else, that might have been a hit below the belt, but Martinez and I had often enough suffered together when Burns had made fun of being able to do pushups with either of us sitting on his back—but that didn't mean Martinez didn't still have a healthy amount of mass on me.

"You're so damn funny," he grumbled. "Anyone tell you that of late?"

"I know. My jokes are killer!" I crooned, but felt my levity drain from me all too quickly. "Seriously, how do I keep him fed? I think my best bet is fresh game, the meat still warm and bloody. It's never been an issue while we were hiding in the middle of nowhere, but he was able to choke down rehydrated rice and pasta back then, although I'm sure he didn't like the taste much. If we stop a little early or set out slings far enough from the camp, we might be able to hunt or catch enough to keep him from losing too much mass. As you so succinctly put it, he doesn't have much subcutaneous fat left. Next up, it's all muscle on the menu, and I don't want to wade into the last battle with him too weak to be of much use next to me."

Martinez considered that for a while, ignoring my running commentary. "Fish's probably the most reliable protein source, and usually comes with great fat content, too," he offered. "If we get lucky and manage to shoot or trap animals, that might work as well, but it begs the question, do we have the time? Right now our downtimes are dictated by what the cars can take, and I don't see Miller making exceptions for himself."

"No, he won't," I agreed. "It doesn't help that he's trying to avoid facing the problem."

"How so?"

I thought about how to best put it. "I think he's afraid raw animal meat is his last resort, and he doesn't want to accept losing that. I think it's safe to say that if Marleen hadn't almost managed to kill me, with him consequently almost losing it, he would have tried to stave off the inevitable by any means available. That means he likely would have ended up starving himself, and I wouldn't have caught on to it before it was too late. I don't mean being too weak to fight. What if something else triggers him and he loses it? I'd hate to do it, but if he converts, I'll put him down in a heartbeat. What if he's coming after one of you but manages to not fully turn? Either way, he's not coming back from that."

Martinez didn't look happy about my assessment but didn't protest its accuracy. "How about this," he proposed. "I'll put out a general recommendation that we take some extra time for hunting. Most of the scavengers aren't in exactly stellar health, and everyone else could benefit from some more protein in their diets. If it prevents another breakfast like we had today, I don't think anyone will protest. And if we only catch a small rabbit or a handful of fish, Miller has dibs on it. We won't tell him, and nobody else will think twice if we don't make a big deal out of it. Should anyone complain about it, I'll take care of that."

I couldn't help but smirk. "Leader gets first dibs? We really aren't in the army anymore."

Martinez looked, if anything, annoyed at my remark. "You really spend too much time with that bunch," he told me in no uncertain terms.

"Yeah? Maybe," I conceded. "But if I take Hamilton out of the equation, they're an all right bunch. And I distinctly remember you all being quite happy not to have to shoot any former buddies of yours."

I realized his ire was focused elsewhere only after Martinez grunted. "If you ignore that your favorite lieutenant is a traitor."

I didn't try to disband the annoyance from my voice when I answered. "I'm not sure Richards betrayed us. It seems a lot more likely that Marleen misled him, and then forced him to tag along if he didn't want her to cut his throat."

Martinez didn't seem convinced. "Don't you think those are your feelings talking?"

"My what?" I didn't have to feign ignorance there—and a hefty dose of anger.

I got a level stare back that could have meant anything, and was way too accusing for my taste. "You were awfully quick to plaster yourself to his side when we met up to storm the camp," he pointed out.

"Because it made the most sense to stick with him since we were all fitting in well with the scavengers," I protested. "And sure, I get along well with him. Also because when Hamilton was doing his very best to be the human incarnation of a massive heap of shit, he acted like a normal human being, and even went out of his way to play nice. Cole and Hill didn't respect me until after we hit that damn lab, and I don't think they actually take me seriously. Richards does." I couldn't help the frustration coming up inside of me, also because I realized how much all that in juxtaposition with him disappearing grated. "Where's this even coming from?"

The question was clearly making Martinez uncomfortable. "A few of the scavengers mentioned—"

"Well, they are wrong!" I ground out, a little too emphatically for my own good, as I belatedly realized. Taking a calming breath, I did my best to center myself. "He kind of laid it on a little heavily when we were trying to infiltrate the camp, but trust me when I tell you, he very quickly saw the error of his ways. And don't you think that Nate would have—quite physically—come after him if he felt himself threatened?" The idea was so ridiculous that it made me want to throw my head back and laugh—except that Martinez appeared, if anything, grim.

"He didn't look particularly happy whenever he saw you tag along with Richards at the camp," he let me know.

"Maybe he shouldn't have stormed off without me everywhere then," I snarked, getting increasingly furious at everyone involved. "He knows that he has zero reason to feel threatened. And he was more than happy to see me tag along with Richards in Dallas."

Martinez looked downright disturbed at hearing that. "He let you out of his sight?"

"Pretty much the entire time until the very end," I explained. "He was way more interested in hanging out with that ass-wipe—as he still does. If I was a little more insecure in our relationship, I'd be concerned, but I guess I should consider myself lucky that I get to spend the nights with him, seeing as otherwise we'd absolutely miss our last chance to unleash our spawn on this world." I wasn't exactly seething but close—and that didn't stop when Martinez broke out in a shit-eating grin, making me realize he'd been leading me on to get a quick, honest answer from me. I glared at him for another second before I crossed my arms over my chest, giving him the "touché" nod that he deserved. "To answer what you actually want to know, no, I don't think Richards betrayed us, but even if he did, it's not even in the top five concerns that are plaguing me right now. Do I hate the fact that I misjudged Marleen and thus gave her the golden opportunity to end us all? Yes, but in the grand scheme of things, it's just one more hitch in the road. I'm not even having nightmares about it, but that's probably due to my body needing every single moment of rest because of the toll wound healing takes. I think Nate's way more broken up about the whole thing than I am."

"I'm sure he is," Martinez agreed, still smiling slightly. Fucker. His amusement dissipated as he went on. "Have you two talked about this, too?"

"Not much to talk about. But I know it hit him hard."

"Of course it did," he remarked, surprised when all he got from me was a neutral stare. "He almost lost you again—and this time it would absolutely have been his fault for trusting the wrong people and giving them the opportunity to get to you."

"He didn't seem that disturbed. More suspicious that something else is wrong," I pointed out—but couldn't shake off the unease that Martinez was right.

I got a borderline belligerent snort for my troubles. "What isn't?" But he dropped the point quickly enough. "Just… I don't know. Part of me wants to tell you not to be a cunt to him about it or the way he keeps acting, but at the same time I don't get it. If you happen to decide to make a run for Bucky after all, let me know. I'll make sure you have overwhelming backup for whatever you plan."

I didn't miss that he used Hamilton's much-hated nickname, and the overall sentiment amused me a lot. "Hate to break it to you, but I won't. Do I hate spending even a single second breathing the same air as he is? Hell, yeah. But Nate is hell-bent on giving him a shot at redemption, and I can't protest bringing another meat shield along for the ride. If it means we have a slightly better chance of survival, I'm all for it."

Martinez looked less than happy at my response but accepted it for what it was. "Guess I'd better set to finding some chow for him," he muttered. "And tell him that if he needs to talk, I'm here."

"I don't quite see that happening," I admitted.

"Me neither," Martinez said with a heavy sigh. "Same as I know I won't get a straight answer out of you."

"What's that supposed to mean?" I complained. "I've been pouring my heart out to you for the past twenty minutes!"

He grimaced. "Keep telling yourself that." When I kept glaring at him, he sighed again but relented. "You two are so damn similar. It's no wonder you hit it off from the very start." I opened my mouth to protest—not quite sure what I was going to say—but he talked right over me. "Sure, on the outside, not so much. But inside you're a damn near perfect match. You're like two wolves, only that you started out bundled in fluff, while he long ago learned to be the loner, wrapping himself up in layers of armor. You lost the fluff and wormed yourself through the cracks in his armor, and what's underneath is like two sides of the same coin. You understand him like no one else—and the same is true for the reverse. The only difference is that you would be able to walk away from his grave, but he won't make it long past your death. So make sure to give him a reason to keep hanging in. We'd all miss you both terribly."

Part of me wanted to laugh at how ridiculous that analogy sounded—except it resonated with something deep inside of me. It was almost as if he'd just put kindling onto the small flicker of hope that kept burning somewhere in the back of my mind—hope that we would, somehow, get through this and not die before we'd made sure to leave the world a better place.

"I will," I promised—no "try" or "do my best" because nothing short of iron-clad conviction would work, that much I was sure. I hated how that made me feel—like we really were on the last leg of our journey together—but that didn't diminish my conviction that I would see this through to the very end. If that meant I had to put up with Hamilton, so be it. I knew Nate well enough to understand that he had his reasons.

I also knew him well enough to realize that Martinez's words also held a hidden warning: to protect me, Nate would try to either push me away or set out on his own, leaving me behind in an attempt to keep me out of harm's way—and if he succeeded, he would leave himself exposed and vulnerable. I would die before I let that happen.

Martinez inclined his head, sure that his message had been received. "I better get going. Try going easy on yourself for another day, and this should be the last time I need to check on your injuries." He let out a humorless bark. "Damn, but that level of healing power would have come in handy when I impaled myself on that damn tree."

"I think Nate's truly jealous of exactly how well I put myself back together," I said. "Might annoy him more than the fact that I might have jumped Richards's bones if all I'd found in the prison cells was a gravestone."

Martinez snorted. "No, you wouldn't have. You didn't even consider it."

"Of course I didn't," I agreed, smiling grimly.

With nothing more to say, I left, checking in with Blake about the watch schedules for the night—and then I went on the lookout for my husband to give Martinez a chance to have a crying, barfing bundle of joy to look out for in the years to come.

Chapter 4

I woke up early the next morning, the sky not even starting to lighten yet. It wasn't of my own accord, but because Nate—after coming back from his watch shift—was hell-bent on giving me a great start into the day. I was still officially off the watch rotation to maximize my rest, but that didn't seem to stretch to where a different kind of physical activity was concerned. Something was definitely different about the downright fervor he put behind his attempt to both peel me out of strategic parts of my clothes and kiss and lick along the side of my neck until he had me panting and squealing in no time. His own injuries were

definitely healing up well, too, leaving my back the only real hindrance.
I was still a little too sluggish with the last dregs of sleep, so rather than
me crawling onto his lap, he turned us both on our sides—making sure
my weight was on my left—and pushed into me from behind, hands
and lips already getting busy again on every inch of me that he could get
to. I gave up craning my neck to steal a kiss from him when he seemed
reluctant to stop devouring me, although it did earn me a growled, "You
taste so damn good." That made me laugh huskily.

"If you follow that up with a claim that I smell fertile and ripe for
the plowing, I'll kick you in the nuts. After we're done."

He eased up for a second to chuckle, which was my chance to
twist and grab his head, almost having to force his lips apart with
my tongue, but he relented quickly enough when he realized I
wasn't taking no for an answer. Sure enough, underneath the near
overpowering scent of mint, I picked up a clear taste of blood,
making me guess that Martinez's plan was already in action. The
nasty voice at the back of my head asked itself how healthy it could be
that, apparently, slaking one hunger seemed to stoke a different one
in Nate, but if that meant I'd get to wake up like this every single day
from here on out, I was ready to sacrifice an hour of sleep each night
to go hunting myself. While understanding why he'd withdrawn a
little from me after we'd taken over the camp, it was only now that I
realized how much I'd missed him.

And if the zombie apocalypse had taught us anything, it was how
to make the most out of stolen moments like this—and that was
exactly what we did.

It was only later, when we were curled up against each other,
enjoying a few more moments of comfortable silence together, that I
realized something: I'd only smelled the mint on his breath—but I'd
absolutely tasted the hint of blood.

My, wasn't that a sobering thought.

I was still contemplating whether to mention that observation or
not when someone knocked on the back window of the car, carefully

outside of the range where he might have caught a glance at anything inside. "We have a problem."

More than happy to postpone that conversation—external or internal—I quickly pulled everything back into place. Nate beat me to it, already exiting the car while I was still busy trying to close my belt without getting up first. It wasn't hard to guess where he went to since people all over the camp were streaming toward the Humvee that Cole and Hill had taken over. Nate had grudgingly agreed to make it our official radio station since it had by far the best equipment, and neither the tech-savvy scavenger nor Blake's marine who knew a thing or two about spyware had found anything wrong with it. It also had batteries strong enough to leave the radio on through the night and still power up the next morning.

"What's wrong?" I asked as I pushed through the throng of people, meeting little to no resistance. Hill was in the driver's seat, Nate standing next to him, listening to Hill trying again to get someone on the line. After another minute he gave up, shaking his head as he glanced down at a handwritten log lying on the dashboard.

"Last confirmed contact was at 0300 and 0320, respectively," he told Nate.

Looking grim, Nate turned to me to explain. "We lost contact with our California settlement and our vanguard both. They've just missed the third consecutive check-in."

I didn't like the sound of that. "Any chance it's on our end?"

Hill shook his head. "That's the first thing we checked. We got through to the radio station back at the camp, and both Dispatch and New Angeles told us to go fuck ourselves. Reception's not perfect, but not problematic. And before you say the cars could be out of battery, that's true, but the settlement has banks of generators with backups. From what your people told me, they never lost radio contact, not even in the fires and earthquakes." He nodded at Santos, standing a little to the side—his apparent source for that. Santos looked worried himself, even though he was trying to hide it.

Nate glanced at the maps Hill had spread out next to him. "How far ahead is our vanguard? And how far are they from the coast?"

Hill must have already checked, his answer coming promptly. "They're three days out of Vegas at the pace they were going, four and a half from the coast. About the same away from us, considering that they can go faster with just three vehicles."

Nate scratched his chin. "Any chance we can make it to the settlement in under a week?"

Hill shook his head. "Not unless we split up again. If we take the strong cars only and pack them light, we can cut the distance down to two days by the time we blow past Vegas, but that's already praying that we don't run into any obstacles."

"Can you get Harris on the line and ask him to send a small recon team over to our people?" Nate asked. "So we know what we're barreling into, running blind at full speed."

"Consider it done," Hill acknowledged, already fiddling with the radio.

I looked at the faces around us, finding everyone at least slightly worried, even the marines. Sgt. Buehler was the one who asked the question that must have been on everyone's mind. "You think that your traitors caught up to them and took them out?"

Nate hesitated but shook his head. "I know it sounds silly considering how she managed to mislead me, but I know Marleen well enough to be sure she's not stupid enough to show her face anywhere near Zilinsky or the town. They're warned, and they know who to look out for. I'm sure she's on her way back to Decker, or she's already there. She knows we'll eventually show up on his doorstep— why bother with coming to us instead?"

Damn, but I hoped he was right, because I wasn't going to let that bitch walk away alive from this.

"So we split up?" I ventured a guess.

Again, Nate took a moment to consider but then shook his head. "No. If this is a trap, it's already set, and we'll need all the manpower we have not to spring it—or survive if that's unavoidable. We proceed as planned. Everyone, get breakfast going as fast as you can. We're moving out as soon as possible." The crowd around us quickly broke up, setting to work as if that would help lessen their unease. Before I could do the same, Nate held me back, leaning in to whisper softly into my ear. "Looks like your grand feeding schedule will have to wait until we've made sure that our people are safe. I have a feeling that won't be too much of a problem once we get there."

I looked after him for a moment as he left to help with breaking up camp. Hill gave me a curious look, but since I had no intention of spilling the beans, I quickly turned to do the same. Oh well—at least we'd gotten one meal into him. And whatever was waiting for us at the coast, it would come with something bloody and raw to sustain him for another week. Just maybe I'd try to sneak a bite or two myself, for curiosity's sake.

And, my, didn't that thought leave me all relaxed and happy.

Chapter 5

Tension was running high throughout the day, but there wasn't exactly much we could do but push on. I agreed with Nate that it only made sense to continue as one closed unit—particularly considering what it meant for us if our vanguard had gotten overwhelmed—but it was torture to check in with Hill and Cole each and every hour, and always get the same message back: no answer. I knew Blake had alerted the Silo, but I was itching to spread the word. Vegas and the large Utah settlement were our closest possible safe havens, both seeming a million miles away considering the terrain—and heat. Summer was in full swing now, turning the days endless and hot as hell. Two of the cars broke down during the day when we kept pushing on beyond what we knew was smart, Nate deciding to abandon them after a brief discussion with Martinez. I tried calling into New Angeles—hoping my name and voice would open doors after all—but the line went to static as soon as I managed to identify myself. That more than anything else made me antsy—Greene and I had had a pleasant-enough talk just days ago, and while I understood him not committing any people to our cause, he always seemed to have considered the coastal settlements as part of their growing network. Absolute silence could only mean one thing—someone must have made them circle the wagons against all incoming forces, us included. My guess was on the Ice Queen herself, deciding that, at worst, the lives of a few hundred were worth less than several thousands throughout the state and New Angeles itself. I also had a certain feeling that as soon as we'd left for our assault on the camp, whoever remained behind had been in a permanent state of high alert. Maybe the unease churning in my gut was completely unwarranted, and what had actually happened was all our people gathering in New Angeles and spending a week on the beach waiting for us to pass one checkpoint or another until they could flag us down to reunite there. It sounded highly unlikely since neither I, Nate, nor Martinez or any of the others knew about it, but it was possible. Nate and Pia both had in the past proven that keeping secrets was easiest if nobody was aware of them—it was hard to torture knowledge out of people who didn't have it in the first place. But—now more than ever—Marleen's betrayal was a constant reminder that we couldn't be careful enough.

That night, we made camp an hour after nightfall, and Nate didn't return to the car until after I'd dozed off. Part of me was curious about what he was doing, but I was happy to give him space if he thought he needed it. Truth be told, I needed a little alone time myself. After taking forever to fall asleep, I was awake by three, finding Nate rolled up on the other side of the vehicle, fast asleep. Too anxious to stay put, I got up and went to volunteer to relieve one of the guards, but since Nate had apparently left word with them not to give me a rotation, they sent me scampering off once more. It just so happened that I was walking by the radio Humvee when I heard the sound of an unfamiliar voice coming on.

"I repeat, anyone out there?" someone said, followed by a low chuckle.

No one else was around, so I took it upon myself to open the door and reach for the mic. "Hearing you loud and clear," I said without identifying myself, figuring that if they were trying to hail us, they'd know who they'd get on the line.

"Thank fuck," the unknown caller acknowledged. "I was getting worried here that you're deliberately ignoring us. Or that you're just human and fast asleep at this ungodly hour."

I couldn't help but smirk, despite the knot in my stomach. "Yeah, what can I say? Someone always gets the graveyard shift."

That seemed to be enough to qualify me as someone worth reporting to. The caller's voice took on a slightly more serious tone. "We just got back to our base truck. Don't have any long-range transmitters on the buggies." I wondered if that should make any sense to me, but he explained before I could ask. "We're the people Harris sent from Vegas to go snooping toward the coast. Since there was a lot of hush-hush going on, we decided to take two dune buggies to investigate. Much lighter, pretty fast, and very hard to spot in a pinch. We didn't find the vanguard group you're looking for, but there's absolute radio silence from the five independent settlements on the coast. It's not due to a signal scrambler; at least we still had radio contact between the buggies. We figured it was best to report in with that before we go any closer. Something's definitely up, but we didn't get close enough for a good look yet. My boss thinks it's someone's contingency plan, but since you called in, I'm not so sure about that. We know where some of their forward watch stations are and we're checking in with them later today. If you don't hear from us by morning tomorrow, proceed with caution."

I didn't like the sound of that, but until we knew more, I couldn't allow myself to start freaking out. "Thanks for the update," I told him. "Looking forward to hearing from you again."

"My pleasure," the scavenger replied. "And good to have you back in the loop, Lewis. Things were way too boring without you around."

I couldn't help but chuckle in spite of myself. "Do I know you?"

"Not personally, no," the scavenger replied. "Looking forward to maybe remedying that soon." He paused briefly. "I'll let you know what we find out as soon as we have details."

He signed off then, leaving me to my pacing. I made it exactly three steps away from the Humvee before a dark shape materialized out of the darkness—Hamilton. The way he stopped, he must have seen me by the vehicle, making sure to keep his distance. In the near complete darkness of our temporary shelter—the outskirts of a small forest at the shore of a reservoir a few miles west of the Texas-New Mexico border—his tall, emaciated frame looked less human and more like it belonged to some kind of woodland creature from a nightmare scape. The usual contempt and hatred burned in his gaze, but rather than engage, he just paused until he saw me draw up short before he stepped around me, continuing on his trek to who-the-fuck-knew where. I stared after him for a moment before I forced myself to relax. In the direction he had come from, I saw Burns make a beeline for where we kept leftover coffee for the night-shift guards in a thermos by the extinguished fire.

He looked up when I joined him, pouring a second mug for me as soon as I held my aluminum cup out to him. "Can't sleep?" he ventured what must have been an exceptionally well-informed guess, judging from the slight grin lighting up his face.

"Just heard from the scavengers that are scouting the coast," I told him rather than reply to his question. "They said all five settlements there have gone dark."

I'd expected a shrug and joke, but he mulled that over for a moment. "I don't know for sure, but chances are good Zilinsky sent all of them scrambling when she heard back from us," he pointed out. "They wouldn't be advertising that after the fact."

"Makes sense," I admitted. "But why not tell us that?"

"No use trying to hide in obscurity when you blare it out over the open frequencies," he noted. "But I'm with you there. I don't like this one bit."

We didn't say anything else, but since I was already awake, it made sense for me to join him on his perimeter route. Somehow that reminded me a lot of the first months we'd spent together, when I'd seldom been left alone on my shifts. It was good to spend some time just hanging out, even if we weren't talking much. Who knew how much time we still had for that?

In the morning, I shared the new information with the others, little as it was. I was met with a round of grim faces, and we broke camp even faster than the day before. The sun wasn't yet fully over the horizon, and already I was sweating in my full gear, not looking forward to how the day would go.

By nightfall, one more car had broken down, and more than one fatigued figure more fell than staggered out of a vehicle when we made camp for the night. Nate was gone before I could ask him to—please!—lift the embargo on me doing perimeter guard, and Hamilton was nowhere to be found as well. I took it upon myself to inform Blake that I was absolutely taking the early shift for next morning, and couldn't help but glare at the radio Humvee every so often. No message came—and the same was still true for when Martinez woke me up, gently knocking on the window of the car. Again I found Nate fast asleep next to me, leaving me conflicted and just a little angry—until I got a little too close to where he'd ditched his jacket in the front seat, the metallic scent of blood tickling my nose. Even sluggish with sleep, it didn't take my brain long to make the connection—he and Hamilton must have been out hunting, and had obviously been successful this time. Relief warred with annoyance as I let myself out of the car and checked in with the two marines who were sharing the shift with me. Sure, I was glad that he'd found a way to feed himself—even if it came at the expense of downtime—but why didn't he take me with him? I was more than capable with a bow, particularly if he gave me an evening to modify it to suit my needs. I didn't need a shrink to tell me what got my hackles up was who he was doing it with, not that it wasn't including me.

Morning broke, and still we had no answer from the scavengers. Nobody said anything, but I could see the latent anxiety growing, jumping from us to the marines in no time. I tried to tell myself that it could still be coincidence—or Pia had caught the scavengers and forbidden them to call in as not to alert anyone needlessly to our plans—but deep down I knew that things were ramping up to be bad.

Another endless day of baking in the sun, just as unforgiving in Arizona as it had been in New Mexico. One more day, and we would be close enough to New Vegas for short-range transmission. Another, and we'd be at the California coast by nightfall. Radio chatter on the open frequencies sounded normal enough, the only reports we snatched up coming from broken-down bridges, tornado warnings, and some flooding in Vermont. My wound was still giving me grief but had healed up enough that I could easily sit through four hours of driving before Nate made me switch, and again in the second half of the day. Nobody from Vegas had invited us, but I was tempted to suggest that we call in and ask if we could spend the night. Particularly if our worst suspicions turned out to be true, getting a good night's rest—and some fresh provisions, and maybe even some backup—would make a difference. Nate considered—which in itself already surprised me—but instead decided that we would continue on our current heading, trying to get just a few miles closer to the coast.

It was only when we stopped for the night when Sonia, of all people, brought up something I'd completely forgotten about. "Shouldn't we be close to the New Angeles beacons now?" That we weren't was obvious. I would have at least felt them, as my experience riding with Red to catch the boat a few weeks ago had proven yet again. I'd never gotten a look at a conclusive map where they had been positioned, but the people from the settlements clearly knew.

It was Burns who finally voiced what must have been on all our minds at her prompt. "Someone must have deactivated them."

The implications of that sat dark and foreboding in my stomach, and I wasn't the only one who kept a weapon ready while eating dinner. Nate was just about to send everyone except the guards to hit the sack—apparently still sated from the last hunting trip—when the radio in the Humvee squawked. Since he was already up, Nate went to get the mic, the vehicle close enough to our fire for all of us to listen in.

"Anyone out there getting this?" someone was repeating—not the same voice as before, if I remembered correctly, but going on the same lack of protocol that seemed to be normal among the scavengers.

Nate—frowning slightly with what must have been annoyance because of that—picked up, but didn't hesitate to go for a casual response himself. "Hearing you loud and clear," he reported back. "What's up?"

"Identify yourself," the voice responded, harsher now.

Nate's frown increased. When he glanced at Amos, the scavenger shook his head. No, that wasn't according to their not-protocol.

"Who's this?" Nate replied, his voice also taking on a different tone—but more like he was stoned, and definitely not gnashing his teeth at the lack of proper protocol.

Silence followed, then, "What's your position?"

Amos had gotten to his feet by then to lumber over to Nate, still shaking his head. Nate motioned for him to speak, indicating that the mic wasn't sending right now. "We never do call-ins like that," Amos insisted. "Not even when we're pretending we're someone who we're not. We have code phrases just like you assholes do," he offered, quite jovial—and clearly excluding Nate from the scavengers as they saw themselves.

Rather than respond, Nate reached into the Humvee, not just ending the call without saying another word but also disconnecting the radio from the battery. Hill looked ready to protest, but didn't when Nate resurfaced, scowling for real now. "We're moving camp. Now," he declared. "I don't think they've managed to pinpoint our location, but I won't risk it."

Nobody complained, and an hour later we'd set up position ten miles farther south, going in the one direction that was least useful for our journey. It was past midnight by the time we were ready for sleep—only that I felt like I wouldn't get much rest tonight. My body was screaming for some downtime but my mind wouldn't shut up. Just as I was about to open my mouth and loudly complain about that—Nate's elevated breathing rate made it obvious that he was still awake as well—he rolled over to face me, concern etched into his expression. We stared at each other for several seconds flat, no words needed. We both knew what that radio transmission was about—someone must have snatched up the scavengers Harris had sent out to do recon for us, and it stood to reason that those were the same people responsible for the radio silence of the settlements. It could all be coincidence, sure—but considering the random location of the scavengers, the frequency that wasn't common knowledge, and a million other things, it sounded like a lot of opposition. More opposition than we with our less than forty people could easily meet—and we still had no clue what we were walking into. The only thing that was certain was that tomorrow would likely devolve into another shitshow of epic proportions.

I was a second faster, pushing up and landing on Nate before he could do more than tense to do the same to me. The sudden need for physical contact was almost painful, and he was quick to respond in kind. With frustration and dread so palpable that I could almost taste them, it was a relief to have one way of dealing with that where before only more of the same existed, twining seamlessly with the knowledge that tonight might be the last chance we got for some extended time together. I was doing my best to keep silent, but didn't really care if the whole camp was aware what was going on.

Right now, it was just the two of us, everything else ceasing to exist—and all was right with the world.

But then it was over, and we both dressed again, ready to either grab a weapon and jump up to defend our position, or run into battle, leaving me feeling hollow rather than invigorated. Nate paused and cast me a glance over his shoulder that so perfectly embodied my feelings that I couldn't help it and cracked up, his own wry mirth mirrored on his expression.

"Do you ever wonder if we're doing the right thing?" I asked, mostly musing to myself.

"Never," he said with a conviction that made me draw up short and look straight at him.

"Never?"

He shook his head. "Not since the day I got the call that my brother was dead. Don't get me wrong. I've made a lot of wrong decisions since then, but mostly because I strayed from what I knew, deep down, is the right path. Getting our people to safety? Coming after Decker? We should have done that years ago."

"We thought we were doing just that," I pointed out.

Nate hesitated—which, in turn, made my stomach cramp up in trepidation—but his voice was strong and full of conviction when he replied. "No. We were biding our time, because I was trying to avoid that ultimate confrontation. Because I knew it would come at a steep cost, and I wasn't ready to pay that price yet."

"And now you are?"

He shrugged. "What choice do we have? And how much worse can the consequences get than what we've already been through?"

I had a feeling that he had just jinxed us—yet at the same time, I couldn't help but agree. Me getting infected; him getting abducted;

all the friends we'd lost along the way... we couldn't exactly have prevented all of that, but more often than not, avoidance had led to things getting worse rather than better. Looking back, our two years of exile had bought our friends time to settle and prepare, and for Sadie to give birth to baby Chris, but it had given the other side a lot of time and opportunity to make matters a lot worse.

Now it was time to put an end to that, once and for all.

I was surprised just how ready I felt for that.

Chapter 6

Nate called for a break during the hottest hours of the day. We were still a good seventy miles from our destination, and judging from the frowns plastered on faces all around me, I wasn't the only one reluctant to halt for two hours, but of course it made sense. We needed to hydrate, eat, and get a little more rest before driving into what might turn into a hell of a long night. My mind still wouldn't shut up and let me sleep, but lying in the relative shade of the ground level of a partially destroyed building, out of the sun, was still better than driving the car through the near-desert. The area was blissfully free of shamblers, making me guess that whoever had deactivated the beacons had either herded them farther north first, or New Angeles had set to getting them out of their backyard for good years ago. Come to think of it, we hadn't seen any on the trek to the camp, either. Since that was nothing I could do a thing about right now—and not exactly a concern unless they came back all at once—I did my best to ignore the nagging voice at the back of my mind. Chances were, a streak wouldn't be the surprise that got us killed today.

Eleven of us knew where the forward sentinel posts were situated. Since three of the positions were more or less in the area we were using as an entry vector, Nate split us up into three groups, making sure that we were staying with Martinez, Burns, and Sonia. We got the southernmost post to investigate while the other two groups split away to the north. It felt stupid to give up the relative safety of numbers, but if that maybe helped with getting closer to the settlement before we got detected... not that I thought it would make a difference. Complete radio silence made it sound like our vanguard had been caught as well, and that last call on the scavenger frequency pretty much confirmed that they had gotten compromised, so why should we be any different? All cars together might have been able to ram right through a roadblock, but splitting up would keep us from that advantage. Yet I kept my opinion to myself, certain that Nate had considered it—and just like the question of whether we should directly involve Vegas, he chose to go our own way. After Marleen, I could more than understand—but I didn't have to like it one last bit.

No need to go hunting for the sentinel post. We were still more than a mile away when Sonia reported in over our coms. "I see smoke up in the air." Ten minutes later, we could all see what used to be the lookout post on top of an old shed clearly—because the whole building was on fire. Nate debated simply going on but then had us swarm out around the area to investigate. When nobody shot at the cars, we got out to check on foot—the drivers the marked exception to that. I gnashed my teeth while I waited an endless fifteen minutes until I saw Nate hoof it back to the car, not exactly stealthy.

"All dead," he told me as he got back in the passenger side. "I can't say more because the bodies are charred beyond recognition, but looks like someone doused them in accelerant to make sure we wouldn't find any traces or could guess at their cause of death. There are no bullet holes that we could see, but since everything's pretty much burnt down to the ground, they'd be easy to miss."

I wondered if I should have suggested that we stay to make sure the fire couldn't spread, but since that was the last thing I wanted to do, I kept my trap shut.

"Where to next?" I asked instead.

"The town," Nate said simply. "Or as close as we'll get."

A few minutes later, both other groups signed in, reporting similar findings. So similar, in fact, that I got the suspicion that whoever had torched the outposts had waited to set the stage for us. Nate gave them the same orders as me, and while I still hated that we were now four cars on our own again, it also set my mind slightly at ease. If they were waiting for us, they'd also had time aplenty to booby-trap all available roads leading to our destination. The more spread out we were, the better the chances of not getting blown to smithereens all in the same instant.

I could only imagine how much worse the handful of people from the settlement must have been feeling when I was already driving on figurative pins and needles.

Unlike the first smaller settlement that we'd helped build, the current one was directly at the coast and easily visible from a distance. On my first and only visit there two months ago, it had been easy to see why Zilinsky had chosen the spot, besides the fact that there had once been a small town there that they had been able to convert to their specific needs: the entire plain leading up to the sea was one gigantic kill zone. Built in a more or less circular fashion, the palisades that served as the town borders now could easily be held by a handful of people if they just had the right kind of weapons and enough ammo for days. Good snipers could easily shoot out the engine blocks of advancing cars at more than a mile's range, maybe even two. Forcing advancing troops to go on foot easily bought the defenders another twenty to thirty minutes to get ready for the shooting-fish-in-a-barrel action.

I had certain concerns that what had once been a great plan of defense might come to bite us in the ass now.

We were still twenty miles outside of that very kill zone when the sun disappeared into the ocean, leaving us at a clear advantage since we had enough people between us to drive in the dark and not give away our position from miles away. I couldn't help but feel that must have been part of Nate's plan—and a good trade-off for the extra exhaustion all of us were rocking, if it meant that we were harder to spot. Split into three groups that were, in themselves, not driving in convoys but with careful distance between the vehicles, I gave us a one-in-three chance to get close enough where the inevitable sounds our cars made would give us away rather than anything else.

"Are we sure this is the only way in?" I asked Nate as I continued to inch the car forward, wincing whenever something on the uneven ground made the vehicle rock, thus making the frame groan slightly.

He cast me a sidelong glance. "Like what? Swim around to their dock? In full gear, without getting the weapons wet? That's a great way to drown."

"What if we walk?" I suggested. "We'd be much more silent than in the cars. We might not trigger any alerts, and there's a much better chance for every individual not to get shot, or become collateral damage in a car hit." I knew he must have considered that option, but I just had to ask. Did I want to spend two to three hours possibly crawling across dust, gravel, and get stuck in prairie grass and cacti? Not necessarily, but I was only just getting used to not having a hole in my hide.

I was surprised when Nate didn't shoot me down right away. "They had time enough to stage the sentries," he pointed out. "If it was me, I'd have mined the plains before that, or at the very least added barbed wire or some other nasty shit like that."

It was a possibility—and I felt vaguely stupid for not having considered that.

"You actually want to do a bull rush instead?" I ventured a guess.

"I… don't know," Nate ground out, each syllable laced with frustration. When I actually turned my head to fully look at him— that admission certainly warranted it—he grimaced. "I'm not shooting down your suggestion. But I don't have a satisfying answer. I don't remember the last time I've been in a position where I've had no intel and no contingency plans. We have nothing—absolutely nothing—to go on, and the fact that I haven't heard anything from two of my best scouts and fighters doesn't make this any easier."

I really didn't like how panic started licking up my spine at his words. "We went in blind with Dallas, too," I said. "France as well. Sure, we had blueprints for the France lab, but no fucking clue what was waiting for us." He glared at me as if I'd called him a liar, making me scramble mentally for another angle. "But you already know that. What makes this different?"

The pause that followed was long enough to make my skin crawl, and seeing the utter frustration in Nate's expression was bad enough, but then I realized what else was in there: fear. And that wasn't something I ever wanted to see from him.

"I don't know," he repeated more vehemently now. "I don't trust myself. My instincts. I know my gut reaction is the one thing I can always rely on, but Decker got under my skin. He's the one who created most of my fallback reactions. He can guess at what I will do better than anyone else. How am I supposed to outsmart the one man who taught me how to outsmart anyone else?"

A different kind of light bulb went off in my head at that sentence. "That's why you've become so chummy with Hamilton, right? You two have been trying to hash this all out. To find the impossible needle in the haystack."

Nate didn't look particularly happy at my exclamation. "You're my needle," he assessed. "And I probably shouldn't tell you this, but it galls him to no end that he has to agree with me on that. Not that it helps us much, seeing as everything you come up with is textbook protocol that I've hammered into your head for years."

"See, that's why you refrain from mindfucking your wife," I told him succinctly, but my hint of triumph was short-lived. "Let's think about this again. We know they must have more people than we do; else they couldn't have overwhelmed everyone swiftly and silently, including our vanguard, the sentries, and the scavengers that went snooping for intel."

A muscle twitched in Nate's jaw. "All it takes for that is a small, very efficient embedded strike force," he pointed out. "If people trust them and never suspect they're moles, they'd have an easy time to overwhelm key personnel swiftly without giving everyone else a chance to rally."

"But they must have more support, or else they couldn't have held their position," I objected. "Unless they slit everyone's throat, someone would have managed to either send us a warning, or set said key personnel free."

Nate mulled that over briefly. "Hate to say it, but I agree with you."

"That bad that I'm right?" I teased.

I got a deadpan stare back. "It means we're likely facing twice as many people. I always prefer a smaller opposition."

"Spoilsport," I muttered under my breath, but did my best to focus back on the question. "We assume they had time to mine the kill zone in front of the town. With what explosives? And wouldn't that hinder them just as much if they had to beat a quick retreat?"

"Who says they are planning for a retreat?" I didn't like Nate's question at all—or rather, the implications—and he gave me a wry grin for my frown. "Even efficient, they must have bled heavily to gain the upper hand. They know we're coming for them. They must have known that coming for our civvies will turn us much less receptive to taking prisoners than we otherwise might be. This is a suicide mission for them—and not one they plan on beating the odds and coming back from. People are twice as deadly when they are fighting with their backs against the wall and their only objective is to take as many with them as possible."

"What you're really saying is that they wouldn't have taken prisoners, either." Damn, but I hated to be right.

He nodded slowly. "Only to use them against us," Nate professed. "And drive the stake even deeper into our hearts. But you have a point there."

"Which is?" I didn't have to feign surprise.

He offered up another mirthless grin. "Knowing Zilinsky as I do, she wouldn't have kept explosives in the town to prevent a situation like this from getting even worse. They would have had to take everything they'd want to use with them, and I doubt they had much room for that, considering they already needed to cram people, gear, weapons, and ammo into their vehicles."

"Unless they got there by boat," I objected.

He shook his head with barely any consideration. "I'm sure they had their port closed for everything short of triple-checked cargo ships pre-arranged through New Angeles. If we figured out the fertilizer scheme, I'm sure others must have at least suspected as much."

I considered that for a while. "That means they probably just mined the most likely entry vectors—the main road to the gate, and the stretches around the two smaller entryways by the guard towers inside the palisade. Plus the very ends where the town borders the sea. If we stay to the stretches of land in between, we'll probably be fine."

Nate snorted. "I hate to bet my life on 'probably,'" he admitted.

"Yeah, well, so do I, but it looks like that's our best way in." I didn't exactly jeer, but it did make the most sense.

"Probably," he echoed, making me roll my eyes. More seriously, he added, "But I'd also drop some mines right in the middle of those middle swaths, just to fuck with people who think they can outsmart me."

"Would be too easy if they didn't," I offered. "So how do we do this? Risk detection at the three-mile-mark and drive until we absolutely have to exit the cars, or get out now in favor of stealth and spend half the night walking up to the kill zone?"

Not much consideration was needed. "We walk," Nate ordered—and I didn't miss that conviction had, for the most part, replaced his previous trepidation. "Pack lightly. We only need weapons and ammo—and we will replenish our stores on the go. Needing to make a mad dash for the town will be more likely than running out of bullets."

Using our close-range coms rather than the car radio, Nate relayed the new plan of attack—we would drive just a little farther, up to what was roughly the ten-mile mark to the settlement. The rest of the way would be on foot, split up into small groups and avoiding any direct, easy routes that would likely be guarded or booby-trapped. We had about enough night-vision gear for half of those who needed it, but the moon was shining just brightly enough that walking across the plains would be feasible for everyone.

I wasn't all that surprised that, as soon as we got ready to depart on foot, Nate put me in a group with Martinez, Burns, and Sonia, deciding to set out with Hamilton himself. Before I could protest—and point out that it was super smart to put the only two people with real first-aid knowledge into one team—he shut me up with a remark whispered into my ear. "I'm not sidelining you. I expect the four of you to head straight to the palisade, be there first, and make it into the settlement before the bulk of us make enough noise to inevitably attract the wrong kind of attention. If necessary, Burns will drop away as a diversion. You get in. You find any potential hostages—or someone we can beat the crap out of—and provide first aid if required. The three of you are smaller and easier to miss, and I'm counting on that. I'd send Buehler with you if her limp wasn't bad enough to keep her back."

Leaning back, I gave him a considering look before I whispered my response. "So, what you actually are saying is that I kill and they patch up what's left over?"

"Pretty much."

I could have done without his smirk—and the answering thrill racing up my spine. I had to admit, it was mostly token protest that wanted to make it over my lips—and that was very easy to silence considering that I knew who might be sitting in the middle of the camp with a knife to her and her kid's throat. I was a very long shot from any turn-the-other-cheek sentiments, but come after the less bloodthirsty of my friends, and you're asking for a knife in the back.

And, my, didn't it feel healthy when that sentiment made me crack up, if as silently as possible.

Martinez and Sonia both had their own night-vision goggles, and because of Nate's intent for them, nobody disputed them using their gear. Burns and I traded a quick look at each other's bare face, him giving the slightest of shrugs as if to say any advantage was welcome. He was downright gleeful as he helped me smear camouflage paint all over my face to keep my skin from turning into a beacon in the night. Asshole. But I couldn't help but grin myself, feeling just a little better seeing as I was setting out with two of the people I trusted the most in the world—and I doubted that Sonia's animosities toward me would be an issue tonight, provided I got neither Martinez nor Burns killed. Lucky me—they could take care of themselves.

The temptation was strong to jump Nate for one last goodbye kiss, but I passed up the chance. It felt too much like jinxing it.

With all three of them very familiar with the terrain, we made good time through the low hills that quickly evened out into the plain leading to the coast. Trees were small, gnarly-looking nightmare creatures in the dark, but there was plenty of shrubbery around that the first hour we could walk for the most part, if as quietly as possible. Nightlife went about its business mostly ignoring us, which was reassuring. No exploding jackrabbits ahead was always a good thing. But then we trotted down the last mile of proper elevation, and the work the settlers had put into securing their town became more obvious. They'd either torn down or carted away all obstacles large enough to count as proper cover, leaving the entire extended perimeter of the town bare and easy to observe from the palisades. We'd been following a few deer trails before but Burns abandoned them, sending us into the dry grass instead. The entire area looked undisturbed by recent trespassers, but just to be sure we spread out farther, the distance between Burns and me increasing from just inside shouting distance to several hundred feet. I didn't look forward to crawling through the grass, but trotting forward, hunched over to give as small a profile as possible, wasn't exactly pleasant, either. Soon, my shoulders, lower spine, and knees hurt, and the wound gave rhythmic, pounding waves of agony in tune with my heartbeat. More than once, I lost sight of the others when someone ducked down for a quick rest, and looking back the way we had come, I had a hard time tracking our trails. Nothing else of note was moving in the night, making me guess we'd beaten the others to the kill zone by a solid thirty minutes of the going on two hours since we'd left the cars.

I almost jumped when I heard someone blow into their mic, making me pause and hunker down immediately. Sonia's voice, barely a whisper, followed a few moments later. "I think I just stepped over a tripwire. Not tripped it, but there's something on the ground behind me. Noticed it when the grass whipped back weirdly."

I held my breath, listening to see if we'd attracted any attention.

"Be right back with you," Burns responded. "You two, advance. We'll catch up with you."

I'd been last in our stretched-out line, Martinez ahead and slightly to the south of my position. I saw him pop out of his hiding spot and move forward before Burns's much more visible silhouette started in the other direction. I was tempted to join him at Sonia's position mostly out of curiosity, but we were on a deadline, and I was sure the two of them could take care of whatever Sonia had found.

I got about a hundred yards farther when I suddenly heard Burns curse, followed by a hissed, "Fire in the hole!" I had just enough time to crouch low when something behind me detonated—presumably whatever Sonia had almost triggered before. The shockwave hit me almost immediately, not strong enough to push me over but definitely unpleasant. I didn't need a warning to flatten myself on the ground, sure that all attention would be on us now. Trying to peer back through the grass, I thought I saw two shapes, next to each other, also lying low, but it was mostly the lack of screams of pain that made me guess that they'd both gotten away.

I was tempted to remain where I was for the next five or ten minutes, knowing that whoever was keeping watch at the settlement would be focusing on this sector now, but instead pushed myself up into a low crouch. "Go, go," I whispered into my mic. "We need to be gone should they send out a firing squad." No protest followed, and I was quick to enact my own command. Ahead, the walls of the settlement were still far enough away to be nothing but a long, slightly curving block of darkness, and I made sure to angle farther north to keep out of what I presumed was the most likely line of sight. All I could do was hope that whoever was on guard duty would attribute it to an unlucky coyote biting it, but I didn't believe it for a second.

No lights came on, and no discharge of a sniper rifle followed, but it was impossible not to feel like a million eyes were on me. Between being paranoid about every straight line I saw—in the grass that was somewhere between ankle and knee height for me, and full of straight lines—and the need to keep a low profile, progress was slow. I looked back at where the mine had blown up, but since the grass hadn't caught fire, I soon lost sight of it. The momentary silence dissipated as animals of all flavors picked up their nightly routines again, allowing me to ease up a little. Every time I paused and looked around, I found only the seemingly peaceful nightly landscape around me, Martinez the only moving target I could pick out every once in a while. That boded well, I told myself.

That was, until the sharp scent of gasoline tickled my nose, making me stop and look around for the source. It was easy to chalk it up to a leaking car that had been used to set up the traps. I hadn't been here long but I estimated that I was a mile south of the main road leading into town. My nose was good, but not quite that good. The wind changed direction slightly and the scent was gone, but I picked it up again a few steps later. It lessened again but returned in force almost immediately. I tried to get a better look around my position but didn't see anything suspicious—which didn't say much since there was grass everywhere, dry as tinder and tall enough to hide someone lying on the ground two feet away from me. I pushed on, telling myself that since Martinez ahead of me hadn't reported in, it must be close yet contained.

The scent slowly disappeared from the air, then came again, but eventually I left it behind. I made it a good quarter of a mile toward the town before I smelled it once more, although logically, it couldn't be the same patch. I halted, trying to better pinpoint the source, but it was impossible with the wind coming and going in small gusts. Then I hit a third patch, the acrid smell so strong that it almost choked me. Trying hard not to cough, I pulled my scarf up over my nose and mouth, hoping to staunch it momentarily. There was something going on, and I didn't like it.

Huffing into my mic, I waited a few seconds, then asked, "Anyone else smell gasoline?"

Silence answered me, making me wonder if I was simply seeing things—or was lucky to have found the trail of said leaking car. A minute passed, then another, until a low, male voice came on—Amos. "Yeah, I smell it, too. Can't find the source, though. We're the northernmost group. You're south, right?"

I gave an affirmative huff, again casting around for anything to catch my attention.

Nate's voice came on next, a surprising amount of urgency in it. "Forward, now! Try to remain low, but if you can smell it, run!"

And just as if he'd jinxed it, a whooshing roar sounded, coming from the road. I had just begun to turn my head to look when bright light started to sear the retina in my right eye. Going more on instinct than command, I bolted forward, trying to keep my torso level with the ground but digging my heels in for a quick sprint. The roar increased exponentially, but was quickly surpassed by light chasing the darkness away, effectively blinding me. Heat followed, blowing over me at an alarmingly increasing rate. Throwing caution to the wind, I ran as fast as I could, knowing fully well how much of a target I must be, a dark body against the fire spreading at my back. Acting immediately on Nate's call got me out of the worst, but even before I could check what was going on behind me, screams over the com made it quite obvious. We were spread too far apart for me to hear anyone directly, but that didn't lessen the gruesomeness of it.

Something was nipping on my left leg, and when I looked down, I saw fire licking over my calf and boot, sparks flying into the grass, leaving a haphazard trail behind. I dropped and rolled, doing my best to extinguish anything that might be clinging to my pack where I couldn't easily check. Grabbing some loose dirt, I dumped it on my leg, the flames going out as soon as they got deprived of oxygen. A quick check confirmed that I was fine, just a few scorch marks around the edges where the spilled gasoline must have transferred from the grass to my clothes.

Glancing up, I got a first good look at the raging inferno behind me. Well, not exactly raging as the flames were already dying down in patches, but in others the grass was burning brightly, sparks quickly lighting everything they touched on fire. It looked like someone had splashed gasoline—or some other accelerant—in three thick lines all across the plains, lighting the entire kill zone brightly. I could see what looked like three fireballs rolling on the ground—the unlucky bastards who had gotten caught in the fire when it had been ignited. The others seemed to be okay, hunkered down but on high alert.

The wind blew hot sparks in my direction, making me back up further, toward the settlement, immediately. Part of me was glad that it was blowing toward the ocean, which might just help keep the entire state from burning. But that also meant that we were potentially caught inside a narrowing noose that kept driving us right into the arms of our opponents—and giving them great illumination to make their shots count.

The rapport of an assault rifle was loud enough to be heard above the roar of the flames, if still far enough away that it couldn't have been a well-aimed sequence of shots. It served as a reminder that hunkering down was no longer an option.

"Martinez, are you okay?" I whisper-shouted into the mic, figuring that the sound of my voice would be the last thing to give me away now.

"Copy," Martinez was quick to reply.

"Burns? Sonia?"

The answer came a few seconds late, making my anxiety surge momentarily. "We're caught just behind the forward-most line," Sonia reported in. "Checking to find a part that we can cross. Looks like we can move forward if we go a hundred yards to the south. Advance without us, if you can."

I was tempted to tell her that I wasn't taking orders from her, but it was sound advice, so I acknowledged and instead tried to find Martinez to join him. It was a horribly easy task, since even partially blinded from staring into the fire, my eyes had no trouble picking him out where he was hunched down behind a scrub maybe fifty feet away from me. The rifle barked again, but since nothing hit me, I continued forward, picking up the pace as I passed by Martinez's position. He sprinted right after me, signaling me to stray farther to my right. That seemed stupid since the road and gate were in that direction, but when he kept insisting, I changed course. The closer we got to the walls, the darker it got, our pace much quicker than the wind could drive the flames forward. I found a convenient cover looming ahead—the base of a forward watch tower, little more than a few slats nailed to some poles, abandoned now. I hadn't been running full out but it still took Martinez over three minutes to join me, his face twisted into a grimace of pain. I was just about to ask him where he'd been shot when I realized it must have been his old injuries giving him grief.

Looking beyond him, I thought I saw Sonia and Burns following roughly in our tracks, if at a much slower pace. I realized why when the rifle barked again. Looking toward the source of the racket, I saw the muzzle flash from somewhere up at the palisades, the guard post pretty much right between where we'd been running and where the shooter was standing. More weapons opened fire, the relative darkness of the barricades making it easy to see them from where I was. My hands were itching to grab the M4 from where it was strapped to my pack, but I remained hunkered down instead, happy not to be in the line of fire right now.

As soon as Martinez looked like he'd be able to respond, I leaned close to him and asked, "Should we try to take them out? From here, I'm sure we'd hit at least five or six of them before they take us out."

Not much of a surprise, he shook his head. "If we can make it onto the palisades, we'll be much more effective," he pressed out between pants. "And you can use your knife, if need be."

Did the very idea of shiving those assholes bring me joy? A little, but it was reason more than bloodlust that had me nod. If we opened return fire, they'd spot us within seconds. If I could stealthily sneak down the line and dispatch them silently, it would take them a while to realize the others weren't just reloading or waiting for their targets to come out of hiding.

Glancing back at the fire, I could make out a few more moving targets, proving just how urgent the situation was. "Can you climb?"

I asked Martinez in what was likely a pure insult. He gave me a look underlining just that as he gave a curt nod. "Great," I went on. "Because I can't. You'll have to go first and help pull me up." It was only at my explanation that he understood, his gaze briefly dropping down to my hands. I gave a pained grin at his apologetic look, forestalling anything he could say with a quick slap on his shoulder. "I go first. I'll throw a rope up. You go up. I come after you. Go!"

As soon as he gave me the thumbs-up, I sprinted toward the barricade, trusting that the now near-constant shooting would drown out any sounds I made. Being a moving target so close to at least three shooters made me physically sick, but they were all concentrating on positions farther out, ignoring me for the moment. The fires likely blinded them too much for them to catch on to what was moving in the near darkness directly below them.

I reached the forward defenses unscathed. The settlement had gone all out and had dug not just one ditch but two, filled with lots of sharpened poles oriented toward the plain. Shamblers might be stupid enough to impale themselves, but for a sentient human it was possible to climb over or squeeze through them with a bit of care. Martinez was fighting his way through the first ditch by the time I reached the heavy, slightly weathered wood beams that made up the wall. Getting the rope from the side of my pack, I wasted twenty precious seconds checking that it had only been slightly scorched but not seared through before I got a good grip and let the grappling hook fly. It went short, knocking against the wood but coming right down again. I quickly sidestepped and pressed myself against the palisade, hoping that nobody was looking down to investigate. Since I wasn't turned into a human sieve, I picked up the blasted thing and threw it again, this time aiming better. The hook caught, staying put even when I used my entire weight to try to dislodge it.

Martinez joined me a moment later, accepting the rope from me, still puffing for air. He was up in record time, not bothering with great leg work as he used only his upper body strength to pull himself to the top. I had noted that his torso and arms had beefed up compared to before, but not how much. I figured it made sense, with months where he hadn't been able to use his legs at all, followed by what must have been a grueling physical therapy regimen. I grabbed the rope as soon as he was over the top, jumping as high as I could and doing my best to get the rope grabbed just right between my ankles. My hands were burning by the time I managed to reach the top of the barricade and pull myself over, nicely aided by Martinez.

We both hunkered down on the dark walkway on the inside of the wall, checking that we were still undetected. The nearest shooter was a good fifty feet from us, close enough that I was surprised we'd made it from the watchtower to the wall without being detected. I debated what weapon to use and ended up getting my knife out. The ruckus caused by incessant shooting—some of which was return fire from the plain below—was likely enough that I could have used my handgun, but I didn't want to risk it.

Still, I hesitated as I glanced toward what would become my first victim. I'd gotten quite good at shooting people who were shooting back; cold-blooded murder was a different affair entirely. I knew it was a moot point—we still had people down there in the kill zone that I was protecting with my actions, and they had at least severely wounded, if not killed, three of us. That should have been more than enough to calm my conscience. Yet as I kept looking for clues of the affiliation of the purported evil in front of me, they were hard to find. From what I could tell—good low-light vision or not, it was dark up here compared to the burning plains below—they were all wearing the typical patched-together gear of traders, scavengers, and lots of settlement people all across the country.

Turning to Martinez, I decided to, this once, get a second opinion. I already knew what he was going to say from his pinched expression that only got more forbidding once he had his night-vision goggles in place—and pointed down into the settlement. "Those are not our people," he whispered, jerking his chin at the shooters up on the barricade. "But they were." Following his gaze, I could just make out two bodies lying in the otherwise unremarkable-looking street. One might have been either a short man or a woman. The other was too slight for that—an adolescent, if my guess was any good.

Fuck.

Well, there went nothing.

Peering one more time into the plains, I tried to make out any of our people but I couldn't even find Burns and Sonia, although I knew where they must have been hiding more or less. Most of the opposition centered further north, which was a good thing—for now. Turning my com to the team frequency, I blew into it first before giving a quick, near-silent status report. "Lewis here. I'm with Martinez up on the wall. We're starting a quick cleanup run, going south to north. Don't shoot us if you can avoid it. Concentrate fire on the shooters north of the gate. I'll keep you in the loop."

Nobody acknowledged, but that was just as well. Martinez had his rifle ready, signaling that he was covering me—and was ready to take care of anything I couldn't quickly overwhelm. I figured I could take out at least two or three of them until I'd have to resort to ranged attacks. After hours spent tensed up without a good way to bleed off energy, my body was singing with the need for violence, and after seeing the bodies in the settlement below, my mind was more than on board with that.

Creeping up to the first shooter was almost too easy. The boards of the walkway weren't completely silent, but even I had a hard time picking up the creaks my weight on them caused, and Martinez remained my silent shadow. I didn't bother with fancy kidney-stabs or the like, but went right for the side of his neck as soon as I reared up behind him. Height difference was no issue as he was crouched over slightly, using the wall as a support for his rifle. Two lightning-fast stabs and a slash across his throat, and I had a dead body right in front of me, still gushing blood all over my arms. I picked up his M16 and threw it over the wall, leaving Martinez to grab any spare magazines he could find on short notice. A careful glance forward revealed that the next shooter was still oblivious, right now busy with reloading. I was on him before he could fire another shot, dispatching him as easily as the first.

I realized I was out of luck when I checked on the next position, and found not one but two shooters, side by side. I considered for a moment but then sheathed the knife and instead drew my Glock. Crossing half the distance to their position, I knelt down on one knee and aimed, hoping that down here they wouldn't see me that easily. Two shots—the first a clean kill in the temple, the second a little too low, hitting the asshole in the side of the neck. He slumped over all right, but ended up partly hidden behind the corpse of his buddy. I came to my feet and moved closer, gun aimed at what I could make out of the bulk of his body. He was still holding on tightly to his AR-15 but hadn't managed to bring it up or even vaguely point it in my direction. His head was turned to the side as if he tried to look for his assailant, but by the time I stepped into his field of vision, his stare had turned sightless. I checked on the next position, but the single shooter was still oblivious to us. As much as I appreciated that stroke of luck, it also made me suspicious. I was good, but not that good. I let Martinez divest the two bodies of their guns and spare ammo while guarding our front, but then signaled him to take over so I could check the bodies once more. One had a bare neck but the other—the one I'd killed with the headshot—had a single X, marking him as a scavenger. My blood ran cold seeing it, and when I looked closer at his gear, I saw streaks of lighter paint across parts of it—red, if I wasn't mistaken, yet it was impossible to tell without additional light. I couldn't help but wonder if he'd been part of the group from Vegas. But why fight against us, then?

The next shooter paused to reload, making me freeze instantly. Yet he didn't turn his head to check to his left or right—just ejected the magazine, dropped it, pushed in a fresh one, and went right back to shooting. Glancing into the dark settlement, I realized he was the last one south of the gate. Since he was on his own, I could have used the knife once more, but I went with the gun instead, minimizing the risk to myself that melee always entailed. He died just like the others, without making an extra sound except for his body slumping onto the walkway boards. Right above the gate, I saw three shooters next to each other, concentrating fire on a position somewhat north of them. I hadn't made it past my last kill when one of them jerked his head around, looking right at me, and I knew my luck had finally run out.

Martinez and I opened fire at almost the same time, me dropping down to minimize the target I was presenting, and so he could spray everything in front of us with bullets. A stray casing hit my cheek, leaving a hot, burning scorch mark, but I didn't even flinch as I kept emptying my magazine into the shooters in front of us. The one closest may have seen me, but he was dead before he could alert the others, who were too slow to react as our bullets bit into them. One of them let out a shout before he died, which I was sure would put a final end to our spree.

"The guard house, to your right!" Martinez hissed to me, making me spring forward and duck through the opening in the wooden box sitting next to the gate. It was barely large enough for the two of us, but it was solid cover with openings to shoot into the area right in front of the gate—that also worked well for whoever was coming along the walkway toward us. As soon as I had a new magazine in my Glock, I aimed and fired, taking the first man who came running in the torso with three shots, and felling the second with one miss and one right between the eyes. Martinez's single-fire shots also landed in their torsos, but I didn't mind the overkill. I waited for more to come, but when the coast remained clear for another twenty seconds, I figured I might as well report in.

"We're at the gate now," I told the rest of our team, still talking in a low voice but no longer feeling the need to whisper. "We also took out two stationed just beyond the gate. Keeping position for now to see if more will come to us. Anyone south of the gate, I think you're free to make a run for the wall."

Since still no resistance appeared at the other side of the gate, I signaled Martinez to check behind us while I kept watch forward. Tense minutes passed while farther north shots were still being traded. Then Martinez gave my left shoulder a slight nudge. "I see Sonia and Burns up on the walkway. They've seen me. I say we let them guard our backs and move on."

No objection to that from me, so that was exactly what we did. In passing, I made sure that both men we'd shot were indeed dead. Both had single-X marks on their necks and their gear was rough, but something just didn't feel right. I considered keeping with my pistol but instead relieved one of them of his M16 and his two spare magazines. No need to fumble with my pack if I could just pick it up on the way. Martinez and I advanced further, with me keeping to the right and him a few steps behind me to the left.

As soon as I got a good look at the next shooter, I aimed and fired, only having to pause for another twenty seconds before the next one came running into his doom. He didn't even try for a strategic position, although there wasn't any cover in the stretch from the gate right to the end of the palisade, where a smaller entrance and similar watch box was located, from what I remembered. But there were two stairs leading up onto the walkway ahead of us yet farther down, still out of sight, obscured by darkness. I was doing my best to locate them. Being able to hunker down on the steps would make for great defensive positions.

Five more shooters in three positions we gunned down, and none of them tried to hide anywhere near the stairs. The night had almost fallen silent when the last one dropped, only the bark of a single assault rifle coming from up ahead. Our people had stopped shooting after I'd reported in, and more than one group had reached the trenches in the meantime. The lone shooter went on, emptying another magazine even after our last shots had killed his remaining compatriots. Chancing a glance down into the plain, I couldn't find what he was shooting at. The fires were still burning but the lines had turned into haphazard patches, leaving scorched earth behind that could be easily traversed.

I raised my hand to signal Martinez to pause and switched back to my Glock. My brain was screaming at me to stop being so fucking stupid as I advanced on the last shooter's position with inferior firepower. I aimed at his shoulder when I shot, squeezing the trigger two times in quick succession. His rifle wavered as he lost control of his right arm, pointing uselessly at the boards in front of him. His attention remained on the plains, which made no sense, as even the most stunned, going-into-shock gunman would have at least looked around in confusion to see where the shots had come from. Advancing further on him, I put two more bullets into his torso but aimed lower, for his hips. The rifle slid to the ground as he folded in on himself, ending in a partially kneeling position. I could smell the blood gushing from his wounds, and still he didn't even acknowledge me. My mind was screaming at me to finish him off— and I would have loved to oblige as his behavior was freaking me out more than getting shot at—but I forced myself to close the distance to him until I could press the muzzle of my gun against his cheek. He didn't flinch away although the hot metal must have burned against his skin. Following instinct, I gave his bleeding shoulder a kick that got him sprawling onto his back, and put another round straight into his chest.

Martinez appeared by my side, inhaling in what I knew must have been to question what the fuck I was doing, but I forestalled him, my gun not wavering from where I kept pointing it at the shooter's head. "Wait for it…"

And, true enough, ten seconds after a gargling death rattle left his chest, his body gave a jerk as he reanimated. I emptied my magazine into his head, reducing it to so much gore, putting a final end to the spectacle.

Martinez looked slightly shaken when I finally glanced at him over my shoulder. "Did you know he'd convert?" he wanted to know.

"Nope. But it was an educated guess." His night-vision goggles hid his frown, but I knew it must be there, so I explained. "I could be wrong, but I think most of them must have been shot up with the mind-control shit that works on the older versions of the serum—and probably on the faulty one the scavengers got as well. Still good enough for mindless shooting at anything that moves in a designated target area. Only the ones at the gates actually reacted to us decimating them."

Martinez cursed under his breath but didn't debate my assessment.

Looking back the way we had come, I saw several people moving on the walkway. "All clear," I called in before I turned to look at the dark settlement below. I was sure that our entrance was no longer a matter of surprise. If there still were people down there, they would have responded to us. Our people, that was. That the intruders hadn't shot at us yet was a marvel, and as soon as I thought that, Nate's voice came over the radio for us to stop fucking around and take cover. There was none, really, but crouching low so that we weren't silhouetted against the sky was a first step. The group closest to us joined us, turning out to be Blake and two of his marines. While they secured the area, I got busy getting fresh magazines from my pack and finally readying my M4. I had a feeling that the time for stealth was over.

Someone down there in the settlement seemed to agree with me as moments after I was done, a succession of explosions went off, lighting up parts of the town.

"That's the docks," Martinez muttered, his face partly turned away so his eyes wouldn't get completely fried.

I had a feeling I knew where we would be headed next.

Chapter 7

"Check the houses closest to the wall. Converge at the gate," came Nate's command a few seconds later.

I waited a moment for Blake to assume command of our impromptu fireteam, but when he just looked at me instead, I gave him a brief nod back. "Understood," I told Nate after identifying myself. "We're at the northernmost part. We'll need a while to be back at the gate. Unless you want us to go snooping to the north—"

"That's a negative," Nate told me, his voice completely void of humor. "Gate. Now."

Far was it from me to protest a direct order—if it suited me just fine—but it soon became apparent that it made sense in a different way as well, when I watched Blake and Martinez both wince their way down the steps to the ground, each man physically hampered in his own way. For a moment I felt bad not even considering that just because I had no issues with running, others might not be that fortunate, but I was the first to admit that I wasn't used to not being the weakest link. That said more about the people I had been running with in both the recent and more distant past than my own shortcomings, but it was something to consider now. Not that I aimed to be rid of them shortly, but I could see how Nate wouldn't forget.

I took point, signaling to one marine to immediately follow me and for the other to bring up the rear. The two of us in the lead could easily case any room we ducked into, and most buildings here didn't have more than that; keeping the other three on the street to keep our backs clear made the most sense, anyway. I still found Blake grimacing as he was sidelined to guard duty, but neither he nor Martinez protested.

Our job was easy enough since there was nobody alive—or undead—in any of the buildings we checked. After seeing the two bodies in the street earlier, I'd expected the worst, but the bunkhouse and two small warehouses we checked were abandoned, with minimal signs of a forced entry anywhere. It made sense—whoever had breached the settlement and set the guards to shoot at us had likely found more resistance in the southern part of the settlement where I knew most families lived, and where all the common areas like the cantina were situated. In the bunkhouse particularly there was some disarray from where someone must have made a quick exit—and a few bullet holes by the door spoke of a not-quite easy exit—but that was the extent of the damage we found.

At the corner of the next house over, Burns and Sonia were waiting for us, having taken the nearby steps down. I motioned for them to fall in line behind me and the marine, building a second group to check on houses. They'd already cleared this one so we went on to the next. As soon as I peeked through the doorway, I wished I hadn't. The scent of blood already gave away what my eyes confirmed a moment later—four dead in the middle of the room, behind the makeshift barricade of an overturned table. I forced myself to check that they were indeed dead for good, but that meant I couldn't ignore the fact that it had been a family with two adolescent girls, both just old enough to try to defend themselves effectively, but they'd gotten mowed down just as quickly as their parents, judging from where the bodies had fallen. None of their faces looked familiar—a small mercy that I knew wasn't something I shared with Martinez, Burns, or Sonia.

The next house was thankfully abandoned, but in the two that followed we found the same—small groups of people killed, and quickly enough that they hadn't been able to put up much of a fight. Not a single body we found was wearing heavy gear, or looked like they didn't belong.

We caught up to the others at the next intersection, the houses between there and the gate already cleared from that direction. Nate was waiting at the broader road inside the gate, currently debriefing the groups that had come in from the south. I joined them to quickly relay our findings, scarce as they had been. Nate took it all in with a stoic look on his face—even the part with the converting guard. "That's likely the reason we haven't found any of them dead down here," he surmised. "They must be busy eating the next best thing that still has a heartbeat." My, wasn't that a positive outlook on life?

It was too quiet for many shamblers to be lurking close by, even the smart ones—and, usually, the freshly turned ones weren't smart. They were still strong enough to go after any prey they wanted, with all the hunger in the world driving them, and that didn't make for stealthy hunters. The explosion coming from the direction of the docks had remained the only disturbance since we'd killed the last guards up at the palisades—but there was still almost the entire settlement to search, and our entrance had been far from stealthy.

"What's up with that?" I asked, glancing at the still-barricaded gate.

Nate didn't even check what I was referring to. "Rigged to blow," he pointed out. "I'll go about dismantling the charges later. If we even need to. Since we won't be staying here, simply blowing it up will be safer."

I couldn't say why that idea hit me in the stomach like a well-aimed punch, but it was only then that it occurred to me that there might not be enough of the settlement left to save—meaning its inhabitants—to bother with recovery.

"How many did we lose?" I asked, trying to get a better idea of who was missing.

"No casualties," Nate told me. "But two badly burned, and one is down from smoke inhalation. They're outside at the northern gate tower." He did a quick sweep of our assembly, singling out Blake, who was trying hard to look like he wasn't favoring his injured leg. "Choose two to guard the gate with. Just because we can't undo the charges now doesn't mean we'll leave it free for just anyone to blow up at our backs."

Blake acknowledged that with a somber nod and motioned for the two men who had been with him before to join him. I would have loved to keep sneaking on with Burns and Martinez, but Nate had other ideas. He assigned Martinez to the team that would go check on the northern parts—more warehouses, the body shop, and vehicle storage areas. Burns he sent as fireteam leader of a larger group of scavengers and what remained of the local people who'd come with us to assault the camp. I got slapped with Cole, Hill, and most of the remaining scavengers, while Nate left himself, Hamilton, and Sonia—of all people—out of the count. She seemed as thrilled as Burns with that choice but didn't speak up. The remaining soldiers and marines each built their own teams. Nate gave us the signal to swarm out, so that's what I did, taking point down the center of the largest street—until I could duck into cover after the second house to the left. I may have been out for blood, but I wasn't suicidal.

Five houses deep from the gate, someone must have cleaned up after them, because that was exactly how long it took us to find the first shambler munching on a dead settler. I heard it before I even looked into the house and might have bypassed the building altogether, except that one peek inside revealed that it wasn't wearing more than a stained shirt with pants tangled around its ankles, and was digging into the intestines of a similarly scantily-dressed woman. The zombie was hunched over in a way that didn't allow me to see the back of its neck, but I was going out on a limb and guessed it didn't have just a single mark there. I couldn't leave one of the super-juiced ones at our back, but I wasn't stupid enough to go in there armed with melee weapons. Signing Cole and Hill behind me that we had a heavy hitter on the floor, I got my M4 ready—and let Hill surge past me into the middle of the room, bringing his shotgun to bear at the back of the head of the still-oblivious shambler. The roar of the discharge was loud, same as the resulting splatter of brains and skull shrapnel was impressive. Dead for good, the corpse dropped onto the woman's body, making the three of us exhale in relief—until she reared up, rage-filled eyes wide, coming for Hill.

He shied away instinctively, backing into Cole, which took them both out for the moment. My mind was still reeling from the sheer incredulity the situation caused—just how out of this world was it to turn and reanimate as your fuck-buddy was busy tearing out your intestines to get to your liver and heart?—and I was slow to act. The zombie was already halfway across the room and aiming for me by the time I had her in my sights and pulled the trigger. Five of the six bullets I sent flying hit home, spraying from the shambler's shoulder across her body down to the gaping hole in her middle. The impacts made it jerk, but none of the hits was lethal, and, if anything, only enraged her further. She let out a blood-curdling scream before she launched herself at me, closing what remained of the distance between us. I was ready, bringing up the rifle to keep it from pushing me to the ground, and kicked at the right knee, putting all my strength in the move. Fresh and sturdy didn't help when my boot broke something important, making the howling zombie fold to the ground. The stock of my rifle, smashed into a fragile temple, was enough to down it completely, so it was easy for Hill to blow its head to smithereens, too. The entire encounter had taken less than twenty seconds, adrenaline only now slamming my heart into overdrive. Hill and I stared at each other over the corpses until he gave himself a visible shake. "Now I've seen it all."

Cole nudged the male zombie with his boot, just to make sure it stayed down, shaking his head before he glanced to me. "Glimpse into your future, huh?"

I stared at him, my wits needing a moment to catch up. "I would have so torn your face off if you'd given me five seconds to come after you. Just saying." Rather than wait for a retort, I stepped back outside, checking carefully that it was our people who came out of the next house instead of an ambush. All around us I heard shots, making me guess they'd found similar surprises.

Twice more we went through the same process until I signaled the rest of my group to keep heading along the street while I took Cole and Hill with me deeper into the houses. Rather than continue with cleanup, I signaled them to move forward, angling away from the sounds of shots. A few times I heard unsavory sounds of feeding coming from a window I ducked underneath, but there wasn't much I could do short of continuing to give my position away. There were no survivors in this part of the settlement; else they would have had ample time to creep out with the distraction our shots created, or join us.

Living quarters changed to houses filled with work stations of all kinds, most for food processing, from what I could tell—going by the terrible stench of rotten fish. I was just coming out of the second house—wishing I'd encountered a zombie rather than a heap of half-processed fish from what I estimated was the day before yesterday—when something pinged against the wall right next to where I was standing, silently surveilling the street. I quickly glanced around, trying to see where the pebble currently rolling away on the ground had come from. I felt ready to kick myself, having forgotten to ask what the inside signals of the people here might be, but in a pinch let out a low whistle.

The answer came swiftly, from the direction of the roofs of the houses on the opposite side of the street. "Marco!" someone whisper-shouted.

Incredulity had me halt for a moment, but at least that cleared up whether the settlers were our people—definitely yes.

"You got to be fucking kidding me," Cole grumbled next to me.

I flashed him a grin and obliged the pebble-thrower on the roof. "Polo!"

A head popped out from behind the roof, eyes narrowed at us. I didn't know the guy's name but I remembered him from my brief stay here weeks ago. He seemed to recognize me as well after some squinting. "You Martinez's friend, right?"

I nodded, hoping he would see it in the relative darkness of the door I was still standing in—but then he had seen enough of me to make sense of my features. "I am. He's farther north, checking on the houses."

A low curse rang out, followed by some scrambling, and in short order three men came sliding down the side of the roof. "Men" was pushing it as only the guy who had been talking was past twenty. The other two weren't old enough for proper beard growth yet, their wide eyes and scared body language speaking volumes. They stopped and almost shied away when they saw Cole and Hill lurking behind me, but when I motioned them to follow us back into the house we'd just cleared, they did.

"You're the ones they were shooting at?" the lead guy guessed.

I nodded. "Took us a little to clear the barricades. The gate's still rigged to blow, but if you go up on top of the palisades, you can use our ropes to get outside, if you want. Not sure I'd recommend it. Half the kill zone outside is still burning. They tried to incinerate us as we snuck up on them," I explained, seeing the bewilderment on their faces.

Lead Guy quickly shook off his surprise. "Fucking assholes got here three days ago, middle of the night," he said. "Not quite sure how it happened, really. Me and my boys, we were out on one of the fishing boats, using the gentle night for some extra catches. Next thing we know, someone hails us with a warning, and then we get shot at when we're trying to dock. We've been hiding in the attic of my shop since then."

"Infiltrators," I presumed. "We had a mole, too."

"Killed him, huh?" the guy presumed.

I shook my head. "Bitch knifed me in the back and took a few others down. Escaped. Long story. Do you know if anyone else is still around? We've found bodies—and quite a lot of fresh shamblers—but by far not enough to account for how many people I know live here."

He licked his lips, nervous. "We saw them round up people. Only the cantina and the gathering hall in the town square are large enough to hold that many people. You know where they are?"

I nodded. "Patrols?"

"Haphazardly," he said. "If you haven't run into any live opposition since the barricades, they must be waiting for you to come to them."

"Yeah, no shit," Cole muttered.

I ignored him. "Anything else you can tell us?"

The guy thought about it but shook his head. One of his sons looked twitchy enough that I stared at him, which made him shrink back, but finally offer, "I think I recognized a few, three guys in particular. They're from the New Vegas bunch."

The way he said it made it plain he wanted to follow it up with "fucking scavenger scum" but something in my face must have made him shut up before he got to that part. "Were they acting normal?"

He blinked, confused. "Normal like what? They're usually fucking high as soon as they get here."

"Well, were they acting high? Because what opposition we've killed so far wasn't."

He didn't respond, but his brother finally piped up. "I saw them, too. They weren't doing a good job patrolling. At least not like Zilinsky always drills us. Just marched down the center of the street from intersection to intersection. Stopped when they startled up a bunch of rats but missed me hiding in almost plain sight down in the shop. They must have been bored out of their minds to be that blind."

Or someone had given them the wrong kind of orders. Maybe it was a complete shot in the dark, but those could have been the scouts I had talked to on the radio—and someone had shot them up with that mind-control shit after they'd been caught.

I really didn't like to think along those lines when, inevitably, the next question was whether they'd also caught our vanguard—and also shot them up with the same shit. It would work on Andrej and Pia both, and I didn't think it beyond those assholes to infect those with their faulty serum who had not yet been exposed to any of the versions. I didn't know everyone well who was along, but Clark was among them; things might not look any better for Collins or Moore, who'd remained here to lend a hand to Sadie should she need it.

Shit, but this wasn't looking good.

I was just about to chase the three hideouts back into their perch—they sounded friendly enough, but after Marleen I wasn't taking any chances—when the team com frequency spewed out static, followed by my husband's dulcet tones. "Where the fuck is Lewis? Has anyone seen her?"

I didn't miss Hill's snicker, but he and Cole both remained silent. One of the people I should have been with piped up a few moments later. "She and the two army dudes went south."

Gee, thanks for ratting me out! Before I could complain loudly— or as much as whispered conversations not to draw unwanted attention could be considered loud—Nate's curse forestalled me. Deciding that my continuing silence was only making matters worse, I spoke up. "We're at the workshops close to the part of the docks that's not blown up, judging from the lack of smoke in the air." I paused, then added, "We found three of the townspeople, alive and well. They've been—"

I didn't get further than that before Nate hissed right over me. "Why the fuck are you disobeying my direct order?"

The other two's mirth was increasing, which didn't help my already not quite sunny disposition—but it wasn't exactly like I had a good base here to defend my actions. "Because I'm a strong, independent woman?" I suggested.

Laughter followed—not from Nate, and probably not Martinez and Burns since they knew better than to keep their mics on for actions like that—but quickly died when Nate's voice came back on.

"And you don't think I give orders like that for a reason?"

"I'm sure you always have a good reason for everything you do," I offered, carefully glancing down the street to see if another patrol was close. "I just didn't see it in that specific order. Plus, we did find those three guys, and they pretty much confirmed what I found with the guys defending the palisades—they're pretty much badly-calibrated automatons, likely due to the mind-control shit the army's been developing. Or, knowing what we know now, I'd say the assholes dug in underneath Dallas. Whatever." Something else occurred to me—something Hamilton and the Chemist's assistant had said before committing suicide. "Or it's all last-stage, faulty-serum scavengers. I don't have a fucking clue. But nobody has found us yet, and that's intel useful to us. Can you keep the chewing-me-out part until it's just you and me and you're not giving Cole more ammo for his exceedingly funny remarks?" The asshole in question flashed me a smirk, but went right back to guarding the doorway.

The fact that Nate had let me explain was testament to his willingness to listen, but even my news didn't change his foul mood.

"We're massively outnumbered and I can't get anything done if we're spread out too far. You need to back-track and follow the path I initially told you to follow. And yes, that's an order."

I had a better idea. Thumbing my mic off, I turned to the guy and his sons. "Did you see where exactly the patrols came from or went to? What about the other townspeople? The bodies we found don't make up for enough that they could have killed everyone. You mentioned the cantina and town hall. What's your best guess?"

The guy shook his head, as did one of the boys, but the older one answered after a guilty look at his father. "I did some sneaking last night, when it was the most quiet after three in the morning. I saw some lights coming from two of the houses at the other end of the port, where we do the port admin shit. Stuff, I mean," he quickly corrected himself. I gave him a look that should have told him plainly he really didn't need to watch his language around me. He quickly went on when he caught his father's scowl. "I also saw some lights coming from the cantina but didn't dare go any closer. I was hungry," he offered apologetically.

"You did good," I assured him, then quickly relayed what he'd said to Nate. "Sounds like that's what blew up after we cleared the palisades," I guessed. "It's not that far from here, or at least I can find a position where I can get a good look." The boy quickly nodded, understanding I meant someone could show me. "The cantina is a good distance from where you are. If you need to split off people to check on the docks, you'll lose time and firepower. We're already here."

No sound came over the line but I knew Nate well enough to perfectly hear how he was gnashing his teeth. "Go check," he finally ground out. "Just to get an overview. Then you loop back to where the rest of your people are, exactly where I told you to lead them."

I swallowed the remark that his exact orders had been slightly different, but now wasn't the time for quarreling. "Sure thing. I'll report in with an update as soon as we can talk freely." No answer came, so I turned to the boy. "Might be too dicey for you to lead us to a possible perch, so do your best to describe where we need to go."

He looked slightly disappointed but was happy to draw us a map in the dirt right outside of the door. I studied it briefly, doing my best to commit it to memory. "Thanks for your help," I told the three of them. "Now go back and hide. Once everything has died down—and you're sure we're the only ones left standing—get out of the town and head to one of the gathering places." I was sure Pia had designated some for emergencies. "If all else fails, make your way to New Angeles."

They were gone in no time, the father leaving us with a hushed "good hunting" before following his boys. I waited until the night was quiet again before I made my way down the street, careful to keep checking our surroundings even with a clear goal in mind. All of the other shops and houses looked deserted, and we didn't find any other bodies. The house with the ladder leading onto a hidden sniper perch on the next house over was exactly where the boy had told us it would be. I stepped aside to let Cole go first. Hill signaled me he would guard the street, leaving me to the shitty task of having to climb up myself, no assistant with a rope for me this time. The "ladder" was little more than weathered slats nailed in haphazard intervals on the walls of the house, on both sides of a corner. They were clearly spaced for someone well above my height, and the weight of my pack didn't help. Halfway up, I had to traverse the entire wall to get up onto the roof, and then continue up the other house's side. Cole was watching our surroundings from up high but kept peering down at me, concerned I would make too much sound so he'd get shot, I was sure.

I finally made it, remaining on my stomach for a few seconds after pulling myself up onto the walled platform, not because I was being stealthy but because my hands were giving me so much grief I needed a few seconds to breathe through the pain and concentrate on anything else. Cole had gotten his binoculars out and handed them to me, silently pointing where to check as I pushed myself into a crouch next to him. The target—the cantina—was easy enough to find, light spilling out of open windows and doorways like beacons in the darkness. I only had to wait ten seconds before a dark silhouette crossed a doorway—a patrolling guard. I tried to follow his path, but before he got to the next door, another walked by it from the opposite direction. I easily counted five people—and that was, at best, a rough estimate, of those smack out in the open. I couldn't see inside well, but I thought I saw movement through the windows—more guards. If they were smart, they'd have any hostages tied up and sitting or lying on the floor. It was hard to sneak out or run when you had a hard time coming to your feet in the first place.

I checked on the main part of the docks next, also visible from up here. Heavy clouds of smoke obscured most of my view, but a few residual flames eating up the wood of the long piers reaching into the bay the settlement was curving around made it obvious that there wasn't much of those structures left. The buildings themselves seemed intact, making me guess they'd set off planted charges there to prevent an incursion from the ocean. In hindsight, my plans all turned out to be shit—the cars would have helped with the fire and gotten us right to the wall—but walking from inland had been the better choice than trying from the water. I waited to catch some movement, but the smoke was too strong. Even up here, it tickled my nose, and as I kept breathing, I felt my throat get scratchy as well.

Unsure how acoustics would work up here, I signaled Cole to follow me once I was down to street level, giving him another couple of minutes to check our surroundings. Getting down was worse than crawling up since I couldn't allow gravity to help along, thus alerting everyone in the settlement to my exact position—and considering how the day was going, I'd end up breaking my neck, anyway.

I was just about to start the last leg of my descent—twelve feet of clinging to that damn corner of the house—when rustling sounds coming from up the street drew my attention. For a moment, I thought it was just the wind carrying some debris along—or rats or other vermin playing hide and seek in it—but then it came again, quickly turning into the regular sounds of footsteps. My body wanted to freeze but that was the worst possible position since I was terribly exposed, easily visible against the side of the house. The same was true if I decided to crawl down—the motion would make me even easier to catch, even to someone who didn't have the same level of low-light vision as I did. Up wasn't an option since that meant crossing the wall again. I was pretty much caught up here, detection almost inevitable.

I wasn't going to make it that easy for them.

If I could have counted on letting myself be caught to get closer to possible hostages, I might have considered that option, but if it was mindless drones out on patrol, they'd probably just shoot me. I was sure that whoever was in charge would want me dead, and I wasn't going to let them turn me into a hostage against Nate. Looking across the streets, I tried to gauge the distance to the next roofs over, both to the east and north. North was out of the question, the thoroughfare below wide enough for two vehicles to pass—and it was the direction from where the patrol was coming. East was the route we'd been following, little more than a footpath between houses.

Trying to be as silent as possible, I took three steps back, then flew forward and across the gap before I could think better of it. Triumph welled up inside of me as I went sailing across the gap easily—only to come down on the angled slate roof with a crash that was loud enough to be heard over by the docks. So much for hiding. And not only was it loud, but my weight was enough to destabilize the shingles, what felt like the entire roof starting to tear loose and slide down into the street. Or maybe that was just me, misjudging the steepness of the roof. I had just enough time to fight for balance to realize it was a losing battle before I slid backward off the roof, incapable of bracing myself. So I did the only thing I could think of, and tucked myself into as compact a ball as I could as I came crashing down.

I heard shots coming in my direction before I hit the ground, the worst of the impact on my right hip and thigh—directly below my freshly-healed wound. Agony exploded through my body, strong enough that for a moment I thought I would throw up. My rolling momentum found an immediate end when my pack hit the ground after something close to a tucked-in somersault, the second shock stoking the flames of the first. I ended up gasping on my side, my vision red with pain. Muzzle fire partly blinded me, but none of the rounds bit into my squishy body. Return fire came from directly next to me, four quick bursts. I was still blinking stupidly when a strong hand grabbed my arm and pulled me up and backward, making me stumble along blindly. Since nobody punched me in the face to knock me out for good, I figured the hand must belong to Hill, pulling me around the corner to the wider street. Terribly exposed in the open only mattered so much when he shot at what remained of the patrol, about to follow us. Two figures fell to the ground. Silence followed, our panting the only sound. Making sure I was standing on my own again, Hill then went to investigate, meeting Cole at the corner. Apparently, my disaster of a descent had given him time aplenty to come down himself. All three of the scavengers making up the patrol were dead, each felled for good with a head shot next to several likely lethal hits in the upper torsos. I trusted Hill to make sure they were gone for good and instead checked their appearance and gear. One of the men looked like your average town guy, no armor but with sturdy boots. The other man and the woman were scavengers, although they were lacking the garish face and body paint I'd seen on Eden, Amos, and their bunch, making me guess they'd become mindless drones long enough ago for all of that to have worn off. They certainly stank like they were in need of a good dunking—not dissimilar to the shooters up on the palisade, but there I hadn't paid that much attention.

We barely had time for a cursory check—and to grab their spare magazines—before the sound of voices coming from the north made us scramble, heading back into the houses to the east, incidentally following the directions Nate had given us. Unintelligible words turned to shouts when whoever was following us must have tripped over the patrol. My mind screamed at me to run, but the three of us were smarter than that, placing feet deliberately to go fast but remain as silent as possible as we went from cover to cover. That strategy went well—until I peeked around a corner and found myself face-to-face with a patrol that looked not just very alert, but also knew exactly how to respond to intruders.

I barely managed to duck back behind the corner before a spray of bullets hit the air where my head had been, a few chewing right through the boards of the wall since I could feel them crash into the wood I was leaning against on the other side of the corner. Shouts behind us made it obvious that we'd gotten surrounded. Rather than try to evade, I dropped down to one knee and leaned forward so I could shoot blindly at the patrol in front of us, counting on the fact that they weren't seeking cover since they wanted to chase us. I felled two and killed one, Cole easily taking out the other two. I was tempted to try to beat the shit out of the surviving guy currently rolling on the ground, screaming his head off, but when Cole ran right past him, I followed quickly. The screaming would be a welcome distraction and likely hide the sounds we made. We were out of the street before the guy could decide that grabbing his dropped rifle and shooting us made more sense than to clutch his perforated intestines. Hill pushed against my shoulder when I wanted to slow down, making both me and Cole speed up into a full-out run.

I lost my orientation ducking around two more corners and weaving between smaller and larger streets, but about that time I heard shots being fired all around us, making me guess that Nate had ordered the others to engage. Patrols were coming after us from three directions, keeping us busy for quite a while until I managed to shoot the last one chasing us. Pressed against the side of a small house, I tried to radio in—including a quick report about what we'd seen from our sniper perch—but no one answered. Looking down at my com unit to see if I'd accidentally switched it off, I saw why Nate had stopped nagging me: the small box was trashed, likely cracking in my fall from the roof, and not getting better since then.

Cole noted what I was staring at, flashing me a quick grin. "Well, that explains it."

"Explains what?" I asked.

"Why you've been so meek and demure over the past few minutes," he shot back. "Give me a moment to save your marriage." He thumped something on his com without waiting for my response. "Cole reporting in. Lewis just realized she smashed her battery pack." He then prattled off the info about the guards at the cantina, the blown-up piers, and no further damage to the port facilities. The pensive look on his face that followed made me guess he was listening to Nate's response. When he finally turned back to me, he did so with a shit-eating grin. "Your husband loves you and cares about you very much."

All I had for that was a grunt. "That's so not what he just said."

"It's not," Cole agreed, still highly amused. "But I think that's what he meant. He may or may not put you on a leash next chance he gets."

"He can try," I huffed back.

Hill shook his head in defeat while Cole continued to be in high spirits, both of them now listening to more directions. I busied myself keeping watch, but the patrols seemed to have lost our trail for good—or we had, indeed, killed all of them.

"Acknowledged," Cole said, then turned to me to relay the news. "We are to rendezvous with the others by the cantina, northeast corner. House with green shutters, second row back from the open space. And I'm to take point."

"That an order, too?" I asked.

Cole, already stepping out in front of me, snorted. "Nope. But it makes sense since you're running blind and deaf."

There wasn't much I could say to that so I shut up and followed, letting Hill guard our backs. Twice we had to backtrack at a corner since we didn't want to alert the opposition, making our already slow progress even slower. My body was singing with adrenaline, the need to run and fight and kill almost overwhelming. Both men with me looked grim enough to make me guess I wasn't the only one who hated being stealthy and careful, but with the entire settlement on alert now, it was the wise choice. Also the only choice, really, I conceded when I realized that the patrols had beefed up, more than ten men passing by the mouth of one alley we were hiding in a few minutes later. They were easier to evade now, so many people carrying flashlights doing their part to give away their position. The fact that they'd rigged both main entrances into the town and cleaned up the streets should have already told me that they came with lots of manpower, but I had underestimated just how outgunned we'd be.

We arrived at our destination what felt like an eternity later, finding seven people already inside the house. Sonia was busy tending to two wounded scavengers on the ground. There was no sign of Hamilton, but Nate's glower at me was strong enough to make me want to run right back out and find the next patrol.

"So good of you to finally join us," he said, forgoing a repetition of the chewing out I'd apparently missed thanks to my busted radio. "Anyone hot on your heels?"

I shook my head. "No. We killed the first few who found us. Since then, we've been able to evade the others. Hard to guess, but there must be at least thirty people patrolling in the southern quadrant between the shops and the docks."

Nate took that in with a curt nod. His momentarily vacant expression made me guess he was receiving another message over his com. I was starting to feel left out, but dismissed that idea when Hamilton materialized inside the door a moment later. He was smelling of blood, which went well with how dirty the baseball bat he was carrying looked. He rocked to a halt next to me incidentally—

it was either that, or step over the wounded on the ground to be face to face with Nate—to report in. "Finished clearing up the outer perimeter to the north, so we should have an exit there." His attention snapped to me. "So you're still alive, huh? Thought you'd bit it since I didn't hear you rambling all over the team frequency."

I narrowed my eyes at him. "Broke my com unit."

I hated how faintly amused he already looked. "I'm almost afraid to ask, but how did you manage that? Shot it while missing your own kneecap?"

No measure of composure was enough to keep the blood from rushing into my cheeks. "I must have fallen on it. When I came crashing down off a roof."

Hamilton's grin was so gleeful it cost me all I had not to try to punch it right off his visage. Nate wasn't pleased—and not just because our chatter was keeping him from business. "Exactly what were you of all people doing up on a roof?" he wanted to know.

"Cole and I were trying to get a better overview of the situation," I explained. "And before you ask, why not Hill? I figured with me being half his mass, it would make more sense for me to climb up since I could hide better."

Hamilton gave something very close to a chortle. "And exactly how did that work out for you?"

Since I'd already explained that, I instead filled them in on our observations. Nate's expression turned, if anything, more grim, but at least he didn't laugh his ass off over my mishap. "Any idea how many of these assholes you killed?"

I shrugged. "High twenties, I'd estimate. I don't think there were any between the docks and here left, but by now they've probably returned and regrouped."

"We need to get into the damn cantina," Nate stressed. He did a quick head count—we were up to fifteen people in here now, a few more having just snuck in. "Take two full fireteams with you and head back to the docks," he ordered. "Then do your best to draw their attention to you. I'll try to rush the building with the rest." His eyes then flitted on to Hamilton. "You go with her."

Both Bucky and I looked ready to protest, but a squint from Nate was enough to shut us up. Since Sonia was about done patching people up, I took her and Burns, plus Cole and Hill with me, filling up the remaining slots with the scavengers I'd come to more or less know. Cole took point, sneaking ahead to make sure the street outside the building was clear, the rest following quickly. Hamilton brought up the rear, apparently trying to put as much distance between me and him as possible. We had to step over quite a few bodies that we'd dropped since the patrols hadn't tried to clean up after themselves, but ran into nobody still alive. It was only halfway back to the dock that I realized I maybe should have counted them, and taken the odd moment to make sure none of them were reanimating, but now it was too late. It took us maybe ten minutes until all of us, split into three clusters, had taken up position by the docks. I signaled Cole to let Nate know we were ready. Waiting for an answer felt endless—particularly since I could clearly hear movement and shots from the northern half of the settlement beyond our destination—but eventually Cole stilled before relaying the answer back to me. "We are to cause a commotion to draw them out, and then make our way along the main road to the cantina." There was a bend in the road so I couldn't see the main doors from here, but we were in direct line of sight of the building.

I acknowledged that with a nod. "Any idea how we should go about that?" I asked nobody in particular.

Sadly, Hamilton turned out to be the one who felt himself addressed. "Why don't you do what you can do best, and scream like a girl?"

I glared daggers at him—but I didn't need to see Sonia and Burns both nod in agreement to realize it wasn't the worst of ideas. Hill was hard-pressed to hide a smile. Cole didn't bother with the hiding part. That they all expected me to do the—literal—screaming was obvious. I had to admit, it wasn't the worst of ideas. I just hated that apparently, they'd already agreed it should be me who did it. Then again, I could see why high, female screeches might draw a different kind of attention than gruff, male shouting. Well, if it helped make this a little easier, it had to be done.

I wasn't stupid enough to leave my cover for this, but remaining crouching behind a small fishing boat someone had dragged up onto the port wall made me feel incredibly stupid as I called out a loud, "Help!" Cole went so far as to shake his head in disappointment at me. Hamilton looked ready to give me cause to holler. With my eyes boring into his, I tried again, this time going for a wordless wail. And then another, because after hours of whispering, it took my voice box a little to reach full capacity. Seeing him smirk back at me made me want to switch to a very different kind of utterance, but I refrained. I wouldn't let him push me as far as to sabotage our mission.

I cut off when my throat started to hurt—and then we waited, collectively holding our breaths, or so it felt. I knew well enough that it was unrealistic for anyone to turn up instantly, but waiting still felt endless. I tried counting down from one hundred, but every little creak and scratch made me perk up and lose count, so I quickly gave up.

I almost missed it when, finally, a patrol did make it down toward where we were hiding, the five men—judging from their height— using slow, deliberate movements as they advanced, staying in the shadows of the houses wherever possible. They missed our outlooks, and were smack in the middle of our position by the time we sprung the trap on them. I was likely not the best suited to try to overwhelm a guy who was easily a head taller than me, but my knife sank into the side of his neck just the same. I knew that there would have been some sense in trying to take at least one of them alive, but I didn't want to risk him alerting the rest. The scuffle was a brief and bloody one, and a minute later we were back in our hiding spaces. When no second patrol followed, Hamilton gave me a pointed look—and I did my screeching routine again. Thanks to me being slightly winded from the action, it sounded more erratic—and realistic enough that it gave me the creeps—and this time, a larger group, composed of at least twenty men and women, came to investigate. It gave me only limited mental reprieve to see that the two female scavengers had the same vacant look on their faces as half of the guys.

We had been careful to hide the bodies, but that still left two enormous pools of blood on the ground where some of them had found their end, and this patrol was less stupid than the first one. Two of the more alert ones advanced, covered by a cloud of five of their drones. I would have waited for them to get to the pools of blood but they stopped close to our hideouts, listening. The lot of us could be silent, but not that silent, so it only made sense to take the initiative. At my sharp whistle, we surged forward as one. I didn't bother with trying to close the distance but aimed and shot instead, using the few moments I'd have before this turned into a black-on-black melee in the shadows. The guy I aimed for went down, but I didn't have time to finish him off before Burns smashed his head in with the butt of his rifle.

Our forces would have been evenly matched if all the patrol members had had their full mental capacity, but like on the palisades, the drones had a hard time reacting to suddenly appearing targets outside of where they had been ordered to look—and we did have the advantage of competence in all things related to killing on our side. From the corner of my eye I noticed that Sonia wisely kept herself to the side of the thick of the fray. I had no such qualms, using my smaller size and increased agility and speed to my advantage. It took us a good five minutes to overwhelm the entire patrol, only taking a few bruises in return.

Looking up after Hamilton felled the last one, I saw ten more people surge down the street toward our position—and if they'd been smart and had proceeded to shoot at us blindly, they would have stood a chance. Yet before it could come to that, Nate and his smaller group gunned them down from the rear before turning toward the cantina. Trusting that he had a better idea about troop strength than I did, I gave the others the signal to advance up the street, not quite running but making haste for the building.

By the time we got there, chaos reigned. The first thing I noticed were the bodies on the ground. At least half of them looked like they'd been guards, still bleeding from wounds, not dead for long enough to have stopped leaking. But just as many dead were slumped against the walls, faces pale after having bled out hours ago, or in some cases, days, the early stages of decomposition already having set in. There was no rhyme or reason to their order, making abject horror claw at the back of my throat when I realized what must have been going on here: they must have killed a few of them each hour that passed since they had taken over—days ago. I recognized several faces, but only passingly. None of them were any of my close friends, which was only so much of a relief.

The next thing my attention snagged to—after verifying that the building was secured—were the two people standing, back to back, in the middle of the room. Although "standing" was a bit much for at least one of them, I realized when I recognized the bloody, beaten male as Andrej. It took me a few more moments to make sense of why he suddenly looked taller; he wasn't standing on his own volition, instead being held up by two meat hooks suspended from the ceiling that had been driven through his shoulders, the ends of the hooks jutting out, black with crusted blood, from below his collar bones. His entire body was slumped, his toes barely reaching the ground, his bare torso smeared with yet more blood and what looked like multiple lacerations and burn wounds. Barely lucid, his face was halfway raised to where Nate was advancing toward him right now.

The second figure, partly obscured by his body, turned out to be Sadie, I realized as I went forward, mirroring Nate's motions on the other side. I almost felt like sighing with relief when I realized that she looked mostly unscathed—and was still standing on her own volition, the blood all over her head and upper torso likely Andrej's from where their bodies were bound together with a multitude of chains that must have further weighed down on him. Underneath the bonds I could see that she had something bulky covering her torso—maybe a plate carrier? Her eyes were wide and red, tears streaking lighter paths through the blood caked all over her face. She was nearly silent in her sobbing, but no less hysterical for it.

And to make the situation perfect, the back wall of the building was going up in flames that quickly spread to the rafters above.

Nate had almost reached Andrej when Sadie—facing the spreading flames—caught sight of us. "Stop! They rigged us to blow up!"

Nate paused for a second, but, if anything, her cry got him closing the distance to them in record time. I wanted to follow but stopped when Nate signaled me to stay back, so I continued my circuit instead, until I got too close to the flames that the heat made me pause. Nate and Burns set to looking at the contraption our friends were caught in, with Hill and Hamilton joining in after a few moments. Sonia stepped up to me, looking equally horrified and conflicted as I felt—there was nothing we could do for them for now, and with four large men crowding in, there wasn't room for us left.

Sadie started to protest when Nate grabbed some bolt cutters from his pack and went to town on the chains, in quick order making them clank onto the ground as they fell away. Andrej gave a low, guttural grunt but otherwise remained passive, while Sadie started to shake uncontrollably. From what I could tell, my first guess had been right—her torso was encased by what looked like a plate carrier, only that instead of extra magazines, blocks of what looked like C4 were strapped to her front, and if I wasn't deluded, back as well. There was no big digital clock spelling out that she only had five minutes and counting until it would detonate, but judging from how gingerly Nate touched the contraption, I figured it was wired and ready to blow.

The heat from the burning wall increased, making Sonia and me step back. Just as I was about to shout at Nate that we should try to extinguish the fire, he paused and looked up, likely because some stray ash had burned him. He cast a longer look around the room, then up to the rafters, before his eyes fell on me. "Get everyone out of here. Radius at least a hundred feet outside the building."

I vehemently shook my head. "I'm staying."

His attention was already back on the contraption, now checking how Andrej and Sadie were connected to each other. "Then get everyone else but your stupid self out!"

That sounded like a plan. Only half of our people had followed inside, the rest keeping watch outside, and in short order I'd sent everyone else but Sonia and me scurrying, someone finally going on the hunt for some fire extinguishers—if not for the building, for anyone stupid enough to remain inside now who might require dousing with foam later. Above the roar of the flames, I thought I heard Martinez protesting from outside as someone must have kept him from entering, but quickly dismissed my concern for him. We had more pressing matters at hand.

Finally ignoring Nate's signal from before, I stepped up to him, trying to calm Sadie down with what was likely more grimace than smile. She did her best to hold on to what little composure she had left. "They're bound together by three leather belts," Nate explained, going right on before I could ask the obvious—why he hadn't cut through them yet. "Sadie's standing on some kind of pressure plate, and since there are wires running up the chains, I think it's a double-rigged system. It blows if she steps off the plate, but also goes off if the weight hanging on the chains lessens."

So much for the idea of putting something Sadie-weighted down on the pressure plate.

I was still at a loss for suggestions when Andrej's croak made all of us turn our focus on him. "Cut the girl loose and hold me down until you get her out of here," he suggested between a series of wheezing coughs. Had the damn hooks punctured his lungs, too? "And then you run. Didn't get a good look at the detonators, but they have a response lag. If you run like hell, you'll be out of here before it all goes boom."

The hard set of Nate's jaw made it obvious that he was having none of that. "I'm not leaving you behind to die." His voice was husky and pressed, almost as if he was the one hanging there.

Andrej gave a short bark of laughter, quickly drowned out by a cough that seemed to wrack his entire body—and got more blood spurting over his front and down his back onto Sadie, who gave a low whimper when she felt it dribble over her head and down her neck.

"You will," Andrej pressed out. "It's the only way to save the girl. And it will spare you having to put me down later. Not worth it. Get her out and leave me." He even went as far as to show a bloody grin, a few of his teeth missing. "I always wanted to go out with a hell of a bang. Looks like I'm getting my last wish."

Nate looked ready to protest while he continued to fiddle with the contraption, but it was Sadie speaking up that made him pause. "He's right," she more sobbed than said, her voice barely regaining strength as she went on. "They tortured and beat him before they strung him up. I think his spine's severed. They only stopped when they realized he was about to die and convert on their traitorous asses. They leashed me to him so he'd try to keep himself alive for as long as possible as they knew he wouldn't want to go for me first."

Her words made it hard for me to suppress a shudder, but on a logical level, it made sense. That didn't take away from the horror gripping me at the very idea.

"'Tis true," Andrej muttered. "Get her out. That's all that counts now." Sadie's quiet sobbing made his words sound all the more final— and right. We could still save her, provided we got the C4 harness off her before it blew up. If we had to drag Andrej out, that would take time—time that we didn't have once the detonators were active.

Nate still spent another five minutes checking and rechecking the contraption before he turned to me, defeat making him look twice as angry as before. "Get me a body that weighs about as much as Sadie with some extra for the C4."

There were several women among the dead settlers, but I ended up dragging one of the female scavengers over to them that had defended the cantina. Somehow, manhandling a stranger felt easier than someone Sadie might have known. Nate and Burns spent another endless minute discussing the cables running all over Sadie's burden before they started cutting wires. I felt like wincing each and every time, but they were too fast and meticulous for that, and besides, I was busy shoving the dead body in my arms at Hill. The belts came next. Nate did that himself, while Burns got ready to stand in front of Andrej, grabbing the top of his shoulders to keep him weighed down as soon as Sadie was free. Just like them to share a few idiotic jokes that grated on my very soul.

As soon as the last belt gave, Nate pushed Sadie away from Andrej, but only a step, immediately holding her back, her feet still on the pressure plate. There were more wires previously hidden between their bodies. Rushing forward, I grabbed Sadie and pushed myself flush against her, both so I could keep her upright and maybe lend what little comfort I could give her. Her cheek sagged down on my shoulder, her sobs almost inaudible next to my ear. Over her slightly slumped body, I could see some of what Nate and Hamilton were doing, but the view of Andrej's back was too distracting. It looked like they'd really gone to town on him, beating him literally to within an inch of his life. That he was still holding on was as much testament to the serum as to how much of a tenacious bastard he was.

Finally, the last wire was snapped and Nate nudged Sadie and me away so that Hill could drop the dead scavenger on the pressure plate as soon as Sadie was off it. Nate checked that Hamilton knew what he was doing as he used some rope to tie the corpse to Andrej before he went to town on Sadie's harness. By then, she felt like little more than a human-sized rag doll between us, not resisting as we kept pushing her back and forth between us so Nate could cut her free. I almost expected another surprise when he finally lifted the harness away—like that they'd punctured her with some wires, too, or some shit—but the heavy, stained contraption came away without a hitch.

Nate then gave me the signal to go, but I suddenly felt frozen in my tracks. Sure, my mind was screaming to run, to get away from the horror and the spreading flames and the explosives, but this was Andrej we were talking about. He'd been the one who first showed me how to handle and maintain a gun. He'd shown me how to skin a deer, and a million other handy things required to make it in this world. He'd always had a smile and an easy joke for me, even after standing by with a stony expression when Nate chewed me out—or us both, on a few occasions. I'd never shared quite as much personal shit with him as I had with Martinez or Burns, but just like them, he was one of my closest friends; an older brother in everything but blood. The very idea of turning my back on him now was unbearable.

As if he'd picked up on my internal conflict, he raised his head and turned it as much toward me as it would go, giving me another grisly smile. "You did good, girl," he grated out in Serbian. "Do one last favor for me?" I nodded, feeling tears start to tickle at the back of my eyes. "Tell Zilinsky—" He paused, then started anew. "Tell Pia that I'm waiting in hell for her with a bottle of vodka and some blinis." I wondered if he was even still lucid, raving about pancakes of all things, but then he added, "She'll get it. Now go."

I still didn't want to, but when I felt Sonia push partly between me and Sadie so she could take some of her weight and help, I nodded and did my best to smile at my friend one last time—and then we hightailed it out of there as quickly as two women could drag a third who got increasingly harder to carry since all strength seemed to have left her, being able to do little more than stumble between us. I only realized how hot it had gotten inside the building when the cool night air felt freezing on my sweaty face. As soon as they saw us coming, the marines guarding the perimeter in this sector quickly stepped aside to let us hasten toward the docks. As soon as we passed by them, Sonia and I both stopped and pivoted, looking back with shared anxiety. Sadie sagged against me but seemed loath to let go, which was fine with me. From the outside, it looked like the entire roof was already engulfed in flames, turning the two figures escaping through the same door as us into black silhouettes. Hamilton and Hill were both running, joining us in record time.

And then we waited, and waited, and I was about ready to scream with frustration and helplessness when, finally, Burns and Nate came hurtling through the door, neither man looking back.

Not a second too early did they clear the frame of the building when an explosion inside went off, the shockwave hitting both men hard from behind and throwing both forward onto the ground. Even further back, it forced me to take a step back as I tried to shield myself and Sadie against the debris pelting us. Every fiber of my being screamed to let go of her and run to check on Nate, but he and Burns were already stirring, two scavengers quick to run over to them, slap out what little flames had caught on their gear, and pull them farther to safety. The roof of the building—where it was still standing—was about to cave in with terrible cracking sounds, two of the walls folding as well.

Checking on Sadie, I found her still staring into the burning ruin, tears streaming down her face. Her lips were moving silently but she didn't seem aware that she was mumbling something under her breath. Once the ringing in my ears from the boom subsided, I could hear her utter a single word over and over—"Chris." It could have been her lover's name, but I was terrified that it was her daughter's.

Turning around—more to distract myself than in search of anything—my eyes fell on a single, tall figure emerging from the shadows from farther down the dock. My eyes went wide when I recognized Pia, swathed in a dark blanket weirdly bundled across her left shoulder. Her eyes were trained not on us but on the flames, and low in my gut I had the sense that she knew her oldest, closest friend had just been blown to bloody pieces. It was only when she had almost reached me that I realized why the blanket looked so weird: rather than carrying her gear—and from what I could tell, she didn't even have a gun on her—it was a child she was holding in her arms, using the blanket to shield them both from whatever shrapnel of still-burning ash was whipping around us all. She looked haggard and drawn, one eye and the jaw on that side of her face dark with bruises and swollen, but still alive.

I must have tensed, or accidentally let go of Sadie, because she turned next to me, and let out a wail when she saw Pia. The Ice Queen noticed her, if only for a second, her motions mechanical as she pushed the bundle from her arms into Sadie's. She visibly shook herself out of her stupor for a moment, quickly assuring herself that both mother and daughter were safe in being reunited before she looked back at the flames, coming to a rocky halt next to me.

My mind was burning with questions, but I wasn't stupid enough to pelt her with them right now. Glancing at Nate, I found both him and Burns sitting in the dirt, still a little stunned from the blast, but looking physically mostly okay. Martinez had materialized from a different part of the perimeter, crouching beside them, checking on a few wounds they must have sustained, either from the blast or before. The guards at the cantina seemed to have been the last, everyone else dead in the streets, with only us still standing. Blake had taken over coordinating a quick search to make sure there were no other hideouts since he still had a working radio.

"He knew that he wouldn't be making it much longer." At Pia's grating remark, I turned to her, but she was still staring into the flames. She must have noticed my motion because she resumed as if I'd asked her what she meant. "Romanoff. The day after you went off to Dallas, he told me. He could feel it coming, his end. Like a winter storm, he said. Raging on and on until you get lost in the endless whiteout. He said he wanted to visit the town one last time because he'd promised the girl he would be back. He'd known it was a lie when we left for the camp, but since he was still standing, he felt he at least needed to try." She paused, her face still an expressionless mask, but there was a world of pain burning in her eyes when they finally shifted and fell on me. "It was my fault. I had a bad feeling but I chalked it up to paranoia, because of Marleen. I led us straight into an ambush. Too late I realized there was something fucked up about most of them. They killed two of my guys but dragged the rest back to the town. I wanted to take as many of them out as I could, but they threw us into one of the houses where they had rounded up more hostages, and I saw that one of the women there had Christine with her." Pia paused for a moment, again glancing over to where Sadie was gently cooing to her dazed child. "She'd been watching the children sleep when they took over, and knew they'd likely use the kid as ammunition against us, so she said she was hers instead. Romanoff told me to stop being stupid, grab the kid, and hide with her. And that's what I did, while they rounded up everyone else and executed them."

While her voice held no emotion, I could tell how much abandoning so many people she'd sworn to protect hurt her, but I agreed with Andrej's choice. Shit would have been so much worse if she hadn't gotten Chris out of there. Just the thought of what they likely would have done to her—and Sadie, since she was no longer the softest chip in the game—made new rage want to flare up inside of me. Staring at Sadie, I couldn't help but feel a smidgen of relief that both of them had gotten away, although it stood to reason that abject terror wasn't the only thing that had left marks on Sadie herself. Pia must have read my thoughts clear off my expression as she gave me a small nudge. "Go check on Miller. I'll talk to Sadie." She paused, then added, surprisingly emphatic, "I'm glad you're okay."

It took me a few seconds to realize she must be referring to my previous brush with death in the form of a knife in the back. That lag alone told me that I wasn't really processing what was going on, but

I was sure that would change eventually. It was a clear dismissal if I'd ever heard one, but rather than follow Pia's order, I hugged her, if only long enough to feel her tense rather than relax. Stepping back, I tried my best at a smile. "Romanoff told me to tell you that he'll be waiting in hell with a bottle of vodka and some blinis."

She stared at me as if I'd gone insane—rightly so, I had to admit—before, out of nowhere, a wistful but surprisingly gentle smile crossed the Ice Queen's face. She squeezed my shoulder, as if in thanks. "My children always wanted blinis for breakfast on the weekend," she explained, her voice so soft it was hard to understand. "I was an abysmal cook. I always burned them. But they loved them."

She turned back to staring at the flames, and since I didn't feel up for any kind of debate concerning the afterlife or whatnot, I trudged over to where Nate was about ready to shove Martinez off if he dared come close to him again. I quickly relayed the news—that Sadie and Chris were both safe, and Pia had hidden with the girl—but all Nate did was give me the curtest of nods, looking over to the people in question to visually reassure himself that it was true before he strode over to Blake, leaving me standing there.

I chanced a glance at Martinez and Burns, both staring after Nate with the same kind of concern that I felt burning deep inside my chest.

Sonia appeared on Burns's other side but he brushed her off, careful not to ruffle her feathers but insisting that he did not need to be doted on. He looked back to me. "Let's make sure that none of these assholes are left standing. Then we torch the dead, and if there's still anything left of this town when we're done, we need to toast that rat bastard with some vodka. I'm sure he had some left in his house. Deal?"

"Deal."

It wasn't like there was anything else we could have done, and that grated on my very soul—and I was sure I wasn't alone with that.

Chapter 8

B y the time the sun came up, I felt like my arms weighed a ton, but I was afraid to give my body the rest it was screaming for—mostly because I didn't want to leave the state of numbness that my mind had disappeared into. There was still much to do, but for now, the pressing matters were taken care of. The fire had been contained to the cantina building where a few scavengers were waiting for it to be out for good, all the wood of the building finally consumed. We'd messed up with the patrols, a lot of the affected scavenger drones reanimating shortly after the cantina had blown up. That—and cleaning the houses down to their crawlspaces of the previously killed and turned shamblers—kept us busy until the early hours of the morning. Pia and Sonia rallied the survivors, both knowing a few extra hidey-holes than I would never have considered looking into. Altogether, seventy-eight people had survived, including our vanguard. It was hard to calculate the numbers of the dead since several people reported sending their kids with shepherds into the surrounding land, and it would likely take days to round all of them up. Seven of our own were dead, including Andrej. There was also the matter of the other settlements, but from what we could piece together of how the insurgents had taken over the town, it stood to reason that most people there were okay and the saboteurs had simply taken out their radio systems to ensure we couldn't call for aid. Blake himself offered to drive to the closest town, a few hours to the north, and report back in once he found out what had been going on there. That call arrived at 9:38 a.m. and was the first bit of good news—the town was safe, only missing two people who Pia later identified among the dead scavengers we submitted to the flames.

Just like Marleen, the moles in our town must have been embedded for months, if not from the very start. It was hard to tell since their first move—after letting reinforcements in through the gate and docks in the middle of the night—was to round up all the scavengers who had already received the faulty serum and shoot them up with the mind-control shit that turned them into moderately useful drones. Whether it was the same shit Hamilton had shot Nate up with back in the Canada base I didn't know, and the man in question avoided answering the question like the plague. He generally kept himself in the background, but since that entailed dragging the dead to the pyres to be identified, stripped of anything useful, and then flung into the flames, I couldn't exactly hold that against him. Not a single of the confirmed insurgents had ever been part of the serum project, as far as we could tell, but that didn't help much. There was a pervasive sense of frustration and grief in the air even though we had saved more people than I had dared to hope at first, but that still meant that two-thirds of the residents of the town were dead, their home mostly destroyed. News of how Andrej had died spread like wildfire, and while not everyone left standing had been friends with him, he'd been one of the cornerstones of the town.

The only definite thing about the insurgents we could say was that the group that had dragged in our vanguard must have been strangers, else Pia could never have escaped with Christine. I could tell that she remained the only one blaming herself for not having saved more people, but the fact that their infallible chief of security had been forced to duck away and hide made everyone even more jumpy. The only thing I could think of that would have made it worse was if Sadie had died as well, but in the face of the gargantuan loss everyone had suffered, that was a small cause for happiness for most.

There was no question about the future of the town. Theoretically, it could have been rebuilt, but with a lot of the important buildings gone and so many bad memories everywhere, it was easier to pack up what could be reused and start anew elsewhere. I wasn't surprised when, just after noon, a fleet of fishing boats drew near the destroyed docks, bringing food for a few days and an invitation to relocate down to New Angeles—for now, or as long as people wanted. My paranoia immediately reared its ugly head—split between the possibilities that Gabriel Greene was profiting from the influx of capable people, and questioning whether the boats actually hailed from New Angeles— but considering my recent talk with Greene, I doubted that his reasoning was of the nefarious kind. I hated that after what felt like years of living in the spirit of people helping people being the only way we would all make it in this world, even neighbors now looked with suspicion at each other. Using our car radios and what felt like a million code phrases, Pia eventually verified that the ship convoy had been sent by Greene himself, and the offer was genuine—and yes, he was aware that, like us, he likely had a bunch of spies ready to pull the trigger on him again. I didn't relay the conclusions I'd drawn after Amos had told us about how the New Angeles docks had been destroyed two years ago, but since that wasn't my concern now, I felt that wasn't necessary.

What was my concern was trying to decide what we would do now.

Nate called a meeting late in the afternoon—command staff only since everyone else was ready to crash by then, most people not having slept for two days or longer. I was surprised not to see Burns or Sonia, but Martinez showed up, he and Pia the only former residents of the town. Of course Hamilton was there, with Amos speaking for our scavengers, and Sergeants Buehler and the recently returned Blake from the Silo marines. If I had to guess, it seemed like the army bunch had resorted to taking their orders directly from Nate, which I could tell he was both pleased with and annoyed by. Judging from how tense he looked leaning against what used to be the dining-room table in the small house he had declared as our headquarters, it was hard for him to remain still, even if it was for just a few minutes.

"I presume most people will go to New Angeles?" he asked as a first point.

Pia inclined her head. "Most are wounded or otherwise in bad shape. Dehydration and lack of food for days, plus the less-than-gentle treatment by those assholes—can't hold it against them. And we'll leave without feeling like we are abandoning them," she pointed out.

Martinez agreed with her. "I know a few will want to come along, but for most it's a matter of leaving here as soon as possible. I'm sure Greene will send a few search parties for salvaging efforts later, when things have died down."

Nate seemed to see that issue solved with their assessment. "Good. That begs the question—what do we do with the people we need to keep safe? Chiefly Sadie and her kid." When momentary silence answered him, he scratched his chin as if he hadn't already come to a conclusion. "I'm tempted to send them along with the others to let them disappear into one of the larger cities we have, but I'm afraid that will get them killed all the quicker."

When he glanced at me as if for confirmation, I spoke up. "That means we take them elsewhere. Utah, Wyoming, or the Silo sound like the best places—but also the most obvious."

"That's exactly what I hate about the idea," Nate professed.

I was surprised when Hamilton was next to voice his opinion. "I'd go with the Utah settlement." When I eyed him askance, he grimaced. "Wyoming is farther away, and since the girl has her parents there, it's the most obvious hideout. From what I know, they did zero vetting of the people streaming in and blowing up their population numbers early on, so you'll have moles aplenty there."

I couldn't help it; while I agreed with his assessment, the Wyoming Collective still felt the closest place to home to me now that the town here was toast, and I couldn't let him bad-mouth my people—even if they'd, quite publicly, kicked us out. "Like that's any different with the other two options."

"But it is," Hamilton half-sneered in my face, then pitched his voice into more diplomatic territory as he addressed the assembly at large, maybe realizing that if he kept this up, the Ice Queen would use his face for anger management therapy. "The Silo's just as bad, although I have a feeling that Wilkes knows way more about who to be suspicious of. But last time I read a situational report, the Salt Lake City settlement was still void of any deep cover operatives. True, that intel is over a year old, but that mayor of theirs has been a pest to deal with from the very beginning."

I wasn't surprised that Martinez was happy to speak up for the settlement his boyfriend was from, but that was not the only reason why he agreed with Hamilton. "Minerva's also been very keen on keeping the core of her settlement rather loosely populated. Charlie's been complaining that they've had lots of issues with wolves during the winters because they kept getting through their fences. What we consider the settlement proper is really closer to at least five different communities, all in walking distance of each other. Making sure to keep Sadie somewhere secluded where nothing can happen to her is easier there than anywhere else. And there's no question that they will help us."

Nate gave that a moment's thought before he nodded. "So it's decided. We leave in thirty."

For a moment, I thought I was hallucinating. "Excuse me?"

I could tell just how tense he was that he didn't even make fun of me for my question. "We leave as soon as we can, which means right now. We know who's up to coming with us—the rest will stay behind and can go to New Angeles tomorrow, or next week for all I care. We're sitting ducks here, with bad defenses, and everyone in the country knows where we are. The cars have been standing idle for almost the entire day, so we can drive them a few hours into the darkness without issues. The sooner we disappear, the better."

I glanced at Pia, but of course she didn't speak up in protest. Bringing up Burns's idea of a wake didn't sound too smart now so I kept my trap shut. It wasn't like much was keeping me here—and I could, and would, grieve just as well on the road, if not better. At least driving, setting up camp, and being all-around busy would keep my mind from getting too caught up with itself, or so I hoped. Martinez offered up a grimace, but since it was a silent one, lacking protest, it was decided. Amos seemed not to care whether he and his people were staying or going, and Buehler and Blake were just as ready to go.

So it was decided, and all we had to do was get back into our cars and leave.

There was the small matter of deciding who to take with us, and what vehicles to stuff them into. Santos, Clark, Collins, and Moore had already declared they were coming with us—between them only having a few scrapes and bruises, miraculously—the latter two likely to stay with Sadie in Utah, if their previous behavior was any indication. I hadn't really paid that much attention before, too caught up in getting out there again to save Nate, but the guys had always turned up somewhere around Sadie and her kid, either still acting like the silent shadows Nate had long ago ordered them to be—or, much more likely, having become a family of sorts, the exact dynamics of which I wasn't privy to. It certainly had been telling that Sadie and her daughter had been inseparable all day long—until Moore turned up, liberated from one of the hostage cellars. She'd still fussed over the kid but with only a little coaxing needed, Moore managed to get her to hand the kid over to him so Sadie could get cleaned up and grab some chow. And really, just what went on between them and how they managed things was none of my business.

Surprisingly, it didn't take much longer than Nate's ordered half an hour for us to be ready to leave. Between those of us who had been on the move in the caravan leaving the slaver camp for California, the vanguard breaking away from them, and our Dallas group, plus a handful of people from the town who were useful enough and ready to head to Utah instead, we made up thirty-nine people, including Sadie and Chris. The vehicles Pia's vanguard had been using were reduced to burnt-out ruins, but Martinez verified that there were enough extra vehicles in their central garage and bodyshop left that could be used. I did a double-take when—except for two trucks—those turned out to be a fleet of ATVs that could also be hooked up to the portable solar panels overnight to recharge. At least their riders would be able to use the wind generated from driving speed to cool off, while the rest would continue to cook in the cars. I wondered if, just maybe, we should leave the batteries charging all day and drive by night, and when I mentioned that to Nate, he looked like he approved.

Unlike the last—and only—time I'd been to the Utah settlement, we decided that we should head straight east, then north after surpassing New Vegas, pretty much crossing Nevada in the south and driving the length of Utah—close to the route we'd taken when rallying for our attack on the Colorado base, but off the trade route most of that had turned into in the meantime. Barring distractions—and I didn't give us much chance to avoid those—the trek was around eight hundred miles long. If we could avoid dying of heat in Death Valley—by not going there, for the most part—we could do it in under a week, even considering the slower speed the ATVs would force on us.

There was both surprise and disappointment on the faces of those sending us off, but just the same I could tell that most were happy to see us gone. It was an understandable reaction—my arrival in the town had led to kicking off the cascade of shit that had rained down on them over the past week, and while a few of us had been their neighbors and friends for a long time, the rest were a bunch of trigger-happy, unwashed assholes they'd be happy to have out of their lives. I was still glad that Pia seemed too worn out to see all that play out on their expressions. The only hitch in our departure had been when it suddenly occurred to her that her constant sidekick in all things vehicular was gone, leaving her without a designated car to ride in. I would have offered up ours but wasn't too unhappy when she decided to catch a ride with Martinez instead. I was sure our chatty medic would get even her talking, even if it was only idle banter; riding with us would have meant me being locked in with the only two people I knew who felt comfortable in complete silence. Sadie and Chris were also riding with Martinez in his snazzy new car, which worked just as well.

It didn't come as much of a surprise that the scavengers fell over each other volunteering for the ATVs, particularly since they could dump their packs on us and just carry provisions for the day and enough ammo for the rest of the century. Even Amos, still recuperating from his injuries sustained underneath Dallas, opted to ride as gunner with one of his guys. That whoever was riding the back would get to do the shooting was a given, although I was sincerely hoping it wouldn't come to that since relative agility and smaller size were the only advantages the ATVs had.

We decided to drive through the night until the first vehicle started to stall on us, roughly following the same route we'd used to get to the town what felt like longer ago than…yesterday, I realized, with no small amount of disturbance. If our opposition had been smart rather than relying on numbers and cheats, they could likely have taken the lot of us out that evening, sleep deprivation making us less than perfectly alert drivers. But no ambush happened, and besides a few scares thanks to wandering deer and dogs, the night was quiet. Too quiet, really, and I was happy to jump out of the driver's seat whenever we took a break to get a few moments of social contact in. Sadie didn't know anything except the most basic details since we'd left for the camp, and Pia wanted an in-depth recount of the shit that had gone down in Dallas, so there was plenty to share in ten-minute intervals.

It was well past three in the earliest of early mornings when Nate called for a longer halt when Pia pointed out an abandoned, derelict farmhouse they'd used in the past. A few miles off any of the trade routes, there was a good chance nobody would come looking for us there. We had to chase away a family of raccoons and some smaller critters, but since some of us were sleeping in the cars, that wasn't much of an issue to begin with. I didn't protest when Nate put us both on the last watch rotation, but felt a hint of surprise when rather than hang out with Hamilton—or Pia, although she insisted she needed sleep—he returned to the car only minutes past the unofficial curfew. Not sure how soon—and with what little warning—we would have to get up, I was sleeping on top of my sleeping bag, boots and pants on, but with my jacket serving as a rolled-up pillow the only concession to easy dressing options. Turning over, I studied his profile as he kept staring up at the ceiling of the car after getting comfy, ignoring me. Or so I thought, until I heard him utter the smallest of sighs—it barely qualified as more than an exhale, really—and he turned his head so he was looking back at me instead.

"I don't feel like talking," he muttered. "And not much like fucking, either."

My first impulse was to laugh—which probably said a lot about both of us. I idly wondered if I should be offended at the rebuke, but then again I was sharing that part of the sentiment, so there wasn't much use to that. He didn't sound like he was spoiling for a fight, but I didn't like how quiet he'd been all night long. Not just Nate-quiet, but quiet even for him. He hadn't even offered an acerbic remark when I'd almost turned two rabbits into roadkill earlier, thus adding to our limited provisions on the road. Thinking about food made me wonder whether I should ask if he'd had anything to eat during our quick stay in town but chose to refrain from it this once. Instead, I bypassed all the possible bullshit I could have chattered on and on about, and went for what I really wanted to say.

"I'm sorry that there was nothing we could have done for him." Meaning Andrej, of course.

Not a single muscle jumped in Nate's face, creeping me out a little. It was almost as if he was ready to shut down—or was already there.

"I know," he finally said, proving me partly wrong—but then nothing else came, confirming my guess.

"It's not our fault," I offered up next. "You heard Zilinsky. He knew he was going to die soon. I know all of us wish we could have allowed him to sacrifice himself in a more active way, but in a sense, I think he was glad he didn't force us to have to put him down later."

"I know," Nate repeated in that same hollow tone as before.

I waited for anything more to come from him, but, surprise, surprise! That wasn't the case. The way he kept staring at me made me first uncomfortable, then started to freak me out, and eventually, something inside of me gave. "Is there anything you can say besides that?"

Of course he had to mutter "I don't know" a third time, but the corner of his mouth was quivering even before I let out a low growl. Another frustrated exhale followed, but at least this time he didn't remain silent. "The fact is, 'I don't know' sums up everything right now, and that's—"

"Aggravating?" I helpfully supplied.

"Killing me," he delivered with a pained smirk. I stared right back at him, but at least he finally broke eye contact, turning to the ceiling instead.

"Because of what happened to Andrej?"

"That doesn't help," Nate professed but wasn't finished yet. "It's everything. I knew something like this was going to happen, but I thought we had better precautions. I thought we could prevent it, or not all fall over like dominos placed in a perfect row. I thought—" He cut off there, speech turning into a low utterance that was too close to a snarl not to set my teeth on edge.

I didn't know what to say. "You weren't the only one in charge so it's not all on you," I tried, but realized I'd missed the mark by a mile when I got a veritable glare from him.

"Do you think this is about blame? I don't fucking care whether it's just me, or me and Zilinsky, or every fucking man and woman out there for themselves! We have nothing, don't you understand? Nothing!"

Color me confused, but I didn't quite get that point. "Well, we do have Sadie and Chris, plus Zilinsky and most of the vanguard we were afraid was already dead. And a third of the townspeople."

Nate's eyes narrowed, as if he was actually pissed off at me. "We have no leads, and no fucking clue who's behind this. Besides the obvious."

That was a sentiment we shared. "It's my fault, too. That we don't know. I knew we should have kept some of them alive, but I was so fucking angry, and I knew we had to get to the cantina—"

"Bree, stop," Nate insisted, interrupting me, now turning our displays of emotion around. When he saw my confusion—next to the unmistakable rage, I was sure—he grunted. "Don't you get it? It was all the same." When he realized that was just adding fuel to my flames, he frowned. "What did you do all day that I have to spell this out for you?"

"Uh, drag around the dead and burn them, maybe? Oh, and hunt down the remaining shamblers? Didn't have time to stop for a chat, you know," I pointed out acerbically.

Nate took the hit with more grace than I'd expected, which was bad as long as it didn't lead to him going off in my face and ending with angry, passionate sex that would do both of us good to blow off some steam. Well, it had been worth a try.

He didn't go so far as to apologize—we may have survived the apocalypse but hell hadn't frozen over yet—but looked a little more mollified. "Nobody knows who the moles even were. That's what frustrates me the most. They must have triggered their attack when they realized Zilinsky and her people were two days away from the town, then let in their support, and were among the first who got the mind-control shit. They lobotomized themselves to ensure that nobody could tell us anything. Or did you see anyone among the competent ones who looked remotely like they were a leader or in control?"

That was a nasty surprise, albeit not quite out of left field. "You mean like the assholes who sacrificed themselves to blow up the fertilizer ships in the New Angeles harbor?"

I was a little taken aback that it took my remark for Nate to make the connection, but then we were all suffering from sleep deprivation, and even if he didn't spell it out, I knew that losing Andrej must have felt like someone had cut out his heart and fed it to him—pun intended, because I was a horrible person and my mind got weird under stress.

"Exactly like that," Nate muttered, momentarily lost in thought.

I waited for his attention to return to me before I picked up the thread. "It doesn't matter that we don't know," I pointed out. "Besides personal satisfaction, of course, but I feel like we've always been running short on that resource. I got to shoot Taggard and you got to tear off Cortez's head, but that's about it—and how much good did that do us?"

Nate put on a musing expression and actually went as far as flashing me a quick smile. "Actually, it was rather rewarding. And it sure makes me sleep better at night."

I offered up a shrug for my agreement. He did have a point there.

"Be that as it may—we don't need any more information. We know where we are headed. We know who we are coming for. If it was as easy as following a trail of breadcrumbs, we would have killed Decker years ago. Yes, not being able to beat the crap out of anyone is frustrating, but that's about it. They are dead. We saved as many of ours as we could. We're making sure that Sadie and the kid are squirreled away where nobody can get to them. And then we ring in judgment day, and that's it. Maybe we'll get treated to one last villain speech of epic proportions that puts every little piece of the puzzle into place. Maybe we just waltz in there, kill that old fart, and call it a day. It doesn't matter in the grand scheme of things."

I thought that had been a mighty fine declaration, but Nate didn't quite go with my enthusiasm. "You say that as if you expect us to survive that encounter," he pointed out, part teasingly, part belligerent.

I couldn't help but flash him a bright smile—and was surprised that I meant it, even if it came with plenty of grim underpinnings. "Failure is not an option, so why calculate for it?" That was definitely something he could have said—and should have, come to think of it. "Besides, I have a feeling that should things go sideways, we won't have time for regrets."

Nate gave me an almost quizzical look. "Bree, I just spent nine weeks locked away in hell. For Hamilton, it was closer to a year. I'm not afraid that if we confront Decker and don't manage to kill him immediately that we end up dead ourselves. I'm afraid of what will happen if they don't kill us on the spot."

I absolutely hated him saying that—and not just because he spelled out the possibility. I knew that, realistically, fear was absolutely a part of his usual emotional spectrum—and I wasn't quite sure whether he'd yelled it at me or not, but there was that saying that he certainly subscribed to about bravery and how it wasn't the absence of fear but acceptance of it that made a difference. But the Nate I'd known for so long had never spoken so openly about it, not to me or anyone else. Then again, we had spent over two years with only each other for company, and that had led to a few late-night dark moments of the soul. Or maybe being locked away, stripped bare in so many more ways than one, had made him realize that he needed to open up to me more to stay sane. Or maybe it was a sign of just how much his control was slipping that things he didn't even acknowledge to himself before now ebbed out to me. It didn't really matter.

"I'm not afraid," I more lied than confessed, but realized it was true as I listened to my own words. "Sure, I'd like to avoid the pain of prolonged torture, but if that's how shit goes down? Fine with me. But we will end this, one way or another. I'm sure of that. I fucking hate what happened to Andrej, but he had a choice, and I don't think he regretted it for a single moment. Considering the life we chose, we don't often get a chance to go out in a blaze of glory, putting our very lives in front of others to save them. I never thought I'd say that, but that's a good way to die. And since we're going to die, sooner rather than later, that's not the worst way to go. I know that you have this romanticized notion in your head of you and me sitting on a mountain, waiting to see who is the first one to go so the other gets to do the murder / suicide thing, and because you're a self-important asshole, you think you will be the one to pull the trigger on me to spare me the mental anguish of the reverse, but I don't mind it ending in another way if it means we ultimately win."

Nate didn't say anything but he gradually relaxed, as if my words had at least some impact on his emotional turmoil. Just when had things changed so that I'd become the one to spell out the uncomfortable truths in our lives? I kind of wanted the times back when he'd had to drill that into my brain, to keep my rampant optimism in check—if that ever had been a problem, really. Looking back, it felt more like a few instances of a much-needed and quite obvious reality check. I couldn't help but smile a little when I remembered the talk we'd had in the middle of nowhere in the Midwest, a month into the apocalypse, the night before we'd gotten our cars.

"It might just turn out better than we think, you know?" I mused, almost immediately drawing the vexed look from him I'd known would come, which just made my smile deepen. "Remember that profound talk you gave me about no place on earth ever being safe again? I call bullshit. The bunker was pretty safe. And going forward, we always managed to get out of even the worst situations—like the factory; like Taggard's white-tiled cell; like France or Dallas. Even that damn prison and arena couldn't absolutely break you. Why should this be any different? Sure, life can be brutal and shit, but we've made it our business to make it a better place. The very fact that we've lived through far worse than either of us could have imagined that night, and we're still standing, and fighting, just underlines how good we are at this."

Nate thought about that for a moment. "That's something Romanoff would have said."

"And toasted the bitch called fate with some booze," I added.

"Absolutely."

This time as silence fell between us, it was no longer filled with guilt, but the all-too familiar low, ebbing pain and sadness of another dear friend lost but never forgotten.

I was a little surprised when Nate didn't use that for an excuse to doze off, but instead spoke up once more. "In a sense, I'm glad that he found his end in a different way than at our hands. No question, I would have done him that last honor of shooting him as soon as he was about to turn, but let's be real here. It wouldn't have been me. It would have been Zilinsky, and I'm not sure she would have walked away from that. She could have walked away from killing me, or you, or anyone else, but not him. I know she likes to blame me for bringing her back to sanity and giving her a life worth living, but really, that was all him. I just happened to be around when they both needed to pivot and change directions. He was the one who found her, picked up the pieces, and made her whole again. I know it sounds like poetic shit, but her being the one who undoes him? That would have undone her, too."

All I could do was nod. That sounded about right. It also made me even more sad for her because I knew she wasn't the kind of woman who would open up to anyone, not even Nate or me. That made me think of his last request to me—the parting remark about the pancakes she'd made for her kids—and I realized there must have been way more to the story than she'd told me. Some shit like her almost starving to death from grief and anguish, and him badgering her into eating some damn pancakes because the memory of her kids was that kind of lasting connection nobody could take from her, even after they'd taken everything else. It made them both so fucking human that it hurt down to my very soul to, yet again, realize that the people I'd in the past elevated to near godhood because my life had depended on my unshakable faith in them were, in fact, mortal. I knew it was unfair that, for whatever reason, Andrej had always been more like the drunk, goofy uncle or older brother to me while Pia had become my unshakable paragon of wrath and destruction when in reality, he was no less deadly and had actually taught her all the tricks, but that very difference in approachability might just have saved my life over and over again—and hers, too.

It also made me realize that, just maybe, the reason Nate was so open and chatty tonight might stem from the simple fear that having each other to be open and honest with was a very limited resource.

"I know you're normally not one for cuddling, and we are both a far shot from wanting to bump uglies instead, but hold me while I fall asleep?" I suggested, leaving out the part where I was sure that he needed it more than me.

Nate gave me a look that let me know he'd heard that loud and clear nevertheless, but after a moment's hesitation—couldn't pass up any chance of being an asshole—he shifted and stretched out his arm for me to shimmy over to him and abuse it for a pillow. Between all the gear in the car, it was more of a climbing expedition that was required, but I ended up cozy and too hot but very content, curled up on my side, with his body fused to my back and half draped over me.

And, wouldn't you know it? In a sense, that helped a lot more than beating the living shit out of any asshole out there ever could.

Chapter 9

A little after dawn hit, I was wide awake, and since there were enough people up and about to relieve the guards, we decided we would set out at eight, which gave everyone a chance to get at least some rest. It became obvious just how well the Ice Queen had spent the last two and a half years, stealthily sending out scouting and scavenging parties that had nothing to do with building up what had started out as our camp and had ended as two settlements. She had more than twenty safe houses mapped out, ranging halfway up to the Utah settlement, some close enough to the trade routes that we wouldn't need to do much detouring, others tucked away that even knowing where they were, we'd likely spend an hour locating them. On some level it was a relief to me that, for the first time in what felt like forever, I could rely on someone else actually knowing where we were going. But there was the latent paranoia that none of the houses would be safe, and we'd only find out after it was too late.

Yet all that was a discussion for a later date. Now, with barely enough sleep to let my body recharge, standing watch was hard, but it was mostly the mental impact that grated on me. There wasn't much to do or pay attention to, so my mind was at perfect leisure to present me with a best-of reel of what had gone down in that damn cantina again, and again, and again, until I was ready to throw my head back and scream, hoping that would make it stop. In the midst of the camp, I saw Sadie get up and retreat from the car she had slept in to the fire, a sleepy Chris on her shoulder. She still seemed reluctant to let go of her daughter, even when Moore joined her a while later and started goofing off with the kid, who seemed blissfully unaware of her mother's constant anguish. Returning to California after losing Nate, I'd been afraid that jealousy and resentment would rear its ugly head inside of me, seeing as Chris embodied everything that Sadie had and I had lost. None of that had come to pass, but seeing Sadie now, bruised and with wide, haunted eyes, made a kind of rage churn in my belly that I wasn't familiar with. It was one thing for those assholes to come after us, or infect the scavengers—but threatening what was as close to a beacon of hope as we had? I could see now why Nate had been all too happy that in the beginning, the guys had adopted me as something akin to a mascot—something to put all their hopes in, something to keep alive. Realizing how close we'd come to losing Sadie and the kid now made me all the more glad I'd learned how to fend for myself.

Our watch schedule was sketchy at best, and I was more than happy when one of the scavengers offered to take over for me. I hesitated, but then went straight over to Sadie, figuring she wouldn't be appalled by me parking my ass next to her in full gear and weapons. She wasn't, although as soon as I stepped up to the fire, she finally stopped fussing over Chris and let Moore walk off with her to look for some lizards ready to warm themselves on the first warm stones of the morning. I'd barely managed to grab a mug and fill it, my ass not yet molded against a crate someone had set up for a makeshift seat, when Sadie leaned closer, her eyes narrowed at me.

"If you breathe even a word of the rape talk I know you are burning to start, I will grab one of these logs and beat you to a bloody pulp with it," she hissed.

Closing my partly open mouth, I instead busied myself blowing on the coffee, forcing my sluggish, erratic thoughts into tracks. "Who beat me to it? Pia?"

"By ten years," Sadie grumbled, then rolled her eyes at me when I raised my brows at her. "Oh, don't be stupid. What you got that first year before our winter together was the sped-up, boot-camp version. I got the lifer version when I was thirteen. And again at sixteen, when I finally had the guts to have a boyfriend. I know what you all think happened. I don't give a flying fuck, thank you very much. I have something more important on my mind than either alleviating your collective fears or confirming them. Keep me and my daughter in one piece until we get to Utah, and consider your job done. I do not need a horde of shell-shocked, jaded nannies trying to analyze my every flinch and frown."

If I'd been Nate—and, realistically, if Sadie had been me, since I figured, despite what she claimed, he was used to pussyfooting around difficult topics with her more than me—I would have pointed out now that all that rambling still wasn't a clear and resounding "no," but dropped the point.

"You okay with staying in Utah?" I asked instead.

Sadie seemed both pleased and miffed at my change of topic but took it for what it was—a peace offering. "It's not like I have much of a choice," she huffed, but then let the aggression leak out of her voice. "I won't lie. I'm scared out of my wits. If you think that's the best place for me to go, that's where I go. I think I would have preferred New Angeles, but I understand why that's a shit choice. I guess Dispatch would have been a good place, too, but considering it's on the other side of the country, I'd rather just spend a single week in terror for my life than two or three." At my questioning look, she shrugged. "I know Rita from when she used to come to Dad's barbecues, too. I'm sure she'd take care of me. But same as with New Angeles, while there is strength in numbers, it also complicates disappearing from the world. I've been to Utah. I'm not sure what to make of Minerva"—the Utah settlement's feisty leader—"but they're good folks. They also have lots of children running around." She paused, as if her next words pained her. "If I can't stay, at least I can make Chris disappear there. Nobody will have a chance of picking one small girl out of a whole crowd of kids." I hadn't even considered the possibility of splitting them up; suddenly, Sadie clinging to her child took on a very different connotation.

"I doubt it will come to that," I tried to reassure her. "Whatever else they may have planned, we won't give them much more time to enact it."

She nodded, but looked less convinced than I would have preferred. "They still hit our town hard."

"They also knew we were trekking across the country, and then back again. We won't give them that kind of a warning this time."

"Let's hope you're right."

I wished there was something else I could offer, but we both knew I was out of platitudes. It felt almost like a relief when Sonia joined us, rubbing gritty eyes after too little sleep. The two women started chatting quite amicably between themselves, silently pointing out that I was dismissed. I took the pointer for what it was, and after filling another mug, went to find Pia.

I didn't get far, as she was just now returning with Burns from somewhere, carrying a bottle filled with clear liquid that she was dusting off. Burns made a shooing motion, making me turn back to the fire. I chanced a cautious glance at Pia but she ignored me. She looked like death warmed over, haggard yet quiet, which was disconcerting on so many levels. Whatever had happened in the past, she'd always been the first up, surrounded by an aura of energy and strength that always forced me to try to match it; now, all that seemed to have been leeched from her very bones, leaving a shadow of her usual self. I was sure that she could still wipe the floor with me, but for the first time ever she didn't seem ready to on a moment's notice.

In short order, the lot of us—pretty much the old gang, with Sonia the only new addition—had gathered around the fire pit, the others keeping respectfully silent. Nobody debated the idea of starting the day somewhat inebriated, but considering that half of us wouldn't feel it, I figured it was just as well. Everyone seemed to wait for either Nate or the Ice Queen to speak up, but all Pia did was take a silent swig from the bottle before she passed it on to Burns. He, at least, found his voice, raising the bottle toward the fire with a low laugh. "To you, old bastard," he toasted, taking a long drag before handing the bottle to Martinez.

"You still owe me two bottles of Scotch," Martinez toasted, coughing when the contents of the bottle turned out to be more potent than he must have expected. "Could be entirely possible they ended up as this," he remarked as he handed me the bottle next.

I considered what to say, but my mind was utterly blank. So I went with, "Keep stoking the flames for us. I'm about done freezing my ass off half of the year," before letting the booze burn me awake. It was damn sharp moonshine—probably meant for engine cleaning, but if Andrej had taught me one thing, it was to never be too picky with these things.

Sonia went next, and Santos and Collins after her, then Moore and Clark, until there was maybe two fingers of liquid left in the bottle as it reached Nate, standing silently next to Pia. I half expected him to go for silence as well, but instead he uttered in low Serbian, "To fighting the good fight," before drinking and passing the bottle back to Pia. She'd given him a sidelong glance but repeated the phrase in English before raising the bottle, and poured the last few drops into the pit. The fire roared up, blue flames licking over the yellows and oranges, as we all echoed her. I knew Andrej would have appreciated the lot of us getting stone drunk until someone almost died of alcohol poisoning, but since this was all we could do, I was sure he'd be satisfied either way.

Just as quickly as our not-so-merry round had assembled, it fell apart once more, people grabbing coffee and fetching some breakfast from our provisions. I shouldn't have been surprised to find Blake appearing at my side, Buehler in his wake. "I didn't get much chance to know him, but Romanoff certainly was one of the good ones," Blake offered.

Pia grinned, if only briefly, while Nate scoffed. "You wouldn't have said that to his face."

"Of course not," Blake insisted, laughing briefly. "Just wait for what we'll say at your eulogy one day."

I had to fight a grin at the disgusted expression on Nate's face. Amos, Cole, and Hill joining us kept me from having to add a witty remark. Somehow, the attack on the town seemed to have done away with some of the raging animosity that had been going on between the army lot and the scavengers, although they still kept a respectful distance from each other. Cole sniffed the air but refrained from offering any wisecracks about wasting perfectly good liquor. They all echoed Blake's sentiment one way or another, then left once they'd grabbed some coffee. It almost felt like an offering to the gods of war, only in reverse.

All too soon, it was time to pack up camp and leave, hoping we'd hit the next stop before the worst of the heat of the day hit us. Before she could collect her kid and disappear into one of the other cars, I pulled Sadie aside, much to her annoyance. "What?" she asked in the same petulant tone I would have used if someone had done that to me back at the bunker. Shit, but things had changed so much…

"You know that we're not just pawning you off to Minerva and her people, right?" I asked. "You're not safe around us. And I hate to say so, but you're kind of a liability until we know you're out of harm's way."

Sadie grimaced but inclined her head with more grace than I could have mustered. "I'm well aware of that. And no, I'm not mad at you for abandoning me, yet again, while you go out and wage war. Happy?"

Not exactly, but since I wasn't trying to incite a fight, I left it at a nod. Much to my amusement, Sadie scowled at me. I flashed her a quick grin. "Hey, you had to contribute to the next generation of the human race—you can't complain that you can't play warrior goddess now."

"Yeah, because that's your job," she harped. It was my turn to frown now, which made her crack a smile. "Oh, admit it. You get a kick out of how the scavengers all get breathless and are about to break out in fanboy squeals whenever you walk past them."

I pointedly looked over my shoulder, intent on proving to her that wasn't the case—only to find a huddle of five scavengers, two male and the three girls we had along, standing together, all staring at me. One of the women went as far as to wave. I quickly turned back to Sadie, a little aghast. "Yeah, I'll never get used to that."

"Might come in handy," she offered.

"Already did, when we cased the camp to spring Nate." I realized we hadn't really had time to catch her up on everything, but that wasn't important now. "Just… I don't know what to say, but I hate that we have to push you away so soon again. If this shitshow has taught me anything, it's to make the most of what little time we still have with the people we actually like being around." I was actually surprised that Hamilton didn't miraculously appear at my elbow, ready to ruin the moment.

Sadie's body language eased up a little, and for a moment I wondered if she'd give me a hug, but she refrained from that. "When we crash over noon, why don't you tell me about the crazy scavengers? I never bought the bull they were reporting on the radio. Most of them we had dropping by from New Vegas were a raucous bunch, but no worse than what I've been used to from before. I'll sleep a little more soundly knowing you'll have them at your back. I got a little concerned when Pia radioed us after you all left the camp and she said you were stuck with Hamilton glued to your side. I'm actually surprised he's still alive."

I couldn't help gritting my teeth in anger. "Yeah, and it's not gotten any more bearable since he's the one who saved my life."

Sadie gave me a curious look but I gestured that I'd fill her in another time. Martinez would likely do the deed as soon as they were in the car together, anyway. She dropped the point, then looked around, her gaze briefly snagging on Pia and Nate where they were standing to the side, markedly out of earshot of us. Her expression was imploring going on cautious, and she kept eyeing them as she whispered to me.

"Okay, this needs to stay between you and me. Promise me. I can't unload this on Nate, because as much as he's trying to appear all calm and composed, it's pretty obvious that he's a mess, and losing Andrej didn't exactly help. But you asked, and I feel like the same is bothering him, so it's up to you to play diplomat and somehow keep your confidence to me and talk him down off his ledge."

I kind of hated where this was going but dutifully nodded. "Sure, I promise. Fascinating that you'd think of me as the stable one, but hey. We all have our moments."

She looked incredulous rather than vexed at my assessment. "You toughed out rotting from the inside out and losing half of your fingers and toes in what must have been your scientist past's worst nightmare. I'd say that qualifies you for keeping a level head—or as level as you can, running with this crowd." She bit her lip, stalling, and eventually resumed when it became apparent that I wasn't going to retort anything. Shit, but I was starting to see why Nate constantly did this to me. It was kind of fun—and rather effective in making the other get to the point. "I know this sounds bad, and in many ways I feel guilty for it, but I'll be kind of glad to be rid of you once we get to the Utah settlement," Sadie confessed.

My first reaction was hurt, although I hoped I managed to cut down on the impulse of showing it. My mind, slowly grinding into gears, quickly hashed out what she was actually trying to say. "Because you are too aware that we will turn into a true menace once we lose it, and you can't have that around your daughter."

Sadie managed to look both guilty as hell and elated that she needn't spell that out since I just did. "Bree, I don't think any of you really get what happened to me. I spent a night, an entire day, and almost another night bound to Andrej while he was fighting tooth and nail not to lose it. And he had already started to turn when they pulled him up and drove those damn meat hooks through him. I could see it in his eyes. He was ready to give in, to give them hell the only way he still could. They knew it, and they turned his last chance at redemption around on him when they bound us together." She paused, licking her lips. "I can't say that I wasn't borderline hysterical when they rigged me with that C4 vest, but that was a hell of an entirely different magnitude. Every time he moved, I felt more of his blood run down on me. And if that wasn't bad enough, I knew that every drop he lost was one drop closer to death. Every groan of agony, every moan or ragged breath, I felt through my entire body, dreading it would be his last. I know that you loved him like a brother, and he's always been the same to me, although probably more the weird, inappropriate uncle always getting drunk at family gatherings. Of all the people in my life that I knew would protect me, he has always been among the first that came to mind. And they not only took that away—they turned that around on me. I don't think I will ever forget exactly how scared I was the entire time. You'd think that decreases as it goes on, as you go numb? No such luck for me since I could tell he was getting too weak to continue fighting the longer we were forced to wait for you like that. It wasn't even a day yet when I was tempted to simply step off the detonator plate and end it, so it would finally be over, but because of how they'd tied us together, I couldn't. Bree, they made me want to blow myself up and even that possibility they took from me! I will forever be so fucking grateful to all of you that you got me out of there, and even more to Pia for saving my little girl, but I don't think I can sleep soundly until I know you're at least half a state away so none of you can suddenly turn and eat my face."

Stunned pretty much summed up how I felt at her confession, if you could call it that. Horrified, too, but mostly feeling stupid because that had been completely outside of what I had considered might be weighing on her mind. No wonder she'd gotten in my face earlier. I was at a loss for words but at least I managed to nod, then took her hands because, hey, physical contact was probably what she was really wanting from me after telling me all that, right? But I couldn't very well recoil from her now, so I squeezed her hands, as if to underline my promise already given.

"Thanks for telling me," I muttered, feeling utterly useless. "And, yeah, it was a sound choice not breathing any of that where Nate can hear. He's… he has a lot on his mind right now, and the last thing he needs is feeling guilty or second-guessing himself for something he can't change."

"You think?" Sadie said, unnaturally acerbic, narrowing her eyes at me when all she got was a blank stare. "I saw him gnawing on a raw piece of meat behind a shed yesterday. They killed all our livestock when they took over the town—I know that wasn't cow or pig. I'm not quite sure that's something you can resolve in couples therapy."

She couldn't know it, but that barb mostly stung because it echoed what Richards had remarked to me after we'd watched Nate's spectacular arena kill. I'd been afraid to find him among the mindless drones in the town but that had thankfully not been the case. Wherever he was right now, I hoped that he was still alive, still of sound mind, and not a lying, deceiving, traitorous asshole. Forcing my attention back to Sadie, I found it relatively easy to offer up a somewhat wry but real smile. "That's my problem, and nothing you need to concern your pretty little head with."

Her eyes went wide, anger sparking in them, setting my mind at ease. I much preferred dealing with her anger than having her afraid of us—although I really got why.

"Just because the scavengers worship you doesn't mean you need to be such a bitch," she hissed, using her momentary indignation to leave me standing there as she marched off toward the cars. I looked after her, shaking my head in silence.

And I had zero qualms about breaking my promise to her as soon as our convoy was underway, Nate driving for the first stretch of the journey. He didn't flinch at my compacted report, taking it all in with a stoic expression. "Well, at least there's hope this takes her off the target list," he surmised, actually sounding amused.

"How so?"

He shrugged, never taking his eyes off the road. "Whoever planned it likely did it to make her hate all of us. That means she's less useful as a bargaining chip."

I didn't miss the frown appearing on his face but it was gone almost immediately. "What's with the doubt?"

Nate mulled this over for a little before answering. "Remember what I told you in the car when we were waiting to leave Dallas? It's a wrong move. It's the opposite of what Decker should have done. Sure, making one of those closest and dearest to me horrified of me is powerful, but it pales in comparison to how much more useful she was before that."

"Maybe the old asshole is losing his edge?" I suggested.

"Probably," Nate admitted. "And it could be as simple as this being his Plan B."

"You mean, Plan A being her blowing up right in front of us, with you having no chance of saving her?" He nodded. "Shit, but I hate being right."

"No, you don't," he teased, but it didn't hold much humor.

I gave him a fake sweet smile that he missed—too bad. "Of course I don't. And that's why we are leaving her behind but I'm coming with you right into the lion's den."

I didn't miss that Nate hesitated before he nodded, but that was a battle for another day. And damn, we still had a way to go until we got there.

Chapter 10

We made good headway at first, but somehow that only added to my paranoia rather than subtract from it. The roads weren't completely abandoned—we saw traders pass by in the distance every day, and Cole kept updating us on what their Humvee caught of Dispatch's chatter, which was also going strong—but somehow I felt like my nerves would have been less frazzled if someone had attacked us. At least the fighting would have done a thing or two to let me bleed off some energy.

It took me around two sets of our haphazard day-and-night driving schedule until I felt moderately refreshed, my body not minding much whether it got the sleep it needed in one long stretch or diced up into three shorter sets. Judging from how Sonia and Martinez were still walking puppets, my recovery was on the quick side, even if I still felt the last dregs of having, once again, hopped right off my deathbed. The wound—well, scar now—still bothered me but I had full range of motion back, even when I got up from slumbering with half my body stiff. My untimely tumble off that roof hadn't exacerbated any of it, leaving only my ego bruised.

We decided to bypass New Vegas in a likely unnecessarily long loop without sending anyone close, and we didn't get a request from anyone to join although they likely must have been expecting us. The scavengers didn't speak up, if anything looking pleased that they got to play my honor guard—or whatever they called themselves—while others were denied that pleasure. Our share of the group was down to what was left of the Lucky Thirteen plus Sonia and Sadie since the others had remained with the survivors in California, their bonds to them stronger than to Nate and me. I honestly felt some relief over that since I trusted Santos and Clark not to knife me in the back, but wasn't so sure about whoever Pia had managed to recruit. I knew that was likely unfair, but after Marleen I was hesitant to make it that easy for anyone else. That of course the scavengers themselves were the most likely host for further insurgent action was obvious, but, if anything, any suspicious glance from anyone in their direction made them stand up a little taller, beaming proud, defiant grins back. And those were surprisingly sober grins; since joining up with us, Amos must have set new rules about intoxicants. Come to think of it, I hadn't seen them smoke anything worse than a conventional cigarette or the odd joint. Of course they were still just as loud and full of swagger, particularly when any of the soldiers were around to see. On watch, they were as disciplined and quiet as the rest of us— just as if they were pretending, which they obviously were. Although none of them had had any affiliation with our townspeople, I could tell that the attack on the town had taken a toll on them as well, once again proving just how vulnerable all of us were in the end, however many weapons we were toting around with us.

Damn, but I was so ready to be done with this shit!

Nevada turned to Utah, but not much changed. It was still dry as fuck and hot as hell, and with our food supplies dwindling as fast as our water, it was hard not to be miserable constantly. Sadie's remark about watching Nate eat meat of questionable origin at least alleviated my concern regarding his energy levels. Two of the springs on our route had dried up but we managed to find water at a third, and got lucky when Hamilton shot a deer too thirsty to stay at a distance although it must have smelled us. Nate made himself scarce when it was time to divvy up the grilled meat, but otherwise he'd stopped lurking around with Hamilton, instead spending most of the time when we were not on the road sleeping or on watch next to the Ice Queen in seemingly silent companionship. Since usually Sadie and Chris were around, too, it didn't appear as if they'd spoken ten words between them, but I noticed, as the others who gave a shit must have. Hamilton surprisingly behaved himself, apparently having found the last shred of decency—or so I thought until I happened on Pia pinning him against one of the Humvees, knife to his throat, hissing something at him that I didn't need to hear to know was as hostile as it got. Bucky appeared appropriately chastised—and maybe a hint scared—but as soon as she let up and walked away, he spit on the ground where she'd been standing and looked ready to come after her, fists flying. I pointedly cleared my throat, making his head whip in my direction, eyes narrowed. I gave him the most level look I could manage before I turned back to my perimeter round, aware that I shouldn't have felt that satisfied that—finally!—someone had put the asshole in his place. I had a certain feeling that whatever truce they had reached wouldn't hold up beyond us reaching the Utah settlement, but I didn't really care, I realized. For how much

Andrej's loss made me feel dejected and raw, I had my people back, and it was hard not to be happy about that.

Setting a punishing pace to California before came with one advantage—all the vehicles that had been prone to breaking down had already been left for scrap metal at the side of the road, with those remaining holding up well. Two of the ATVs started stalling out, but Martinez fixed one using spare parts from the other over one hot midday break, forcing the two scavengers now without a ride to hitch with the marines.

And then we were on the last two-hundred mile stretch almost true north, our destination tantalizingly close. I could tell that Nate was tempted to have us drive through the night and forego two longer rests in favor of reaching our destination sooner, but decided against it. It was only when he mentioned it that I realized it had been over a day since the last trader caravan had made us veer farther off track. Just as if my rising paranoia had conjured it, Cole hailed us on the radio, letting us know that he had someone from Salt Lake City on the open frequency.

Nobody tried to pretend they were not listening in as people crowded around the Humvee, Pia needing to bark a few sharp orders so someone would do a passing impression of keeping watch. Nate accepted the mic from Hill, remaining standing outside the vehicle in the afternoon heat baking us all.

"Thought you would be dropping by my humble abode sooner or later," Minerva herself offered instead of a greeting.

Nate's expression was completely neutral but he had that fake jovial tone going that he so often used when he was sure someone was spying on us. "Must be a real surprise since you're the only waypoint of interest going pretty much anywhere from where we were last."

Minerva laughed. "That is true, and also the reason why we are one of the most important trading hubs in the country." I wondered for whose benefit she was mentioning that since it couldn't be for ours. "Do you have an ETA for your convoy? Just so we know when to put out a few extra placemats."

I wasn't surprised when Nate lied. "Likely another three to four days."

"Splendid." I couldn't help but smirk at Minerva's exclamation. "Then you'll be just in time to help us with some cleanup."

Silence fell, everyone seeming to hold their collective breath. That didn't sound good. Nate briefly looked in my direction but didn't say anything to me before speaking into the mic again. "Sure, we're always happy to help. When do you need us?"

"Three days from now sounds about right. Let us know if you need anything when you get here."

"Some chow and a place to crash is more than enough," Nate stated.

"Good. Safe journey until then, and don't let the zombies bite you," Minerva offered and signed off.

Murmurs rose all around us but quieted immediately when Nate spoke up. "Opinions please on if I've deciphered this right: they have vermin sitting outside of their settlement and need us to be there in less than two days at the most or else we don't stand a chance to break through. My guess is with undead sheep in tow, but that might just have been her way of being funny. That woman has our kind of humor."

A few of the scavengers grinned at the last bit. Nobody spoke up to negate his guess. Hamilton finally piped up. "Sounds about right. It's likely for the best if we cut it down to one day. Whoever is getting ready to prevent us from getting there likely heard that transmission. They likely won't believe our three-day estimate since they know where we're coming from, and also have estimates of how long it took us from Alabama to California."

I hated to agree with him. Thankfully, Pia spoke up before I had to. "We should drive through the night and chance getting in trouble with some shamblers on the way there. If they have an undead problem outside of town, getting there in the morning will be the best time. That gives us the entire day to cut and shoot our way across the plain to their gates." That she'd been to the settlement before was obvious from that statement—which likely put her ahead of me since I could only vaguely remember the one time we'd dropped by there. Somehow, that whole business about rotting from the inside out had overshadowed that part of the trip.

"Then let's not waste perfectly good driving time," Nate called, thus shooing us back into the vehicles.

We made surprisingly good time, but it still took us until four in the morning, the sky still dark, until we reached the territory officially claimed by the settlement—literally, a series of sign posts and openly positioned lookout towers proclaiming their presence. All of them were unmanned but showed recent signs of habitation, making me guess that when the California coast towns had gone dark, Minerva had pulled her forces inward to ensure that they could defend their core settlement at all costs.

Nate had us set up camp to refuel and get some rest but shooed me right back into the car after I relieved myself, Zilinsky and Burns following in Martinez's Ford after ousting a sleepy Sadie and Chris and our very unhappy medic. Our cars weren't exactly the best vehicles for going cross-country, but with only ten miles to the plains in front of the settlement, we took the road, trusting that going slowly enough that the tires made minimal sounds would let us be sneaky enough not to be discovered.

I could already see the terrain even out in front of us when my gut suddenly seized up, Nate next to me sitting up straight. I gave him a curious look but kept creeping forward. Just as we broke through the light cover of rocks and the odd tree, I felt it again, and this time it was unmistakable. "That's a beacon." I gave Nate another sneaky glance. "And you definitely felt it, too."

He nodded, not looking disconcerted that I wasn't the only one who could feel them now. I was less happy about that but kept my thoughts to myself. The other car stopped beside ours and we all got out, binoculars at the ready. There was no moon out and with the sky slowly starting to lighten, it was actually harder to make anything out than if it had still been pitch black. Even so it was hard to mistake the mass of shapes moving on the far side of the plains, drawing toward this side—the same side the settlement was on, only another few miles farther north—by what I tried to discern as either three or four attracting beacons. They were by far not as strong as those that New Angeles employed to keep the vicinity of the city well-controlled, but since we were too far away to make out a source, they must have been stronger than the few portable models we'd found strapped to zombies in the past. It shouldn't have been much of a surprise to encounter more of them now but I still didn't like it—not at all. Pia and Burns seemed oblivious to their siren call, making me hope that Nate—and maybe Hamilton, too—was the only one besides me who was susceptible to them.

"How long until they reach the settlement?" I asked no one in particular.

Pia, still looking through her binoculars, gave me the estimate I didn't want to hear. "At their current speed? Before we can be back with all of our people." She then glanced toward the mountains of the Wasatch Range to the east. "But by then the sun should be rising, so maybe that gives them a pause. We were right to get here as fast as possible."

"We've seen what we need to," Nate said, making a gesture toward the cars. "Get on the com and tell the others to come to us. No need to waste any more time. If they don't know yet that we're here, they will find out soon enough. Speed's our best defense now." The Ice Queen immediately set to it, leaving Burns and me to play lookout for now. I was a little surprised when, maybe five minutes later, Nate pulled me aside and told me to stretch and limber up. Sure, I'd spent most of the last fifteen hours in the car, either driving or trying not to fall asleep in the passenger seat, but I had a good ten more of the same in me with no issues. But when your man tells you to stick your ass up in the air and turn yourself into a human pretzel, who was I to protest?

I realized Nate had something different planned than what I'd figured when, as soon as the others arrived, he commandeered the car he and Hamilton had been sharing on the way to Dallas, telling the soldiers who had been using it in the meantime to split between that one and ours—leaving me pointedly out of the seating chart. He ignored my imploring gaze—well, glare—until everyone was assembled, safely out of where we could be visible from across the plain.

"The plan's as simple as they come," he explained to us before singling out Sadie and Chris. "We have one objective above all else— we need to get you two into that settlement and out of the killing ground that the plain will turn into as soon as we clash with the shamblers and whoever else is hiding out there. I'm sure Minerva has a sortie planned, so at the very least they'll give us cover fire up to their gates." He glanced at the brightening sky. "The sun will come over the mountains in about thirty minutes. By then we need to be ready."

"Ready for what, exactly?" I asked as soon as he fell silent.

Nate gave me the kind of smirk that let me know I wouldn't like what he had to say. "We'll be using the ATVs—and decoys." He let that sink in, but when all I had for him was a blank albeit murderous stare, he elaborated. "You're driving one of them, with Sadie behind you. Since the passenger is always more prone to fall off, we'll strap Chris to your front so that you can best protect her, even if Sadie should get thrown off; one of the others can pick her up and take her along. We'll use the other four ATVs as decoys, so I need everyone who's small and light on them. Martinez and Sonia will take one; the others I'll leave up to you to fill. To make you harder to identify, I need everyone to cover your heads and faces as much as possible, and we'll use backpacks in the front for the drivers and back for the passengers to make it as impossible as we can to tell who is actually carrying the kid. Strap your weapons to the ATVs—speed is key so you won't get much of a chance to shoot at anything. The rest of us will try to give you as much cover fire as possible as you race toward the settlement. Best case, you get to the gate just in time before the first shamblers reach this side of the plain. Get ready."

He left me exactly one breath's time to protest—which I didn't, partly because I agreed with him that it was a good plan, partly because I was still stunned that he expected me of all people to drive an ATV, and that with a wailing child strapped to my chest. Then he turned to the others, talking attack vectors and strafing runs. I couldn't hold it against Sadie when I looked at her and found her frantically clutching her child to herself, but she at least tried to give me an encouraging smile. I didn't tell her just how badly she failed.

"So I guess earplugs it is," I muttered, more to myself.

I was surprised when Pia stepped up to us, pulling a small object out of her pocket. It took me a moment to realize what it was. "Poppy seeds? I may be nervous about this but I don't think being all calm and relaxed for this is a good strategy."

The Ice Queen looked ready to bite my head off, but instead she turned to Sadie, plucked the kid out of her arms, and offered the small seed pod to Chris as if it was a pacifier. The sleepy kid didn't protest much, starting to suckle on the pod after minimal fussing. I didn't know who was more appalled, Sadie or me.

"You do know what the active ingredient is in that? Fucking morphine!"

Pia barely glanced at me, instead cooing softly to the sleepy child. "Do I like the idea of subjecting her to this? Not at all. But how do you think I got her to remain quiet while we were hiding in the town? She'll be fine." Sadie still looked upset—and honestly, the same was likely true for me—but Pia made a shooing gesture with her free hand. "Go get ready. We need to be alive a few hours from now for you both to chew me out for this." She had a point there, so rather than protest, I grabbed Sadie's arm and steered her back to the car so she could get fully dressed.

Even in the relative cool of the morning, I was sweating in full gear, an old balaclava over my head with an extra scarf tied across the lower half of my face to serve as a gore splash guard that I dearly hoped I wouldn't need until I got rid of my soon-to-be burden. I kept my knife and gun in their thigh holsters but otherwise forwent arming myself, except for the M4 pinned directly to the chassis of the ATV right alongside the driver's seat, a spare magazine each in my jacket pockets. Sadie had a shotgun strapped to her backpack, but I doubted she'd get to use it even if she needed it. Martinez and Sonia were ready on their vehicle, both bringing rifles and plenty of spare ammo that we could share if we didn't make it. Pia had in the meantime transferred Baby Chris into one of those carriers people probably used for hiking with their small kids, the girl fast asleep. Absolutely not familiar with the gear, I simply stretched out my arms to the sides and let Pia and Sadie strap that contraption onto me, securing it with a built-in belt around my hips and lower back. Looking down, I gently stroked a finger over the sleeping girl's cheek, but she didn't react. At the outside of the carrier I could plainly feel the ceramic plates someone had installed underneath the outer layer of kevlar, doing their best to shield the baby's head and body. I could only hope that she wouldn't be able to bat me in the face with her tiny hands or that her legs sticking out of the carrier wouldn't get in the way, but honestly? A scrape or broken bone would heal easily, particularly at her age. If I crashed the ATV and we got swarmed by zombies, those relatively small injuries would be the least of my problems. But I would have been lying if I'd said that having that little helpless bundle so close to me didn't do a number on me.

I didn't need further orders or encouragements to hop onto my ATV, doing my very best to familiarize myself with the controls while it was still turned off and Sadie got busy climbing on behind me. No surprise that the other three ATVs remained mostly in possession of the scavengers, the three females and two slighter males not giving up their favorite rides. One of the shorter marines was delegated to riding shotgun behind the third woman, but, if anything, she seemed mighty pleased with having her own marine gunner on board. I was a little surprised that Buehler hadn't jumped at the opportunity, but when I saw her follow hot on Pia's heels to what used to be my car, I figured she had found herself an even better opportunity to let her inner war-pig out.

We were ready before the sun crested the mountains but judging from their bright halo, it would be any minute now. I had my com switched on to the general frequency and no real way of changing channels or turning it off, which meant I would get to hear the whole plethora of people screaming, shouting orders, and dying. Part of me wanted to remain optimistic and rule the last part out, but considering that, even here, a good five miles outside of the settlement fortifications, we could already make out the mass of shamblers moving on the plain, I didn't see much chance of that happening. For a moment, I questioned the wisdom of making this a full-frontal run for the gates, but Nate must have a good reason for it, and the same was true for Minerva. Even a much smaller territory back in the day, our bunker had at least five exit vectors that we kept both maintained and mined at all times. Maybe it was a simple matter of the Utah people being incapable of giving us a good, safe route into their territory outside of the plain. That would also explain why they had, for the most part, suffered few losses over the past years—they were too tough a nut to crack. Clearly, that also came with disadvantages once that nutshell was closed.

For a last time, I glanced down at Christine, her face mostly obscured by how she had nestled into the carrier. As if she'd felt my attention, one bright blue eye cracked open, but almost immediately fell shut once more. I vaguely remembered that babies were born with blue eyes but couldn't be sure. Both her parents had less impressive color schemes, although that could be due to her age entirely. I cut down hard on the impulse to wonder if my own child would have had eyes like that. It was much easier to idly wonder how afraid Sadie behind me must be that I would bite it and end up eating her daughter, if not outright kill her on the spot. Ah, fun times, indeed.

Glancing back to the shamblers, I decided I was done waiting. "I say we start now," I proposed, hoping my mic would pick it up. Sonia, from the quad in front of mine, gave me a thumbs-up, likely both in response and to signal that my com was working. "The way is clear for the first mile, and maybe that's exactly the head start we'll need."

A low if agreeing chorus of grunts answered me, until a few seconds later Nate gave us the go-ahead.

Feeling something between scared and excited, I started the ATV's motor, using a few moments to get a feeling for the controls as we rolled along the road until we reached the actual plain. The ATV with the two male scavengers was going first, then Martinez and Sonia, followed by Sadie and me, the two female scavengers right on our heels, and the one with the marine gunner bringing up the rear. I doubted we'd keep anything resembling a formation up for long. Martinez, of course, had no problem with the quad, but I'd never driven one myself—and the last time I'd ridden on one, it was tied-up in the back when those assholes had grabbed us at our treehouse and carried us off to the slaver camp. Theoretically, I knew how they worked—Bates and Andrej, who had been responsible for most of my driving lessons, had taken some pains explaining pretty much every possible vehicle out there to me—but there were a few growing pains to deal with that I could have done without, considering that, a few minutes from now, we would be almost as blinded by the light as the shamblers, racing at top speeds across flat yet uneven country, possibly getting shot at and likely having to evade the quickest of the shamblers... and all that with a baby strapped to my chest. I told myself that, at the very least, possibly erratic driving would make me a harder target to hit, and the ATVs were harder to topple than motorcycles.

Yeah, this was so going to end in disaster.

But it started out well enough. It took me a little to catch up to Martinez after I fell back when I was still fighting with the perfect balance of accelerating and not hitting every little bump in the state, but the controls were more responsive than I'd had to work with in the past, and even when we went off-road, we were still following a track that similar vehicles must have plowed into the hard-packed earth, so it went relatively smoothly. The pulsing of the beacons was a constant annoyance both at the back of my mind and low in my gut, but while it got increasingly stronger, it wasn't getting harder to resist. Sadie was clinging to me as if her life depended on it, and if I wasn't mistaken, the hand she didn't use to grab onto the carrier strap she had cradled around Christine's right leg. I felt like my entire body was getting shaken and stirred, but this wasn't so bad.

The sun crested the mountains when we were maybe ten minutes into the plain, our little column finally traversing from the shadow into the light. I did my best to try not to squint too much, the tinted goggles doing their own to help protect my retinas. Ahead, the shamblers started to take on shape, and from what I could tell, they really didn't like being out in the sunlight that gained intensity quickly with each passing minute. The steady advance toward the settlement had slowed, leaving the center of the mass maybe a mile outside their forward guard towers. A few crafty individuals had likely made it to the gates, but right at the line where the light continued to eat away at the shadow of the mountains, a stretch of free land remained—and that was exactly where we were heading.

Whether it was instinct to try to guard the weakest member of the pack—or just spoke of the eagerness to get to the gate—the two vehicles behind me were close enough that I could have called out to them, while the two in front continued to drive at somewhat of a larger distance from us. That way, when the lead ATV drove over a mine buried in the ground and disappeared in a massive explosion of dirt and undefined organic and inorganic shrapnel, Martinez still had a second to veer hard to the left, avoiding getting pelted by what used to be two people and were now large chunks of scrap metal. Sadie screamed as I instinctively wrenched our quad to the right, going around the sudden obstacle on the other side. The only reason my hearing was preserved was that it was only her voice close to my ear, without the amplification of the com. In hindsight, it made sense not to give her a com to keep her from hearing everything, but it still felt like an error to me.

Suddenly on my own without a pacemaker or guide—and quite shaken from the shock and the shockwave both—I slowed down a little, but then gunned the accelerator, surging on ahead. I tried to remember whether I'd seen any markers, but I'd been too far back from the exploding vehicle for that. Just to be sure it wasn't some kind of previously set-up defensive system, I aimed the ATV a little farther into the plain, which gave Martinez the perfect excuse to shoot by me but slow down almost immediately, falling back to match the speed I was going at. The other two quads were following at a little more of a distance now but they were still there, continuing the surge forward.

"There was a patch of turned earth there, I think," Sonia's partly breathless voice came over the com. "Just like the one up ahead to our two. Let's avoid that." Martinez was already course-correcting and I followed suit. Looking farther ahead, I saw a lot more of those the closer we got to the shamblers—and a moment later, one of them tripped another claymore, disappearing into a mist of red, not all of it dust.

"What the fuck was that?" an unknown, gruff voice asked—likely one of the soldiers.

"Claymores, buried all over the plain," Martinez reported back in. "That's gonna be a problem for you more than us."

Cursing followed but cut off immediately when Pia came on the line. "All cars come with four people—one driver, one navigator, and two gunners. Navigator keeps track of what's going on, easy as that. They won't have mines where the thick of the fray is, but still keep an eye out for any."

Ahead, the sunlight flared across the palisade making up the main defenses of the settlement, setting the slightly weathered wood seemingly aflame. At first I thought I was simply seeing things when something was moving, but then I realized they were opening their gate, a convoy of cars coming out. The ATV ride was too uneven to properly count them but there must have been at least fifteen—and they weren't done yet. Following at a slower pace behind the cars, two massive harvesters came rolling out, barely fitting through the gate. That confused me at first but I was sure that Minerva knew what she was doing—and I doubted they had chosen this morning to go get some crops. The cars started fanning out to the north and northwest, one of the harvesters slowly trundling after them, while the other continued straight out from the gate. Something about it continued to distract me, but I didn't have enough focus left to pay much attention to it. Between keeping the ATV at as high a speed as I dared risk and continuing to dodge the patches of turned earth that may or may not have hidden mines underneath, I was about fully occupied.

And then there were of course the shamblers.

We were almost at the halfway point when the first didn't just glance idly in our direction but started surging toward us. With the center mass of the streak toward the settlement, those turning to us were the slow, skeletal ones, too slow to be much of a bother for Martinez and me, but it wasn't long before the assault rifle of the marine at the very back started barking in uneven intervals, interspersed by the low cursing of its wielder. Apparently, our bumpy ride wasn't that great for picking out moving targets.

Then a few more substantial shamblers made a run for us, forcing Martinez to slow down so Sonia could aim. My instinct was to slow down along with them, but I had nobody behind me who I trusted to keep the undead off us, so instead I gunned it—and narrowly missed driving over another mine, partly hidden under some sorry excuse for a shrub. I instinctively wrenched the ATV to the side as soon as I registered the abnormality on the ground, sending it into the higher grass toward the mountains. That was the wrong decision, I realized, when I almost brought it to topple over when the tires got stuck in something I hadn't seen—some branches or whatnot. Cursing, I reversed, losing precious seconds as I slowly made it around the hidden obstacle and turned the ATV back toward the dust of the plain—only to see two rather beefy zombies vault in huge steps toward us.

Neither of them reached us—the first's head exploded as soon as I became aware of it, and the other's followed a few seconds later just as I ambled the ATV back into the grass. I stared at the fallen corpses stupidly for a second, then wised up and gunned the throttle, picking up speed once more. Between finding where best to drive and avoid further mines, it took me a little to deduce where the shots had come from—and in actuality, it was only after another zombie was felled, maybe twenty yards to our left: someone was shooting from the top of the harvester.

A little closer now, I could finally make out what had irritated me about the harvester before—besides its very existence on the battlefield: there was movement on top of the huge machine where several people stood, probably lashed to the vehicle with belts or whatnot to prevent them from falling off. From what I could make out, four men were slowly but steadily picking out targets with sniper rifles, while a smaller figure—too small even for most women—was waving colored flags. A quick glance over to the second harvester confirmed that they had a similar setup going on. Too bad that I had no fucking clue what they were coordinating between the two of them, but it didn't really matter.

Trusting for now that the snipers had our backs—or fronts, or sides, or whatever—I increased the speed to as fast as I dared go. A second ATV pulled ahead and fell in beside me. It wasn't Martinez as I'd hoped but instead the one with the marine, still happily chewing into the shamblers slowly turning toward us. I slowed down a little, letting them pull ahead. The com frequency lit up as our cars started to engage with the zombie streak, coming in from the rear. I picked up from their calls that the Utah cars were also gearing up to cut into the mass. Yet the free corridor leading to the settlement was getting smaller and smaller, and we were still a third of the way from the gate. With a sinking feeling in my gut I realized we wouldn't make it. Well, if I had to, I would smash and kick my way there, dragging Sadie along behind me.

At first I ignored the pressure on my right thigh, but when Sadie added a loud shout close to my ear, I finally slowed down a little so I could glance back, if not in her face than at least so she'd realize I was paying attention to her. "I think that white flag is for us!" I thought I heard her shout, hard-pressed to make out the words over the com chatter and the assault rifle spewing lead a few feet away from us. Looking forward to the harvester, I saw the flag wielder—likely the adolescent child of one of the snipers, I figured—let out another flurry, but this time I realized that it ended with a repeat sequence, using a set of two white flags, pointing repeatedly away from the grass and toward the shamblers. That seemed like the most idiotic idea ever—until I topped a small rise, and realized that the mines we'd previously circumnavigated were only the beginning. The strip of land in front of us looked partly churned, making it impossible to estimate what was safe ground and what wasn't.

So into the fray it was, or at least as close as I dared drive.

Not that it came to that, as I almost collided with two of our cars that came blasting by us, first putting a kind of physical barrier between our ATVs and the streak, and then opening fire on them. I didn't get a good look at the first, but the second came with the Ice Queen and Sgt. Buehler pretty much hanging out of the rear windows—secured with rope harnesses to keep them from falling out—shooting into the mass of zombies as fast as they could reload, which was plenty considering who we were talking about here. Someone was stealing a page from my distraction playbook, it seemed, and I so didn't care.

I didn't even attempt to hold back a feral grin as I did my best to match my speed to that of the cars, trying to concentrate less on possible shamblers bypassing our honor guard and more on the terrain. Farther ahead, I saw the snipers up on the harvester switch to assault rifles as well, going for more close-quarter tactics—which were necessary now that they had reached the mass of undead. The harvester managed to keep going forward but at a slower pace, and considering how quickly the bottom half of the vehicle was covered in gore, they were applying the vehicle's intended purpose to its most grisly use. I could see the driver up in his cabin, barely above the splash radius, looking concentrated but calm.

And then we were past the harvester, and past the guard tower, the cars falling away from us to remain close to the vehicle while we blasted on toward the gate. Already, I saw the massive doors opening, a handful of guards on foot stepping out to join those on the palisades above in killing any shambler getting too close for comfort. A hundred feet, fifty, and then we were through, careening into the huge open space behind the gate meant for traders and scavengers to get ready, or as a very convenient space not to crash into each other right now. I let the ATV lose speed as I eased up on the throttle, the steep elevation directly at the gate helping. Swerving in a gentle curve, I let it roll to a halt at the very back where more armed guards were waiting, but also a bunch of civilians, although they didn't look any less fierce or less armed, to be honest.

Exhaling slowly, I felt a single shake run through my body as there was suddenly no use for the adrenaline poisoning my blood, but a moment later I was off the vehicle so I could help Sadie scramble down. She almost fell as she stumbled, her legs too shaky to hold her up. I made sure that she was safely leaning against the ATV before I checked my hands to make sure they weren't caked in gore—they were covered in dust, but that was true for my entire body—before I set to undoing the carrier, doing my very best to reunite mother and daughter as fast as possible. Two guards were quick to join me, helping once they realized what I was up to. I felt like screaming in frustration when my fucking useless fingers wouldn't let me undo the belts of the harness, but someone else did the trick, and Christine was off me and delivered into Sadie's shaking arms a moment later.

Whipping around to look back at the gate, I tore the damn balaclava, scarf, and goggles off my head, only now realizing how stifling the hood had been. Warm morning air hit my skin, doing nothing to cool or calm me down. I should have been able to relax now that we'd made it here, but my mind and body seemed to have a different idea, making me feel like I was just now starting to gear up for a fight for real. Behind us, two other ATVs had come in and stopped, but the last was still missing—Martinez and Sonia. As soon as I realized that, I felt panic twined with rage flare up in my gut, so strong that for a few seconds they drowned out the constant thrum of the fucking beacons—

The last ATV came sailing through the gate just as it was about to close, Martinez sending it into a masterful, elegant bank, ending with him facing the gate as if ready to depart any moment now. Sonia clapped him on the shoulder once before she hopped off, maybe a little unsteady but definitely safe. Martinez remained sitting, the only one of us smart enough to let his body acclimatize to the sudden relief that came with being out of harm's way.

But just because my rage had lost its target didn't mean it was ready to leave me the fuck be.

I forced myself to take a few calming breaths as I turned back to Sadie. She was crying again, but this time with obvious relief. That was a very natural, very understandable reaction, but it made me want to slap her, and yell at her to stop being such a baby. A woman and man who had that unshakable calm determination about them that seemed so universal to doctors, nurses, and other first responders were looking after her and the kid now, making it clear that she was no longer my concern.

Looking back to the gate, I found one of the guards who'd been outside and quickly stepped up to him. "Give me a status report."

He gave me a slightly curious look, but whether it was my demanding tone that left no question that I thought I was in command, or the crazy look in my eyes, he was quick to respond. "All the cars are engaged now, three broken down but I think they got the men inside out and into other vehicles. Our snipers have taken out at least three of those undead fuckers with the beacon vests but that means they are staying right where they fell. We need someone to drag them back out into the plain so we can get them away from the gate and further spread out."

I slapped him on the shoulder to show I'd understood, which made him look at me cross-eyed. "Perfect. Any more vehicles going out that I can hitch a ride on? If not, get that gate back open for me to run outside in five."

The guy didn't have time to respond when suddenly, the three female scavengers popped up beside me, already armed to the teeth. "Awesome! Where are we going?" the closest one to me—a girl barely past twenty with vaguely Asian features—asked as she pushed an M4 at me—not the one that was still strapped to my ATV. When she saw me glance at the vehicle, she let out a giggle that fit more into a mall or beauty parlor. "We took some spares along for you, seeing as you had your hands full." She proceeded to shove a pack—filled with minimal provisions, lots of ammo, and some first-aid basics—at me. Pia would have approved of how well it was maintained. Actually, it stood to reason that the Ice Queen had packed it. So much for surprising me with my part in the cargo run scenario. I felt vaguely stupid, only now realizing that Nate and Pia had likely planned it in all the hours they'd apparently not just sat together in silence. Fine with me if it meant I had a gun, plenty of ammo, and what was as close to a fireteam as it was going to get ready to head back out with me. By the time I was done suiting up, the marine had joined us, equally not ready to sit this one out.

Just then a pickup truck—heavily reinforced for withstanding a shambler onslaught at least for some time—was readied, the gate was pulled open once more, admitting three cars. I didn't recognize the first two, figuring they were local, but the last was one of the cars that had helped get us to the settlement. I was only so surprised when I saw Nate jump out of the driver's seat. He wasted only a second glancing to where I was clearly doing fine, and another on Sadie, before he ran over to the other cars, helping them unload their badly wounded cargo—seven men, presumably those from the cars that had broken down. Hamilton was right behind him, helping along, and I could see why in a second. The wounded had not just gotten mauled but were also splattered in gore from what must have been the rescue effort, turning them into one viral hot zone. Glancing at where Martinez and Sonia had perked up, I was glad to see both of them hesitate, the same as the medical staff who were still looking after Sadie and her kid. Fact was, the initial outbreak of the virus had killed too many doctors and nurses that no one could in good conscience risk their lives if it could be prevented. I'd heard Martinez himself rant about it on more than one occasion—and he dutifully ignored the advice, for the most part, where we were concerned—but from what I could tell at a distance, those seven men were going to die, and likely long before the fever from the infection could set in. But there were still some things that could be done for them, like to help them clean up and get comfortable, and anyone not afraid of the virus could lend a hand there.

Part of me was aware that should have been my cue to run over there, but instead I swung myself up onto the back of the pickup, my scavenger harpies and the lone marine quickly following. The truck was equipped with an entire jungle of belts to let anyone riding on the truck bed shoot or move around without fear of being thrown off, and in short order we'd all found a spot. By the time the truck rumbled toward the gate, Nate and Hamilton were on the way back to their vehicle, ready to join the fray again after a quick respite. I had a certain feeling Nate had used this as an excuse to check up on me rather than a need to lend a helping hand, but maybe I was getting a little cynical in my old age.

"We're ready to leave the settlement again," I talked into my mic after making sure that my com was still working. "Where do you need us?"

Pia answered less than five seconds later while we were still waiting to get back outside. "Wherever the fuck you want. It's a free-for-all out here. Make sure to bring melee weapons, because even with all our ammo, we won't kill more than a third of them."

Before I could, one of the girls called down to the guards that we needed axes or baseball bats—and with a few more seconds of delay, we descended back into hell.

Chapter 11

On principle, I never doubted the Ice Queen's assessment, but even less so where all matters of war were concerned. Of course, she had been right with her warning about just how big of a problem the zombies were—but a few minutes into the fight I felt like she massively understated the gravity of the situation. With all the attention that went into driving the ATV, I hadn't had enough focus to get a good picture of the entire situation, and in hindsight, our decision to go as early as possible with our cargo run had been right—and the only reason that we'd made it through.

Like with all streaks, this one also had the weak, frail, easier-to-kill shamblers that barely got enough food to keep on being a menace to all living things. The core of the large mobs was usually built around a group of either super-juiced zombies or at least unnaturally smart ones that had developed tactics that let them hunt food rich in protein and fat, drastically slowing down their deterioration and turning them into a real menace.

All of us had counted on finding a few of them—but not fresh, super-juiced zombies that were smart and could easily wipe the floor with us, seeing as the virus had fried their pain receptors for good and broken down any inhibitions even the most ruthless human still had. Because, lo and behold, a good third of the zombies seemed to have been scavengers as little as a few weeks ago. Now that was a nasty surprise if I'd ever seen one.

It made me a little afraid that I'd come face to face with someone I'd known.

It also made me want to get on the next long-range radio to call Harris and ask him exactly how many scavengers—infected with the wrong serum or not—they'd lost since after the winter we'd been to France. I vaguely remembered that someone—had it been Richards? Greene? One of ours? I really couldn't pin it down—had mentioned that a lot of the scavenger groups I had personally known and who had supported us were gone, but not in a million years had I expected to encounter them again like this. There was a chance that the faulty serum had killed some, true, but I doubted that had happened within a span of mere weeks.

Quite frankly, I was glad that I didn't have the brain capacity right now to consider the ramifications, because this was not something I wanted to consider. One thing was sure: we needed to take care of this problem, just as Minerva had said—likely not getting exactly how much of a problem it really was.

As much as I wanted to waste all my ammo on any undead asshole, it was obvious that we needed to conserve it for the harder-to-kill targets, so what had started out as a quick sequence of strafing runs soon ended in me and the scavengers jumping off the truck close to where the settlement defenders had rallied, and joining the melee fray on foot. I could feel that two beacons were close, so it didn't exactly go against our initial plan. As it turned out, so could one of the girls. We decided to split up the larger group, with her going for one target and me aiming for the other. Even though we couldn't get infected, we could still get killed, so for now our immunity was only so much of an advantage. Thankfully, one of the defenders was happy to trade his light ax for my bat, making my work a little easier. Somewhere on the other side of the mass of undead was a car with the rest of my gear, but until we'd either dispersed the crowd or killed enough of them to get through, I'd have to make do with this one.

Even with the need to conserve ammo, the cars still had the huge advantage of being both fast and a large target, getting the shamblers to run after them as soon as they drove close by. A pass or two were usually enough to loosen up a knot, and distract the stupid ones so they were easy killing. As soon as that tactic worked twice, the com frequency was alight with people relaying the news, Nate and Pia both updating us with strategy solutions depending on where someone got bogged down, or someone else managed to pull more than a handful of zombies away from the mob. That meant a lot of running for me, but also a lot of hacking; the latter got easier about an hour in when the Ice Queen came screeching by and dropped off my spare pack, complete with my tactical tomahawks and plenty of water for everyone else to hydrate. By then, I'd lost count of how many shamblers I'd killed, but there seemed no end to them.

Just before noon, we managed to decapitate the last of the zombies wearing beacon vests, and then things got a little easier when we dragged all seven outfitted corpses onto the pickup truck and had it race off across the plain, hundreds of shamblers running screaming and groaning after it, never mind the gazillion degrees and blinding sunlight out here. That, in turn, allowed us to take a break to refuel and rehydrate, although more than one valiant fighter hurled water and food right back up, considering that we weren't just splattered but drenched in zombie guts. I doubted I'd ever feel clean after this again.

Leaving the slower, more stupid shamblers to those more concerned about getting infected, I hitched a ride on another truck following the one with the beacon zombies to where the first of the corpses had been dropped, around two hundred shamblers now flocking around it. Half an hour later, the last one lay dead for good on the cracked dirt. One group down, six more to go.

By the time the plain was aflame with the rays of the setting sun, the only ones left standing were alive and mostly human, and not a single one of us wasn't either limping or favoring one arm over the other, or in desperate need of a long beach vacation.

And still, adrenaline was roaring in my veins as if I'd only just now crawled off the ATV, leaving me very concerned and deeply disturbed.

I tried my best to hide both as I joined the throngs of fighters slowly making their way back to the settlement. A lot fewer people came dragging their stinking asses through the gate than had left it. The three female scavengers were still alive, having more or less fought right beside me the entire day. But the marine was gone, as were about half the defenders from the settlement who'd ventured outside. Pia had earlier done a tally of our people, coming up short by three more marines, two army soldiers, and five scavengers. None of my friends, and sadly, Hamilton was also still very much alive and looking surprisingly unscathed when I walked by him to where troughs of water and bottles of bleach had been set up as a preliminary cleaning station. I didn't even get as far as sneering at him as the mere sight of his smirk aimed at me got my harpies to close ranks and glare right back at him. Still covered in gore and weapons in hand, they made quite the impression—although less on Hamilton and more on the male half of the settlement people who had come to lend a helping hand wherever possible. That gave me an idea of why Nate had stopped making fun of me whenever I got all angry and feral. If I hadn't been very dedicatedly married, I'd have hit that in a second, and I doubted that the ladies would have to seek long and hard for food and entertainment tonight.

But first, cleanup, and then more thorough time with soap and warm water and less public displays of nudity, covered in scrapes and bruises as we peeled ourselves out of our gear and layers of clothes underneath, dumping everything that was ruined for good in a growing heap by the gate. Since I didn't see Nate anywhere, I decided to stick with the harpies, sure that sooner or later he would track me down.

The settlement wasn't just large enough to have separate bathhouses for men and women, but also a decontamination station set aside just for the ladies, which made sense as a good fifth of their guards and fighters were women. I'd seen very few of them in the melee fight outside, but most of the guards keeping watch up on the palisades turned out to have been women, same as the drivers, and all but one of the snipers up on the harvesters as well—pretty much everywhere it wasn't all about superior strength maybe being a survival advantage. Most of them didn't even have single marks on their necks, making me guess that they'd never joined the ranks of the scavengers—and had also not gotten infected with the faulty serum. The one time I'd been to the Utah settlement before, I'd already gotten the sense that everyone here was very self-sufficient, but having to wait for an hour until we could get into the decontamination station to do our thing down to scraping zombie guts out of our toenails hammered down just how few actual civilians the settlement harbored. In a sense, I was almost miffed that I would be dead in a few months' time and couldn't accept the offer Minerva had talked about in the past—finding a secluded hut for Nate and me where we could do whatever the fuck we liked, for as long as we didn't get bored of it. Ah well.

Tired as fuck didn't mean that the three scavengers weren't still very much up to being their vivacious selves. Jokes rang loud and lewd between them, and I had absolutely no qualms joining in. We were among the last few out of the station, down to pretty much our underwear, as a concerned matron shepherded us into the normal bathhouse to get a good soak—and escape our stupid chatter while she and her squad hosed down the remains of blood and grime in the other.

Bathhouses, plural, really, and we quickly found one that we had just to ourselves, which I was kind of glad about as I peeled myself out of the last of my layers, the landscape of scars that was my body now on full display, with a few new ones added to the collection. I spent some quality time with a sponge in front of one of the floor-length mirrors provided, cleaning what scrapes needed extra attention, doing my very best to ignore the stares of the others—and stare they did, quite unabashedly so, which I figured came with the territory of being all brash and honest. At least my hands were mostly out of the picture with the sponge and the suds.

When I turned around, the three of them were still staring at me, but with frowns on their expressions rather than the curious fascination I'd noticed before. With my temper barely in check and my pulse still going way too high, it was hard to try for diplomacy— so I didn't. "What?"

While the other two exchanged glances, the Asian girl—I still didn't know their names, and by now it was beyond awkward to ask— narrowed her eyes at me. "Why are you so damn self-conscious? So what, you have scars. How you got them is beyond legendary. Hell, I've been known to flaunt the few bite marks I've gotten over the years. If I had yours, I'd probably run around in a halter top and cut-off shorts to show as much of that off as possible."

"Yeah, and then we'd all need brain bleach constantly," the Latina sitting next to her on the bench piped up, earning herself a sponge in the face for her trouble.

The third shook her head at her friends before she looked back at me. "Your husband, he's not making fun of you because of it, right? All hero worship aside, if he does, he has one hell of a beating coming from us, just saying."

The very idea of that made me laugh, and I was almost tempted to let them try. The outspoken, semi-nudist girl spoke up then. "He does have a certain reputation. No judgment from us. Nice and gentlemanly only gets you so far in this world. Particularly if he makes up for it elsewhere. Which, presumably, he does. Because, you know. Reputation."

It was a damn shame that Nate wasn't here to listen to this. I had a hard time not to roar with laughter—but should maybe set them straight. "All his many flaws and admirable qualities aside, he actually gets mad at me if I show even a hint of self-doubt."

The women nodded at each other in shared satisfaction, as if they'd expected no less. They also seemed a little let down that I didn't expound on what qualities I was referring to—and there was no question what either of us meant by that—but quickly got over it.

"I'm Adalynn, by the way," the Asian girl—very belatedly— introduced herself with a bright grin. "And this is Tessa," she nodded at the Latina, "and Snow White here is Ingrid." The—actually very fair-skinned—woman scowled at her for that. Judging from the hair south of her neck—what little was visible—the jet-black of her mane came from a bottle.

Grinning, I nodded at them in turn. "I'd say nice to meet you, but since we've been on the road together for weeks now and spent the entire day bashing in zombie skulls together, I'll leave it at that." Come to think of it, it was entirely possible that it had been the three of them who I'd seen getting really cozy with Hamilton back at the camp, before we'd split up and set out to Dallas. While slightly revolting, that made their show of scorn toward him an hour ago all the more hilarious.

Adalynn and Ingrid exchanged glances, until Ingrid finally said what seemed to have been on her mind for a few minutes already.

"We know who your husband is. I mean, obviously. But I mean, about the arena. None of us made the connection before you came down on that shithole and closed it up for good." I just looked at her, not quite sure what to answer to that. Good for her? When she saw my confusion, she offered me a mirthless smile. "We are aware of the fact that any food he gets from the provisions is usually what you end up eating. We're cool with that, is what I'm saying."

Adalynn, clearly at the end of her patience, punched her in the arm to make her shut up before she turned to me. "What the bitch is trying to say is, if you need some help with procuring something else, just let us know."

The third—Tessa—gave a nasty little laugh. "Our collective star-struck hero worship may not go as far as a willingness to donate a juicy ham, but I know a wicked recipe for extra spicy jerky seasoning. Pretty much tastes the same for whatever meat you slap it on."

Once more I was hard-pressed not to laugh, but maybe with a note of hysteria now. "I appreciate the team spirit, ladies. And I might get back to you on that eventually."

"Anything you need," Adalynn enthused, chuckling. "Within reason. We may be crazy, but everyone has limits. But you can count on us. When we pledge our loyalty, we don't just mean it at face value."

I took that with another nod—and then paused, when something they might help me with came to mind. "Actually—"

"Just spit it out," Tessa enthused, a step away from gleefully clapping her hands.

I grinned. "Any of you ladies got any red hair dye in your packs?"

I'd expected them to be on board. I'd not expected them to erupt into shrieks of glee, with Ingrid jumping up and running outside— clad in nothing but enthusiasm—while the other two fell over themselves letting me know that, absolutely, the dish-water blonde I was naturally blessed with so wouldn't do. I couldn't help but smile to myself—what my life had turned into that in almost the same breath we could talk planned murder for cannibalistic purposes including spicy recipes and beauty advice. But, really, after spending the last couple of days feeling like I'd again lost a part of my soul that I'd never get back, it was good to have a few silly laughs.

Chapter 12

I remained soaking in the by-now cool water of the tub I had commandeered after the girls had wrought chemical warfare on my hair, and after rinsing it until the water ran clear again, had also braided it up once more, cutting down any maintenance I'd have to do for the foreseeable future to simple dunks, unless I decided to get drenched in gore again. They'd seemed disappointed when I wasn't ready to follow them quite yet on their mission to get some food, get high, and get laid, but were quick to reassure me that it was okay for me to want some alone time to decompress. In Adalynn's case, I had a feeling like she knew exactly what I was talking about—but if she could feel the beacons, she was probably not going to be around by winter herself. I didn't ask, but I got a sense that she knew exactly what was in store for her—and her devil-may-care attitude seemed all the more genuine for it. Maybe I should simply take a page from her playbook and be done with overthinking everything.

But as I slid into the tub until the water was up to my chin, and then deeper so that my entire head was submerged, cutting me off from the rest of the world, I couldn't help but face the truth: I was hearing it, too, that roar in the distance. Not just hearing it, but feeling it thrumming deep inside my bones. That final, eternal rage that I knew I would eventually succumb to, throwing off the last vestiges of what little remained of my humanity.

What surprised me was the realization that I wasn't afraid of it anymore.

I couldn't help it; in my mind's eye it was as if I was suddenly standing in front of the embodiment of all that—a feral warrior, uncompromising, ready to face her end with her head held high—and as such things go, it could have been so much worse. It was easy to imagine her cocking her head to the side and smirking at me. "Really, this is what you're shitting your pants over?" she'd say. It really wasn't. And with loss so fresh in my heart, being able to divorce myself from all that didn't sound so bad, either. What remained was something akin to grief—for those I'd leave behind, for whom I couldn't cushion the blow, but that had always been one of humanity's cruxes. We all die, and we seldom get to say our goodbyes first.

My lungs were slowly starting to remind me that I wasn't quite there yet and thus needed some oxygen to keep fighting the, if not good fight, then the fight that needed to be fought. But I didn't quite want to let go of that pervasive sense of tranquility yet that, slowly but surely, pushed the roar in the distance farther back until it had almost subsided, little more than a low-grade buzz that I was barely aware of, if I concentrated on it. Truth be told, it was a familiar sensation, only the intensity and stubbornness to ebb away completely new.

So I stayed under water just a little longer, until I felt a slight burn start at the very ends of my extremities and in my lips—

A face appeared above the water as someone leaned over the tub, staring straight down at me. My expectation went with either one of the female scavengers, deciding that I'd had enough me-time, or Nate, investigating along similar lines but with likely other intensions. But while painfully familiar, those weren't features I associated with spending an entire day neck-deep in zombie guts. That soft, wavy blonde hair up in a messy bun, gentle light-brown eyes wide with concern...

Sam.

I had, of course, known that she was still living here. I hadn't outright inquired, but between Pia and Martinez, I'd snatched up enough throw-away comments clearly aimed to make my curiosity rear its stalker-y head. With Martinez in particular I was sure he'd been fishing, knowing way more than he let on. I'd refused to ask because this was one mess I'd decided not to deal with. She had her life and I had mine, with zero overlap. On our trip to the Silo that fateful late fall, she'd made herself scarce when we'd spent the night there, and I figured had come to the same conclusion as I had. Yet here she was in what was obviously a very deliberate act of tracking me down. If all she'd been after was a casual greeting and five minutes of small talk, she could have done that any time later tonight or tomorrow.

Dealing with my possibly still pissed-off ex-girlfriend? Not what I'd thought would be on my agenda tonight. But then again, what I'd had planned—get food, jump Nate's bones—would have been too easy.

Listening inside, I waited for the anger to roar back to life, but except for that pervasive sense of unease preceding potentially uncomfortable emotional situations, my mind was quiet. I was kind of proud of myself that my immediate reaction hadn't been jumping into the—possibly quite physical—defensive.

And, just maybe, it was about time that I resurfaced and let my oxygen-deprived mind have some of its necessary fuel, or else things would get really weird really fast.

Gripping the sides of the tub, I heaved myself up while simultaneously drawing my knees to my chest, then underneath me so that I managed to go from lying fully submerged to vaulting out of the tub in one glorious splash of water, coming with the twin benefits of not just being super dramatic, but also making sure that Sam, anticipating getting drenched any moment now, quickly retreated several steps, giving me the physical space that I definitely needed. Joints cracked, tendons complained, muscles burned, but overall my body was responding as it should, which gave me a hint of satisfaction—which was much needed considering that I now found myself facing the woman who, with Nate being the exception, knew my body better than anyone else in this world... or had known it, before it became hard and tough and then mutilated and covered in scars. It was one thing to feel slightly silly with the scavengers who made fun of my unease, knowing full well that this was the best balm on my soul available, but quite another to see the appropriate amount of horror in Sam's eyes now. Like them, she stared at me unabashedly, familiarity long gone, allowing her to forget that it wasn't the modest or appropriate thing to do as her mind was cataloguing all the many changes from what she remembered.

And, wouldn't you know it, one thing that hadn't changed was that she still held the trigger to my instant defensiveness in her hands, and kept accidentally pushing it like there was no tomorrow. Granted, that was likely one hundred percent in my mind, but didn't change a thing now.

"Like what you see?" I drawled, fighting hard not to curl my hands into loose fists to hide my fingers, or cross my arms over my chest to make them disappear in my armpits.

Sam's gaze zoomed from where she had, indeed, been staring at my fingers to my face, physically drawing up short. She looked more horrified—in a sympathetic kind of way—than guilty for having been caught ogling me, and it took her a second to rein in her features. And because I could be a royal bitch when I wanted to—and suddenly, I did—I kept flexing my fingers, as if they needed any extra attention drawn to them.

"Of course not," she whispered, her voice hoarse but quickly gaining strength as she did her best to compose herself. "But I doubt you need me to tell you that it's horrible what happened to you."

I almost laughed at how terribly predictable she was—but the same could have been said for me as I found myself doing what I'd just sworn I wouldn't do as I cocked my hip and crossed my arms over my chest, pretending like I was so very much at ease in my nudity. I was totally not hiding my tits, or what was left of them after spending years on the lower end of subcutaneous fat percentages healthy for my height and weight—and the odd months way below that.

"No, I really don't," I answered her when nothing else came to mind. What was she doing here? I could tell that I made her uncomfortable, and probably the scars and other changes were only the most obvious but overall negligible part of it, as far as emotional impact went. I felt taken aback when I realized that I was likely physically scaring her—and while that did come with a hint of satisfaction since I'd absolutely earned that kind of reputation, it wasn't anything I wanted to see in someone I'd once loved for real. Quitting my damn posing, I made a grab for a towel, slightly stained red from our previous not-quite beautification efforts, quickly drying myself off so I could start getting dressed.

Sam watched me for a moment before noisily clearing her throat. "You're likely asking yourself why I'm here."

"Naturally."

She grimaced at my slightly acerbic tone—looked like I wasn't the only one with those triggers still intact—but ignored it. "I think we need to talk." When she saw me pause and look up at her, she quickly explained. "Or, I need to talk and I need you to listen. I'm not quite sure I even want a response from you since I doubt what happened in the meantime has made you any less defensive than you used to be—" All it took from me was to give her a blank stare like the one Nate so loved to direct at me, and she pretty much fell over her own words in her haste to get them out. "As am I, yes. I'm aware of that. Whatever—"

"Sam." Saying her name out loud felt vaguely weird, like something long forgotten but suddenly remembered, but it only came as fragments, not a whole picture. She halted, briefly gasping for breath, allowing me to stop her right there. "It's okay. I'm not mad at you, or anything. Not for anything you said to me in Halsey"—that damn cultish settlement in the middle of nowhere in Nebraska, where we'd met again after I'd escaped from Taggard's white-tiled prison—"or on the way back here." Which had been after we'd attacked the base in Colorado and forced that truce on Hamilton that had done nothing, or nothing good at least. All that felt like it had happened a million years ago. "You had no idea about what had happened since we last saw each other, and with the settlement at least, you met me just after I'd gone through the worst few weeks of my life, and the—" I paused, trying to compile a quick list. "Something between third- and fifth-most traumatic experience until today. It really wasn't a good time for me, and I was way outside of the emotional range required to deal with the fact that you were still alive. Which I was insanely glad to see, and still am." I winced at how that came out. "Guess what I'm trying to say is, no hard feelings?" It was more of a suggestion than a statement, really.

She stared at me for several seconds flat even after I'd fallen silent, likely having to fight impulsive reactions while at the same time rearranging her inner talking-point cheat sheets on the fly. It was okay. I wasn't quite feeling at my intellectual height, either.

"No hard feelings," she finally offered, looking relieved for a moment. I could tell that she wanted to snap that she had done nothing to warrant the same on my side but wisely swallowed it, which I figured had more to do with the fact that she was feeling uneasy because of what she knew I could do now, rather than emotional maturity. Who was I kidding? She wasn't exactly wrong there, although I sure hoped I wouldn't fly off the handle and physically attack her.

Mostly to stave off the threatening lull in the conversation, but also because I was curious, I asked, "How are you doing these days? You look happy." And she did. Thankfully, someone had found more sensible clothes for her than what she'd been wearing the last time I'd seen her, and she looked stronger and healthier as well, speaking of better food choices—and better psychological conditions as well, not that I'd expected any less from the people here.

"I am," she admitted with a small smile, but it disappeared almost immediately, as if it made her feel guilty.

"Oh, come on. Just let me have it," I teased. "It's entirely unfair that you probably know details of my life that I'd rather not be public knowledge, and you're not even telling me what made you smile like this?"

Sam grinned, almost bashful, before she inclined her head with purpose. "Okay, you asked for it. I'm actually happily married. To a woman who I love, also because she doesn't take me seriously. And we have five kids together. Two are biologically hers; one is mine." She paused for a moment with the goofiest grin on her face. "The eldest two we adopted, since there are too many orphans in this world and we wanted to get our little family started as soon as possible. My little girl's just over eleven months now. And, I'm not quite sure yet, but she might be getting a new sibling soon. It's a little early to tell yet."

I had to admit, what I was the gladdest about was the timeline of her pregnancy, because that meant that, however that baby had been conceived, it was long past when Sam had gotten away from that fucked-up cult that I was still convinced was the extended breeding program of whatever Taggard had been up to. It vexed me for a moment that I still didn't know if it was all connected, down to the scavenger zombies we had to kill today, or just random offshoots of the same crazy tree, but it didn't matter.

I could tell Sam relaxed—outwardly and inwardly—when I smiled back at her, trying hard to push away my speculations. "Turkey baster, huh?" I half-joked.

She chuckled. "Actually, yes, but our three… well, maybe soon four biological kids all have the same father. Vince lost his son and wife in the outbreak and I think he's sworn to himself he'll never cheat on her memory, but he always wanted to have a large family. Since we needed a donor and are very happy to have another pair of helping hands, it was a great solution. We co-parent the whole ragtag bunch together. Right now they are all too small to need any specific explanations. That's a conversation for another day in the far, far future." She sounded happy rather than wistful.

"Hey, no judgment from me," I was quick to offer. "Two moms and a dad who love you? Sounds awesome to me. Then again, my definition of family nowadays is an unwashed horde of somewhere between ten to thirty people who I love, like, am able to stand, or absolutely hate their guts on a changing spectrum depending on the situation, so maybe don't ask me about such matters."

She shared my grin for a moment but then it slipped, and I could tell that we were closer to her real reason for accosting me. "That's actually part of why I'm here," she explained. She hedged around for a moment but then went for it, probably to get it over with. "I was with Charlie in the radio station when Alejandro called a few weeks ago. Martinez," she clarified.

I gave her a hard stare. "Just because I'm used to calling most of these assholes by their last name doesn't mean I'm not at least passingly aware that they do have first names, too. Only took me about three seconds to catch up."

I could tell that my snide remark vexed her but she went on rather than reprimand me. "He's taking it really hard, that all-of-you-dying thing, you know? You make up more than eighty percent of his closest friends, and it's not helping that you're all simply accepting it, and expect him to fall in line, too."

I couldn't help but snort. "Yeah, not so sure about the acceptance part of that. I'm maybe seventy percent into coming to grips with shit. But I presume what he meant was that we just up and decided to ignore it and went to get killed in Dallas. No need to cry over spilled milk when someone smashes your jug before you get to it."

I could tell that my attempt at gallows humor didn't sit well with her, but again she chose to surge on rather than bicker. "Be that as it may, he's hurting. And I can only imagine how much worse it must be for all of you after what happened in your hometown. I'm so sorry for your loss. Words can't describe how that hurts me, and I'm not even directly affected." She paused, but before I could do more than nod in silent acceptance, my throat momentarily tight, she went on. "Anyway, listening to their conversation got me thinking. I never expected to talk to you again, truth be told. I think I know you well enough still that you would have been perfectly fine with us forever avoiding each other. But that's almost like cheating, you know?" Now she did look guilty, but still wouldn't shut up. "I just… I actually don't know what to say but figured, this is likely my absolute last chance to sit down and have a talk with you, and for better or worse, here I am! Rambling, incoherently, making an ass of myself."

She seemed taken aback when I smiled at her, and it wasn't even a sarcastic emotion. "I'm not sure we could have had this talk any sooner than now," I admitted. Look at me, all mature and ready to make concessions! "Sam, I should have had the guts to break up with you years before everything went to shit. But I wasn't ready because I wasn't mature enough, and because it felt like failure and I was afraid of feeling rejected, and it was so much easier to just ignore shit and thus condemn us both to being miserable. Or, I don't know. We could have agreed to continue our cohabitation thing, maybe with benefits, maybe without, but with the open and honest agreement that you could date and have sex with whoever you liked, without it needing to be some kind of rebellion, or out of spite, or whatnot." I hesitated, but she deserved to hear the rest, too. "I loved you, really loved you— once. On some level, I still do. But I fell out of love with you a long time ago, and you deserved better than being locked in a cage of cozy convenience." She looked ready to protest—ever the good samaritan, needing to share the blame, so I let her have the rest as well. "But you could have done the same, or at the very least you could have told me, to my face, that you wanted an open relationship, and there was no need for you to constantly rub my face in the other pussy you were licking, so to speak."

She let out a little guffaw in response that was part relief, part offense. "You've always had such a way with words," she remarked.

"It's my special superpower. Including inevitable foot-in-mouth moments. Half my reputation is based on that."

"And the other half?"

I considered just how honest to be with that, but decided that, going with the honesty theme, she deserved to hear this—and be glad our lives had taken very different turns. "Following up on my threats in the most efficient, brutal way possible. And running with a crowd who see that as a virtue, not a horrible flaw." It was obvious that this wasn't something we'd ever see eye to eye on—but I was oddly okay with that. I wasn't seeking anyone's approval with my actions, least of all hers. And if all the shit we'd been through had taught me anything, it was that in the end, all I could do was be true to myself—because that was exactly what had gotten me through the worst of it.

"Want to hear the full story?" I asked, a little surprised at myself for the offer.

Sam hesitated but then said, in a slightly shaky voice, "Yes, I'd love to. Whatever you feel comfortable sharing with me."

I almost balked at the implication that I wanted to hide anything— but then realized there were a few things I either didn't much feel like rehashing, or had no business telling her as they weren't exactly my story to tell, like Nate's imprisonment at the camp, and all the many absolutely convenient aftershocks of that we were still dealing with. But there was so much else that I could share, starting at the fateful Friday morning when I'd been so hell-bent on getting to work so I could be rid of my sick girlfriend that I'd missed that, for all intents and purposes, the world around us had already gone to shit. It had just needed another twenty-four hours for all hell to break lose.

So I told her about how it had come that I'd fallen in with that crazy lot I was still running with. How I'd learned to be strong and self-sufficient, and later deadly and brutal, but didn't leave out the toll it was taking on me. How I'd grieved for her; how, in a sense, underneath all the grand speeches, she'd kind of become my personal reason to call for a change and rally scavengers from all over the country for my crusade. That, of course, I'd been out for blood and vengeance—but finally getting it had done little to heal me and had, for the most part, left a bad aftertaste in my mouth. Then sheer survival had become a new priority, and I'd been forced to compromise on things I hadn't thought I could ever compromise on, not after what had happened mere months before. I even told her a little about the madness of crossing the Atlantic ocean in search of a cure that I knew didn't exist, and how, maybe, or maybe not, that had played into our current problems. She listened to all of it in silence, never offering more than a nod or expression of sympathy—not like a priest hearing my confession; not even a therapist acting as a neutral sounding board. No, like a friend; like someone who, even though she no longer knew me as I was now, had once known me better than anyone else in the world, and some of that understanding was still there. I could discuss all this and more with Nate, and most of it also with Martinez, but somehow it was different now with Sam. Maybe because, of all the people who knew me, she was the least personally affected by it.

And still, she was who I hoped would very much profit from what would likely become our final mission.

"Are you afraid?" she asked when I finally fell silent. "Of dying, I mean? Because from what you've just told me of what you'll do once you leave here, I'm not even sure that you'll get much of a chance to worry about the details."

I couldn't help but laugh, and it wasn't a nice sound. "There's a huge chance none of us will walk—or even crawl—away from this. But I'm okay with that." She made a disbelieving face, making me reconsider how to better explain it. "Sure, would I love to live another year, or even a decade? Fuck, yeah. I'd give a lot for that, but it's not like this is a bargaining game. I can't influence or negotiate like that. But what I can do is try to put an end to what's been going on, what's been dragging the world further and further into the abyss. And I'm so fucking over constantly having a target painted on my back. Although, it's mostly just flakes that have rubbed off from the target that Nate has painted on his back. It doesn't matter."

She still looked rather skeptical. "Are you sure that's all true? Or can even be true? No offense, but it does all sound like one huge conspiracy... made up by a paranoid circle-jerk by people too traumatized to still believe in the good left in this world."

That made me laugh out loud—and partly in agreement. "That's an entirely realistic possibility," I admitted. "Maybe we're all just psyching each other up, and then we'll arrive at that doomsday bunker, all bent on raining down destruction on it, and all we find is an abandoned construction site that was never more than a scam. I'm not even sure that's the worst thing that could happen, if I'm honest. Maybe it's all just in our minds. Maybe there never was an overarching conspiracy. Maybe there was but has long since fragmented, and we've killed off all but the last remaining cell of it. I don't know what we'll do if that happens, but at least I can say for myself, I tried. I tried to make the world a better place. It sounds so damn idealistic and naive, but honestly? Looking at what you've all accomplished here with this settlement, I have to agree that just maybe, that's all any of us can do, and maybe that's even all it takes. If

I have that option, I'd like to go out with a bang and leave the world a better place. If I've already done everything I can, just as well. I'll die with very few regrets, and that's a lot more than I could have said for myself the last time we met. That's something."

I hadn't expected to see her agreeing with me, but maybe I should have. While she still refused to carry a weapon beyond a utility knife—from what I could tell—she'd always seen her pacifism as a very personal thing that needn't necessarily encroach on anyone else's different view on life. It was kind of hilarious that I'd gone from being with a woman who wouldn't hurt a fly but was getting off on emotionally manipulating me into being a victim so she could have someone to take care of, to, well, being with a manipulative asshole who mostly did it so he'd get me to where I was happy to fully accept myself, which he'd kind of done from the very beginning. Despite all the mistakes that Sam and I had both made in our relationship, I was sure that, eventually, we would have found a way to happily exist alongside each other—but it was only after I'd met Nate that I'd started to fully become confident and happy inside my own skin.

"I think I need some food," I muttered, grinning at my own · weird ruminations. "I can't tell, but I must be starving by now, and my blood sugar is likely below what is advisable for anyone, let alone someone who should keep a balanced diet to prolong what little time she still has left. And some booze, too, although I doubt I'll manage to get more than slightly buzzed. Unless there is something else still on your mind?"

Sam shook her head. "Not really. It was nice to air our old laundry—"

"Nice?" I echoed, smirking.

"Necessary," she corrected herself. "And thank you for sharing. But I think you will agree with me that we don't really have much in common anymore. Of course I could regale you with tons of funny baby stories, but I know you likely can't relate, and I understand that must be painful for you on several levels. Village life doesn't hold a candle to being out there, fighting the good fight or whatnot. And that's about it."

Part of me was tempted to blab out that, just maybe, there was a slim chance that I'd get to understand more of her life, but I cut down on the impulse as soon as it appeared. There was no sense in it, and in a way, it even seemed cruel of me to mention the possibility of me having a child myself. I was so happy for her and her family, knowing that she'd get to not just have her kids but watch them grow, and likely even take care of their children, and maybe their children's children. At best, the knowledge that my baby might already be an orphan upon birth would just mess with her head—and really, if Martinez and Charlie got to adopt and raise my spawn, she'd learn of it soon enough. And if it was just a futile dream, or I died long before that child had a chance to live, then it was all the same whether she knew about it or not. It was my dream, not hers, or even ours, and while it felt stupid to jealously guard it like a treasure, that's exactly what I did.

I could have offered up a myriad of platitudes now but since they all felt tainted with passive-aggressive undertones to me, I simply walked up to her, gave her a long, heart-felt hug, and then I left, walking out of her life in every way possible.

Chapter 13

I found Nate sitting by one of the many fires roaring in the middle of the settlement, a lot of familiar faces all around. I took my time greeting Minerva and thanking her for her hospitality, then got some quality bear hugs from Jason and Charlie. I'd seen them both fleetingly on the battlefield today but there had been no time for chatting, and none of us had wanted to get killed over exchanging pleasantries. No surprise about finding Martinez sitting next to Charlie, and I gave him the most conspiratorial look I could manage without shouting at him to stop being a wuss and finally spring the question and make it official. Martinez chose to ignore me, but it was in such an overt way that I knew my message had been received. I didn't recall the name of the woman sitting next to Jason but I remembered her from our last visit, and there was no question about who the father of the two small children on her lap was, seeing as they had both inherited the shocks of ginger hair on their heads from Jason. I almost felt like griping that everyone was hell-bent on unleashing the next generation on this planet, but really, I was glad about that. We were still losing way too many people as it was, and a massive increase in pregnancies was to be expected now that birth control was pretty much back to middle-ages standards. Sadie was also sitting there, a very much awake and lively Christine climbing all over her, still a little timid about joining the other kids that were running rampant all over the town but likely less than a day or two away from joining them.

Sagging onto the log next to Nate, I snuggled up to him, nudging his arm until he relented and lifted it onto my shoulders, laughing softly. "You seem awfully relaxed for someone who looked ready to never ever come down from her high again," he teased—for the most part. Looking up, I saw the cautious concern in his eyes. At my "don't worry about it" look I sent back, he eased up, going as far as to nuzzle my head with his face before planting a soft kiss against my temple. "Love the hair color. But, shit, it smells like you doused yourself in all the bleach left in this world."

"Too bad for you," I quipped, then skipped on to the important part—food. He had a bowl full of jerky strips sitting next to him that, even at that distance, smelled… interesting. Since he made no move to hand it to me, I got up once more to fetch something from one of the huge pots simmering over the fires, full of stew, curry, chili, and whatever else could be easily thrown together and taste good. Everything was chock-full of vegetables, very important for those of us forced to subsist on shit that couldn't easily rot on the road. Upon my return, I eyed Nate's jerky again, as if it would tell me where it had come from if I just stared at it long enough. He pointedly pushed the bowl further back, as if to say, "You're not getting any of that." Fine with me—for sustenance, the chili-curry-stew would more than do. And when he finally let down his guard and idly chewed one of the strips, I just so happened to steal a kiss from him when he was distracted, joking across the fire with Jason—and yup, there was definitely something there that tickled my taste buds.

"What exactly was that about?" Nate asked as he pulled away, his voice sounding neutral enough but his gaze imploring.

I shrugged, but then forewent playing coy. "You can feel the beacons. And although I still feel no hunger, I can taste just a hint of your questionable mystery meat. I thought it was just a fluke a few days before we got to California, when you came back after hunting. So I suspect it's blood rather than the mystery-meat part per se, or a combination of both. I was just a little curious, is all." And because it wouldn't have been me without adding a little pizzazz to the observation, I added. "By the way, one of the scavenger girls has a family recipe you might want to look into. I didn't ask for specifics, but I have a feeling it is more along the 'Hills have Eyes' lines than her abuela's special spicy chicken."

It was hilarious to watch Nate's expression go from curious to fascinated to slightly concerned and then right on into a deep dive into condescension territory, but what was missing was the disgust so often present when we'd talk about the topic of how to get him fed. Maybe that wasn't even mystery meat in his jar, and he was guarding it jealously because it was the first thing in a long time that he liked to eat and could stomach and thus didn't want to share with me, who could easily chew cardboard and not find it revolting. Or—what sounded way more likely—with a good portion of the settlement people here being scavengers, someone else had developed a certain taste for certain special flavors, and they'd found a way to take care of that. Logically, that made the most sense. Huh. The more you know—or don't, in this case.

"How did your talk go with Sam?" Nate asked, carefully neutral, but I could see he was trying to change the subject and at the same time get back at me for bringing it up in the first place.

"Better than being ambushed in the bathtub usually has a right to go," I admitted. "I presume you saw her asking around for me?"

"And spend twenty minutes trying to decide whether she should actually go in or not," Nate pointed out. "I almost took pity on her and told her to just get it over with, but that might have set her in the wrong mood. Glad you got your chance for closure."

I was a little surprised he'd jumped to that conclusion, but then again, if I hadn't, I likely would have come stalking over here, fuming, and in need of some way to work through the added level of aggression. Perceptive, my husband was, but sometimes I was simply very easy to read.

"Speaking of tangents," I started, looking around. "How much more time for socializing did you plan for tonight?"

Nate gave me a calculating look that made me guess I wasn't the only one who was finally in the mood for something other than spending the entire night locked inside my head. "Why, that eager to jump my bones?"

"Generally speaking, yes," I enthused, incapable of holding in a low chuckle. "I mean, that right there is the cabin where we last made love when I still had all my fingers to poke and prod you with, in all the places you like, don't like, and insist you don't like but secretly love."

As intended, I got a pained look for that worst of puns—but it didn't take away from the glint of interest in his gaze. "For the record, the latter never happened, and I think the worst 'prod' I've ever gotten was an accidental elbow in the face while you got dressed inside a car. And besides, how much longer do I have to suffer through these less than clever and certainly not entertaining jokes?"

I struck a musing pose before shoveling another mouthful of food down my gullet. "How much longer do you still intend to live?"

Oh, I so loved him glaring at me like that. "Who even got this shit into your head?"

Now it was my turn to be slightly annoyed for real. "You, of course."

"Me?"

I nodded. "Sure, you. You can't go all 'well, at least that shit shook you out of your depression!' in my face and not expect to get that dish called revenge, served cold."

Nate stared at me for another moment—pretty much like he was considering if I'd actually gone insane—before he burst out laughing, loud enough to turn heads all around us. My turn to be playfully annoyed—and to poke his arm with what was left of my left index finger, which made him shut up in favor of grabbing my entire hand so he could plant a kiss on my palm. "You're not wearing your gloves," he remarked, and it almost sounded like it came with a hint of praise. Couldn't be, since we were talking about my husband here.

I shrugged, extricating my hand once more so I could continue my meal. "First, it felt ridiculously inconvenient to get them off, clean them, then put them on again, and then off again half an hour later when we slink away to do the dirty. Also—and this is a much bigger point—I left them soaking in bleach for half an hour to get out the shambler gunk, and then had to dunk them in water forever to get the bleach out so it wouldn't eat away what's left of my fingers as soon as I donned them, and it takes a while for them to dry after that. Last but not least, I'm not ashamed of how my hands look. I wear them in combat because I have a much better grip that way and I need the extra protection, but right here, right now I trust that you will defend me, if the need arises, with your questionable jerky strips. Happy?"

"Excessively so," he professed, grinning.

Silence fell between us as I continued to shovel dinner into my mouth while Nate listened to conversational snippets going on all around us. Pia joined the round, returning from somewhere else in the settlement, wherever that had been. I was a little concerned for a second, afraid she'd spend another night brooding at the fire, but maybe a minute later Blake and Buehler joined her, the marines reengaging her in a conversation that seemed to have been going on for a while now. She caught my gaze for a second and went as far as giving me a wink before she laughed at something Buehler remarked that I didn't quite catch. Needn't worry about this old dog, it plainly said.

"You never answered my question, you know?" I quipped at Nate.

He let out a long-suffering sigh, as if I'd been nagging him about something for hours, before he leaned in. "Since I don't intend to sleep a single minute tonight, I think we still have a little more time for socializing. But while you were holding court in the bathhouse, I got us a cabin—an entire one this time, not just a room so everyone else gets to listen in to our deep philosophical conversations all night long."

That made me snort—and pat his knee. "Good man."

Nate groaned. "I swear, one of these days I will put you over my knee, in front of all these people, and spank you, and then we'll see just how well you do with being a brat."

All I had for him was a bright, saucy smile. "Bring it on, old man."

I expected him to drop the point—as he usually did at this turn in our banter—but instead found myself being not just dragged off the log but hoisted up and onto Nate's shoulder so that I was dangling upside down from it, the last spoonfuls of my meal disappearing into the night. My yelp got everyone looking over, to which Nate responded by offering up a quick bow—that almost sent me off his shoulder and toppling backwards into the flames, if he hadn't quickly gotten a better grip on me—much to everyone's amusement. "I'm sorry, ladies and gents, " he called out. "But I'm afraid I need to teach my wife some manners since she does nothing but bad-mouth me, day in, day out. I know you'll understand." And as if that wasn't bad enough yet, as he turned to step over the log and leave, he slapped my ass, and it was not a gentle pat.

"You're such an asshole!" I protested, drowned out by everyone's laughter—and quite a few suggestions how he should go about that task. "You're all assholes!" That just made them laugh all the more. I tried to wriggle myself free but Nate clearly had no intention of letting me go, carrying me off as if I weighed nothing.

Well, clearly we were feeding him the right stuff to keep up his strength.

Nate didn't stop until he'd reached our cabin—which was a good five hundred feet away from the fire pits and well out of shouting distance—and only let go of me to throw me onto the bed. Maybe not exactly throw, but I wasn't being set down gently, and I had about two seconds before he pounced on me, pinning me to the mattress effectively. Any protest that I might have uttered—not that I had much on my mind—disappeared when his mouth came down on mine, as hungry and demanding as his hands on my body. I was more than up for the challenge, giving as good as I got, loving the feel of warm skin on skin once we were both peeled out of our clothes. As convenient as screwing around in a car was, it didn't hold a candle to getting it on with lots of room and no care for what you might bump into. Nate didn't give me any chance to get up to any shenanigans, covering my body with his, his lips skipping down to the side of my neck. I was more than happy to wrap myself around him, opening myself up to his eager fingers, quickly replaced by his cock when he realized I was more than ready. As he thrust into me, he bit down hard—hard enough to hurt, but also enough to make me let out a guttural laugh. I had zero qualms about sinking my fingers into the strong muscles of his upper back, then rake my nails down to his ass, urging him on to take me hard and fast and deep, and make me forget about this shit—

My climax hit me with the strength of a lightning bolt, and it wasn't just the sheer physical satisfaction. No, this was us again, like we should be, abandoning all reason or care in the world for a few minutes of bliss—and then a few more, and more, until everything else ceased to exist. I felt my body key up, adrenaline flooding through me, the roaring in the back of my mind intensifying once more, but the anger remained like a distant memory, not important now. There was a small part of my mind that was still working, that was concerned about this, and when it made me pause for a moment, Nate froze above me, staring deep into my eyes—and I could swear I could physically feel his body sync to the beat of my own drum. He grinned, and I answered it with a feral grin of my own, rearing up to drown his resulting moan with my mouth. He flipped us over so that I ended up kneeling above him, but rather than let me rear up and move, he pulled his arms around me and held me close, leaving only our hips to move freely—but I didn't exactly need more than that. I couldn't tell whether it was his lip that caught on my tooth or vice versa, but suddenly, there was the metallic taste of blood in my mouth. I could taste it—actually taste it as it hit my tongue, mixing with saliva, thinning out, then getting stronger again as our kiss intensified, driving me wild… and I definitely wasn't the only one it had that effect on.

We didn't exactly maul each other, but by the time I found myself breathless and on my back, my legs too shaky and weak to stand, with Nate stretched out contently next to me, I definitely had a few more bruises and bite marks than when I'd dragged my tired ass into the bathhouse—and so did Nate. I had to admit, he did look a little worse for wear. Oops.

"Guess the part about the scintillating philosophical discussions was a lie, huh?" I wryly observed once my breathing had properly slowed down.

Nate let his head fall to the side so he was looking at me rather than the dark rafters above us, his attention briefly locking on to what I was sure was blooming into a substantial hickey on the side of my neck before skipping on to my face. "Are you complaining? Give me five"—he considered for a moment—"three more minutes, and I'll give you something to complain about."

Reaching over, I idly smeared the tip of my finger through a trickle of blood leaking from a scratch across his ribs before sticking it into my mouth and sucking on it, my gaze never leaving his. He let out a low, rumbling growl that should have made the hair at the back of my neck stand up but didn't. Before my mind could wise up, I pushed myself up and leaned over him to directly lick up the smear before crawling up his body, swinging one leg over him. Turned out, three minutes was a pessimistic estimate after all.

As it was, those teasing quips were the only words we exchanged that night, and I couldn't find it in me to regret it.

Chapter 14

The morning dawned too bright, too soon, particularly to my bleary eyes and overall sore body. I was sure that Nate would have loved to claim he was the reason for the latter, but while he'd definitely been a contributing factor, my arms and back hurt from hacking and slashing at zombies all day long. I would have loved to make up on the socializing front what I'd missed out on last night, but when I dragged my sore ass to the fire pits, I already saw the first trucks leaving, hauling firewood and people out onto the plain.

Right, we still had some cleanup to do—a few thousand rotting shamblers worth of cleanup. The range of my taste buds might be limited but my olfactory system was working just fine, so I simply opted for some black coffee and called that my breakfast. No sense in wasting food by eating it now and hurling it up thirty minutes later.

Nate was gone by the time I returned to the cabin to change into my full gear, but I didn't mind since I'd gotten more than my fair share of him all night long. I almost laughed at the goofy grin I felt spreading across my face. At the very least, I could claim increasing mental decline for acting like a teenager on hormones, but I doubted anyone would buy the excuse.

Back by the gate, I didn't bother with looking for anyone I knew but simply hopped on the closest truck, figuring that I'd have plenty of time to either make new friends out there or find comrades-in-misery already hard at work. Since the truck driver stopped next to where Pia and Burns were already dragging bodies into a heap to be weighed down with wood to later be incinerated, I figured people recognized me better than I did them. Fine with me.

Burns paused after heaving yet another body onto the growing stack when he saw me sauntering up to them. "You're doing it wrong if you can still walk straight the next morning," he drawled instead of a greeting.

Looking over my shoulder to where, a short distance away, Sonia was helping with unloading wood, I couldn't help but laugh. "You sure you don't want to take that back?"

He kept grinning but held his tongue. Before the Ice Queen could add a barb that would leave us both hurting, I walked over to the closest shambler and started dragging it backward by a leg. Since it used to be moderately substantial, that even worked without me having to return for the second half. It happened. It wasn't often that I'd had to help with shit like this, but when it had been just Nate and me, we'd never dared to leave the remains out in the open unless carrion feeders had already beat us to the punch. If those assholes hadn't dragged us away from the treehouse, we would have returned to the plantation to burn and bury what was left of the shamblers we'd found there.

"Why the sour face?" Burns asked when we crossed paths once more.

"Isn't being knee-deep in rotting undead reason for that enough?"

He shrugged. "Too much wistfulness in it, not enough outright disgust."

I couldn't help but laugh. "I was mourning my salad."

He actually paused and gave me a strange look. "I can take a lot from you—bloody revenge, ice-cold murder, cackling with glee while you descend on your enemies—but if you keep going on about that fucking greenery, I'll have to consider our friendship null and void. I have my limits."

Grabbing another shambler—this one by the upper few inches of the spine, ending where someone had lopped off its head—I started dragging again. "Seriously? You'll abandon me over my priceless, perfectly organic, hand-watered romaine or lettuce or whatever the fuck it would have grown into? You wound me. You absolutely wound me."

Pia, always the show-off, caught up to me where she was dragging her own corpse. "You didn't even know what kind of salad it was? Stick to the meat. We're not going to survive your moaning and complaining if you accidentally eat poison ivy."

"Oh, you're just jealous because I didn't bring any of my amazing salad with me," I muttered.

"Green with envy," Burns agreed. "Just like your salad."

We kept our rapport up for this and the next three pyres but then it was getting too hot for shooting the shit, our grisly work turning all the worse for the lack of distraction. But it had to be done, and since we didn't want to needlessly endanger anyone who could get infected by handling the undead, it was up to us to do it. The settlement people more than pulled their own weight, bringing more wood and digging trenches to make sure the fires we lit couldn't escape and set the entire state ablaze. I could tell they had more practice than I did—but so did Burns and the Ice Queen, I had to admit.

Farther away from the settlement, the corpses were in better condition, which made the work so much worse—and not just because they were heavier. Yesterday, all of them had been damn hard to kill and almost as deadly as we were, if not more so in some cases. It had been easier to ignore that a few weeks prior, they had likely been walking among us. A lot of them were still wearing the typical haphazardly assembled scavenger gear, in some places with red paint still visible where it hadn't been completely covered in fecal matter and dried blood. Many of them had been younger than me, and more than I'd realized the day before had been women. I tried hard not to look in too many pallid, often destroyed faces, but more than once I felt the low gut-punch of memories stirring. Because of my absence in this part of the country for the past two years, it was unlikely I'd actually known any of them, but considering I'd run into my ex-girlfriend of all people out in Nowhere, Nebraska, one could never know. I really didn't want to know, but that didn't keep my brain from being stupid.

Every few hours, we took short breaks, Martinez driving out from the settlement with fresh, cold water. The first time I bothered with wasting some water on cleaning up. By the third time, I had him hold the bottle for me so I could drink, my arms hanging uselessly and heavy by my side, with me likely resembling a shambler myself. We were almost done by then, and I felt about as grimy as the day before, although not fighting for my life helped. The more heat and exhaustion sent my mind into a stupor, the more I felt that damn droning come back, but since it came with enough adrenaline to keep me up and working, I told myself I didn't mind so much.

I knew it was a mistake to let Martinez dump the rest of the water onto my head to cool off a little when I realized he was scrutinizing my hickey, only visible now since I'd pulled my jacket open a bit to let the water dribble inside. Part of me wanted to zip it up with resolution and forestall any comments that might follow, but I was too tired and hot for that shit, to be honest.

"You maybe should let me clean that up for you," he advised, his voice bland enough that I wasn't quite sure whether he knew exactly where the scabbed-over bite marks atop the bruise stemmed from, or if he was mad because he thought I'd gotten careless about after-battle care just because I couldn't catch the virus.

"I'm sure it will be all healed up by tomorrow," I offered.

Martinez let out a mirthless chuckle. "You mean like the two tantalizingly similar ones I stitched up for Miller today? Yes, don't go all doe-eyed on me. He needed two stitches on his left shoulder and one on his ass. I can think of a better way to be woken up than that."

Burns guffawed behind us, making me glance at him over my shoulder. "Stop it, or I'll mention the salad, and where would you find your entertainment if not from me, huh?"

Martinez shook himself as if to say "I'm not even gonna ask" before letting out a dramatic sigh. "I never thought I'd say I miss the days when you were a rookie and all twisted around yourself, worried that you'd lose street cred you didn't yet have if anyone thought you were his girlfriend and at the same time stalking around camp, glaring at that Madeline woman if she even dared look in the general direction of your man, but I kinda do. I can deal with pretending like I don't care that he's sitting there, munching on his bandit or raider or other assorted asshole jerky, but if you're now literally tearing chunks out of each other, I'm done. You heard me—this is where I draw the line."

I got that he was serious but I couldn't help but grin—and yes, the term "asshole jerky" would become a thing, if I had a say in it. "So I'm not allowed to have life-affirming, deal-with-grief, post-fight sex now? You're such a prude."

Of course Burns found that statement hilarious—and I caught Pia turning away a little too slowly to completely hide the smile crossing her face—but Martinez would have none of it. "Fuck however the fuck you like, but don't end up in my triage station afterward!"

Burns continued to chortle—and, of course, found the perfect remark to make it all worse. "Maybe we could pick up some chew toys for them? You know, like what you'd get for a dog? Or we could head into what's left of Salt Lake City and go look for a quality sex shop. I'm sure that nobody thought to raid those, and at the very least, they should have some gags left."

I was ready to join Martinez in trying to pretend he hadn't heard that, but instead smiled brightly at Burns. "You calling me a bitch now?"

"Kinky bitch," Burns corrected.

Thank fuck that Sonia wasn't around or we both would have been back in the dog house—which of course cracked me up now, which lead to a round of demanding looks so I had to explain, and the lot of us ended up sharing goofy grins—except for the Ice Queen. "If you have energy enough to act like idiotic fifteen-year-olds, you can go back to work. Scoot!"

Properly chastised, Martinez sent me a last warning look before he hopped back into the car. I turned to Burns one last time as we trudged over to where the next corpses were waiting for us. "While you're there, you could pick up a whip for her. I feel like it would suit her."

Burns was about to agree—grinning from ear to ear—when Pia turned around and glared at us, obviously having caught that part. "You should," she told us, calm and collected, and thus scary as hell. "It will come in handy when you two slack off digging latrine pits for the next two weeks."

Burns grimaced—but only where she couldn't see—while I went ahead and saluted her with a bright grin. She ignored me, but again, she was too slow to hide a hint of a smile. As much as I hated getting permanently delegated to the worst job on the go, at least that was something.

Chapter 15

Grime, sweat, and corpse fluids aside, cleaning up that evening went much faster than the day before since dragging around corpses was still cleaner than having them bleed all over you while they were still moving. I also didn't feel the need to decompress, so I got a good four hours of sitting around the fires, everyone telling jokes and anecdotes while eating unhealthy amounts of food and drinking what felt like half the moonshine the Utah settlement must have distilled last year, although I passed up the booze since it wouldn't affect me anyway—such a waste. Sadie was still hanging around with us so I figured her grand reveal to me had been a lie—or, more precisely, the excuse she needed to tell herself to be able to stomach the fact that once we left, she'd likely never see us again. I couldn't fault her for that, but it still kind of rankled. I didn't see Sam again and thus got no chance to scope out the woman who had ultimately replaced me, which was probably for the best. While I was sure all the others were very aware of who Sam had been to me, nobody mentioned her. There were plenty more interesting topics to discuss, and it was well past midnight by the time we were back in our cabin.

We did go at it again, although at a more leisurely pace. While I had been right and I was mostly healed up after cleanup this evening, we didn't give Martinez any more reason to go off in our faces, but I didn't miss how Nate—lovingly—continued to nuzzle that spot. I had to admit, I wouldn't have minded if he'd bit down hard again when I came with him fucking me from behind. That was all just normal, passionate behavior, right?

Since "wrong" wasn't an option, I chose not to dwell on it. Exactly how long could it take us to get to that damn bunker? Three weeks? Four, tops, if we ran into any serious trouble? We'd easily hold out until then. What were a few love bites between a loving husband and wife?

It was one thing to know that we could both run several days on sleep deprivation but it made no sense to push ourselves further, so we caught some quality sleep, once more curled up around each other, sweating profusely on top of the sheets because of it, but both loath to let go. I had to admit, I got a kick out of Nate being more physical, even if it was mostly happening when it was just the two of us. Just to myself, in the dark of night, I could admit that I'd been concerned—and just a little hurt—when he'd withdrawn from me after we'd liberated the camp, particularly en route to Dallas. I got that he'd needed some time to get his head in the right mindset again—and it irked me to no end that I still had no clue what he and

Hamilton had been up to whenever they'd vanished—but that didn't change my feelings. This wasn't even about our mad daydreaming about missing our rapidly closing procreation window; I had to admit, since Andrej's death—and finding Sadie hysterical over believing her child dead, if only for a few minutes—that desire had greatly diminished. If it happened, great. If not, just as well. And with that droning sensation ebbing and flowing inside of me with everything that made my pulse spike, I didn't feel too confident it was even on the menu still.

Nate woke me up just as the sky started to lighten—accidentally, as he slipped out of bed and then thought better of it, returning to place one last, lingering kiss on my shoulder that roused me from my slumber—but it was just as well. I felt marginally more rested than when we'd decided to call it a night, which meant my batteries were well on their way to being fully recharged. We'd finished with the cleanup yesterday so, technically, our work here was done—from what "conditions" Minerva had named in exchange for offering us her hospitality—but we weren't in that much of a rush. One day more or less wouldn't make a difference.

I realized I was wrong as I watched Nate dress, then halt at the window that let him stare at the mountains where the sun would be rising in an hour or so. It was then that I knew we would be leaving today. I waited to feel disappointed at not getting another day off—this one preferably also including not working my ass off—but found only excitement fluttering in my chest.

What was way less exciting was seeing worry and indecision on his features, but the mere fact that he didn't close up when he caught me watching him counted as something.

"What's with the doubt?" I asked as I slid partially out of bed, angling for the discarded underwear I hadn't really gotten much use out of since dressing after decontamination last night. "Aren't you a few hours too late to have one of those 'dark night of the soul' moments?"

Nate allowed himself a small smile—probably prompted by me almost falling off the bed to reach my bra and tank top without actually leaving the bed yet—but his expression was somber when he spoke. "Not doubt, exactly. Indecision, for the most part."

I couldn't help but pause and stare at him. "That's a first."

"That I admit it to you, maybe," he teased, but his heart wasn't in the brief show of levity. "It's one thing to send a bunch of trigger-happy idiots gunning for what they want to be gunning for in the first place. It's quite another to actually try to decide how much my own life is worth—and how much yours is."

I didn't like the sound of that but decided to give him the benefit of the doubt. "Am I missing something here? We know where we're going. We have backup, and you know that we're one radio call away from easily tripling that in size, if need be. This may be a little more complicated than storming the slaver camp, but it can't be impossible."

He shook his head. "That's not it, although I'm sure that getting in by force will be excessively hard to pull off."

"Again, what am I missing?"

"I'm just playing guessing games here," Nate admitted. "But I can't help but feel like the other shoe is about to drop. And it drives me fucking insane that I don't know where it will be coming from, and I'm having a hard time coming up with any kind of plan when I don't know who I can trust."

"But you do know," I pointed out. "You can trust me. You can trust our people. And considering how much of a beating they have taken for us, I'd say you can trust what's left of the soldiers who've set out for the camp in the initial run. I admit, that's less than thirty people, but it's better than nothing."

Nate slowly inclined his head. "It's more people than I had for half of the non-sanctioned missions I've been sent on in my entire life."

"Then why the long face?"

I'd almost given up hope on getting an answer—in the meantime I finished dressing—while Nate was back to staring at the brightening sky. When he finally turned back to face me, Nate stared at me with an intensity that made the spot between my shoulder blades itch that was impossible to scratch. "I need an honest answer from you. No bravado. No grandstanding. This is just between you and me, and won't leave this room."

I was tempted to crack a joke, but he was way too serious and strung out to appreciate it. "Sure. Shoot."

"If we have a choice—and I'm not sure we'll get one, but say we do—to go all in and sacrifice ourselves for the greater good, would you? No guarantees, but say I have one last ace up my sleeve that could give us that option."

That explained his sourpuss mood. Knowing Nate, we were talking contingency plans more than wishful thinking here.

I gave it some thought, but realized not much of it was required. "I presume this was brought on by losing Romanoff?"

"In a sense," Nate admitted. "But it's less about him going for the ultimate sacrifice, and more about the general circumstances. Call me inspired."

Now that wasn't sounding cryptic at all, yet if he didn't want to spill the beans but keep this theoretical only, I was happy to work with that. "Realistically, we won't live much past the huge showdown, whether we survive it or not, right? No bullshitting me now, either."

He shook his head. "I give us maybe three months? I doubt we'll get to ignore another Christmas as is." Since it had just been him and me, and neither of us big on arbitrary celebrations, we'd ignored those dates passing for the past two years. With no one but us around, it had seemed sad rather than festive to go hunt for a tree and craft ornaments out of shell casings.

I waited for my stomach to seize up, but all I felt inside was, at best, a vague sense of unease. "I say we go for it then. Three months as the prize for getting the single last item checked off our to-do list?

Worth it. If we can make it count, that is. I won't go for a needless, stupid sacrifice. If I go out willingly, it has to be with bravado and grandstanding, or nobody will believe I did it on purpose."

I could tell that my joke annoyed him, but at the same time it made him crack a smile. "Good."

"Good? That's all you have to say to me agreeing to some clandestine suicide pact you still won't tell me the details of? You can do better than that."

"I can," he agreed. "But I'm not going to, unless I have to. I still plan on us surviving this and going for that mountain-top, mutually assured destruction ending."

"I'd be okay with a beach, too," I offered. He turned back to the window without comment, making me sigh. All my great humor, lost on this man. "I presume we're leaving today?"

Nate inclined his head. "I still have to discuss some things with Minerva, but after breakfast we hit the road. If you still need to do anything that requires civilization, I'd get to it now."

I was tempted to snark at him that I hardly required a mani-pedi treatment with barely any nails left, but since I'd have to spend the rest of the day in the car with him, I found it wiser not to annoy him too much. I could have asked to join them but figured he would have invited me if he thought it was necessary—or a conversation I'd enjoy. So instead I stole a kiss on the way to the door, and went to hunt down whoever would get me my first cup of coffee of the morning.

Nobody was surprised that we weren't staying any longer, but trepidation came mostly from those who had decided to stay—Moore and Collins. I knew something was up when Collins was already waiting, steaming coffee in hand, when I made it over to the fire pits, an appeasement if I'd ever seen one. Still sore from fighting and dragging corpses for two days straight, I let him fidget his way through my first mug, and only relieved him when he almost spilled my refill.

"Nobody's holding it against you if you want to stay, you know," I pointed out wisely, hoping I wasn't accidentally lying through my teeth. "I for one will rest more easily knowing that Sadie has a few familiar faces around. And once things settle in, you can decide whether you want to stay here, go back to join the others in California, or take a trip over the mountains and head to Wyoming. I'm sure Bert and Emma can't wait to see their granddaughter for the first time." I'd been surprised when Sadie had told me that neither of the four of them had crossed state borders since she'd bailed on her parents, deciding that the safety of her child was her highest priority. I was sure they'd gotten some chances to talk on the radio, but that was hardly the same.

"We'll see," Collins offered. "Shit, but I thought it would be hard to 'fess up that we want to stay behind. Now I feel like an asshole for kind of wanting to come along."

That made me laugh. "Can't help you with that." This, at least, was one dilemma I didn't have.

One after the other, the rest of our group turned up, Pia markedly missing. Since Nate's meeting with the leader of the town here was likely all about taking care of what was left of the people from the California town, it made sense for Pia to join them. I was glad to see that the scavengers—with very few exceptions—looked mostly sober, and while there was the mandatory grumbling about lack of leave going on, nobody seemed serious about it. Then again, we'd all known where we would be heading for a couple of days now; California had been a necessary detour that had cost us time, ammo, and lives. We didn't have any more to spare. In an hour or two from now, we'd be back on the road, but for now we could still eat, drink, laugh, and joke around, and that's exactly what we did.

Nate and Pia joined us about an hour later, and while their arrival produced the expected momentary lull, since no orders were given, we resumed stuffing our faces. Pia joined in enthusiastically while Nate nursed his psychopath-black coffee, seemingly content to watch me make an ass of myself next to him. Most of the residents who had joined us earlier were leaving to go about their day, but some from the night duties were dropping by still, so it was all a pretty loud affair.

That changed when Minerva herself came to join us, looking grim. "A call just came in on the radio for you," she told Nate—and me, I realized, when her attention didn't remain centered on him. "Sounds like you should take it."

The radio station wasn't far from the fire pits, in easy walking distance from the gates and parking spaces, so we made it there in under two minutes. And by "we" I meant pretty much our entire entourage, a few already with their weapons in hand, others still sipping coffee and meditatively munching their bread. I was surprised when one of the operators directed Nate to a receiver setup on the outside of the building, but figured it must have been rigged to the speaker systems used for alarms—and the odd entertainment event. The amps were off so the entire settlement wouldn't be listening in, but it worked well for the fifty-odd people crowding in around us. Hamilton slipped through the ranks just as Nate grabbed the mic, doing his best to ignore me. I had a certain feeling that would be the only blessing I'd receive this morning.

"You want to speak to me? Here I am," Nate said, sounding harsher and colder than I'd heard him in quite some time.

I hadn't quite made up my mind yet who to expect on the other end of the line, but hearing Rita's voice was one of the better options. I'd had a feeling that we weren't done yet with Dispatch.

"Good to hear your voice," she enthused, giving me slightly weird vibes with that semi-seductive undertone she so loved to use around Nate.

Usually, he was happy to ignore that, but not so today. If anything, he sounded more hostile as he responded. "You mean, after you opted to let my ass rot in a seven-by-three-foot cell?"

Rita laughed, the sound a little too sharp. "I trusted that your wife was more than capable of springing you with the support she had already gathered. Turns out, I was right."

Nate didn't look too happy, and neither did Hamilton, I noticed, realizing for the first time that I had absolutely no clue how Bucky and Rita stood with each other. I knew they'd been fuck buddies in the past—after she'd rubbed her cooties all over Nate, which didn't endear her more to me at all—but had no clue if that still meant anything for either of them. Dispatch had been scavenger central from the start so I doubted they'd had much official contact, but that didn't necessarily have to mean much where personal sentiments were concerned. Hamilton looked neutral enough not to give me anything to speculate on now, either. I almost missed his constant sneer in my direction—which was to say, until he noticed me scrutinizing him, which brought on a sudden return of my favorite expression. At least that I could still rely on.

Nate—as usual ignoring our glaring match—didn't laud my prowess in freeing him, but then neither I nor my ego needed it right now. I was too curious what this was about to care much, truth be told.

"Why are you calling, since this doesn't have the feel of a courtesy chat?"

The radio picked up a low sound that reminded me of a vexed grunt. "Can't I be contacting an old friend to express my sincerest condolences?"

I was surprised to see Nate tense. "You're a week late for that," he ground out. "I'm done playing games. State your reason, or get off the line."

I expected her to be pissed off now, but while her tone cooled somewhat, that made it sound hollow rather than annoyed. "You're right. I am. Part of that is because I didn't want to paint even more of a target on your back by pointing a finger in your direction. A useless effort, I had to realize, since you couldn't have been long inside the Utah settlement's walls before a visitor announced they would like to have a chat." She paused, but didn't force Nate to ask what she meant by that. "I was asked to extend an invitation to you. I don't know the specifics beyond that it exists, and that it comes with a deadline. A very close deadline, and one I think you should take seriously."

Now that didn't sound good. Murmurs rose all around us, but cut off immediately when Nate replied. "What does the invitation say? And what kind of deadline?"

The following pause was a pregnant one. "I don't know, honestly," Rita admitted. "All I was told was to tell you an invitation is waiting for you—a literal invitation in a sealed envelope—that I was asked to inform you about and hold until I can directly give it to you. You have seven days exactly from today to come get it from me, here in Dispatch. You will not be harmed and you will not be hindered on whatever route you decide to take to get here—barring natural disasters or free roaming critters that cannot be influenced, of course. The invitation is for all three of you—Miller, Hamilton, Lewis; so if your plan was to ditch your wife somewhere along the way to keep her safe, don't. That won't do either of you any good."

That didn't sound foreboding at all—and absolutely not like a trap. Hamilton wasn't the only one who was grimacing, although Nate did his best to keep his tone level. "Anything else? Like, your opinion on this?"

"I don't have an opinion," came Rita's flat reply. "And I wouldn't threaten the lives of those that depend on me by speaking it out loud if I did have one." So much for guessing how much free will was involved in this call. What irked me the most about it was that I was burning to know what Decker had against her—and that it was he who must be behind this was no question. When it became obvious that Nate wouldn't respond, she spoke up once more. "The best route would be to head straight through Colorado. It will save you up to a day."

"Thanks, but I can plot my own routes," Nate said gruffly, but something about his tone rubbed me the wrong way. He briefly glanced at Hamilton and me, but really, he needn't have bothered. It wasn't like either of us would speak up against what we both already knew would be his answer. "See you seven days from now."

Silence followed as Nate handed the mic back to the operator who, presumably, killed the line before retreating into the background, without a doubt to eavesdrop.

"Do I need to say it?" I offered when nobody else would speak up. "I doubt it, but I kind of want to. It's a trap!"

I got a few grins and chuckles for my effort—not so from Nate, of course. He stood there, considering, for almost a minute before he turned to fully face the crowd silently surrounding us, with himself, Bucky, and me still in their midst.

"Yes, I'm well aware of that," Nate acknowledged, his tone utterly devoid of humor. "But I would be lying if I claimed I hadn't been waiting for something like this. And I intend to exploit it since it's likely the only chance we get to end this in our favor."

Nobody protested, and there was minimal muttering going on. That quickly changed when Nate turned to where the marines had congregated around their two sergeants and told them, point blank, "You're not coming with us." He paused for just long enough for the worst to die down before he explained. "It's not that I'm not trusting you—on the contrary. I don't need to spell out to you that if what we think is our final destination is in fact the location of a well-reinforced bunker, it won't matter whether there are ten more people along, or a thousand. This is our mess—and has been so from the very beginning. I appreciate the help all of you have lent us, but this is where we part ways." He briefly glanced at the army soldiers standing next to the marines. "And the same goes for you. Go with the marines back to the Silo, or return to whatever base you were stationed at before this started. Wait there for how it ends—if it ends. There's no need to risk your lives any further. But I may very well need you as a last contingency if nothing we do makes a difference."

"That sounds ominous enough," Blake offered in a gruff voice. "And unnaturally pessimistic for someone who didn't bat an eyelash heading into Dallas, hunting after a lead that was paper-thin at best."

Nate held his gaze evenly without flinching or fidgeting. "I've spent what feels like an eternity ducking my head and running as low to the ground as possible. I'm done aiming for diplomatic solutions." I almost laughed out loud there—Nate's version of diplomacy wasn't exactly Ambassador to the United Nations worthy. Thankfully, he kept talking before I could interject anything along those lines. "It wasn't enough that they came after my family—first, my brother; then, my wife—no. They came after our civilians, and they came after anyone likely to lend us a helping hand, and this is where I draw the line. Yes, I have a plan, and even if that goes horribly wrong, I'm convinced I can pull it off and end this, once and for all. But if it doesn't end with this, or if I've miscalculated and my own worst-case scenario comes true and they manage to turn me into a weapon against you, I need you to be ready. If worse comes to worst, I need you to nuke that fucking bunker back into the stone age, and if that leaves half of the country an irradiated wasteland, so be it. There are few enough of us left that we can do with a handful of states that will be uninhabitable for a while."

I had to admit, that declaration stunned me a little—and there was no doubt that he was serious. I wasn't the only one. Buehler picked up on what seemed like the least of the hitches in Nate's plan. "And where exactly would we get those nukes from?"

Nate gave her a scathing look that I was all too familiar with, making her draw up short. "Your headquarters are in a decommissioned missile silo. Don't tell me you don't have the locations of at least twenty others just like it that were only cleared on the outside. I'm sure that someone, somewhere might even still have launch codes lying around, if you don't want to get your hands dirty. We never got to ask Scott where exactly his people had their home base. And I can't be the only one who's been wondering all this time where the SEAL teams disappeared to."

Blake allowed himself a grin that was very much like the cat who'd just licked the cream. "Not wondering, no. But we're not going to tell you."

Nate looked momentarily annoyed but chose to ignore that topic for another day—that would likely never come. And considering where we were going, it wasn't a bad idea not to collect any more clandestine information that could be beaten and tortured out of us.

While Blake seemed satisfied with Nate's explanation—and Buehler was reluctant to speak up against him—Cole took it upon himself to be the voice of dissent from the army corner. "What's stopping them from simply killing you on sight? Or just after they let you waltz through their gates? The three of you may think that you're unstoppable, but recent history has proven otherwise—repeatedly." I sure didn't need that reminder, but he wasn't wrong, I had to admit.

Seeing the murderous rage shining out of Nate's eyes for a second before he reined himself in made me glad I hadn't voiced that thought. "Wanna know something funny?" he asked in Cole's direction, but went on talking before he could get an answer from anyone. "One of my wife's favorite sayings is that her superpower is people constantly underestimating her. She's not wrong with that. I myself have underestimated her—more than once, and I'm not afraid to admit it. I've also used other people's penchant for underestimating her against them. Knowing all that, what makes you think that I'm any different?" The silence that followed wasn't entirely comfortable, and Nate broke it after doing a quick sweep of the crowd with his gaze.

"I think it goes without saying that I have a certain reputation, or else none of you would ever have considered following me. But has no one amongst you ever asked yourself why I have that reputation when most of my actions over the past years speak a very different tale? The only thing you can hold against me is my dishonorable discharge, and you very well know that I planned for that to happen because it was my only way out so I could do what I thought needed to be done. I've spent the last ten years cleaning up other people's shit, trying to minimize any possible fallout, and atoning for sins that, if I'm honest, I didn't commit. I've tried my damnedest to turn my life around the only way I know how. But underneath all that— behind every decision to do the right thing—the old me... the real me has always been lurking. Decker recognized that potential in me decades ago and did his best to hammer me into a tool that's good for only one thing: destruction. More to spite him than to do what's right, I turned all that around on him, step by step, when I was finally done being someone else's pawn. That spite eventually took on the face of atonement, but if I'm honest, it only ever went skin deep. But for a while, that was enough. When the fucking zombie apocalypse kicked off, I thought I'd been granted a new lease on life. I survived; I rallied some of my closest friends and confidants around me; I got the girl."

He paused for a moment to grin at me, but the fervor of his speech never left his gaze.

"I would have been content to go on doing my thing for the rest of my life—to live free, passingly help others in turn for some creature comforts, and forget that anything before the damn outbreak existed. But that wasn't meant to be, because one dirty old bastard couldn't bury the hatchet and let sleeping dogs lie. He had to send my former best friend after us to kill my wife and turn my people against me, and when even that failed, he made damn sure that I'd end up going insane, alone, in a deep, dark pit of my own despair. He made one mistake: he should have killed me when his henchmen had all the chances in the world. But he didn't, because death would have been the easy way out, or the absolution that he didn't feel I deserved just yet. I'm done turning the other cheek. I'm done waiting for the other shoe to drop. If he's stupid enough to let me get close to him, he dies. I'm out of fucks to give about anything else—and I will succeed. For some reason or another that I cannot quite understand, he thinks I'm some kind of bleeding heart who will beg for mercy—if not my own, then for my wife. I don't need to tell you this because you've met her—she's the last one who needs anyone to step up to protect her. Because if I can't kill Decker, she will. And that's exactly what we're going to do."

No one cheered or applauded—although that speech definitely deserved one of those "I'm thanking the Academy" bows—and more than a few of the soldiers looked happy to have already been granted permission to sit this one out. Our people—which, to my surprise, included Sonia—and the scavengers looked satisfied instead, chief amongst them the Ice Queen herself. That made me wonder just how much resentment she must have felt—for years now—watching Nate pretend to be a bystander rather than to jump into the game head-on. I'd never gotten the sense from her that it irked her overly much, but that had changed since Andrej's death. Had he meant that with his cryptic mark about inspiration?

A little late, I realized that, maybe, I should offer my expressive, quite public support for Nate's endeavor. "We will. No doubt about that." Hamilton echoed my sentiment, if silently and with a gruff nod instead, but that was all that was required. While dread did settle into my stomach, it was mostly relief that flooded my mind. Relief that finally the time for waiting and indecision was over. Even if we all got killed, at least it wouldn't be while churning frustrated ruts into the dirt.

Taking another look around, Nate nodded to those of us who would follow him. "Grab your gear and get ready. We have some work to do."

Chapter 16

As inspiring as Nate's speech might have been, leaving turned out to be an undertaking in itself, a certain sequence of essential tasks that needed to be checked off first and couldn't be skipped. Like trying to decide which cars to take, and who would ride with whom. With Moore and Collins staying behind, what had once started out as the Lucky Thirteen could have fit in a single vehicle if we'd opted for clown-car style conditions, or a large truck. It made more sense to keep to our usual MO of fitting somewhere between two and four people per car, with ample room for gear and sleeping space if the need arose. I fully expected to return to the car Nate and I had been driving since we'd liberated it from the laboratory underneath Dallas.

Other people had alternate plans in mind.

I knew something was up when the flurry of activity ground to a halt, and everyone was suspiciously waiting close by at the same time as Martinez had suddenly disappeared. I would have claimed amorous reasons for that but Charlie was standing right there behind Sonia, shooting the shit with Burns, so that couldn't be it. Nate picked up on my sudden irritation but seemed clueless himself, which made my paranoia skyrocket—until it deflated in the best, and most unexpected, way possible.

The crowd, for what it was worth, parted as two vehicles came lumbering toward the fire pits from somewhere deeper inside the settlement. At first, I figured they couldn't be ours since those cars were all parked in the enclosure meant for that very purpose by the gate. But then the make and model of the lead car registered, making me laugh out loud with delight.

It wasn't my Rover, of course, because I'd trashed it to where it wasn't even useable for spare parts—Martinez's words, not mine. Upon closer inspection, it was obviously not the exact model, the grill and window proportions slightly different. But it was a Rover, painted in matte all-over-camouflage pattern, and on the driver's side door I could just make out our old scavenger unit decal. Not in garish red as we'd gone for in the initial run, but the darkest gray used in the pattern, impossible to make out from more than a few feet away—a number thirteen inside a circle, the lines tilted slightly in an approximation of speed. Underneath, also in dark gray, an alpha symbol and "Lewis" in clear stencil. I was sure that the other side had Nate's name on it. So much for any future discussions about who would get to drive this baby.

I didn't know what to do first—jumping up onto the hood and trying to hug the windshield sounded weird even to me—so instead I grabbed Martinez as soon as he slid out, doing my very best to crush every bone in his torso. A million questions raced through my mind—and I knew it was just a matter of seconds until someone started wondering aloud why I'd never shed a tear about losing a single piece of gear but was now ecstatic at the sight of the car—and he started answering them as soon as I let him draw breath once more.

"We found it last year, rotting away in a field," Martinez explained, lovingly patting the car's chassis. "Took some work to find the spare parts to get it moving again, but it was a welcome excuse to spend a little more time up here than down at the coast." He allowed himself a grin in Charlie's direction, as if that explanation was necessary. "We knew that, eventually, you'd come back, and we figured it likely wouldn't be by sneaking in through the back door late at night. Guess we were wrong about that to a point, but hey. You still need a car, and if we're driving to our doom, might as well do it in style."

I didn't know what to say so I hugged him again, and did him the favor of not following that up with a kiss. "That's simply—"

"Amazing," was what I'd wanted to say, but Martinez finished my sentence for me. "What friends do for each other."

Looking from him and past the Rover to the other car, I felt my heart grow heavy for a second when I realized that, of course it was a Jeep, albeit a slightly smaller one than its first incarnation—that I had totaled as well, although it stood to reason that having a bridge collapse underneath us was in no way my fault. Glancing at Pia, I found her staring at the vehicle with a hint of resentfulness, although it was obvious that she'd known of its existence—and whose name must be printed on the driver's side. Before I could say something, she shook herself out of it, glancing at Martinez with her arms crossed in front of her body. "I presume you will insist on keeping your very sorry excuse for any driving that's not on a race track?"

"You bet," he said, grinning.

She grumbled something under her breath and turned to Burns next. "Any chance in hell that you'll shut up if I ask you to ride with me?"

She got a bright smile for her bother, and a slightly more gentle one from Sonia. "It will do you good not to spend the entire trip brooding in silence," Sonia enthused. "Besides, if you don't feel like talking, the two of us can more than carry a conversation."

"That's exactly what I'm afraid of," Pia muttered—but also looked kind of pleased.

Santos and Clark would ride with Martinez—as they had expressed they would love to do since we'd left California—and that almost took care of the lot of us. The exception—Hamilton—turned to where Cole and Hill were the only two of the army faction who hadn't started to drift away. I almost expected them to do some bona fide grunting exchange with no actual words involved, but Hamilton let me down. "You two okay if I catch a ride with you?"

"Fine with us," Hill offered. I hated that it sounded more like, "Honored to have you along, Sir," but then some habits seemed to die harder than others. I figured they'd continue to take their Humvee since it was a perfectly fine vehicle with a perfectly working AC. Assholes.

That left the scavengers—all nine of them that were in good-enough shape to join us—with enough surplus cars that we could leave the ATVs to the Utah settlement to put to good use. I wasn't surprised that my three harpies were over the moon when Nate offered them our car, although I could tell they were miffed I hadn't been the one to hand them the proverbial keys. The other six scavengers split two-by-four into the prize cars we'd taken from Dallas, leaving plenty of room for extra provisions.

Glancing over to the marines, I could tell that Buehler was seething with resentment for being left behind, but Blake had a certain relaxed air about him. I hesitated, but then walked over to where Buehler was pretending to ignore me so I had to directly approach her. "Sergeant? If you have a moment, I have a favor to ask of you."

She grimaced but then dutifully stepped to the side, out of the bustle surrounding Martinez and Clark driving the new cars and over to the others, all of them getting filled up with provisions and gear now. Nate, noticing my absence, gave me a nod that told me he'd take care of my shit, leaving me to do damage control.

"Can't say I will miss missing out on another suicide run," Buehler offered while I was still stalling. "No offense, but I think your husband is right in one regard. This is your mess, and if you have a chance to resolve it, you should absolutely take that opportunity."

"Sounds better than nuking half the Midwest," I only half-joked.

Buehler grinned, making me guess she was either on board with that backup plan, or not taking it serious at all. "So what's up?"

Looking around, it didn't take me long to single out Sadie where she was standing, Chris safely clutched to her shoulder to keep her out of the fray, watching the rest of us get ready. Turning back to Buehler, I did my best not to let a sudden wave of emotion choke me up. "I know this may sound strange, but I need you to take care of Sadie and Chris for me." Buehler looked ready to protest, although I was sure it wasn't about the task in general. "I know, they will have a great home here, or wherever else they will end up. That kid will grow up with a lot of love, never feeling like she lost anyone, and I'm glad about that. But honestly, I'm a little afraid Sadie won't ever let her out of her sight, and she'll get coddled way too much by an overprotective mother who has every right for her actions but won't see what damage she'll do. I need to know there's someone around who'll take the kid aside and teach her the necessary shit. You know, like take her to the range, teach her all the self-defense shit that's not sanctioned by the official authorities, things like that. If either of us were around, that's what Zilinsky would be doing, and me, too. Her mother and the people here will only ever tell her the good stories, always feeling for the poor kid who lost her father before her mother even knew she was pregnant, and most of her aunts and uncles before she could form more than vague memories of us, if even that." When I saw Buehler's confusion, I chuckled. "Christine's father was one of us. He died defending my life when we came after the cannibals that were killing people left and right in Illinois, that first spring after the long winter, when nobody was organized enough yet. He's the reason we have the thirteen in our unit name but only twelve people ever signed the sheet."

Buehler's eyes widened with recognition. She must have heard one version or another of that in the past, but never quite made the connection. It wasn't exactly something we loved to advertise. "Sure, I can do that," she promised, still sounding slightly perplexed. "And I'll tell her all the things her mother won't want her to know." We both looked at Sadie and Chris then, a little lost in thought.

"Fuck, but I wish I could do at least some of that myself," I muttered.

Buehler chuckled. "That reminds me of my first Sergeant, back on my first deployment in Iraq. He was dying of a gut shot out in the field. The corpsman had done his best to patch him up but there wasn't much left to keep it all together. He told me what he regretted the most about dying wasn't the fact that he'd never get to see his wife and kids again, but that he wouldn't be around to teach them everything they really needed to know to get ahead in life. Shit, I wish I'd been on my usual post when the shit hit the fan. Then maybe I could have gotten them out and someplace safe." Her eyes focused back on me. "I'll make sure that little girl won't need anyone to come save her. You can count on me." I didn't hesitate to shake her hand when she offered it, her grip strong and firm despite the fact that she knew what was missing inside my gloves.

"Thank you. I can't tell you how much I appreciate it."

"Don't mention it," she muttered. "I don't have kids and don't really plan on changing anything about that in the near future. Having a surrogate to look after is almost like you're doing me a favor. Gives me a good excuse to get back out there once in a while. We do our best to keep the roads in this part of the country free and as safe as we can, you know."

I wondered if that was a barb at us, but then decided not to dwell on it. "I'm sure the people here appreciate it. Even more so after the shit that went down in California."

She grimaced, and I realized she might interpret my statement in the wrong way. "I hate that this could happen on my watch," she offered. "Or what would have been my watch if we hadn't been chasing after ghosts with you. I don't regret leaving my normal post, don't get me wrong. Might even have ended up saving my life, although I could have done without getting shot." She paused, making sure nobody was close enough to eavesdrop on us. "Wanna know one thing I regret? That you had that fight with Hamilton while you were still recovering, and not on the way back to the States. You could have wiped the floor with him if you'd waited a little longer, but I'm starting to see why you didn't."

I couldn't help but laugh harshly. "I wasn't really jonesing for a fight on the way back anymore. But for him, I would have made an exception."

Buehler grinned, but also looked slightly confused. "I still haven't quite worked out the details of your hierarchy. Back when we set out to France, that caused a lot of discussion among my men. They told us next to nothing except that you're all army, plus some technical advisors, and we should let you take care of any issues. To say I was surprised about your rampant lack of respect for your commanding officer is putting it mildly."

That made me guffaw. "Bucky Hamilton has never been, and will never be, my commanding officer, or anything even resembling that."

"I know that now," she admitted. "Getting some of the details from Richards helped, too." Again, she paused, as if she was considering how much to share, but more likely she was gauging my reaction. She must have found it favorable since she continued. "You fascinated him, you know? I hate to admit it, but at first, that made me jealous, although I had no reason whatsoever for that emotion. You know how strange the human mind can get at times, particularly when it cannot understand something."

She looked quizzical enough that I decided to let her off the hook. "I get it. I've had my fair share of issues, finding myself, unfairly, scrutinizing other women. But I've never had anything but sheer fascination and respect for Zilinsky. Well, and fear, but that's partly her fault for shooting at me while I was hiding behind a trash can and inside some air ducts. Long story," I added when she gave me another weird look. "We've since become tight friends. But I still wouldn't dare antagonize her and expect to see the end of it."

"Wise choice," Buehler offered, smiling slightly. Then her expression evened out once more into a neutral one. "As I said, Richards found you fascinating. Although, less in a chick-he-wants-to-bang kind of way as I first suspected, but more like a hard-to-make-sense-of specimen. I know that probably makes him sound worse than he is—"

I interrupted her with a smirk. "Don't get me wrong—I like him. And if that's what you're fishing for, I don't think he betrayed us. But I am very much aware who his superior was, and in whose footsteps he was treading. 'Specimen' is likely the best term for how he sees me. I'd like to think that we've become friends over the years, and he's the charming, good guy, sometimes womanizer, always straight shooter that he likes to show the world. But I know that, at the very least, he's not just all that."

The look of surprise on her face was borderline offensive, but quickly got replaced by a shrewd smile. "Considering who you—willingly—married, I should have figured that you don't take anyone at face value. But let me repeat what I said earlier—you are a hard woman to understand. I'm glad I met you when your quirkiness was at what must have been an all-time low. I'm normally better about judging people, but you've sent me on quite the run for my money there."

"I get that sometimes," I said, not without pride. "What do you think about Richards? Did he betray us?"

She shook her head, quickly enough to make it appear genuine. "It took me a while to understand that he wasn't just a pretty, ambitious face with a helluva nice body," she hedged, laughing at herself. "Just saying, I normally don't make a habit out of sleeping around. But it was a damn long, boring time on that destroyer, and with him being from a different branch, there wasn't that much issue with fraternization and shit. I'd never bang one of the soldiers under my command."

"No need to defend your choices, not to me or anyone else," I offered. "But even less to me, really. I'm not pointing any fingers any time soon."

I got another considering look from her. "None of us saw the betrayal coming, you know? That bitch assassin, I mean. I didn't like her but only because I knew she'd banged Richards and I felt like she must have been jonesing to encroach on what I falsely believed to be my territory. Not sharing that bias, you didn't stand a chance seeing through her. The way she was portraying herself, she was immediately too much like you for you to get suspicious."

While just thinking about Marleen was making me angry, that statement got a good laugh out of me. "Oh, you mean because my husband clearly has a type? Spunky psychotic?"

"Something like that," Buehler agreed, chuckling. "She played us all, but even more so, she must have played you from the very start. And not just you, considering how murderous Zilinsky gets whenever her name is mentioned."

"Yeah, I don't think she would have taken it lightly if I'd died, whether it was on her watch or not. And considering the shit that happened in California, I'm not sure how much worse off we'd be now if she hadn't been racing to the city, but I doubt that even half of us would still be standing."

"Maybe tell her that, too," Buehler advised. "I have no business whatsoever imposing on her grief. But you're her friend. Just like you rely on her to keep you on the straight and narrow, I think she needs you to tell her to loosen up a little, let go of all of her guilt. She's an admirable woman. I mean, the stories people tell about her... and having been around her for a few weeks now, on and off, I can tell they are true, all of them. But what's that saying? Metal that turns too hard also becomes brittle. Saying she needs to soften up a little is akin to anathema, but I think you know exactly what I'm talking about."

I nodded. Did I ever. I was sure that Buehler had no fucking clue about the details of my friendship with Pia, but I was one hundred percent certain that if she hadn't followed me and told me the story about her children back at the Silo after my miscarriage and subsequent recovery, I doubted I'd have been able to get through all the shit that I'd had to deal with since then. It maybe sounded stupid, but realizing that the Ice Queen, of all people—my nickname for her long since having turned into an honorific—had once started from scratch, with even worse odds against her than I'd been facing when the zombie apocalypse had happened, had made me question my conviction that the only way I could move on was to let myself become hard, cold, and deadly. Ninety-nine percent of what she'd taught me had been about survival and proficiency in all aspects of war, but it was that one remaining percent of humanity that was responsible for me standing here today. And it was about time that I'd make sure to repay her for that. Or maybe not; suddenly, it made a lot of sense why she'd—pretending to be annoyed by it—asked Burns and Sonia to hitch a ride with her. If there was someone who could get that job done, now that Andrej wasn't around anymore, it was Burns. But that didn't mean I couldn't at least give it a try.

"Looks like you've overstayed your welcome here," Buehler remarked wryly at something that must have been going on at my back. Half-turning, I found Nate waiting, obviously annoyed, next to the Rover, with Hamilton looking about to volunteer to come get me and drag me, kicking and screaming, to the cars. When I glanced back to her, she gave me another brief smile. "As promised, I will do as you asked of me. Gladly. In turn, why don't you make sure we won't need to nuke anything? As if zombies weren't bad enough as it is. If we need to add radioactivity to the decontamination mix now, those of us who've so far survived will die of bleach intoxication."

"I'll give it my best," I promised.

"Wouldn't have expected any less of you," she offered, ready to turn away, but then pausing once more. "If you find Richards, and it turns out we're both right—tell him to get his ass over to the Silo if command doesn't agree with us. We can always do with some able-bodied, bright-minded young men. Like those three scoundrels you left with us. They've come quite a long way, Blake recently mentioned. Your fault for not keeping them for yourselves."

I grinned, and didn't do a thing to tarnish my own reputation by letting her know I hadn't wanted the three idiots along for the ride because I didn't fully trust them. We had gotten off on the wrong foot, true, but reading people wasn't necessarily my strong suit.

With a final nod of thanks, I left to join Nate, ready to get this show on the road.

We were pretty much ready to roll, everything stowed away and checked over twice, when I saw Martinez halt next to his car, seemingly hesitating to get in. Suddenly done thinking about missed chances and where we'd all gone wrong, I changed course and stalked over to him. He saw me coming, first offering a smile, then frowning when he realized I was about to put my war face on. "What's with the—" he started, and that was about as far as he got.

"Are you fucking insane? I'm not letting you go just like this," I bit out, underlining my words by poking him in the chest. "After this shitstorm has blown over, that's what you said, right? That's not going to cut it. Have you learned nothing from our combined idiocy? Just look at Sadie, who never got a chance to tell Bates that he was going to be a father. Or my damn husband who would have let me die without ever telling me that I am the one for him, and he had to fucking ask me to be his wife after I crawled up from my deathbed! Man up, you fucking coward!"

I didn't know what exactly had set me on the roll I was on, but after a few concerned moments, Martinez relaxed and let me prattle on. When I finally shut up, he offered me a tight grin. "Are you done?"

"Depends on whether the message hit home or not," I quipped back. "You still have, I don't know…" I glanced at where Nate was glaring at me, as usual annoyed by my antics. "Five minutes or so? Go make the most out of them."

I knew something was up when Martinez continued to grin at me. "Are you done making an ass of yourself?"

It took me a moment to decipher that. "You… popped the question already?"

He gave me a tight—and rather self-satisfied—nod. "Two days ago, actually. After all the carnage, and your dear husband carried you off so you could do whatever ungodly things you two do to each other, Charlie and I got talking because I remarked how fucking romantic that gesture was." He paused, smirking. "Because it wasn't. Don't lie to yourself, chica. Anyway, I joked around about what would come next, seeing as there was always something next coming to massively complicate our lives, and I was kind of sick of it. And he said, well, that is life, whether we like it or not. I admit, I was a little drunk, but that sounded like some really deep shit to me, very profound. I thought some more about it, and asked myself, what am I waiting for? That either of us dies before we get to the good parts? That we survive but virtually all of my friends die? Right that very moment, it was as good as it was going to get, because I was there and he was there, and then I said, fuck it. There is one single thing in my life that I would regret not having done if I did end up dying the next day, and I was not going to let the idiotic wait for the perfect moment take that away from me. So, there you have it."

I stared at him for several seconds straight, then echoed what was, without a doubt, the important part. "Two days ago? And you're only just telling me this now?"

Martinez let out a guffaw, but it had a good-natured tone to it. "I'm under absolutely no obligation to share every single thing with you that happens in my life."

"Yeah, but… two days?!" I was sure people were starting to get interested in our conversation, but I couldn't let this slide. "Who else have you not told? Does Burns know?" Because if there was one man in the world who'd be pissed at him for not having been in the know, it was Burns. Well, and me, but this once I kind of understood how this might have been a bro code thing—and I had been a little unapproachable of late, too busy with my own concerns.

Martinez shook his head, cracking a smile. "You, right now, are actually the first person I'm telling. And I'm only doing this because I know you're five seconds away from making a scene, and it's probably easier to get this over with while we're still inside the gate, not out there getting chewed up by the undead."

Narrowing my eyes at him, I was hard-pressed not to complain that I would do no such thing, but I knew it would have been a lie. "So is this just a proposal, or did you guys decide to take a page out of our playbook and go all the way, vows and ceremonies and all that be damned?"

Martinez shrugged—and I could tell that he was just a little nervous now. "If you ask me, I don't need a document or a blessing from some idiot who got ordained five minutes earlier by the power of what used to be the internet. I know Charlie wants a bit more of some kind of official thing. We both agreed that now was not the time for that, with everyone's nerves frazzled, too many people mad with grief, and the entire valley stinking of zombie guts. So, provided I don't bite it in the next few weeks, I'll come back, and then we'll make it official. This way, I got what I wanted and he gets his wish, too. And I'd much appreciate it if you didn't shriek now and started a mad hunt for some empty cans that you can use to deface my car, which makes no sense whatsoever since he's staying here while I'm leaving in it, but it's absolutely some fucked-up shit you would do."

He wasn't wrong with either accusation, but I did my best to keep a lid on the enthusiasm bubbling up inside of me. "Do I get to hug you, at least? You owe me that since you're already robbing me of being your maid of honor."

"You would so not have been my maid of honor," he said, slightly incredulous. "Honestly, I have no clue what part in my wedding you could have played. They don't normally have court jesters, right?"

"Har, har. Very funny," I grumbled—and went to steal that hug anyway. He hugged me right back, and I was surprised to realize that there was a lump in my throat. No way I was starting to bawl like the mother of the bride now, but at least I had a few moments to compose myself. "I'm so happy for you both," I whispered close to his shoulder.

"Me, too," he snarked back, pushing me away with maybe a tad too much emphasis. "Now go. I didn't spend an entire winter restoring that car only so you'd continue to ignore it."

"Sure thing," I quipped as I turned around, marching over to my Rover—and in passing hollered at Burns, "You know that Martinez got hitched without breathing a word to us because he was afraid we'd mortally embarrass him and do all kinds of weird shit?" I saw his eyes go wide before Burns whipped around and glared at Martinez, while Sonia started to laugh her ass off—and for once didn't glare daggers at me.

Martinez was less amused. "Lewis, you fucking cunt!" he called after me, somewhat amused but still angry.

I blew him a kiss and skipped the remaining way to the Rover, stroking a quick line along the side of the car before pulling myself up into the driver's side. And damn, it was neat to have a car again that was high enough that I could roll out of it and end up in a defensive crouch, without first needing to heave myself up. Nate looked somewhat bemused, as if he didn't quite know what to make of my antics—but what else was new.

"I think we should be going now," I tartly told him. "Possible roadblocks or not ahead, it only makes sense to be quiet while we're out there as not to draw any unwanted attention. He can't really be quiet and scream at me, right?"

Nate shook his head but spared himself a verbal response. I started the car as he gave the gate guards the signal that we were ready to leave. I felt the car come alive underneath me, and while it made sense that the electric motor only gave a low hum, I really missed that familiar purring that my old Rover had come with. It didn't matter, though. Those were all just details.

I waited for Nate to sign in on the radio, but of course, he didn't. "Where to?" I asked as I started easing the car out of the settlement, needing a few moments to reacquaint myself with it—or so it felt. All changes aside, it really did feel like my Rover.

"I-80 into Wyoming," he ordered. "I think you know where to turn from there."

Was I a little surprised that he didn't follow Rita's advice to take a slightly more southern route? Not at all. But I hadn't expected that he wanted to swing by the bunker once more before we hit Dispatch. Then again, with his talk of aces up his sleeve, he had likely been referring to triggering literal contingency plans, not just something obscure like the joint power of our willingness to sacrifice ourselves.

I had a feeling I'd soon find out.

Chapter 17

We left the settlement—and soon the state of Utah altogether—without really saying goodbye to anyone. It stood to reason that, if we survived, we'd still have time to drop by once more and get that over with—and if not, that was fine by me. I knew it was superstitious nonsense, but deep in my gut I always felt like I was jinxing my chance to return if I didn't just up and leave. Look what had happened to us with the bunker.

And no, it wasn't coincidence that I was thinking about that, since that was exactly where we were headed next.

"We're trusting them—whoever they are—that there's nothing lurking out there that we're driving straight into?" I asked about thirty minutes in, more blasting than cruising down the highway.

"Since they managed to stage the undead streak right outside of the settlement, I'm sure they have posted lookouts around here, too," Nate observed while idly looking over the landscape speeding by us. "The route Rita suggested is the most likely one for us to take, but this one isn't that far off, either. Since we have no idea how the situation is in Colorado, it makes more sense to swing north into Wyoming in the first place. Then again, I'd be surprised if our departure remained a secret for longer than it took for the first three cars to rumble outside, so it doesn't really matter. So, yes. For now, I say we trust them, and give them all the chances in the world to fuck up."

The first few miles from Wanship toward Echo had been slow going, too many wrecks on the road to do more than clear a path in the middle, but a short time later, I got my first chance to see just what the new Rover was capable of. It was just us and the road, no shamblers in sight with the late morning sun blasting down on us. The next car—Hamilton in the Humvee—was over a mile behind us. It was one thing to "trust" the message Rita had passed on to us, but quite another to be stupid enough to traipse into any possible traps that were waiting for us before the obvious one. All the transponders in the cars had been deactivated to make sure we would be moving in the black. We still had our coms but those were switched off right now as well, making it very easy to pretend that it was just me, Nate, the car, and no care for anything in the world.

"I find it disconcerting just how content you are to have that damn car back," Nate remarked a while later. "You weren't that ecstatic to have me back."

The note of anger in his voice made me grin. "Oh, come on. I was high as a kite back then. And, as I remember, you were more important to me than food at the time."

"Since you don't get hungry, that's not a feat," he grumbled. When I just kept on grinning without taking his bait, he grunted, glaring at me. "You're practically purring with contentment!"

"That's the engine, my dear," I teased.

"Just how much can I even trust you, huh?" Nate continued with his griping. "All it would take for anyone to turn you against me is to offer you an unlimited supply of cars to crash, and I'd be history."

I gave that some thought. "Just how unlimited are we talking here? And I have only destroyed half the vehicles I've used since the apocalypse started. Our buggies must still be sitting right where we left them at their charging station, and the harpies are quite happy with our previous ride. Wanna know what this is about, besides you loving to hear yourself complain about me? You're just jealous because I'm driving, and it's officially my car, and you have no claim to this throne whatsoever."

Nate continued to glare at me through slitted eyes. "I'm running this show. It stands to reason that any car I choose is mine."

"Yeah, but this one has my name right here on the driver's side, so you're obviously wrong."

Silence fell, making me wonder what he was musing about—likely how to usurp my position somehow—but when I looked at him again, he was smiling. "I've missed this the most, you know?" he said, a lot softer than before. "I know it's a false sense of security, and I'm not falling for it. But being out here, on the road, with you thinking you're a good driver—"

"I am," I insisted.

Nate ignored me. "Those were the best days of my life, I think. After we left the bunker, and before shit went sideways at the factory."

I was a little surprised that he didn't extend that window to the winter before, but, looking back, I could tell that he'd spent the time at the bunker pacing up and down like a tiger locked in a cage at the zoo. He had been much more at ease once we'd set out to Sioux Falls, and even the shit with Bates and that damn town with the lab in Kansas had only thrown him for so much of a loop. Maybe if we'd all lied about identities… but I knew this was wishful thinking. It wasn't like we'd had much of a choice in the first place.

Nearing the border to Wyoming at Evanston, I slowed down, hoping that we would be able to stay on the highway through town if we didn't attract much attention. That turned out not to be a problem since the town looked completely empty. A few miles east, I turned north, leaving the highway for US-189 where it went north, then northeast after switching to WY-28 toward Riverton. I didn't mind so much that Nate remained lost in thought while idly checking the horizon for anything that might require our immediate attention. There were no good places to stop out here, not even much shade to park the car underneath to let the engine cool off a little, so I just kept on driving. The Humvee caught up to and even overtook us a few times before falling behind once more to let the next car do the same, thus making sure that our spread-out convoy was still all accounted for. One or two cars, driving at intervals up to ten minutes apart, didn't exactly leave much of a dust plume to track, and right now, this was working well.

Once we got close to Riverton, I couldn't help but look around with a little more interest, trying to pick out familiar landmarks. We hadn't ventured farther south than the imaginary line between Riverton and Casper, where our territory had about ended. The landscape didn't look much different from when we'd arrived here years ago, everything flat and dry and dusty. After looping around Riverton and as we turned north toward our destination, I couldn't help but feel a familiar ache start up in my chest. We may have given up on it willingly, but this had been our home for a while, and I couldn't help but feel like it had been the only real home for me since the outbreak. Nate didn't comment on my change in mood but I was sure he was aware of it.

One thing that had changed were the guard towers and sign posts—forward positions of the core territory of the Wyoming Collective. I found it a little eerie to drive past what should have been manned checkpoints but looked deserted now. Was Decker's influence really reaching that far? Or had Rita herself pulled strings?

No way to tell now, and with no people in sight who we could ask, I doubted we'd find out.

The last time we'd come through here had been to deliver a stack of what we'd hoped had been secure radios, at the gate to the central town of the collective, formerly a handful of houses in the middle of nowhere. We didn't head for that but instead, Nate pointed me to one of our old roads that led directly to the bunker, a few miles to the south, into the foothills of the mountains. I could have found that road blind in a snowstorm—also because I'd, more than once, had to drive it, blind, in a snowstorm—but if not for memory, I could have easily missed it now. Someone had taken great pains to erect some fences and even rerouted one of the dirt tracks, prompting us to wait for the Humvee to catch up so they could waltz them down, sparing my snazzy new car's paint job. It belatedly puzzled me that Hamilton had no problems finding the road. Then I remembered that just because he hadn't come here after the outbreak didn't mean he'd forgotten all about the bunker's existence. The last two miles of winding road I took point again, letting Hamilton follow what I hoped was still the one true pass through the gauntlet of mines and traps we had prepped the territory with. Somehow, I couldn't see Bert ordering anyone to risk their lives disarming their best forward line of defense.

We arrived, unscathed and unhindered, at the meadow in front of the cabin sitting atop the bunker, a strange kind of feeling bouncing around in my chest—homesickness, I realized, with quite a lot of bewilderment. Since the last stretch of our journey had been slow going, the other vehicles were right behind us, with the Jeep bringing up the rear. Grabbing a shotgun from the rack in the middle console—old habits were very easy to pick up again, it turned out—I followed Nate out of the car. He swung by the trunk to get a sledgehammer out of the back—not disconcerting at all, that move—before he aimed for the door, Hamilton falling in step right behind him, equally armed.

The door burst open when they were still a few feet away from the steps leading up onto the porch, two guards accosting them, looking nervous as fuck. I couldn't hold it against them; it was unlikely that there hadn't been any random, unannounced visitors here for a long time, maybe even years. As governor—or whatever she called herself these days—it made sense that Emma, Sadie's mother and another one of my favorite people in the world, albeit not one I wanted to kill, was living in the town now rather than out here. Still, it was a bunker, the entire setup a refuge for fifty people if necessary, and easily housing twenty on a permanent basis, if they didn't mind sitting on top of each other. The good old days, for sure.

"Stop right there," the older one of the guards said, trying to sound like he meant it. That he did was obvious, but he also seemed to be aware of the fact that their guns wouldn't help them much if we decided not to heed their order.

Nate had no intention to do so, it seemed, but he paused for a moment, looking up at the guards, exasperation plain on his face. "You know who I am?"

The younger of the guards looked puzzled, but the one who'd spoken gave a grim nod. "You're not welcome here."

Nate flashed his teeth at him in something that wasn't even an approximation of a smile. "If you know who I am, you also know that I helped build this fucking bunker, and I will come and go whenever the fuck I please." He let that sink in—and didn't even go so far as to raise his hammer to add to the unspoken threat—before he went on. "We won't be long. If you stop being a nuisance, you'll be back to your lonesome selves out here before the sun sets."

The guards still hesitated, but when Nate continued forward, they let him brush by, then quickly stepped away when Hamilton aimed to plow right through them. I followed, because, damnit, I was so fucking curious about what we were here to fetch. A few more people followed me although most remained outside, and the high whine of a dirt bike disappearing into the hills made me guess that at least one of the guards was getting backup.

While Nate went straight down into the lower level, Hamilton followed at a slightly slower pace, curiously looking at everything. The interior hadn't changed much, the location clearly no longer in use. I could see a few familiar coffee mugs by the sink, waiting to be washed, and what little furniture was in here was still the same. I caught up to Nate in what used to be our bedroom, or rather, dormitory—one of two large rooms that made up the bunker portion of the building. The other had been used as a pantry and alternate living space. A glance into the pantry revealed that food stores were minimal but the armory was still stocked, and some older gear was stashed on the shelves beside it—spare clothes and things that would still work in a pinch. The dormitory was empty except for a threadbare mattress in a corner with a disheveled comforter and sleeping bag on it—another emergency setup, or maybe what the guards used, one at a time, to crash.

Nate ignored all that, instead walking to the very back of the room. There, he turned, and took three measured paces toward the middle, where he stopped—and started to smash the concrete floor underneath us. Hamilton joined him, the two of them falling into an easy, alternating pattern that soon had the surface cracked, cement chunks and dust flying everywhere.

"Exactly what have you hidden underneath there?" I asked after watching them for a while. "A thermonuclear warhead?"

Nate paused, drenched in sweat from the hard work, briefly glancing over to me. "Depends on what you consider as a warhead." He picked up the sledgehammer again and continued. "And drop the 'thermo' part."

My teeth made an audible "clack" as they snapped together. I had been joking, obviously. Apparently, he hadn't.

"Are you for real? You buried a radioactive bomb, or whatnot, underneath the place where we slept for more than half a year? I know you weren't that concerned about the possibility of procreation at the time, but the cancer risk alone…" My thoughts trailed off there, and you could have definitely considered me alarmed. "Are you fucking kidding me?!"

If anything, Hamilton was amused by my outburst. Nate paused again to give me a vexed look. "Basic physics. And chemistry, too. Did they let you skip that in school? Alpha, beta, gamma radiation— and how to contain it? Stop making such a fuss. The background radiation in the ground from the mountains here is way above what this could produce if it was leaking—and it's not leaking."

I stared at him for another moment, ready to whip around and run outside, but I was way too curious to pass this up—and the fact that both of them seemed relaxed despite the heavy physical labor helped set my mind at ease... somewhat.

"I still can't believe that you never told me that we were sleeping on a damn atomic bomb."

Nate went on working until he needed a break, a now sizable portion of the floor ruined. "It's not an atomic bomb. And as for why I never told you, well, it kind of never came up in casual conversation," he said, doing a very bad imitation of me.

Hamilton chuckled under his breath. "This is just too precious."

Ignoring them, I looked at who else was in the room, realizing that only Amos and Adalynn had followed us into the house and were still upstairs, well out of earshot. I turned back to Nate. "So what is it, then? And, you know, I didn't pass up basic chemistry or physics, so feel free to go into as much detail as you like."

I had to wait another five minutes until Nate was tired enough to need another break, letting Hamilton have a go in the meantime. "Actually, it's a case inside a case—both made of lead, of course." He paused, smirking at me. I rolled my eyes at him, not hiding just how annoyed I was right now. "And inside of that, there are four vials filled with enriched, weapons-grade plutonium that can be inserted into a small, detonatable device that's also included in the outer of the two cases. It's all safe to handle since I have no intention whatsoever to add radiation burns to my current collection of scars."

If anything, that explanation left me confused. "What's that useful for? And don't you dare say to make shit go 'boom,' or, I swear to God, I will make you regret that you haven't used that shit on yourself yet."

Hamilton smirked at me between two swings. "You should ask him how he got it. That's the better question."

I pointedly glared at Nate, prompting him to do as his bestie had just suggested. The fact that Nate was reluctant to do so made my interest flare up. Maybe Hamilton wasn't that useless after all if it meant I finally got to hear about some of the shit they had gotten up to long before most of the others had ventured into the picture.

"That case was the backup case a bunch of terrorists were using, trying to get some very important persons killed. We busted their operation, secured the primary charges before they could come to use, and saved the world." That part Nate said in an appropriately wry tone. "And later, we found the backup case when we were rounding up a few more leads. The paperwork was already filed and we didn't want to sit through yet another endless debriefing, so..." He trailed off there, and gave me a surprisingly boyish grin.

"So you just happened to make it disappear in your pocket and nobody has missed it since?" I hazarded a sarcastic guess.

Nate snorted. Hamilton laughed. "We did cause an international incident but not because of that," Hamilton told me—and promptly shut up. Typical.

Nate had a hard time not chuckling himself but turned back to me as he continued his explanation. "It really has very limited use. You'd need the proper facility and at least two hundred of those vials to make an actual fusion bomb out of it. But what makes atomic bombs special is based on plutonium's properties, and that also goes for quantities too small for a weapon of mass destruction: it's an insanely powerful explosive, several times more so than C4 at a fraction of the size. Those devices in there are pretty useful as anti-personnel explosives."

I was still fuzzy on that, but Hamilton was only too happy to enlighten me on their use. "As in, if you're in the same room with someone you want to kill by turning yourself into a small, vaporized dirty bomb, this is what you need."

I almost heard myself deflate, or at least that's what it felt like to me. "So that's what you meant with that talk about how much exactly our potential sacrifices are worth," I noted.

Nate inclined his head. "If my suspicion is right and the invitation that Rita is holding for us says something along the lines of going to a face-to-face meeting, I will make sure that Decker has no chance of walking away from it. My preferred plan is to not blow myself up, but if I only get one chance, I'm not going to miss it." He snorted. "We're fucked if that letter tells us to kill each other, and once we're dead Decker might consider letting the rest of our people live, but that's not his MO. I'm ready for pretty much any concession, if it means I can trigger that bomb. I hate to say this, but I hope so are you."

I was saved from giving an immediate answer by the arrival of more people, suddenly turning the vast, empty space into a crowded room. I would have been alarmed otherwise but was sure that Pia would have called down had it been someone out to get us. And it wasn't hard to guess who would come knocking, guards riding off or not.

Bert managed a modicum of authority even though the dust cloud he stepped into made him cough. He focused on the guys first—"Nate, John"—before giving me a slight nod. I considered being just a little offended but since we were technically trespassing, I cut down on the impulse, mostly playing off Bert's relaxed demeanor. The guards from before were with him, and two more we hadn't seen yet, all a lot more tense than Bert himself. He remained standing just inside the door while his guards tried to fan out. They looked absolutely miserable when neither Nate nor Bucky dropped their sledgehammers and pretty much ignored them—but also made no move on them, either.

"Hi, Bert," I offered conversationally when the incessant pounding stopped for a few moments. "Nice to see you."

He offered me a sardonic grin. "I'd say the same if it was under different circumstances." He watched the proceedings for a moment before gesturing me to precede him. "Why don't we take this outside? I'm not sure anymore whether we used asbestos in the insulation, but either way, I can do without inhaling any more of this shit."

His use of profanity made me smile, if only for a moment. It looked like Nate and Hamilton would be busy for a while here still. Also, Bert and me exiting meant the guards had no reason to linger, which I presumed was the reason why Bert was doing this. Still curious, I kind of wanted to see what they'd unearth, but I had a certain feeling I'd see more of it in the coming days than I liked— after making sure that box got nowhere near the Rover.

Back in the early evening sunshine, Bert stretched, then made a show of walking over to my car and looking at it from all sides, drawing the guards farther from the bunker as they tagged along at a distance. The rest of our people were spread out and mostly relaxed, lingering in the shade or enjoying a few rays of sunshine that weren't baking us alive anymore.

"Martinez mentioned that he'd found a wreck to restore," Bert noted after his circuit was complete. "He and Clark dropped by with a bunch of traders to get some tools and the odd spare part still left in the garage. Looks like their work paid off." The fact that he didn't mention Andrej's name made it obvious for me that he knew what had gone down a week ago. No way Andrej hadn't been involved, considering he loved cars as much as Martinez. Had loved, I corrected myself, my heart giving a painful pang.

"Sadie's okay," I more muttered than told him, hard-pressed to change the topic to something he must have been more interested in than my ride. "Not good per se, and I'm sure she'll need a while to deal with the trauma, but she's physically okay, and she's with people who care about her. Chris is doing just fine. I think the fact that in

Utah, there are easily five times as many kids her age than she's used to makes it easier to forget what she's been through. For Sadie, too, probably."

Bert nodded, almost pensively, but I could see the pain plain on his face. "I hate that it's come to this," he offered. "My own kid feeling the need to run off to save her own kid—and she wasn't wrong." The way he glanced at me made me guess he wanted me to protest. When I didn't, he sighed, suddenly looking ten years older than he actually was. "You don't need me to tell you this, but end it, if you can. I understand it if you have little love left for us—settlements in general, but us in particular—but we've all lost people and paid a terrible price for sins we didn't commit." It struck me as strange that Nate had, just this morning, used almost the same phrasing, but maybe they were quoting from a poem that I wasn't familiar with. Stranger things had happened.

"We'll try." That statement didn't seem enough, so I did my best to lend my voice conviction that I didn't necessarily feel. "You know Nate well enough that he wouldn't lie to you concerning something as important as this, and neither will I. I can't tell you that we will put an end to this—but you have my word that I will do my very best to make it happen. You know the same is true for those two assholes currently ruining the floor of the bunker." That, in turn, made him grin. "You knew what was underneath all that concrete, didn't you?"

Bert nodded. "Who do you think had the idea to bury it there?"

"And you let your wife and daughter sleep right above it?"

Bert gave me a smirk that lured me to expect him to point out they had slept in a different corner of the room, but in actuality, he was way too much like Nate to go for it. "We have a Geiger counter in the pantry, if you want to check. I wouldn't have risked Sadie's health for anything in the world. But I don't need to tell you that none of us ever thought we'd need this bunker—or any of its secrets—not in a million years."

"Hey, we also thought the zombies would be the real problem, and look at us now," I joked.

I got a smile for my trouble, but I knew he was just humoring me, not really feeling it.

"You can stay the night," Bert offered when I didn't have anything else to say. "We can send over some provisions, if you want any. I hope you understand why we can't invite you over to dinner."

As a matter of fact, I still didn't, but kept my comments to myself. "Thanks, but we're only wasting daylight if we stay. We'll camp somewhere out in the plains. It's been a while since we've been here but I still know a handful of good locations that I doubt have changed much in the meantime."

Bert looked relieved, then guilty. Nate and Hamilton returning from the bunker was a welcome distraction for both of us, although in my case, it was short-lived.

"That thing won't come anywhere near my car," I shouted when I saw the case Nate was carrying in his left hand, the sledgehammer in his right. He cast me a sidelong glance as he continued toward the cars. At first, I thought he was aiming for the Humvee, which didn't sit right with me, either. Did I trust Cole and Hill? With my life, yes, but maybe not with other things. I needn't have worried since he passed by the behemoth without stopping, only to hand the case to Clark. Part of me wanted to protest that I didn't want Martinez and the other two irradiated, either, but it was a good choice. The Rover, same as the Jeep—and, in a sense, the Humvee—were the obvious choices, leaving the snazzy Ford as a good alternative.

Bert had meanwhile used the opportunity to leave my side and was standing next to Hamilton, who, at best, seemed vaguely uncomfortable in his presence, if he was even capable of such an emotion. I hated that I was starting to be able to read him. Things had been so much easier before I'd seen little more than the caricature he so loved to portray. "It's good to see you two working together again," Bert offered.

Hamilton pretended to ignore him but then answered nevertheless. "Don't get used to it." Bert looked slightly disappointed but was quick to hide it when Nate returned. The two men stared at each other for a few seconds before Nate extended one cement-dust-caked hand. Bert shook it, and whistled for his guards to leave with him. Only the two who had already been here upon our arrival stayed. Ten minutes and a quick wash-up later, we were back on the road, my bewilderment on a higher level than it had been in quite some time.

"Well, this was strange," I finally said when I couldn't stand the silence any longer.

I was surprised to find Nate smiling slightly as he briefly looked from the horizon to me. He had done a lot of that during the day, and not just because we needed to make sure not to attract attention. "For you, maybe."

"Sure, extricating nukes from underground bunkers is what you usually do before 11 a.m."

"It's not a nuke," he insisted. "Do I wish it was one? Fuck, yeah. But plutonium needs over twenty pounds to achieve critical mass, so no grenade-sized thermonuclear warheads available, I'm afraid." I waited for him to say more, but when nothing came, I decided to drop the topic—for now. I knew it would come up again—inevitably so—and until then I would do my best to ignore the implications: if we needed to use that shit, we would all end up dead.

Acceptance was one thing, but I very much wanted to live long enough past our victory to at least get a good cheer out of it.

Chapter 18

The trip to Dispatch took us five more days, leaving us one entire day to spare. After leaving the bunker, it had made sense to head south rather than north as the settlement was kind of in the way otherwise, so we ended up pretty much backtracking along the very first route we'd ever driven after the undead had risen. The northern trade route wouldn't have been much better since we'd taken that to Sioux Falls, with only a slight detour for the cannibals afterward. My paranoia wanted to jump at the fact that, while never traders ourselves, our most iconic trips had ended up being everyday thoroughfares now. In reality, it made sense; Nate and Andrej had, of course, picked out routes that had been easy to follow and as far away from population centers as possible—the same principles that, even years later, still appealed to travelers of all walks of life. And since we had a full set of maps of the current trade routes—and Rita's promise continued to hold up—why not make this as easy a road trip as could be had? A few times we saw traders on the go, but as soon as we—or the Humvee—zoomed by them as the lead car, they usually stopped and retreated to the side of the road, no further stunts like on our way to Dallas required. They obviously knew who we were, or had made it their business not to bother anyone who looked like they were going somewhere fast. I didn't care, my need to socialize completely filled up by having my old crew back with a few additions. Hamilton, I could ignore. After the first night on the road, Nate returned to disappearing with that asshole in tow, while I was up and had someone to keep me company at the fire. Each familiar face from years ago that was missing was grating on my soul, but, honestly? It was fun to share all our weird tales with Amos and the scavengers, and while Cole and Hill both pretended to be annoyed by it, I could tell that they always lingered to hear the end. I was well aware of the fact that it was only a very brief respite, but if the last few weeks had taught me anything, then it was to get the most of the few opportunities that presented themselves. For now, I was healthy, I was free, and I was able to joke about apple sauce and graphic T-shirts, and the odd time I'd crashed into a wall or puked my guts out, hanging from the hood of my old Rover—although that last bit I heavily debated, my memory of our visit to Dispatch sketchy at best.

It was impossible to miss that we were coming close to Dispatch in the last few hours of driving the day before we actually arrived. First, there were the signposts—a dead giveaway even now. But it was the subtler signs that both put my mind at ease but also got the back of my neck itching, feeling watched. Even in the very first year after the apocalypse, the territory around the sprawling scavenger city that had once been Grissom Air Reserve Base in Indiana had been remarkably well prepared, with forward watch towers aplenty, the roads cleared so that larger groups of cars could quickly get there and leave once more. They'd accomplished that by towing the wrecks off the roads, and I'd seen firsthand that they'd siphoned off what fuel had remained in them. Now, even the wrecks were gone, likely repurposed in whatever way possible.

New were not just increasingly more guard towers but entire groups of buildings, not unlike forward bases, and several rows of trenches and fences that left the road free but could be barricaded within minutes. The Dispatch I'd visited had been a somewhat guarded free-for-all festival. Now, it was a veritable fortress. As we got closer to the gate, I saw that the town had by now grown right to the border of what had been the base beforehand, and on the other side had not just extended to the buildings of the former prison next door but completely incorporated it. With New Angeles, it was always impossible to tell just how far the settlement reached, but here it was obvious just how much it had grown. From the amount of houses altogether, I wouldn't have been surprised if the number of permanent residents had surpassed ten thousand easily. But people weren't only living on the other side of the fence; an entire shantytown had grown outside the gate, presumably where those who weren't welcome went. The entire last mile up to the gate was jam-packed with market stalls, potential customers and vendors alike jumping in front of my car, forcing me to slow down to a crawl if I didn't want to run them over.

Trying to do the right thing and letting them pass made it so that I was almost at the gate when I realized that our arrival hadn't gone unnoticed. I hadn't expected them to let us in without some posturing and threats, but from the roadblocks dragged in front of the gate and the well over fifty armed guards in evidence, it didn't look like they were planning to let us inside at all. Rita herself was waiting smack in the middle of the crowd, the hard expression on her face as impactful as the defenses on display.

Up until then, I'd thought she was refusing to help us because she was afraid. Seeing how she'd built up Dispatch's defenses, I realized she must have decided she was done being pushed around, and what little she'd done had already been a courtesy—probably because she figured we might still come in handy, like to take out the one threat to her reign that still existed. I didn't know why that left me a little conflicted. For some reason, I liked my internal narrative better when we'd been too dangerous to deal with.

Glancing at Nate as I brought the Rover to a stop in the middle of the wide open space in front of the procession, I found his face unreadable. There was tension in his body, but that was all I got from him. Noting my focus on him, he briefly turned his head to look at me. There was anger in his gaze, more than I'd expected or seen him exhibit before. What must have looked like a concession to me was clearly an insult to him.

At his nod, I turned the car off and reached for the door, opening it in sync with Nate. For once, my body didn't sabotage me, my exit one flawlessly executed sequence of motions. Stepping around the car after slamming the door shut, I ended up on Nate's left while Hamilton assumed position on his right—a leader flanked by his attack dogs. As much as I hated to be lumped together with Hamilton in any way, I definitely liked the impression we left.

Nate halted exactly one third of the distance between the cars and Rita's position, forcing her to come walking toward us herself—but also giving her the option of stopping at an equal distance from her people, turning the space between us into some kind of neutral ground. That was exactly what she did. I wasn't surprised that she came alone, her position portraying strength and ease. The queen deigning to step in front of her castle to hold court, nothing less.

I'd expected some additional show of strength—and maybe a greeting—but Rita waited exactly five seconds after rocking to a halt before she reached inside the pocket of her jacket and pulled out an envelope. She and Nate stared at each other before she extended the hand holding it. "I have been asked to give you this."

Even though it wasn't my task to do so, I positively vibrated with the need to come forward to collect it. Nate simply remained standing, staring at her rather than the envelope.

"Impressive setup," he remarked, still focusing on her alone. "I can see why you'd be afraid to lose it all."

A muscle jumped in the corner of Rita's mouth, but rather than become offended, she seemed to relax, letting the hand drop to her side—just as if she knew something we didn't, but direly needed to.

"So good of you to notice the obvious. And the only thing I'm wasting is my time with this. If my call earlier this week has left you with the impression that I'm acting as someone else's errand girl, then I have to inform you that you're sorely mistaken. I was asked—nicely—to deliver a message since I have established Dispatch as a neutral ground. The fact that you'd come here of your own free will made it interesting as well, but I'm sure that if not through me, the message would have reached you through other channels. Since that likely would have involved even more senseless bloodshed, I agreed. Too many people have bled for this already."

I could tell that her words grated on Nate's conscience, but I doubted he felt guilty for what she accused him of—and, just like me, he wasn't responsible for this.

"Then why don't you finish your errand that isn't one so we can be done here?" Nate suggested with all the arrogance I knew he was capable of—which was a lot.

Rita stiffened but started walking forward. Nate didn't move a muscle, remaining standing between us, not giving her an inch. With every step forward, Rita's demeanor grew colder and more aggressive, until she rocked to a halt right in front of Nate, just close enough so the envelope could be exchanged with outstretched hands. I half expected her to turn around now and stalk off, her proverbial tail swishing like a cat's, but instead she remained right where she was, considering Nate calmly. Was her demeanor all just for show? It would fit, I figured—and grew increasingly more annoyed with it.

"Want a word of advice?" she offered, her voice pitched low now, not carrying back to her people, but also not to the rest of ours. Nate gave the smallest of nods. "Run." When he just stared at her uttering that literal one word of advice, she allowed herself something between a sad smile and a smirk, as if she was conflicted herself with which emotion to go. "You know that at the end of this road, there's only death and pain. You've been expecting this for a long time, and have been planning well for it, I'm sure. But you will not find what you're looking for. There won't be a chance to reason with the powers that be, and there won't be a chance of redemption. But it's not too late yet to simply turn around and run, and live out your remaining days together in as much happiness as you're capable of. There's nothing but darkness if you continue following this road."

That sounded cryptic enough—and very much like crap—that I wanted to laugh, but Nate kept staring at her as if she'd given him some profound truth. That was annoying in and of itself—until he replied.

"You've talked to him. And you've known for a while exactly where he is."

Rita grimaced, but it didn't look like in response to his statement.

"I would have done a shit job fortifying my home if I didn't know what's lurking on our doorstep," she offered. "But yes, I've known for a while. Which is also the reason I have done my very best not to get further pulled into this shitstorm. Because I know this is a fight I can't win."

"You let yourself be paid off," Nate accused, his voice turning soft and deceptively calm.

Again, she wasn't perturbed by the unspoken threat. "Yes," she responded, plain and simple. "To save myself, but more so to save my people." She cocked her head to the side, studying Nate intently.

"How many people have already died because of your pride and arrogance? If I've learned one thing from watching you from the sidelines, it's not to make the same mistakes myself."

"You still think you're so much better than me?" Nate's tone definitely sounded like a growl, and I realized he was a step away from physically launching himself at Rita, either to strangle her to death or smash her head in. That realization bewildered and alarmed me, and not just because it kind of came out of nowhere. It really didn't fit the calm, collected front he'd always displayed around her.

Rita must have realized what was going on, a look of caution replacing her outward calm. "No," she finally said, more even than I could have managed in her position. "I don't. In fact, I've tried very hard to break that compulsion for years—to always measure myself against both of you so I can devise a way to come up ahead. I'm not your competition, and you're not mine. Do I understand and support all the actions you've taken in the past seven years? No, but then I don't need to, either. As I said, leave me out of your fucking war. And before you get all high and mighty, consider this: how many people have you saved? And how many have you condemned to death? Because Dispatch comes with a rather steep headcount, if you need something to measure your success against."

Nate simply stared at her, as if that could deflect her barbs. Maybe it did, because he sounded more composed than before when he replied, "Good for you."

Shaking her head, she sighed with annoyance. "Whatever you think is waiting for you, you're wrong. This isn't a war that you can win, or even fight. Trust me. Turn around and run. I can't offer the three of you sanctuary, but we're happy to keep your people here until the air has cleared once more. Just... it's not worth it."

Nate gave that a moment's consideration but I could tell nothing she said had changed anything about the situation. "As touching as your concern is, it's unwarranted. You didn't give a shit about

Hamilton or me rotting in that prison cell, either. What should have changed in the meantime? Besides us likely inconveniencing you if we kill your cozy next-door neighbor."

Rita looked ready to fling something at him—at the very least some expletives—but then she shrugged. "What do they say? It was nice knowing you."

"That's a lie," Nate noted.

She didn't deny it. "You're only going to make it worse, you know," she started again, but then shook her head, mostly to herself. "I've tried my best. Can't save you from yourself."

"No, you can't," Nate offered, still staring at her. "What's with the second envelope?"

I almost startled with surprise and glanced at his hand, but since this seemed to be a hush-hush thing, I tried very hard not to.

Rita seemed, if anything, slightly annoyed. "It came with the other, if not as a package deal. It's addressed to someone named Cole. Ring a bell?" Nate shook his head before I could give anything away. Rita gave another shrug. "Maybe you'll know once you've opened yours—far, far away from here."

"We're not welcome to keep loitering in your driveway?" Nate asked, amused. "You wound me." Before she could respond, he turned around and started marching back to the car. I had to hurry to catch up, figuring that if I hadn't said goodbye to friends, I didn't need to wish Rita a good rest of her life, either. Hamilton followed at a slightly more sedate pace, apparently at ease that he was reduced to a silent bystander.

"Where to?" I asked as soon as the car door closed behind me. Was I burning up with curiosity about what was in that envelope, likely dictating the terms for how the rest of my life would play out? Yes. But it made sense to get away from here first where there were less bystanders, and not a million sniper perches all around us.

"Back the way we came, then turn south at the second guard tower. That should get us out of here."

Nate remained as silent as our coms, which irked me more and more with each passing mile. Ten minutes passed, twenty, until I could finally turn off the road onto a much smaller one. Nate kept pointing straight ahead whenever I checked with him, the others following behind. It was a good hour outside of Dispatch—and a while since I'd seen the last of their forward positions—before Nate told me to stop at the side of the road, literally in the middle of nowhere. As soon as I'd brought the Rover to a halt, he got out, with me following hot on his heels.

It took what little patience remained inside of me to manage to hold still while he tore open the envelope. Inside, there was a card—as in, a fucking stationery card, thick cream paper and gold print. It spelled out our names, and an invitation to "dinner, tomorrow evening." Things couldn't get any more surreal than that.

"Think it's black tie?" I joked. "Not sure a ball gown would go well with my combat boots."

Hamilton, reading the card over Nate's shoulder, snorted. "I'd be more worried whether it went with all the parts you're missing, if I were you."

I was only mildly annoyed by his remark. He was really letting me down. That didn't even warrant a response.

Nate turned the card over, pausing when a map was printed on the back. Squinting at it, I realized that it was a road map, Dispatch and the doomsday bunker clearly marked, the same as a few waypoints in between. "At least we know now that we are heading in the right direction," I pointed out. Somehow, getting that address before in Dallas now left a bad taste in my mouth. Again so many lives lost, and for what? I had to remind myself that this wasn't a zero-sum game—and our arrival had led to the death of the serum project, probably quite literally when its lead scientist had bit the dust. Going forward, that may very well be the single most important thing we'd accomplished—no more people getting infected with faulty versions of the serum.

Once he was done looking the card over, Nate handed it to Hamilton, who continued to scrutinize it until Pia held out a hand in silent demand. Curious as I was, I figured I'd seen everything there was to see. Nate had in the meantime gotten the second envelope out of his pocket, handing it to Cole. "Since that's addressed to you, you might as well open it."

Cole looked at the offering like it was a basket full of snakes but finally accepted it when Nate seemed ready to tear it open himself. He paused with the single sheet of paper that he found inside halfway pulled out. "What the—" he said, confused, but stopped himself when something must have occurred to him. "I'll need a while, but I think I can decipher this." He looked up, searching for something. "Who has a spare charged battery in their car? I need to plug in my laptop, or else this will take fucking forever."

The Ice Queen was already signaling him to follow her. As he turned away, I got a glimpse at the paper. It was full of numbers and what looked to me like random signs—gibberish that a printer possessed by demons might spit out. Nate saw my confusion and answered it with a barely perceptible shrug. He clearly didn't have a clue, either, but since Cole sounded confident, it was best to let him work instead of demanding answers now.

After setting Cole up with the battery pack, Pia returned to us, a bundle of maps in her hands. Splaying two of them out on the hood of the Rover, she and Nate quickly noted down all the marks on the invitation card, and with Hamilton joining them, they started tracing routes. I watched them for a bit until Burns handed the card to me, after pretty much everyone else had gotten a good look at it. Considering our current situation, it looked like right out of a sci-fi movie—a world where you could still call or email a printer and pick a stack of these things up the following day. The letters were embossed, the paper around them in enough relief that I could even feel it through my gloves. It even had that fancy-card smell, a little like old books; something I'd never noticed before, but now it was impossible to ignore. Flipping it over, I stared at the map, noting that we had already diverged from the marked course, if not by much. The bunker was exactly where we knew it would be, near the southern end of Daniel Boone National Forest in southeastern Kentucky. With Cumberland Lake just a stone's throw away, it could have been some upscale resort, but then that might have been a selling point. If the roads remained clear and we ran into no other obstacles, we could make it there in a little over a day, although I really didn't feel like driving well into the night if that meant that tomorrow evening I might already be dead. As much as I'd yearned to finally know what message Rita had been told to give us, now that we had about thirty hours left—going on the cryptic "tomorrow evening" countdown—I wouldn't have minded to have another week, or decade for that matter.

Nate was quick to fold up the maps once more, signaling me to get back into the car. "South," he told me once more when I asked for directions. "Then west. I'll tell you where." That puzzled me a little—also because the route on the invitation card had gone east, then pretty much clear south between Indianapolis and Cincinnati. It hadn't been a very detailed map. Nate gave me a bland look. "I'm not going to play 'Simon says' with him unless I absolutely have to. We pass by Indianapolis to the west and hunt for a place to crash either at Lake Monroe or Patoka Lake, and then amble toward the Appalachians tomorrow." He followed that up with a surprisingly acerbic smile. "If I go to my execution tomorrow, at least I want to do it not stinking to hell. A good night's sleep in the cooler air by the lake will be good, too, and we can supplement our diet with fish, if we catch any."

"Unless the alligators eat us first."

Nate sighed, but I could tell he was loosening up a little. "Bree, there are no alligators in Indiana and Kentucky."

"There could be," I pointed out. "Maybe they escaped from a zoo. Or from a private owner's estate. Would be just like us to get eaten by an alligator two states over from alligator country."

He shook his head at me, laughing softly. "Just drive. And I'll make sure to keep you safe from anyone's bites other than mine. And maybe a million mosquitos."

"You say the sweetest things," I quipped as I started the engine. That blasted thing was still way too silent for its own good. And off we went.

Chapter 19

After having spent the last five days pretty much blasting at full speed through the Midwest—whatever "full speed" meant on any given road; sometimes it had been little more than a crawl for a mile or two, but more often than not we'd stuck to broader roads—it was oddly relaxing to spend the remainder of the day meandering through the countryside. Because that's exactly what Nate had meant when he'd said he'd tell me which roads to take. I knew it wasn't about enjoying the landscape, although past the Indianapolis metro area it was quite nice cruising. It also wasn't about enjoying our last two days of freedom, although being out and about, ambling through the forests and hills, was a nice change. It was even less about keeping me busy, although I appreciated that. It was obviously for operational security purposes, our mad, near random to-and-fro hopping between country roads left us incredibly hard to track, the terrain making it near impossible to follow us except at direct line of sight distance—and we paused often enough to make sure that didn't happen.

By the time we got to our destination for the night—Patoka Lake, since we'd almost crashed into the end of a streak slumming it at Lake Monroe's western edge—I was very ready to get out of the car and into the blue water of the lake. We spent another thirty minutes finding the perfect spot to make camp—which was an elaborate way of saying we ditched the cars in the forest far enough away from the next larger road not to be seen, but close enough that should we have to bail, we wouldn't end up stuck between trees or have to drive into the water to become sitting ducks there, quite literally. There was a certain air of levity going around as we established a perimeter—without running into alligators, or anything larger than the odd critter quickly disappearing into the underbrush. Like many recreational areas, it had remained mostly untouched by the apocalypse at first glance, not many visitors having been around to die out here due to summer season not having started, and a week of what people had believed to be a flu epidemic ravaging the country. Oh, if they had known... I was sure a few more would have chosen lake houses to bite it in.

Our provisions were starting to dwindle, but nobody seemed to have the appetite to go cabin raiding. We had two fishing rods with us and Burns and Clark set them to good use, which was to say they were standing knee deep in the water, joking around, shirking their duties in camp setup. I was surprised that none of the scavengers suggested finding a boat to row out and drop some explosives into the water to make fishing just a little interesting. Maybe they just didn't do it where I could hear. I was happy to walk through the forest farther back from the water to make sure nothing unpleasant was hiding in there for us, and by the time I returned to the shore, we had a fire going, some coffee brewing, and the first three fish were slowly turning to charcoal over the flames. No bean-rice-mystery-meat stew for tonight. And what did they say? Tomorrow we might dine in Valhalla.

I'd kind of expected the mood to be somber—or rather, dreaded it—but the opposite turned out to be true. Was our ecstatic-going-on-manic chattering fueled by a latent sense of dread and unease? Yes, but I honestly couldn't remember a time anymore when that hadn't been a constant in my life. Even before Nate's grand speech to me about there no longer existing any safe places in the world, the fact that billions of people had died and way too many of them had refused to stay dead had drastically changed my perception. It had taken less than a year after that to turn my paranoid sense of being chased—by the undead; by assholes out to rape me, or eat me; by someone misguided trying to protect their territory—into reality... and still, we prevailed. It was impossible to forget about all the shit that had happened since I'd thrown my lot in with Nate, but there had been good days as well. Actually, some of the best days of my life I'd spent with the people sitting around the fire with me now. I hadn't let the rise of the undead stop me, and I sure as hell wouldn't let that asshole in his doomsday bunker change anything about that now. In a sense, knowing that tomorrow things would come to a head was a relief. Finally, no more guessing games and feeling like I constantly needed to look over my shoulder. We'd go full frontal into confrontation mode—and whoever was left standing won. I had a certain feeling that Nate would make damn sure that only we would be able to limp away from this. And if we didn't? Then getting the most out of tonight was all the more important.

Because of the fish we caught, we kept the fire burning well into the night, trusting that we could easily defend the small peninsula which we'd chosen between the twenty of us. Once everyone had their share to fill our stomachs, Martinez got a little creative with seasoning the last two fish, turning one spicy enough that it became a dare for everyone to eat a bite of it. I, of course, went about it with all the cockiness that dead taste buds had lent me—and almost choked on my bite when it turned out hot as fuck, much to the raucous laughter rising around me. Coughing, I managed to find the bits I'd accidentally spewed out and swallowed them, not willing to relinquish that victory. My mind was still reeling from the sputtering as I idly wondered if that was a repetition of being able to kind of taste blood, when Martinez patted me amiably on the shoulder. "Should have warned you about that," he teased. "Just because you can't taste for shit doesn't mean you can't smell it. It's the oil in the seasoning that draws out the heat of the spices, and when the fish is still warm enough, it keeps evaporating in your mouth and fucks with your upper airways."

Of course I had to reward that with a rather crude and graphic remark about where he could shove his spicy fish—which sounded even more painful than eating it—but since even Hamilton and Sonia kept their barbs to a minimum tonight, I wasn't actually annoyed. We of course didn't have any milk to tone down the burn so most of us were sitting there with tears streaming down our faces, which just added to the general sense of hilarity—until Martinez's explanation triggered something in the deep recesses of my brain.

And, just like that, I was very happy I'd passed up the bottle of moonshine making the rounds, objecting each time that since its taste and effect were lost on me, someone else should get wasted on my share instead. I'd always found that a very curious thing, those reports about a heightened sense of smell, leading to anecdotes about cravings for pickles just because someone at the other end of the train was eating a sandwich with pickles in it. No idea why that of all things had stuck with me. Nothing I could do about that now, except curse to myself about the timing. Somehow I didn't see our current travel schedule having room to go hunt for a stick to pee on. I briefly considered saying something, but then cut down on the impulse. What did it matter if I ended up dead tomorrow, anyway? And leaving the others with one less nuance to mourn seemed like a blessing.

Second watch shift turned to third, and begrudgingly, we decided to call it a night. I figured it was probably an oversight so I turned to ask Pia for which shift I was penciled in—it was always either the last, or the one just before that—but got a smirk from her in return. "Everyone here knows that you're not standing watch tonight," she told me, her attention briefly flitting over to Nate. "And neither is he. So why don't you finally leave us to enjoy the evening in peace and get on with christening the back row of your snazzy new car?"

I couldn't help but laugh. "What makes you think I haven't already rubbed every inch of me all over it?" Then I had to pause because I burst out laughing at myself. "And that came out so very wrong."

I was met with agreement, but Pia was adamant about shooing me away—and didn't meet with much resistance, Nate and me both quick to get up. She then turned to Hamilton. "You hit the sack as well. It won't do anyone any good if you fall flat tomorrow because of lack of sleep."

He gave her a tight smile that was far from humorous but retreated toward the Humvee without a word of protest. That puzzled me all the way to the Rover, my thoughts clear on my face since Nate paused by the door and looked back at me, a wry twist to his mouth. "You know that they need to do their plotting without us hearing even a breath of it, right? Can't spill any secrets that you're not aware of."

Gee, that was the kind of reminder that I'd needed just then. Nothing like thoughts of torture to get my groove on.

"So our plan is to simply show up there, the three of us, and see what happens?" I asked.

Nate shrugged. "What else can we do? And before you start to speculate—don't. Let Zilinsky handle this. Trust that, by now, she knows what's in that note that Cole got delivered from whoever was made to play errand boy, and she'll likely spend half the night and most of the day briefing the others about it." His smile was more of a grimace. "Do I absolutely hate this? Yes, every single aspect of it, starting with having to walk into what may very well be our certain doom absolutely blind, with no clue about what our team might have planned to support or rescue us. Am I arrogant enough to be certain that I could come up with ten better plans? Yes, but the problem is, all the strategy planning I've ever done was based on what Decker and his cronies taught me. My mind is poisoned by his doctrine, and anything I can think of, he will have already planned for. Zilinsky? She's a brilliant strategist in her own right, and her ideas have always been as bloody as they are efficient. That was one of the first things that fascinated me about her. It's part of the reason why they accepted her and Romanoff into the serum program. I think the only reason she ever even glanced at one of our manuals was to come up with ways to subvert all the standard strategies and know what to do should she ever again find herself on the other side. Let her do her job so we can do ours."

I didn't really need that reminder and got the sense Nate was mostly droning on for his own good. All I did in response was quip a brief, "Okay," and pull open the back door of the Rover to get inside. Nate looked slightly puzzled at my lack of protest but wasn't far behind.

Things got pretty heated pretty fast. Was I tempted to inform him of my suspicion that, strictly speaking, our activities were no longer required? Yes, but the day I'd have sex for any other purpose than having sex was the day I was ready to clock out for good—and that would never happen. After spending the entire evening with my best friends, making fun of each other and sharing a million stories we'd already heard a million-and-one times, this was the perfect ending to what might very well be my last full day alive. Nate was just as eager as I was, if not more, to chase that high and pull each other along, years of familiarity going great with the rising need to forget about the world one last time. And then one more, and one more, until we were both panting with the need for breath, exhausted in the best kind of way, sweating all over each other and the Rover's back seats—and not giving a shit about anything in the world except for each other. It was amazing—no, divine—and my body was still soaring on its endorphin high when my mind crashed, sudden and unrelenting, from one moment to the next.

Staring deep into Nate's eyes, I heard myself whisper without even giving my voice box the command for the words. "I don't want to die."

Pain cut through his haze of lust, his eyes, a moment ago unfocused, now staring deep into my own. "Neither do I. Want you to die, that is."

Maybe now was the wrong moment to split hairs about phrasing, but with the iron grip of dread squeezing my heart to the point where I couldn't draw breath anymore—or so it felt—I couldn't let this go. Yes, I was fully aware that I was having a panic attack, but that didn't mean I wasn't thinking rationally anymore… somewhat. "And you?"

Nate's expression remained carefully neutral for way too long before he looked away. I was afraid he would withdraw from me, physically the same as emotionally, but instead, he rolled over onto his back and pulled me close so that I was mostly lying on him rather than at his side, our bodies molded against each other from my cheek on his shoulder down to my toes against his shin. He brought his other arm up, actually holding me, as if the very thought of letting me go was impossibly painful.

"I don't want to die, either," he finally said in a low, raspy voice, speaking to the dark ceiling above us rather than me. "But considering what I'm afraid I will have to do tomorrow, that doesn't really sound like a good option."

I was silent for a while, waiting for him to elaborate, but he didn't. We were both still wide awake—and I doubted I would get much rest tonight, not with my mind getting weird like this—and when he refused to say anything, I was the one to budge. "Which is?"

I hated watching his throat move in a convulsive swallow right in front of my face. Not much in this world fazed him—and I wasn't sure I wanted to know about the few things that did.

"Over the past week I've been thinking a lot. I can't help it, but there's this nagging doubt inside of me that I've been seeing things wrong."

"Like what?"

Again he hesitated but then let it all out. "I've been trying to come up with exactly why things happened the way they did. I've shared the theory with you that I've had for the longest time—that when I refused to do as Decker wanted me to, with Bucky's sister, and then went on and refused to lead a strike team and went for search and rescue instead, I deeply disappointed him. And then I added insult to injury when I did everything possible to make them kick me out so I could come after the people who killed my brother. He gave me one more chance to come back, and I not just blew it; I used him and his resources to further my plan, until I'd gotten what use there was out of it. I figured I'd never live to regret all of it. When they started coming after us, and Hamilton let it slip who was behind it all, it made sense—extenuating circumstances warranted Decker giving me another chance, only that I did my very best to keep wriggling out of the noose he tried to knot around my neck. But there are so many inconsistencies in this, and so little that fits perfectly. I… I fucking hate to admit it, but I think I've been looking at it all the wrong way, and for a lot longer than since we've met."

"It made a lot of sense to me," I offered, not quite sure what else he saw in this.

Nate frowned, mostly to himself. "It's just… I always thought it was a competition. His way of forcing Hamilton to try to keep up with me. I'm not proud to admit it, but while I applied myself, if you want to call it that, he never had a chance of surpassing me."

"That's a lie." I didn't know what made me say that, but I couldn't help but snort when Nate looked almost offended. "Admit it. You got off on being the best, even if that meant excelling at being a monster. You've never not been honest about that."

"True," he admitted, faintly amused now. "I'm not denying it. It just lost all meaning for me that day. That's why I quit the race, and from what I remember, Decker accepted that. He said he'd miscalculated. And while I'm sure he'd meant it to rekindle the fire, he let me walk out on him—twice." A brief pause followed. "But what if I'm wrong about that? What if he only pretended to let me quit?"

"I don't get it. He lost you, and for all intents and purposes, you've been a nuisance, constantly crossing his plans, ever since."

Nate shrugged. "Or he just gave up on me for a while, to let me simmer, so to speak. And then he slowly upped the ante, like with the frog slowly getting cooked in a pot. This invitation? That's his way of letting the jaws of the trap snap shut once and for all, forcing me to become what he'd always wanted me to."

As much as he seemed to believe that theory, it didn't gel for me. "First off, that thing with the frog? Not actually true. Frogs are not that stupid. And second, don't you think you're being a little too dramatic?"

I got a soft laugh for that. "True with the amphibians. And yes, it's entirely possible I'm just coming up with the weirdest connections, but hear me out. What if the stunt with Hamilton's sister wasn't meant to put me—or us—in my place, but as a last, final stepping stone to becoming a cold-hearted killer, with no remorse or regrets?"

"How should raping a teenage girl accomplish that? Sounds like BS to me."

"I don't think I was meant to rape her. I think I was meant to kill her." He said that softly enough that it gave me the creeps. When I just stared at him, he made a "just think about it" face. "She was innocent—in every sense of the word. She was the one person in this world who her brother absolutely, unconditionally loved. If I had killed her, there would have been no going back. I could never have flagged or tried to tell myself that I'm still a good person, deep down inside. I'd always have the memory burnt into my brain that I'm capable of anything. And me doing so would have broken Bucky to the point where he'd have known forever that he'd never be a leader, only good enough as a henchman—beta to my alpha. Because I fucking killed his sister and he was powerless to stop it from happening. But I didn't, and I folded, content with stepping down although I'd been just a single step away from the finish line. And yet—the game isn't over. Only the stakes changed. Because, now I have you—the single most important person for me on the planet. The woman I love more than life itself—and don't roll your eyes at me for spouting off mushy shit, I mean this literally: if he gave me the choice, I would gladly trade my life for yours. The thing is, I don't think he will let it come to this. Actually, it makes a lot of sense if you look at everything that's happened to us over the past four years. He's still hell-bent on turning me into his perfect killing machine, and he's going to do it by making me kill you."

That… sounded like a lot of nonsense, or so I wanted to scream at him—but I remained silent, thinking.

"Why would you? Kill me, I mean. I know I can get damn annoying at times, but I've always thought that you'd be bored without me, and that's why you put up with my charming self," I tried to joke.

Nate snorted, but the humor didn't reach his eyes. "Just think about it. Why did he send Hamilton to the factory to kidnap you? Even then, I knew how tough you are, and that he could absolutely have tried to turn you into the perfect instrument against me, but Decker didn't know that. What he did know was that there was a new opportunity to turn me inside out, by forcing me to kill you. Then again, the shit with Taggard. Hamilton tried to warn me in Colorado, I think, and when that didn't work, he made me almost strangle you before Raynor cut you up and put you back together.

How much more literal could he have gotten? None of that worked, so Decker must have reasoned that I'm still clinging to too much of my humanity. In steps Cortez and his arena, and I must say, he did a damn good job dehumanizing me. You could say I'm primed and about ready for that last, final step, or as ready as I'll ever be. Before you protest, just think it all through again. It does make sense."

Except for one thing. "It would kill you. Killing me, I mean. Not in a literal sense, but you'd turn brittle rather than hard. You'd be fucking useless to him in that state."

Nate considered my argument briefly. "I don't think he sees it this way. It would break me, yes, but he must be reasoning that he'd be able to put me back together, reforge me like a broken blade. Nothing he's ever tried has managed to crack the armor around my soul, if you want to call it that, but me killing you would do the trick just fine. And, really, what does he stand to lose? At best, I'm dead and no longer a disappointing reminder of his failure. But he stands to win what he always wanted: me as his perfect soldier."

"Yeah, except that in a few weeks' time, you'll turn and someone will have to put you down. Not really worth all the trouble," I pointed out.

Nate's smirk was bordering on evil. "Unless, of course, he has the antidote."

That made no sense. "What do you mean? We know it doesn't exist."

"Do we?" Nate made that not just a question but also a suggestion. "We went to France for a reason, and you got very busy with poring over the notes and scribbling suggestions for Raynor to implement. We think there is no antidote because you are convinced none exists. But maybe she didn't find one in the meantime and didn't lie to you—maybe my brother already had discovered it. That's a good reason to have had him killed, right? Before he could tell me or anyone else that he'd had his breakthrough—the magic bullet to end all negative side effects of the serum. I never quite understood why they'd let him research that, even if having him on the development team for later iterations must have been a boon for them. That antidote—that possible cure—was way too dangerous to exist. So they used him as long as he was useful—and then decided to bury that part of the research with him, and sent me to clean up what remained of the mess. If it meant I came out of it feeling vindicated but with my hands even more bloody and my soul more soiled, all the better. They even sent Hamilton to collect me, to make sure that I wouldn't just slip away one last time. I admit, if things had turned out just a little different—if I'd never met you, and if Zilinsky and Romanoff hadn't used the months before we executed the mission to make me see that I couldn't let anger and grief destroy my life—I would likely have come out of this like a piece of clay, ready to be molded further."

I had a lot to say to that, but that little nugget toward the end was too good not to jump at it. "Why, what did Pia and Andrej do to get you back from the brink?"

Nate gave a non-committal sound. "In detail? No one single action they took really did the trick. And maybe it was just incidental. Maybe they simply showed me that I had a lot more to live for than I thought—which had boiled down to pretty much only vengeance after my brother's death. If you want me to wax poetic, I'd say that just as Romanoff managed to not just keep Zilinsky alive but teach her how to keep on living, they both paid me back the same way after I got them out of a hairy situation—and gave them a much better chance to keep surviving what they both excelled at doing." He paused for a moment. "I miss him like crazy. Never thought I would. Over two and a half years of not seeing him, or hearing even a peep from him—no problem. We picked up right where we left off as if less than a day had passed in the meantime. But I'll never have to deal with his absolutely horrible jokes, and now more than ever I could use someone who just laughs at me when I get all moody and lost in thought."

We shared a few moments of silence before I made myself speak up. "I get why Decker would want to force you to kill me. But why the fuck would you do it? You just said it yourself—you'd die to save me. There's no sense in killing me in your view of the universe." And just as I said that, I realized where I was wrong—and the reason why he had his proverbial panties in a twist. "Ah, I think I see it now. You kill me, and Decker thinks he has you right where he wants you. So you can get close to him, and kill him. And that's why we are having this conversation."

I both hated and loved how Nate was looking at me—glad he didn't have to spell it out, a little proud of my powers of deduction, and utterly unhappy of the consequences.

"Pretty much, yeah," he drawled.

I gave that some thought, which was a very surreal thing indeed. I had few problems anymore with risking my life, including using my life as a bargaining chip. But this was pushing it, even for me. The strange calm I felt spreading through my mind felt less like acceptance, and more like the calm before the storm made out of pure, unadulterated hysteria.

"What does he need Hamilton for in this scenario?" I wanted to know. "No offense, but you can more than kill me by your lonesome self. You don't need backup."

"But I might need an incentive," Nate pointed out. "Or an inciting incident, if you will. Plus, if all else fails, Decker still has Hamilton if he ends up losing me. But I think his idea is, he'll offer Bucky and me the choice that whoever gets to kill you first gets to live. Hamilton will go for it; I will kill him; you'll likely end up wounded seriously enough that it would be closer to a mercy killing; mission accomplished."

I hated how his theory was starting to make sense. "You mean exactly like with Hamilton's sister? Decker didn't just order you to outright kill her. He set it up as a segue back then, too. Her life was supposed to be ruined and over, anyway, so why make her last moments any more painful than necessary." Nate inclined his head. "Only one problem."

He was more than happy to finish the sentence for me. "You'd want to fight to your very last breath," he stated—no question about that. "You didn't commit suicide when you knew you were dying from getting savaged by zombies and infected with the virus, and even then you couldn't pull the trigger of that gun. You didn't even try. That's why I keep telling you, I will hold out until after you've turned to kill you then, and make sure you can never be an undead menace. Because you'd absolutely kill me, but you wouldn't kill yourself, thus only solving one problem yet creating another."

True—just as what I said next was also true. "Tough luck. Looks like you're going to have to kill me after all."

And, damn. Saying that out loud didn't sound any better than knowing it deep inside my heart. But at least I'd managed to keep my trap shut about my epiphany from earlier. If I really had to die, at least I'd be the only one bearing that loss this time.

Chapter 20

I didn't get any sleep that night, and neither did Nate. Whenever one of us moved, the other used the evidence of our mutual wakefulness as an excuse to start pawing at each other once more. I couldn't in good conscience call it lovemaking—there was too much desperation between us, too many words that still needed to be said but never would. Turns out, since I was already too chickenshit to say goodbye to acquaintances and distant friends, doing the same to Nate was impossible. On the plus side, while we were twisting around each other, I had a very good excuse not to talk and offer up inspirational remarks like that he only needed to survive me by long enough to take down Decker, so if everything went perfect, he could commit suicide before my body had fully cooled. I had a certain feeling he was aware along what lines my thoughts were running, and getting me off one more time might just have been his attempt to spare himself having to listen to that. If that was the case, my fate could have been worse.

As soon as first light broke, we were both out of the car, checking in with the last guard shift—who weren't the only ones awake—before hopping into the lake for a last, long dunk, and then it was time to get ready. Or at least to break camp, chug down coffee, chew listlessly on tasteless breakfast, and drive the one hundred and fifty miles until it was time for the three of us to split from the others.

That was one depressing morning, followed by a tediously annoying day that managed to both drag on forever, and be close to over way too soon.

As much as last night we'd all been doing a great job pretending to forget what waited for us today, whatever had made that work had long worn off. There was a constant air of strain and tension lingering, both around the others but also between Nate and me. Beyond telling me where to drive, we remained silent for the most part, and the few times we halted to keep exhaustion to a minimum, the same was true all through our group. I could tell that some had serious trouble keeping their plans from us, chiefly among them Martinez—not much of a surprise—but also Sonia. I was glad that no one but me and Nate had been privy to our conversation last night, but I had a feeling Hamilton knew the gist of it.

With only thirty more miles to go, we stopped for a last break together—and then it was time to split.

I'd hoped to be able to just remain sitting, staring stoically forward, behind the Rover's wheel, but that was, of course, not in my cards. Did I want to bitch about Nate getting that damn nuke-that-wasn't-a-nuke in its case from the other car? Yes, but my enthusiasm about that had drastically reduced itself. There was a quick debate about whether we should strip down the gear we carried inside the Rover, but it made little sense since the others had by far enough ammo and guns. I doubted we'd be able to carry any of that with us, but, who knew? Maybe I'd make a repeat performance of my escape from the factory and end up dragging myself to my car to try to bring down our entire arsenal on whoever came after me? Slim chance, but stranger things had happened.

Few words were exchanged—like Martinez whispering to me, "This is not goodbye!" as we hugged one last time—but I was surprised how calm and composed I felt. I honestly hadn't expected to have any kind of fatalistic composure left by afternoon, but here I was, feeling an awful emptiness inside but little of the emotional anguish I'd been dreading. There was always time for that later, I was sure.

I didn't know what was worse—having Hamilton or that case in my Rover, both securely stashed away in the back row. As I started driving, I saw the others remain behind, their need for secrecy going as far as not even letting us see in which direction they would set out. Two more bends, and they were gone, leaving only the three of us in one lonely Rover as the center of my world. At least driving distracted me somewhat, but that only went so far.

"So," I started, having to pause to clear my throat to stop sounding like a frightened child to my own ears. "How is that business with the nukes going to happen? I presume it's not as easy as simply carrying them in our pockets."

Nate allowed himself a small smile—likely having been waiting for days for that question—but it had to be Hamilton who had to answer. "Security's likely about what you're used to from most settlements. How often have they asked you to bend over and spread 'em?"

"Thought so," I muttered under my breath, not giving him a chance to think I was scandalized. "What do we do if they use metal detectors?"

Hamilton's grin from before spread. "Then we're, quite literally, fucked."

"Or maybe not," Nate offered. "The metal in your femur will throw any detector off, and I think they'll believe you when you say you're not carrying any other weapons than what you are yourself."

I couldn't help but chortle. "That would be stupid." When I caught Hamilton's smirk in the rearview mirror, it turned into a full laugh. "Don't tell me I'm the only one with razor blades hidden in my bra and boot soles. Well, I am likely the only one of us wearing a bra, but, you know…"

I didn't get an answer, which pretty much confirmed my guess that I wasn't alone. Problem was, a single razor blade wasn't exactly useful, particularly if I couldn't easily get to it. A gun or knife I could easily draw. Something shoved up my colon? Not quite that easy.

"How do the detonators work? I presume a dead man's switch isn't exactly what we're going for with this here," I rambled on.

"Implants," Hamilton provided, rather unhelpfully.

Nate glanced at him briefly before explaining. "Small subcutaneous chips that are triggered by a series of taps. And, yes, they have a built-in dead man's switch as well, but one that only activates after twenty minutes have passed."

"Let me guess—they didn't come with that?"

Nate shook his head. "We had someone modify them for us. Let's hope they still work."

I hated how much about this plan was hinging on things we knew shit about, and could, at best, only guess at. But that was all we had, and we would have to make do with the cards we'd been dealt.

Twenty miles from our destination, Nate told me to make a quick detour in the thick of another forest. He got out as soon as I cut the engine, rounding the front of the Rover to get to the passenger side back seat where the damn case with the nukes was still strapped in behind me. I slid out of the harness and seat much slower, not for the first time asking myself just how insane we were to consider a plan like this. By the time I joined him, Nate had the outer case open, revealing a small box—presumably made of lead—next to a surprising amount of other things, including what must be the injector for the trigger chips. He and Hamilton set to fiddling with that stuff, doing whatever they needed to do to test or arm them, I had no clue. I remained standing there, watching them mutely, trying to decide what to do.

It should have been easy. I stood the best chance of smuggling anything inside, for a million reasons. I didn't doubt Nate's assessment of Decker's plans—and if there was a different solution, Nate would go for it. But I was ready to make the ultimate sacrifice, so this should have been a very easy decision. A very rational decision. But with fear paralyzing my limbs and thoughts alike, it was one of the hardest choices I'd ever been forced to make—and it wasn't even because of things not discussed or even mentioned. Or not just because of that, although it kept bouncing around in my head like a ball in a very small cage. It certainly made me feel like I should not be granted a second chance like it since I was clearly not the responsible type. Better let me shove two of those nukes up my orifices.

Satisfied with the chips working and whatever other setup they'd done with the small electrical device coming with the case, Hamilton held out his left hand so Nate could implant the chip in the callused flesh of his palm underneath the thumb. The needle used wasn't even that thick, and Hamilton barely winced, which gave me some hope it wouldn't be too bad. He waited for Nate to open the lead box and hand him one of the vials, which disappeared into a casing that made it look like a stainless steel cigar. Grabbing that and a tube of lube— for whatever purpose we had been carting that around, I didn't ask— he shimmied out of the car on the opposite side while muttering, mostly to himself, "Oh, how I've forgotten how much fun this is."

I waited until he had disappeared into the woods before turning to Nate. He already had the next tracker loaded, but held out the syringe to me rather than waited for me to offer my hand. I took it, studying it for a moment, before mimicking Nate's motions from when he'd chipped Hamilton. Yet rather than putting it back in the case, I handed it to Nate—and after a moment's hesitation, held out my right hand. "Do me next."

He didn't halt as much as scrutinize my face before reaching for one of the remaining chips. "You sure?"

"Fuck, no," I admitted. "But it's the rational thing to do, right? You said so yourself—they'll underestimate me, and I have the excuse with my trashed leg. If all else fails, wait those twenty minutes and then use me as a distraction. Promise, I won't mind by then."

He actually flashed me a grin for the joke, if a weak one. The chip hurt like hell going into my hand, and it didn't get much better with the second one right beside it. I stroked over the raised welts with the tip of my finger before halting, suddenly afraid. "What's the trigger sequence again?"

"SOS," Nate said. "Three quick, short taps, followed by three slow taps with pauses, and three more short taps. Maybe don't drum your fingertips on your palm for the next few hours, unless you need to."

Surprisingly soon, Hamilton was back, even before Nate had prepped the other three charges. I silently accepted the lube from him, refraining from commenting on his speed and proficiency in hopes he wouldn't offer to lend me a hand. My fingers trembled as I accepted two of the sleek tubes from Nate. They looked light but were surprisingly heavy, but then the atomic weight of plutonium was quite a distance from, say, carbon or magnesium. They also seemed a lot less sleek then they'd looked in Nate's hands.

Cursing my own bravery and stupidity out in my head, I walked a short distance away from the Rover to hide behind a few bushes, and got ready to drop my pants. And yes, of course I needed a full five minutes, way longer than Hamilton, and as it turned out, Nate as well. So much for me not being the uptight one. And no, that wasn't all that funny to me, either.

I knew it was mostly paranoia about possible leakage and instant immolation from the inside out, but while I waited for Nate to be done before trudging back to the car, I couldn't help but shift my weight from one foot to the other, very, very uncomfortably so. Even using what had felt like half a tube of lube had helped only so much. How was anyone expecting me to act normal and be able to, quite possibly, fight like this?

Easy, as it turned out, as the guys continued to act as if everything was normal and there was no reason for me to dread sliding behind the wheel of the car. At least Nate didn't insult me by suggesting that he drive the remaining distance. Hamilton kept smirking at me, even after we were—gingerly, in my case—settled in our seats once more.

The miles crawled by, until we finally reached Cumberland Lake, following one of the roads that passed by its southern shore. Ten more miles, five, and then all there was in front of me was a dirt track, somewhat overgrown. I told myself that we were still on the right track; if the cars that had remained with the Dallas lab had been the only ones to come here often, then it was well over a month since their last visit, if not longer. Of course nature had been crafty to reclaim what it could in the meantime, and it made no sense to advocate any bunker front or back door. Still, I couldn't help but ask myself what we'd do if we found nothing at the end of the track. Getting jostled this way and that helped somewhat since I was all out of worry for finding nothing with what felt like the acute panic of instant immolation weighing much heavier on my mind.

There was one last bend, and the underbrush and few trees fell away, a sweeping meadow before us. I hadn't expected to be able to, but I recognized the site from the documentary back in the day, but only because I knew what it was supposed to be. Maybe half a mile in, a single shed stood, built against the slope of a hill behind it—and that was it. There were no power lines or additional buildings housing generators. No parking spaces, but also no ditches or fences as outwardly visible defenses. It was anticlimactic in the sense of appearing exactly how a hidden doomsday bunker should be looking like—not there.

I didn't need it, but at Nate's grunt I brought the Rover to a stop and turned the engine off. I couldn't help but stroke the steering wheel one last time. Technically, we'd only spent a week together, but new and old memories had already started to mingle in my mind. A shame to never return to the car again. It was a really nice car.

And damn Nate for joking that I could be bribed with a fleet of them, because right now I really wanted a better bargaining chip than my life. Since nobody presented me with that option, I swallowed my ire and got out.

We left all obvious weapons in the car, which meant we spent another five minutes actually pulling them and their holsters out of various open and concealed carrying places. I was so used to the weight distributed all over my body that I felt naked, even fully clothed with my jacket zipped up once more right to my chin. We could have done that already at our last stop, but since we hadn't known what waited for us until we got here, it had seemed like a good idea to wait until the last minute to disarm.

Then we set out, Nate walking in the middle, me on his left, toward the shed.

I made it all of ten steps before I froze in my tracks, my mind going haywire with panic—but it was something else that sped up my heart into a frantic pulse. I simply couldn't do this. I felt like a coward, and like I was letting Nate down, but if I was really going to die, I would do it with no regrets, and with a clear conscience. And if that meant dumping more shit on his shoulders, well, he'd better think quick on his feet about how to deal with that.

"Wait," I hedged, the guys already a few feet ahead of me. Nate stopped immediately, turning to me, while Hamilton took another step forward, grumbling something that sounded awfully like "cowardly cunt" to me. I ignored him, instead staring at Nate, trying to come up with the right words. I could see disappointment etched onto his features as he jumped to conclusions, but he was quick to hide that from me. He looked glad for a second before even that was swallowed up in his neutral mask.

"It's probably better if you stay with the car—" he started, but I cut him off with a vehement shake of my head.

"Oh, I'm coming. I just… I need to tell you something first."

That's about as far as I got before Hamilton started to cackle, although less in a "oh, this is funny" way, and more like he was about to lose it completely. I glared at him—which he ignored—but Nate's weirded-out expression made him laugh all the harder, going as far as needing to wipe a tear off his cheek that had escaped. "Ah, this is too precious," Hamilton grumbled, and when Nate still stared, he sobered up. "Congratulations," he more jeered than wished. "You knocked her up. And now she's going to ruin our entire plan. Perfect timing."

"How did you—" I started but then cut off, because I had to. I had thought I'd already reached peak annoyance with Hamilton in the past. Anger—and fear; no sense about lying there—lapped at my mind, turning the panic in my stomach into a roaring inferno of rage. It was hard to take a calming breath but somehow I managed, the much bigger feat certainly that I didn't launch myself at Hamilton and tried to beat him to a bloody pulp right there. But then my gaze skipped over to where Nate was staring at me, and the rage died, once more doused by a wave of fear. Fear of rejection, but also fear of finding him passive, like this was just one more nuisance he really didn't want to deal with.

Instead, a grin was blooming on his face the likes I hadn't seen in… a very long time. It was an expression of carefree joy, the kind that was reserved for children too young to know better and the odd stroke of luck that came out of nowhere and left you feeling like you just won the lottery. He was back by my side in no time, grabbing my face and kissing me, deep and passionate and without a care in the world, as if he'd forgotten all about Hamilton, and Decker, and what else was waiting to kill us. And for a moment, I was right there with him, my soul singing with hope and joy that I'd forgotten I could still feel.

The moment passed, and Nate pulled back, if only far enough to start whispering in a low voice, almost too fast to make out single words. "Why the fuck didn't you tell me? You must have known last night. Why did you let me drone on for hours and not say a thing? That's why you freaked out about the nukes? Why didn't you tell me half an hour ago, back in the woods?"

With my mind reeling and torn between heaven and hell, it was hard to find the right words, but I knew I only had a few more seconds. If they weren't watching us already, they must have been alerted to our presence, and it was only a matter of moments until we were out of time.

"I didn't tell you because until last night, I didn't know. I thought it didn't matter. What you said was convincing, and I'm sure it is a solution. But I couldn't walk in there with you none the wiser. I'm sorry, but you have a right to know." My thoughts were racing, and suddenly, something else came spewing forth than the speech of acceptance that I had planned. "You know what? Fuck your fucking plan! You think you're the shit? You think you're better than Hamilton, and Decker, and anyone else in the world? Prove it! If you're really that strong and smart, get us back out of there, alive. I don't give a shit about Hamilton, but I forbid you from getting me killed, or yourself, because I'm not doing this on my own! You better be ready to get yelled at and your hand squeezed and smashed nine months from now, do you hear? Now, think. You have maybe five minutes until we've reached the door of that hut. That should be more than enough time to come up with a new plan."

Somewhere during my speech—around the part where I revoked my permission for any murder-suicide pact he might have come up with—he'd started to laugh softly, but dutifully stopped at the end to instead lean in and kiss me again, making it count. The retching sound Hamilton provided in the background just made it perfect. I allowed myself to linger for a second longer—a silent "I love you" since I could say that about as well as goodbye—before I pushed Nate away, doing my best to get back into the right mindset and stop my heart from wanting to burst out of my chest. No surprise that Nate looked calm and collected by the time we caught up to Hamilton, falling easily into step beside each other. While Nate's expression remained passive, I could almost hear the cogs in his brain churning, a million scenarios conceived and discarded with every step. The thing was, I hadn't just blurted that out to appeal to his vanity—I believed it. He would get us both out of this, I knew it. And then, we'd have a very long, likely very loud and heated conversation that had better end with bodily fluids all over the Rover's interior. That lube really had no business going to waste elsewhere.

The door to the hut swung outward, admitting a single person. As he stepped out into the late afternoon sunset, I saw that it was a young man, maybe in his early twenties. Nobody I knew, but the fact that he looked soft, with slight pudge around his middle and the lingering softness of baby fat in his cheeks was stating quite plainly that this wasn't anyone who'd had to live rough on the road for the past several years. He was wearing army fatigues with no rank, insignia, or name on them—also not a surprise, but on him they looked like a costume rather than everyday wear. He watched us approach, seeming not at all frightened, although even I must have had more muscle mass than him—and both Nate and Hamilton had bulked up once more since leaving the camp, if not quite to prime strength yet. I was sure that, Nate's little outburst back there notwithstanding, we were looking like doom had come to knock on their door. He obviously felt like he was in no danger from us at all.

"Welcome," he simply offered once we were in talking distance. "You are expected. Please follow me."

Nate didn't miss a step but he briefly glanced at me, a hint of bewilderment recognizable in his gaze. I gave a small shrug back. If they were stupid enough not to pat us down, well, it just so happened that I'd forgotten all about the knife in my left boot—and I was sure that between the two of them, Hamilton and Nate were still carrying a small arsenal. Better safe than sorry—and nobody would have believed us not to be carrying in the first place. Let them have a few triumphs…if they found them.

Just inside the door to the shed, there was a freight elevator waiting, and we followed the young guy inside, the door behind us closing with an ominous boom belying the flimsy look of the shed.

The elevator started its descent, and with a hint of amusement I realized that the churning in my stomach had stopped. Sure, I was still on the verge of panic, and any second with my mind being idle was bad, conjuring up a million ways to die. But, deep down, the conviction that we would make it was strong, my will to survive as unbroken as ever.

Well, maybe drinking my own Kool-Aid wasn't the worst in situations like this. I had a feeling I'd soon find out how wrong I was about that—or how right.

Chapter 21

I wasn't quite sure what I'd expected, being invited into a bona fide doomsday bunker. But for the first maybe five minutes, it all held up to my expectations… until it didn't.

I was honestly surprised that when the freight elevator—after descending what felt like maybe twenty or thirty feet—came to a rocky halt and the doors opened once more, there weren't a million soldiers waiting for us, guns at the ready. It was closer to twenty, and while they did stand at attention along the sides of the long, industrial-looking corridor, none of them got fidgety with his rifle.

Why became apparent soon enough as we passed by the first one, and looking into his face, there wasn't much staring back at me. Drones, again, like the scavengers who had overrun the California coastal settlement. Only these were all wearing the same uniforms with no scavenger mark in sight, and whoever was responsible for their PT regimen was going way too lax on them. While I did feel more with the scavengers, this was no fate I wished on anyone, and seeing so many young men who were—as far as we knew—a step away from brain-dead was like a punch in the gut.

What I'd also expected were a few literal punches in said region, but at least for now they seemed all about courteous behavior.

I was sure that would change when, in the very middle of the corridor, our guide stopped in front of the single break in the walls—a small room, complete with a desk right by the door. Anywhere else I would have guessed it was a coat-check room, but that couldn't be it, right?

Wrong, as it turned out, since our guide turned to us, indicating the table. "If you would be so kind to leave your jackets and any bulkier clothes you are wearing underneath here? You can collect them again on your way out." His gaze then skipped to my hands. "You can of course keep your gloves on. We are very considerate of our guests' well-being, and that includes not making anyone uncomfortable."

I cast a questioning look at Nate—who stared blankly at the guide, but I could tell he was equally as bewildered as I was—but then unzipped my jacket and dropped it on the table. It was a relatively new jacket, only mended in a few places and carefully scrubbed clean to avoid getting zombie guts all over the inside of the Rover, but it wasn't in as pristine a condition as the soldier uniforms around us. While I was a hundred percent sure this was a measure to both make us uneasy but also make concealed carry much harder, for a second the idiotic idea zoomed through my head that, just maybe, they were asking us to leave our old, stained gear out here as not to drag any dirt inside. Ditching the jacket meant I was down to the tight black T-shirt over my somewhat ratty tank top and bra, quite obviously not having strapped three guns to my ribs and lower back. I was disappointed that Hamilton wasn't wearing a white shirt with pink hearts underneath, but hey, a girl could dream, right?

Once we were done, the guide still wasn't satisfied. "Please drop any weapons you are carrying here as well. I will perform a quick pat-down. It would be a shame if I had to actively filch you." Going with his casual tone, I was surprised he didn't offer to fetch a female colleague for me to do the deed. Neither Hamilton nor Nate made a move to put anything on the table, so I didn't, either. The guide didn't bat an eyelash as he did a—very lax—pat down, starting with Nate. He looked oddly satisfied not to have found anything. He barely touched me when it was my turn, which was all very gentlemanly, but not efficient at all. While he was doing Hamilton, I caught a look of doubt crossing Bucky's face that I understood all too well. What the fuck was going on here? I didn't buy the nice act at all. It set my teeth on edge more than a brutal, thorough takedown would have. I'd expected that. But this? This was bordering on creepy.

It got way worse as we reached the end of the corridor and stepped through an airlock that appeared as if it hadn't been closed for years, judging from the lack of scuff marks on the floor and ceiling. I forgot all about that when I caught a glimpse of what was waiting for us beyond.

My first impulse was to try to puzzle out with what kind of nerve agent they had just gassed us to make me hallucinate like this, but judging from the look of abject horror on Nate's face before he managed to hide it, we either shared that hallucination—or it was real. Impossible, unbelievable, but real. There was mood lighting and soft elevator music playing in the background. Leather sofas and plush-covered chairs. Potted plants, artfully arrayed in corners and on decorative side tables. Hardwood floors, thick floor runners, cream-colored wallpaper, tasteful if bland art. There was even a hostess in a pretty if conservative uniform behind a reception desk, who cast us a glance that belied the casualness of her stance but then pretended to ignore us.

What the ever-loving fuck was going on here?

All three of us must have been staring at the hostess for a little too long as our guide paused in the middle of the room and glanced at us over his shoulder. "Please refrain from enacting any and all hostage-taking plans you might have. Anyone you will be coming in close enough contact with to grab is deemed as utterly dispensable and thus useless to you."

Neither Hamilton nor Nate reacted to that barb, but I couldn't resist. "That include you?"

I got a tight-lipped smile for that. "Of course." No further explanation—and he still didn't look uncomfortable walking with his back fully exposed to us. My guess was that, however genteel it all seemed, we were three seconds away from someone who'd empty a magazine into the back of our heads; maybe five.

The level of surrealism increased as we left the foyer behind to step out onto some kind of gallery. The pastel-and-burgundy theme picked up here, the walls held in tasteful, dark colors now to make the already massive space seem even larger. Through the glass balustrade I could see into the two—no, make that three—levels below us, arranged in different styles and different "room" heights depending on what was going on there. One corner seemed to be a bar—including mahogany furniture—while another served coffee and cake; seating areas were arranged all through the room, and even a small bistro in the corner. But even worse than the seemingly extravagant-but-everyday commodities were the people milling around, more and more turning to casually regard us. Not just because of the glass that kept us well above and away from them, it all seemed like an exhibit to me, or like a museum: see what the apocalypse ripped from our grasp. The people fit perfectly into their environments, decked out in casual clothes in the sitting area, or wearing an elegant evening gown or tux in the bar. And it wasn't just any random people: I recognized quite a few, but not from ever having met them. A few politicians, yes, but mostly celebrities from all walks of life—singers, movie stars, CEOs of Fortune 500 companies exposed enough that they themselves had been better known than their work. Athletes, socialites, and about everyone else who must have had enough money to buy a ticket to this place, or had otherwise been deemed important enough to… "preserve" was the word that came to mind foremost. Not a single one of them showed any signs of starvation or hardship, making me doubt they'd even set foot outside the bunker since the shit hit the fan. An arc of the wealthy and important—making the three of us stand out like a dirty, sore thumb. And while all of them were staring, it was curiosity on their faces, not even a hint of trepidation or disgust. It was as if we were the odd thing to be ogled and discussed over dinner.

There were no soldiers walking below—or even standing at mindless attention in corners—but five more lingered up here, with two guarding the staircase at the other end of the glass walkway, well out of clear sight of the carefree minglers below. One of the guards twitched as he saw us come onto the gallery, making me presume that he and the fellow beside him still had enough computing power to realize who—or what— had just come strolling into their lair. We continued on past them, leaving the large, open space behind as we followed the gently curving staircase—only to step into a similar space, this one more geared toward entertainment. A yoga class was going on in one of the larger spaces, next to a spinning class in another. There was a golf range simulator, and a weight room, although that was empty at the moment—and not much in use, if the general condition of the people seemed any indication. The other half of the room was taken up by several computer stations and two separate partitions for movie theater setups, seating maybe twenty people. I could also see a playground for children, but only two kids sat there, listlessly driving trucks around. Again, people stared at us as if we were three very interesting specimens.

One more staircase, and the building around us changed. The floor remained hardwood but the walls and ceiling looked more utilitarian, huge open space giving away to smaller rooms. I wondered if this was where, finally, we'd find all those four-star generals waiting that I'd expected here. Scott and his marines had mentioned that they'd been guarding the president—well, plural, since they seemed to have gone through a few—but apparently, that hadn't been going on here from the lack of brass in attendance. Looking back, my guess had been that Marleen had killed Scott to keep him from recognizing the address we'd found in the car SatNavs, but it looked like that hadn't been the case. Maybe that was a second bunker, even more exclusive than this one, too lavishly furnished to let us in. The very air we breathed out might have smudged anything.

Whatever this part was, it seemed to be used for more mundane administrative purposes. What I hadn't seen yet was a medical wing or infirmary and any lab spaces; it would make sense not to guide us through those—if they existed. There must have been private living and sleeping quarters for the well over five hundred people that we'd seen somewhere, too, but it all looked way more like a luxury resort than, well, a bunker to weather out the apocalypse in. The admin wing here was only a single level, conventional room height, and seemed to end with what appeared like a large conference room— which seemed to be our destination. The door was open, but since it was slightly offset from the corridor leading there, all I could see right now were four soldiers, at attention, next to each other. Unlike those up on the galleries, they were armed and in full riot gear, if without plate carriers or packs to carry extra ammo. Since I doubted they were alone, that would have likely been overkill.

Bewildered as fuck from what we'd just walked through—and with dread rising with every step I took forward—I did my very best to steel myself for what I knew was to come. Unexpected and weird as it had been, what they'd paraded us through didn't necessarily mean that doom wasn't waiting for us in that room. While the two huge, open spaces had looked extravagant to the point of gaudiness, I hadn't missed that everything was reinforced and built to last an eternity—and easily withstand waves of assault, if not a bomb dropped on the entire complex. Our little nukes-that-weren't-nukes seemed so very inadequate to cause much damage here—but then, they didn't need to.

I cast a last, sidelong glance at Nate, trying to read his expression. He looked very much the embodiment of everything he'd ever strived to be—including the merciless killing machine, his eyes that careful kind of neutral that betrayed no emotion but spoke of iron-clad control. I could only guess at how he must be feeling, about to stand in front of his mentor again, who had, in all things that counted, tried to utterly destroy Nate in every way possible. I had to admit, as much as I was of course dying with curiosity to, finally, come face to face with the man responsible for the apocalypse, and, in so many ways, my life and death—but if I could have, I would have turned on my heel and walked right out of the bunker, and never looked back. Whatever happened in that room wouldn't undo the damage done; wouldn't resurrect the billions of people killed, wouldn't kill the millions of zombies plaguing every corner of this world. It would change nothing about our ordeals; it wouldn't take away the pain from our losses. All we could do was hope that we'd get a chance to put a final end to all the shit that the man hiding like a spider in the middle of his web had flung at us—and to make sure that what was left of humanity had a fighting chance to survive, going forward. If that came with a hint of personal revenge, fine—but I wasn't counting on it anymore. Killing Taggard had done virtually nothing for me, and I couldn't help but feel that with Nate and Decker, it would make even less of an impact. His former mentor had long since become a burden Nate needed to deal with, nothing more—and, at worst, leave an emptiness that nothing else could fill but the endless guilt because of everything that had happened because Nate hadn't killed him sooner.

Suddenly, that tiny, little life hopefully growing inside of me took on a very different meaning. No, we couldn't really change anything for us—but we damn well could make sure that our kid would grow up in a very different world; a better world, a world that was large and dangerous, but also full of wonder and opportunity. And to make that a reality, any sacrifice necessary would be worth it.

Now all I could do was hope that Nate would see it the same way—and do what needed to be done.

Our guide stopped just outside of the door. He was still that annoying, pleasant kind of neutral, not a hint of anticipation or nasty glee visible. "They are ready for you now," is all he said as he stepped away, and with something akin to a flurry, grabbed the handle of the second part of the door to pull it open, letting the three of us advance abreast, taking the need away to work out who'd go in first.

It took me a single look at the raised dais at the other end of the room—past the double rows of soldiers lining the walls as an unnecessary honor guard—to realize one thing: We had been so wrong—about everything.

Chapter 22

There were four people up on that dais, and I knew who all of them were, although I'd only met three.

Marleen was the least surprise. I felt the anger in my gut flare alive as soon as my eyes met hers, and the way she grinned back at me—not unpleasant, and still not like the psycho bitch I knew she was—looked very much like an invitation for me to try.

Richards also wasn't a surprise, and like Marleen, he was easy to read—as in, he was standing there, ramrod straight, radiating unease and something bordering on panic. Yes, it absolutely could have been a show that he was putting on for us, but my gut reaction was to believe that he wasn't the traitor Marleen had halfheartedly set him up as. Maybe he'd had no other choice; maybe he'd decided to try to infiltrate the other side to later be able to help us. My guess was that he'd been the one to deliver the envelope to Rita in Dispatch—a somewhat reluctant lapdog, caught on the leash others had put on him. He must have known that Cole would still be with us.

But the envelope addressed to the impertinent Delta operator? My bet was that it had come from the woman on the far end, dwarfed next to Richards' tall stature—Gita, Gabriel Greene's hacker, former activist, and my self-proclaimed fangirl number one. That explained why I hadn't seen her at the New Angeles docks, or at the very least gotten a chance to chat with her on the radio. I couldn't remember the bullshit excuse Greene had given me when I'd asked about her, and what had become of her since coming back with us from France. If Richards seemed vaguely uneasy, she looked a step away from a nervous breakdown, and working very hard on trying to hide it. She was attempting to look all high and mighty but was clearly crapping her pants—and I doubted that it was from being afraid we'd brand her as a traitor. She must have known what was about to happen, and was likely afraid she'd become collateral damage in the consequences. Again, my instinct screamed to trust her—but what did we really know about her? She'd admitted in the past having been a part of the hacker group that had brought down the internet when the shit hit the fan. That she'd turned against them in the end could have been a lie that none of us could ever disprove. A long time ago, she'd called herself my biggest fangirl, but then it was entirely possible that she also blamed me for losing Tanner. Where did her loyalties really lie?

And the last person—sitting on a bona fide throne while the other three were standing, Marleen to the left, seen from us, Richards and Gita to the right—was not a wizened, old bastard of a man, but that didn't mean that I didn't recognize her immediately. I would have loved to claim a striking family resemblance, but while her hair was dark and her eyes a light brown not unlike her brother's, it wasn't physical clues that tipped me off. She was a little younger than me—late twenties or so—but then she must be, given the time that had passed. Sitting there, with her legs crossed and her hands splayed on the armrests, it was hard to tell, but she looked fit, and without a doubt she was attractive. But the hate spewing from her eyes destroyed what even features created easily.

I didn't need anyone to tell me who she was: Hamilton's sister.

Because Nate stood between us, I couldn't see the reaction on Hamilton's face, but he missed a step, making me guess that he hadn't had a clue about any of this, either. Nate pretty much didn't show anything, but I could see his eyes widen for a moment before his expression closed down as he must have thrown years' worth of plotting and analyzing to the wind, starting from scratch. It was then that I realized I didn't even have the timeline straight—how long ago had it been that they must have last seen each other? Ten years? No, it must have been closer to fifteen, considering the apocalypse was already five years ago, and Nate had left the military two years before that, and he had been part of the serum project for more than a measly three years. That would have put her in her early thirties—and that was pretty much the least interesting detail about any of this.

It wasn't every day that I was left completely clueless, feeling as if someone had pulled the rug out from under me, but that was a pretty accurate description for how I was feeling right now. I could only guess at how much worse it must have been for Nate, not that he was showing any of that.

Not for a single second did I think this was some kind of elaborate ruse. One thing was obvious—we'd been wrong about Decker being behind any of the shit that kept raining down mercilessly on us. I very much doubted he had been alive to see any of it—but I had a sense we would very soon know more about that. I mean, if you go so far as to destroy the entire world on your crusade for revenge, the least thing you would have time for when things finally came to a close in one last, penultimate showdown was a villain speech, right? I'd know; I'd incited a—albeit very toned-down—version of it myself.

And that this was about revenge was obvious from the abject hate in her eyes, on her face, and seemingly screaming from every fiber of her being. That woman had done literally everything in her power to make the lives of those she thought responsible for her misery a living hell.

And it made sense. So much sense. Fuck Nate's cobbled-together theories. I didn't need to hear a single word of explanation from her to see it clearly now, how it all fit together. And the worst of it? I was nothing but collateral damage myself. That pissed me off way more than if Decker himself had presumably been using me to torment Nate.

Marleen raised a hand when we were roughly halfway across the open space to the dais. "That's close enough," she called out. "We wouldn't want to invite any accidents, now, would we?"

I was ready to tell her that any and all violence that would come from us would be very deliberate, but for right now I decided to leave the talking to the others. Marleen's attention was fully focused on Nate and Hamilton, which left me to glance at Richards instead. Our gazes locked for a second but he looked away quickly. I had to cut down on a frown, but when I looked back once more, his eyes were still downcast. Was he trying to tell me something? Like that there was a smudge of something on my left pants leg, presumably lube? More out of vexation than anything else I glanced at his thigh—where I found his fingers, featherlight, drumming a pattern where, at best, Gita could have seen it, but neither of the other two women. Maybe it was because I was hyper paranoid about the nukes, but that definitely looked like that same pattern Nate had drilled into me—the Morse code signal for SOS. No shit, we were in trouble—but then I started thinking. What else could he mean? Maybe I was just being a know-it-all, but I remembered, someone had told me once that its sister signal—Mayday—was really coming from the French m'aidez which translates into "help me," and since we had been to France together, it made sense... that if Richards was actively trying to help us, he would have to be sneaky about it. Or he was asking for our help—or something. It wasn't like I could ask for clarification.

"So we meet again." Hearing those words in an unfamiliar voice made me focus back on the resident evil mastermind. She had a good voice for it—alto, but not too deep or smoky; definitely some public speaking training since she spoke in a way that even the last soldier in the corner could have understood her. From what I could tell, the effort was wasted on half of them since nobody was home in that meat bag holding a rifle. But enough did show emotion on their faces, if mostly carefully neutral not to give away too much.

My mind was still reeling, trying to reorient itself, but Nate seemed to have settled on a strategy, taking on a more relaxed—and unnaturally cocky—position, with one leg slightly extended, his elbows out, fingers touching the tops of his thighs. He was still keeping his expression neutral, but there was an arrogant tilt to his chin, and he looked a little more physically imposing than I was used to—not that hard with me standing beside him, I was sure. It was a pose demanding attention, quite literally so. "Looks like it," he said simply, but it had a certain "and I'm not impressed" ring to it. I honestly wasn't sure if antagonizing her was a smart idea—but it seemed to be effective as far as drawing everyone's focus to him went.

"Aren't you the least bit surprised to find me sitting here?" she asked, her eyes briefly flitting to her brother, but leaving me out completely.

Nate gave the approximation of a shrug, as if he couldn't be bothered with more. "A little. But I doubt that what I think matters to you, after everything you've been up to."

She pursed her lips, not very satisfied with the answer. "A little birdie told me you were operating under the assumption that Decker was the root of all evil. I can see how you'd jump to that conclusion"—her gaze zoomed to her brother for a moment—"but as you must have realized by now, it's completely and utterly wrong." Judging from the satisfaction in her tone, it was obvious she had had something to do with that.

Nate let his gaze skip over the entire group on the dais. "And which traitorous asshole would that have been? Or should I say bitch, since Richards happily let you cut off any balls he ever had."

The man in question stiffened—and I didn't miss that the drumming of his fingers stopped, only to start anew… and I had no clue what that could mean. I did my best to widen my eyes at him—my most hilarious owl impression ever—trying to portray cluelessness, but then noticed that, really, all he did was point to his left—to Gita. At the very end of the lineup, she had an easy time using hand signals, and the hand she had partly hidden behind her body was moving, using some of the modified sign language that Nate had adapted after I'd lost a few too many fingers to rely on the usual signals. At first I didn't get it, but then I realized that she was giving us the "stay put" signal. The bright lights in the room flickered for a moment—nothing remarkable, considering the electricity down here must be requiring an entire bank of generators, if not more—and nobody else seemed to notice, but Gita's hand stilled, and then switched to a "wait for my mark" signal. I hoped that Nate singling out Richards had been his acknowledgement that he was aware that Red tried to tell us something, and not just plain anger. Then again, if I noticed, chances were good that Nate had noticed as well.

Hamilton's sister—whose name I still didn't know, and now that seemed very much like an oversight—wasn't impressed by Nate's slander of her henchpeople, but far from fazed. "Of late you've been surprisingly open with publicly discussing your suspicions, so it could be virtually anyone. Exactly how sure are you that all the members of your merry band of misfits aren't actually my band of misfits?"

If she thought she could shake Nate's confidence that way, she was sorely mistaken—and he let her know as much with a smirk, not deigning to spell out the words. Instead, he took a moment to look around, as if the barren conference room would let him see all the secrets of this installation. "Quite the hideout you've built here. I guess leading us around like a menagerie for all to gawk at should have made us feel small, and so very impressed by your accomplishments? I'm not. Anyone can sit on their lazy asses if they have someone else to get slaughtered for them instead."

All she had for that was a snort as she leaned back on her throne. "And yet, you're the one who's out there, losing how many of your closest confidants now? Some of them aren't even dead. They simply wised up and kicked you out. I must say, I thought Bert and Emma were just putting up a front, but they really must have meant it since they've made no move to even contact their daughter, let alone get her back in the fold. Can't fault them, really, seeing as the girl was so eager to forever soil herself. Guess once this is over, I will personally send them my condolences. They've earned that measure of trust."

At first, I was surprised that she knew the names of our people in Wyoming… but probably shouldn't have been, I belatedly realized. They were important on the grand scale of things, but that wasn't what had triggered my memory. Of course she knew—at least of, if not them personally—Emma and Bert since Hamilton had helped build the bunker, the fact that he'd known about the nukes buried underneath it just one more reminder. But it was a different detail that stood out to me—the fact that, for whatever reason I'd never really questioned, there had been an entire set of survival gear in the bunker that fit me well enough although not a single female member of the group was anywhere my size. I didn't need Nate's statement from last night about his sister being the only woman Hamilton had ever loved to realize whose box that must have been, although it did make me wonder if now was the right time to say, "Hi, I'm Bree, I may have accidentally crapped your pants twice a few winters ago." Come to think of it, I doubted she had known about the bunker, considering that she must have been maybe twelve or fourteen when it had been built—and the fact that we had survived there the first winter of the apocalypse was kind of a dead giveaway for that as well.

Nate didn't react to the name dropping, and instead switched topics.

"I presume Decker is dead?"

She looked very pleased with herself as she nodded. "For years."

"You killed him?"

She nodded again. "And it was easy, really. Both actually killing him, and getting to him first. You see, that was the one thing I'd been dreading for a long time—facing the man who had given the order that, for all intents and purposes, ended my life. I spent years in therapy, trying to deal with all that shit, but it turns out, all I needed to do was to flay him alive to be able to sleep soundly again. Who would have thought?"

Yeah, who indeed?

Nate took the news without a hint of reaction. "That was before you kicked off the apocalypse, I presume?"

"A while before that," she replied, almost lost in thought. "You helped with that, incidentally. If you'd stayed with him, after your brother died, I'm not sure I'd have stood a chance. I'd hoped my actions would lead to this, but there was no way I could have planned for it. It was plan B, really. The leads I laid out for you should have led you in a different direction."

"You expected me to kill him?" Nate presumed.

She made a face, as if the disappointment still rankled. "Hoped is more like it. That you didn't was confirmation for me that you still were his creature, unable to rise up and rid yourself of your master. You sealed your fate with that, you know? I still would have killed you, eventually, but that kept things on a nicely personal level." She allowed herself a bright smile. "Oh, how he bled. And how he begged. Pathetic, really. To think that someone so weak did such a good job pretending to be strong. But then he never did anything else but make others do his dirty work. Physically, it wasn't hard to overwhelm him. It wasn't much harder to break him, either. But I have to give him that much, until the very end he was too short-sighted to realize where he'd gone wrong. He didn't even try to recruit me, nor was he wary of me, when I showed up on his doorstep. He recognized me, you know? 'Ah, you're that girl that broke my most promising tools,' he said. He didn't consider that I was there to kill him. Probably thought I was doing this because my therapist had told me to confront him. For closure, or something. In a sense, it was closure, but it didn't undo anything that had happened, of course." Her gaze then turned considering. "I know that you're smarter than him. At least you were smart enough not to discredit a potential ally just because she's a woman. Of course you never actually did anything with that intellect of yours. What a shame. But how does the old adage go—boys will be boys?"

Nate shrugged off her criticism, as it was. "I'm not sad to see him go, if that's a kind of vindication to you."

"It's not," she was quick to state, her voice suddenly ice cold.

Nate shrugged. "If he was weak enough that you could easily have gotten to him, he deserved to die."

Her eyes narrowed, but she looked pleased rather than antagonized, as if Nate had merely confirmed her suspicions. "And yet, you thought it was him, hunting you, all these years."

Nate considered his answer for a few seconds. "It made sense that he would. You know this, because that has been your strategy all along—to imitate his style, and to use the power his very name held with so many people." He paused. "I admit, I was easily fooled because I was vain enough to believe he'd still be after me, had he still been alive. And you picked your allies well." He ignored those standing beside her, so he must have been referring to someone else.

"Not that I need your validation," she muttered. "But yes, if I may say so myself. And except for very few people, most of them still don't have a fucking clue that I'm the one holding their leash—or that they even have a leash around their necks. General Morris has turned out to be a godsend for that, buffoon that he is. He never once questioned whether those were genuine orders I gave him, or if they actually came from Decker. He still thinks I'm his secretary, who so happened to survive the outbreak by his side. And not even my brother dear has suspected anything for the longest time." Her eyes briefly flitted to Hamilton, and, shit, compared to that look, he and I were really tight friends. "Only that, for whatever reason, he thought it was a good idea to subvert orders rather than follow them, going as far as to warn you. Not only that—he started snooping around. While I was sure to leave no traces for him to find, that kind of disobedience needed to be punished. Too bad that ended up reuniting the two of you, but considering the circumstances, I can't find it in me to regret that. How does life on the other side of the equation treat you?"

Neither Nate nor Hamilton rose to the bait, but I couldn't help but feel like she'd just spelled out her motivation—and damn, I hated how that left me feeling conflicted. Not about the certain knowledge that we couldn't leave her alive—she had killed billions of people, and all for the sake of personal revenge. But while I certainly hoped that the consequences were something I hadn't been able to ignore, I could kind of identify with her need for vengeance. Shit, but really, this was a dumpster fire of epic proportions.

Without acknowledging her point, Nate steered the conversation in a slightly different direction. "What you did, you needed to do through others. That's the reason why you fucked up so much, isn't it?"

Anger sparked in her eyes, but it was a glancing blow at best. "I'm only one woman. To accomplish more than any single person ever in the history of the world is not something you can take away from me, just like that. But yes, I've had to rely on others. That ability to delegate is the very reason my plan worked, and why you would have failed. I didn't need to be the strongest, toughest, most evil bitch on the block. It sufficed that I knew who to give the right tasks to. That has also left me ready to pivot and react to changes as they were required. Just look at us here. While you've been crawling in the dirt, life for us hasn't changed at all. We live in lavish luxury. And, if you were wondering, we will continue to do so through several generations. We don't depend on your scavengers to bring us garbage. The bunker is outfitted with several layers of hydroponics to grow our own food for generations, and a manufacturing plant for all the goods we could ever need. After all, somehow we need to keep the families and dependents of the staff here busy, too. You wouldn't expect how easy it is to recruit new people if you just promise them paradise."

So much for the question of how they kept this institution running. Nate looked about as impressed as I was. "Slaves, whether they still have the capacity to understand it or not."

"And how is that different from everyday life for virtually everyone before the outbreak?" she wanted to know. "We have fair conditions here. Labor laws, very strict rules for how long anyone is even allowed to work. We have had virtually zero complaints, and a lot of people have professed that their quality of life has much increased. Take away money, and you immediately solve the living-wage crisis. But someone who's only used to taking everything he thinks he deserves won't understand that concept."

Nate ignored that barb as well. "I think I'm starting to see how things could have gone to shit as they did, but there's still one detail I'm unsure of. Why kill my brother? If you'd ever met him, you would have known that he had no love lost for anything even remotely connected to the serum program."

A satisfied twist came to her mouth. "And still he was helping them, with fine-tuning the serum."

"That's why you killed him?"

She shook her head. "No. Because he was trying to save you." The smile that followed gave me the creeps. That she wasn't exactly sane wasn't hard to guess, but that looked like it was coming from the far side of the psychopath range. "And want to know the best part about it? He succeeded. Not in saving you, of course. But he could have, because he made that breakthrough just days before he met his well-timed end. That forced me to greatly accelerate some of my plans, but as you know, he never got to tell a soul about it."

So far, it had been easy to keep my trap shut—confusion will do that even to me, and since it was obvious that Nate was putting up some play, it made sense to let him lead without getting in the way—but that was too good a nugget to ignore. "Are you sure? Raleigh Miller actually found a cure?"

Uh, she didn't like having her little one-on-one with Nate interrupted. The way she stared at me should have made me drop dead on the spot. But after a few seconds of me just looking back as neutrally as I could manage, she gave an imperceptible shrug, as if deigning to include me in the conversation. "For the terminal run of the serum, yes. Him hiring you was the reason why we had to kill him before he could share his breakthrough with you. His own assessment of you stated clearly that he trusted that, with your help, he would be done with testing and troubleshooting within months. Since your name came out of nowhere, I had no way of assessing how true any of that was, so he had to be dead and his research destroyed before you could catch even a glimpse of that. Catastrophe avoided in the nick of time, as they say." She seemed very pleased with herself for that. Rather than focus back on Nate, she continued to stare at me, now more like a collector scrutinizing a particularly interesting new specimen. "How does that make you feel, knowing that your possible involvement got one of your heroes killed? You know what that kind of research would have entailed. I saved you from having to soil yourself like that. But then, you didn't exactly show much sense of self-preservation, considering what questionable choices you made going forward."

I didn't need to read her mind to know she was referring to Nate. The anger in her voice made that rather obvious. Since she wanted a response, I was ready to give her one—if a cautious one since I still had no clue how Nate wanted me to react. "I hardly knew the man. What I admired was his intellect. I got the job I was officially hired for and loved working on that. Not much to regret there, if I'm honest."

My response bored her and she looked away from me, which almost made me breathe a sigh of relief. She thought she was so clever? But she was not. Because what suddenly made me want to vibrate with tension was the fact that she believed she'd killed Raleigh's research with him—but that wasn't true. Because in the lab in France, we had found the letters he'd sent to his research partner, and I had been able to recover a lot of notes that had gone way beyond what Nate had shown me of his brother's research. Those notes I had been working on during our return, sending them and my thoughts on to Emily Raynor. If Raleigh really had made that breakthrough, it was in there. I just hadn't recognized it for what it was. But I had added the contribution he had hired me for, in a sense, so there was still hope for Raynor to make the connection. Maybe it was too late for us, but this was actually the best news I'd gotten in years—and all the better if this bitch here wasn't aware of any of it.

"None of that changes anything," Nate said, drawing her attention back to him.

"Oh, but it does. Or did," she replied, again with that eerily happy smile on her face. "Stopping the research for the cure for the serum was vital. It ensured that you assholes couldn't simply step away from all the shit you had done. If that had been the case, how could I have systematically targeted you all to wipe you out with one fell swoop?"

I was sure that the momentary glee on Nate's face was fake, but it weirded me out. "Huh. So that's what you tried to do with the weaponized version of the virus? Single us out and kill us? Hate to break it to you, buttercup, but you accomplished the opposite." He wasn't done yet, cocking his head to the side, a wry grin on his face. "Actually, what you did was kill billions of innocents, and we are still standing. People see us as heroes because we are the ones who helped them rebuild and continue to provide them with anything they could possibly need that we pick up from the ruins. But you already know that. And that's the reason why you've been doing your very best to poison and kill everyone who might have even a hint of admiration for us."

The scavengers and the faulty serum—that explained it. And really, it was the extension of the insane explanation that the mad scientist at NORAD, Dr. Alders, had given, his fervor going as far as to infect his own son—who happened to have been one of my favorite people of all time: Taggard. I fucking hated that we'd known this; we'd been right there, and we had made sure this ended with him—or so we'd thought. But we'd missed that he hadn't been alone, of course, the serum project group under Gabriel Greene's father still operational. I still couldn't understand how she'd managed to make them do this—knowingly condemn thousands of good people to insanity, death, and worse.

No time like the present to ask, I figured.

As soon as I cleared my throat, her attention was on me again, and she looked even less pleased than before. "I have a question regarding that," I offered, and went right on talking before she could tell me to go fuck myself. "How did you get Walter Greene to turn on what must have been the central part of the research of his lifetime? You must know that we found their secret hideout underneath Dallas." No question, with Marleen standing next to her.

She gave a curt nod. "Yes. They took the ultimate sacrifice to ensure that you couldn't mess with their accomplishments," she said, notes of praise and gratitude in her voice. "They accomplished so much. I'm indebted to them, and will never be able to repay them."

I couldn't help but glance at the two soldiers closest to me, both standing in the exact same position since we'd entered without even twitching once. "You mean, they gave you your drones?"

Her tight smile was answer enough, but she was happy to elaborate on that. "I'm not a weeping heart pacifist, if you're stupid enough to think that." I was not. That woman was responsible for what pretty much amounted to World War 3 in my books, but I was careful not to say that. "I know how vital protection is. And that if you want to accomplish anything, a show of force is necessary. As your husband put it, yes, I had to eliminate those imbeciles that worshipped him and those like him. But they weren't lost causes. I could still put them to good use, if I could break some of the protection the serum conferred. It was a truly lucky coincidence that it turned out said protection came with a back door that we could exploit, and now turn into the perfect vehicle to undo the damage."

"How did Emily Raynor get her hands on it?" I asked. "I presume you know that whole spiel of your brother shooting my husband up with that shit and then telling him to strangle me."

Annoyance briefly clouded her relaxed show of satisfaction but was gone after a few moments. "The problems you run into when your resources are limited and your potential allies are spread all over a nation that is suddenly moving at walking speed." The smile returned. "Yes, of course I know about this delightful little anecdote, and it has annoyed me for the longest time that he didn't finish the job. Then again, I wouldn't have been there to watch him go insane with grief over what he had done—or not." She allowed herself a little smirk. "I saw the best-of reel of the surveillance footage. He put on a great show, pretending to be the anxious husband. But there's a segment, around five minutes long, where you can see that he has already shaken off the effects of the drugs, yet that whole display of emotion isn't there yet. He must have been pretending to still be under while plotting the course of his next actions. I can show it to you, if you don't believe me."

Since I had all the excuse in the world to look from her to Nate now, I did, desperately hoping he'd give me a hint of how to proceed. Her words and accusations bounced right off me—I knew they weren't true. I was sure that footage existed, portraying exactly what she described, but knowing Nate as I did, those must have been five minutes he allowed himself to wallow in self-pity and run through worst-case scenarios before pulling himself together and locking all that away so he was ready for anything else they'd fling at him, and to find a way out for us both. She thought she had him all figured out. And that persona was exactly who he was pretending to be now, I realized.

It wasn't really a hard guess where she got all that from—and why it seemed easy bordering on natural to behave like that. My guess was, this was how Nate must have been before shit went sideways that fateful night—and, maybe to a point, it hadn't even been an act. He loved to call himself a bastard. It stood to reason that "cocky, uncaring asshole" wasn't a long shot from that. And no, I didn't find that even the least bit appealing. The realization that, had I met him years before Raleigh hired me, I would have absolutely detested Nate was rather hilarious—but then, I'd always suspected that, to a point. It wasn't like he was any less of an asshole now—he'd just honed his edge to a very fine point, and kicked out most of the machismo.

Looking at him now, I could see the real him simmering underneath the mask he'd donned, without a doubt disgusted by the whole situation, but also by the reminder of who he'd been. His gaze was challenging bordering on belligerent—and yup, that was my hint right there. I knew that look all too well. It usually surfaced early in any escalating discussion we had—and we had had a lot of them over the years. It was his annoyance with me hanging on to a talking point with the tenacity of a small, yippy dog, biting into it to then never letting go, even long after the point had become moot. I could have been wrong, but I thought he was trying to tell me to keep yapping. And yes, once this was over we'd definitely have a firm talk about that.

The light flickered again, and beyond Nate's shoulder, I saw Gita stiffen—and then she signed something that looked awfully like a countdown, eight going on seven. Was that minutes? It was possible. In retrospect, we should have made sure to ask Cole what message he'd received, but that was a missed chance now. It made sense with Gita here—and both of them knowing a thing about computer systems—that it must be something to do with that. We hadn't seen a glimpse of the control room of this bunker but I was sure that it was stuffed to the ceiling with what used to be state-of-the-art computers. Maybe she'd managed to find a back door—or built one—to the system, and had given him the password? Well-timed fluctuations in the lights could be an easily disguised signal, triggering a perfectly-timed countdown. But countdown to what? I had a feeling we'd find out in a little less than eight minutes. Now we just had to keep everyone distracted until then, at least from shooting us on the spot.

Right. Yippy dogs can be very distracting.

Turning back to Bucky's sister, I did my best to appear confident but let a hint of doubt and anger leak into it—not hard since that was, to a point, exactly how I was feeling, if one discounted the raging anger deep in my gut, and the lid panic kept on it. I allowed myself a long sigh—as if I had spent the last seconds debating with myself how to react to her offer to prove to me what an asshole I had married—and shook my head.

"I should probably not be saying this, but I am aware what an egotistical asshole my husband is. I mean, just last night he pretty much made me give him my permission to kill me—sacrifice me, really—to get close enough to Decker to get a chance at killing him for good. Finding out now that reality is a long shot from that doesn't exactly endear me to him or that plan in general very much."

Nate growled—which again gave me an excuse to check in with him—and while his expression screamed that he was disgusted with my betrayal, his eyes sent me a clear "go on!"

The queen bitch gave a surprised if satisfied huff. "Interesting."

I looked from Nate to her. "You have no idea."

"I don't?" she asked, doubtful.

The sarcastic laugh I offered was real, for sure, if coming from a different place than she hopefully thought. "Do you have any idea how much shit I've had to put up with since throwing my lot in with him? If I could go back, I'd do a hell of a lot different the second time around." Pursing my lips, I glanced in Richards and Gita's direction. "Let me guess. You've started collecting allies among those you know also have a reason to hate his guts, just like you do? I'm a little insulted I never got an invitation for that."

Now her laugh held a note of delight, but before she could answer, Marleen interrupted me. "You know that she's lying," she told Bucky's sister while still looking at me. "Right from the very beginning, she's never shown any indication that she doesn't want to stick with him. And why would she have rallied whoever she could reach to get him out of Cortez's camp?"

I got a shrewd look from the queen bitch. "Why indeed."

That was a good question. As much as I tried to remain calm and sound confident, I couldn't help it—my attention briefly flitted to Gita, trying to see if I had been right about the countdown, and for how much longer I had to stall—and of course both Marleen and Bucky's sister noticed, staring at me. I knew I had to come up with something good now— and went with the first thing that came to mind. "To retrieve his corpse, really. I didn't expect to find him still alive. That has actually complicated things a little." Their blank stares gave me nothing, so I laid it on a little more heavily, offering up a nervous if hard laugh. "Oh, fuck, Richards didn't tell you? My, isn't this awkward." That gave me a reason to glance at the man in question—and yes, Gita was signaling me that I had another five minutes to fill. Looking back to the other side of the dais, I singled Marleen out. "I didn't expect I'd get to repay your stupid, 'oh, sorry, how do you like that I fucked your guy?' thing, but, well, here we go. I know this doesn't put me in the best of lights, but while we were gallivanting through the French countryside, Richards and I, well, kind of got to know each other better, but I never thought I'd get an opportunity to further explore that. But then I found myself in the middle of nowhere, needing help after escaping that damn camp, and he was the first on my list to call. Which was easy, since we'd had set that up as a kind of security net before we disappeared." Not even a lie; just my involvement was exaggerated. "What can I say. Things… changed. When it was time to infiltrate the camp, it only made sense that we'd team up, since we could hardly explore anything with my husband's people breathing down my neck constantly. Consider me surprised to find out I wasn't a widow yet."

Bucky's sister seemed to consider that but Marleen cut right through my reasoning. "Remember that I was there to help you break him out of his cell?"

I couldn't help but laugh. Yeah, what a coincidence that must have been—although I still didn't quite understand why. "What exactly did you expect me to do? I tried telling Cortez that he could keep him, but that didn't work out."

"You were all over each other as soon as we got back to your people," Marleen went on pointing out.

I offered up a derogatory huff. "And exactly how would it have looked if I'd refused, huh?" Fuck, but I hated saying that. Then again, considering who I was putting this show on for, it seemed like less of a stretch of the imagination—and it was a great lead to the next point. "Never wondered why, on the way to Dallas, I stuck with Richards? Yeah, I wasn't lying when I said I didn't trust Hamilton not to stab me in the back—which you took way too seriously, I might add—but that wasn't the real reason. Which reminds me…" I trailed off there, going for a slightly musing pose as I addressed the queen bitch. "I presume you want those two assholes gone? I'd consider you letting me kill your brother as a kind of signing bonus. And before anyone accuses me of lying about that, I am on public record, repeatedly, saying that I want to be the one to end his miserable existence. The only reason I changed my mind was because the very idea he'd have to live on with the memory of what Cortez did to him for ages sounded very satisfying to me, but that was before that asshole tried to redeem himself by saving me. Just consider how pleasant that was to be lying there, paralyzed and in incredible pain, unable to shake his hands off. Am I glad I survived? Yes, and I've done a lot to ensure that in the past. But I'm more than ready for some payback."

Marleen was frowning at me now as if she had a hard time reading me. Bucky's sister seemed intrigued—and much more inclined to believe me. "You'd really do that? Turn against your people?"

"It's debatable who my people really are," I ground out. "Much good it has done me, sticking with them. And yes, the offer to join you would have been much more interesting before your pet assassin there knifed me in the back."

Marleen's frown deepened. "It interests me how you survived that. I'm excellent at my job."

I couldn't help but snort. "Yes—when you have good intel. I hate to tell you this, but whoever gave you the file detailing my injuries gave you the wrong one. Emily Raynor's notes were fake. Richards can confirm this."

Eyes all over the room turning to him, Richards gave a curt nod. "What she says is true." He paused, and when he looked at Nate, a hint of a smirk appeared on his face that was so very unlike what I was used to from him—but what I had long since suspected he was capable of. "All of it. I couldn't in good conscience continue to stand idly by, watching you undermine such a brilliant woman. If Cortez hadn't stripped us of our weapons, I would have killed you in that cell and told your people that it was one of the guards during our escape." His attention then went to Marleen. "If you'd told me earlier who you really were working for, we could have ended this shit right at the camp, or at the very least in Dallas."

Marleen's shrug in return was unperturbed. "I have trust issues," was all she said.

In all that back and forth, I went to check back with Gita—three minutes. My stomach seized up with a bout of anxiety, which made me slow to pick up the slack—which gave Nate the perfect reason to reinsert himself into the conversation. Rounding on me, he gave a good impression of a seething grizzly about to maul me.

"You fucking traitorous cunt!" he pressed out between gritted teeth—and honestly, I had a hard time telling whether he meant it or not. "Everything I did for you! Several of my men died because you were such a bumbling idiot in the beginning. Because of you I went to war against my best friend! And this is how you repay me?"

The nasty voice at the back of my mind was quick to inform me that, while not completely true, what he said must have crossed his mind at least once in the past for him to sound so fucking honest and personally insulted now. Like nothing else, that kicked the hinges off the gate behind which my rage hid, coming roaring to the forefront within seconds now.

"Yes! And I should have done so years ago! Don't you dare talk to me about sacrifices! What did you lose, huh? Men die. That's the reality of war. And you can ask any one of them—I never got anyone personally killed. But me? I lost my fucking child! My entire identity got annihilated when that bitch up in her ice fortress cut off half of my fingers! I almost died twice—three times if I count you strangling me!—and you had nothing whatsoever to do with my survival. Did you ever ask me if I wanted to betray the company I'd worked for, or my principles? If you'd told me what fucked-up shit your brother had been working on, I would never have tried to help you, not breathed a single word of anything. And whose idea was it to drag me off into the wilderness instead of letting me go with the other scientists? I should have been leading that lab in Aurora, and if I'd gotten a chance to work with Walter Greene, I would have perfected that serum within months, rather than them bumbling around in the dark for years. And I would have loved to personally inject you with the first dose of it and watch the light go out in your eyes, to be sure that you'd never drag me to hell again. You know the best part? Richards didn't need to do anything remarkable to seduce me. All he needed was to act like a normal human being, who doesn't slam my face into marble floors to break my nose and then threaten me with more violence if I didn't help him. All it took was for him to be nice. Now choke on that, you rat bastard!"

Yeah, maybe we'd need the couples therapy that Richards had joked about what seemed like a million years ago now—but it felt kind of good to fling all those half-truths and misinterpretations into Nate's face—and see him get angry for real in return.

It was impossible to gauge how much time we still had left, and if I was honest, I didn't dare look away from Nate right now. I wasn't afraid he'd lose control, but I would have been lying if I'd said I wasn't intimidated by him.

"We're fucking done," he ground out, eyes narrowed. "You're a useless piece of trash that I should have discarded years ago. You'll fit right in with the other garbage here. Washed-up wannabes, has-beens, and never-will-bes—that's your crowd all right."

"You'd know," I hissed back. "Because that's exactly what you are. I fucking hate you!"

Behind Nate's shoulder, I saw Hamilton smirk at me—until I realized, it wasn't one of his usual grimaces. He was silently voicing something to me—"Shout." I couldn't be sure, but that was the closest I got in the moment I had time to focus on him. He then stuck out his tongue and rolled his eyes upward, completely confusing me. What the—never mind.

Nate blew me a kiss, and for a fraction of a second, a real smile was peeking through the smirk soon taking over his expression—and then the lights went out, casting us into complete darkness.

Chapter 23

Silence fell, and I suddenly had an idea what Hamilton's clue could have been about—and really, if I was wrong, I likely had less than five seconds to regret it. Inhaling deeply, I did my very best to put every ounce of authority into my voice as I shouted, "Soldiers! Stand down and drop your weapons!" I had no fucking clue if this might work, but their leader and chief of security were women, and back at the Canada base, when Hamilton had shot Nate up with the mind-control shit, he hadn't responded to my pleas—but he'd done exactly what years of training had ingrained as his default program: to follow orders by his superior officers.

But, just to be sure, I threw myself on the ground, hoping that I'd be fast enough not to remain standing there by the time the first shot was fired.

Light blinded me—followed by the boom of a weapon discharging, hellishly loud inside the relatively small room—coming from in front, then somewhere above me where Marleen must have instinctively fired at where she'd last seen me. Before I could think about how to react, I was pelted with assault rifles dropping from drone hands, my plan working better than I could have hoped for. At least I had choices. Before I could grab a single one and fiddle with it to point it in the right direction, shots went off all around me when the soldiers not affected by the faulty serum opened fire, making me hunch in on myself instinctively. Through my arms that were still coming up, illuminated by the muzzle flashes, I saw a dark silhouette vault forward, toward the dais—Nate. The impulse was there to remain still and watch, but I knew that if I wanted to survive, I needed to do something—and if I wanted to keep him alive, that meant to go into offense. Getting a good grip on the rifle close to me while letting my body roll fully onto my back, I opened up fire, blindly, at the soldiers on my side of the room, trusting that Hamilton would do the same on the other. Considering their overwhelming numbers, it would have been harder to miss than hit anyone.

That went well for about three seconds. Then they started shooting back.

I couldn't tell how many soldiers I'd hit—and how many of them were dead—but there was a body slumped on the floor next to me, so I did my best to roll over and behind it, using it for cover. I had a moment to try to orient myself. Then a small, light body descended on me—Marleen. One of her knees landed in the pit of my stomach—what was it with this woman and the softer parts of my torso?—and as soon as she'd regained her balance, she brought her elbow down toward my face. Thank fuck I had an assault rifle of unknown make to ram up and between us, using it like an unwieldy club. Something connected—her shoulder, maybe?—and I felt her rear back. Twisting, I managed to dislodge her from me, giving me the chance to come staggering to my feet—only to feel a random spray of bullets pass by and chew into the wall next to me, the chunks of concrete and insulation hitting my side and shoulder. The rifle was gone but there was another one right by my left foot, so I hunched down to grab it.

Someone—way more substantial than Marleen—barreled into me and took me down. I tried to push the body off me but since it was trying to get away from something, that didn't quite work. Then it went still, rocking as more bullets bit into it. I tried to shove it off, but it was—literally—dead weight... only to reanimate moments later. Shit!

The only warning I got was a growl before teeth bit into my unprotected lower left arm, right down to the bone. I screamed—which I myself didn't really hear over all the shots going off—and blindly punched with my other fist in the direction of the pain radiating from my arm. The pain increased, pushing away panic and confusion, letting the rage deep inside of me take over. Twisting, I managed to grab a chunk of hair belonging to the biter, and kicked with my right leg, hitting it square in the face—and a second time when the first didn't quite do the trick to dislodge it. I was sure that it managed to take a chunk out of my arm but at least I got free of it. Blindly grabbing for the next available weapon, my fingers closed around something smaller—a handgun, either from Marleen or one of the soldiers, I didn't give a fuck. I aimed at where I heard my attacker growl, getting ready for another pounce, and pulled the trigger twice. There was resistance the first time, making me guess the gun had a safety trigger. On the second pull, it shot all right, hitting the fresh zombie square in the face. While the afterimages of the muzzle flash were still seared into my retinas, I fired twice more, and the damn thing dropped onto my legs, dead for good. Rolling up into a crouch over my left shoulder, I tried to orient myself—

which was pretty much impossible. A high-pitched scream rang out somewhere to my left—Gita. I saw her cowering in the corner, a large form looming over her—Richards. It took a few muzzle flashes for me to make out that he was trying to shield her with his body—that couldn't be a good idea.

Before I could react—not much that I could do from across the room, half-blind in the dark—I felt something move close to me. Letting instinct take over, I twisted, shooting before I even had something to aim at. It was probably stupid, with likely less than ten bullets left in the magazine, but I didn't care. I wasn't sure if I hit anything, but not getting grabbed or kicked felt like a triumph. Then my wrist hit something hard—the wall. Easing up on the trigger, I pushed myself onto my feet, standing up, hoping that against the wall I wouldn't get shot immediately. With crying, screaming, grunting, moaning, and still more shooting going on all around, it was impossible to orient myself well.

Then I saw her, crouching in front of me, still staring at where I had just been. Not hesitating for a moment, I brought the gun down and pulled the trigger. At the last moment, Marleen suddenly moved as if to get up, so what was supposed to be a perfect head shot hit her in the shoulder and chest instead. The gun clicked empty as she screamed, but that only sounded like an invitation to me. With a primal shout, I launched myself at her, my shoulder hitting her fresh wound. Marleen dropped onto her back, gasping—which soon turned into a bloody gurgle as I pistol-whipped her with as much force as I could. That wasn't enough, but there was another discarded rifle on the floor, which I grabbed, and using the stock now and much more momentum, drove it into the bloody ruin that used to be her face, over and over again. I felt her try to shake me off once but then she went still, and I likely wouldn't have stopped smashing the rifle stock into her until it met concrete if a stray bullet hadn't burned its way across my already bleeding arm, distracting me.

Right. My job here wasn't done yet.

I tried to get a better look at the situation. A lot of bodies were on the floor, most of them still with only a few writhing in their death throes. The problem was, the drones had been easiest to hit since they hadn't made a move to defend themselves after they had dropped their guns—at least those that had done that and hadn't started to shoot. Unlike the other soldiers—who stayed down—they were starting to reanimate, at an alarming rate. The blood saturating the air made most of them fall on the next best body to gnaw on, but a few were looking around for other targets. Glancing at the dais, I realized that there was a commotion going on, at least ten of the soldiers involved. Nate, if I had to take a guess, so I couldn't exactly fire at them. Richards was still busy trying to keep Gita safe in the corner, and as I kept scanning the crowd, I saw Hamilton drag himself out from under two dead bodies, aiming for the next freshly-turned shambler coming for him.

I had no intention of saving him, but every zombie that stayed down was one less hazard for all of us, so it only made sense that I went to help him.

Not bothering with checking the ammo of the rifle, I brought it to my shoulder and aimed three shots at where I'd last seen the shambler come for Hamilton. In the bright flashes I produced myself, I saw that I had to course-correct, but the last one hit it in the back of the head, bringing it down. Immediately, I aimed away from Hamilton and for the next moving target, and then the next. Something roared way too close to my face on my side of the room so I quickly dropped to one knee and shot an entire salvo blindly, seeing the outline of a shambler jerk as it fell. Two more shots and the magazine was empty. I was kneeling right next to one of the dead soldiers so I blindly groped at him with one hand, elated to find a fresh magazine quickly. Hamilton had started shooting in the meantime, killing the last two standing soldiers in the half of the room with the door. I saw three more shamblers move so I hosed down the general area, hearing their grunts and moans die.

Looking back toward the dais, I saw that the knot was starting to loosen up, thanks to Richards—having grabbed a discarded assault rifle himself—aiming what I hoped were precise shots into the fray. Two more soldiers died, but a third realized where the shots were coming from and brought his rifle around. I was already moving, pivoting myself, a scream of warning on my lips—but I was too late. No more muzzle flashes came from the corner, Richards likely having run out of ammo himself—and then the soldier shot, two bursts of full-auto salvos going off. It was too dark in the corner to see, but I heard the impact of bullets on flesh, with a wet gurgling sound underneath that must have been his dying breath. My own scream finally made it over my lips, my rifle spitting death, chewing through the soldier and his comrade beside him, dropping them to the ground seconds too late.

Then it was silent for a moment, all weapons spent or people reloading. That made it easier to hear the motion of several bodies dragging themselves across the floor, and the sounds of chewing, swallowing, tearing…

Something hissed, and a second later, I had to whip my face away as light blinded me—someone must have found a lighter. Squinting, I realized that it was Hamilton, currently backing away from a dead body on the ground that he must have just set alight, first scortching part of its uniform to catch, then breaking the lighter over it to accelerate the rapid spread of the flames. Suddenly being able to see once more helped, and I quickly killed two more zombies that had gotten way too close to me for comfort, but were now staring, transfixed, into the flames. I didn't want to look, but I knew I had to, my attention drawn to the back corner of the room.

The entire front of Red's body was a mess, the bullets having shredded his torso and face. Horrible as that was, it didn't compare to how my stomach seized up when I realized that he was still moving. No, scratch that—moving again, and with Gita currently trying to squirm out from underneath and behind him, it was a very easy guess who he'd go for first.

"Hey, asshole!" I shouted, my heart seizing in my chest. "Why don't you take on someone a little more your size?"

Stepping over the dead in front of me, I advanced on him, sparing a momentary glance at the other end of the dais. Only three soldiers were left standing now, and I could see Nate throwing punches and kicks, trying to keep them too closely engaged to bring their weapons to bear. I didn't see Hamilton's sister but presumed that she must have been hiding somewhere around there, likely between the wall and the soldiers where Nate couldn't get to her—yet.

Disbanding all thought about them, I focused on Richards. He had Gita in what looked like a painful grasp but hadn't started chewing on her yet, instead staring at me. Fuck, but I hated seeing that all too familiar inhuman stare in his eyes, nobody home except rage and the need to feed. Even the drones looked more human than that. I knew what I had to do, but that didn't make it any easier. Exhaling slowly, I stopped so I could aim properly—and pulled the trigger. What was left of Richards's face turned into a ghastly ruin, leaving a spray of dark red on the wall behind.

Gita gave a choking sound as Red's body fell on her, making me curse under my breath. Before I could get there, Hamilton was already pulling her free, using brute strength I couldn't have mustered. He sent her stumbling toward the door, making sure she was out of the way. He and I stared at each other for a moment. There was no smirk on his blood-stained face now. I'd actually never seen his face that expressionless. Oh, he was still home—but he looked like he had nothing left to fight for. In a sense, I got that. And still, he moved toward the dais, getting ready to help Nate.

Nate must have seen us come to his aid—or it was sheer desperation that made him lash out, a series of kicks sending the soldiers staggering back, far enough so that we could shoot them without fear of hitting him. He was swaying, his bare arms and face stained with blood, and I realized he must have been stabbed or shot—or both—several times… and he was still standing.

Turning around slowly, he focused on the figure lying prone on the dais. She was still alive; still moving, actually, trying to crawl away from him even though there was nowhere she could have hidden anymore. Nate was on her in a second, using his weight to pin her to the ground. I expected him to punch her now, to let off steam, but instead, his hands closed around her throat, choking her. Her body started to convulse, her heels drumming uselessly on the floor, her hands first trying to claw at his face but—like me—she couldn't reach it, so she tried to pry off his fingers. He kept crouching there, unmoving, staring down at her.

"I'm so fucking sorry for everything that happened to you," I heard him whisper, his voice raw with guilt and utterly lacking anger. "It should never have come to this. And I'm sorry that I never tried to reach out to you later. Never tried to ask you if there was anything I could do to help you deal with the shit that you never deserved. Maybe if I had, it would never have come to this." He paused, likely to swallow.

Her mouth was open as if to scream as she continued to gasp for air, but it was obvious that she wasn't getting any. Her motions were already turning sluggish, even less effective than before.

When he continued, Nate's rasp was still gentle, but the emotion was leaking out of it now. "But none of that gave you any right to do the fucked-up shit that you did. I could see past you killing my brother, although that's already pushing it. But everything you did after that? Trying to kill thousands of soldiers who had done nothing to deserve it, just to wipe out a few assholes who did? Adding billions of innocent civilians to that? And then continuing with those that survived? Where's the reasoning in that? None of them had anything to do with you. And all of them deserved so much better." He swallowed again, and now there was anger—only a tendril at first, but quickly growing stronger. Judging from how the muscles in his arms bulged, he was squeezing her throat harder, probably already having broken her hyoid bone. "You killed my friends. My wife, twice, if she wasn't so damn hard to kill and even less likely to give up and stop fighting. And trust me when I say I am not a man who subscribes to any 'turn the other cheek' mentality—so this is also for what you did to me! You did not deserve to get raped, but you absolutely deserve to die. And I'm fucking glad that it's at my hands, and my face is the last fucking thing you see!"

He fell silent then but remained like that for another minute—well past when her body stopped moving and then went utterly slack. I doubted she'd been able to process even half of what he'd growled in her face, but that was okay. It wasn't really for her benefit, but for his.

And then it was over. Technically, we'd won—but I'd seldom felt this empty inside.

A creak sounded behind us, making Hamilton and me whip around and Gita shy back from where she was leaning against the wall, close to the door. The door had swung open, and illuminated by red emergency lights outside and several beams of flashlights, a woman stood, silhouetted against the backdrop of several confused-looking civilians in plain clothes, likely admin staff. The fire from the burning body on the floor cast shadows into her face as she took one more step forward, but paused before the blood on the floor could reach her sensible, cream-colored pumps. Her silvery-white hair was gathered in an elegant twist at the back of her head, and she was wearing light but tasteful makeup, the kind that cost a fortune and took hours to apply. Her dress was conservative yet stylish, a scarf casually thrown over her shoulders. She must have been in her sixties, maybe early seventies, but still very spry for her age. She surveyed the scene with a casual calm that belied her obvious civilian status, and she barely more than glanced at Gita, Hamilton, and me, ignoring the weapons now trained at her. Her focus was drawn to Nate, who was still crouching over the dead woman's body, his hands still around her neck, squinting into the light and looking very much like the monster he so loved to call himself. I could see liquid glisten against his side and leg where he was still bleeding, but he didn't seem to care about that.

The elder woman cleared her throat once she was done with her assessment of the situation. "Took you long enough," she said in a clear clip, not a trace of horror in her tone. If anything, she sounded annoyed. "I expected you to take care of this years ago. One might go so far as to say I had almost given up hope that you would. A shame, really. So much time wasted sitting on your hands idly, rather than doing what is important."

"Are you done?" Nate ground out, somewhere between a rasp and a shout. What her voice was lacking in fear, his was filled with anger.

Unperturbed by his outburst, the woman inclined her head. "Obviously, there is no sense in berating you about your tardiness. It just had to be said. I'm sure you knew it already."

I almost expected him to bark the question at her as to why she'd said it. Instead, he let go and came to his feet in one fluid motion, but then almost staggered off the dais, pain catching up to him. Yet he remained standing, refusing to clutch any of his wounds as he kept staring at her, slowly coming to stand between me and Hamilton once more. I didn't know what to do with my rifle, yet was reluctant when Nate signaled me to lower it. We'd seen plenty of soldiers outside, and I was sure that many more were on the way from wherever they had their barracks.

The woman noticed, although she seemed to focus more on my face now than Nate's gesture. "Oh, there's no need to shoot anyone else," she assured me, sounding like she meant it. Actually, as if it was a ridiculous concept. "There's no one left standing who would dare lift a finger against you. You can go now." She paused, switching from talking to all of us to Nate specifically again. "Or, you could stay. We easily have room for a handful more people. And since you killed our beloved queen, the people need a new leader." There was sarcasm in her voice, stating plainly that she wouldn't spill a single tear. Interesting... but also so very confusing.

Not so much for Nate, it seemed. "Fuck, no," he uttered. "You can all go to hell in your arc here."

She shrugged, as if it was all the same to her. "Then please close the door on your way out. We wouldn't want to catch a cold in the draft."

Nate glared at her some more, then looked at me, then over to Gita and Hamilton, and then paused. Feeling my heart seize up, I nodded toward the corner, where most of Richards's body lay. Nate's face froze for a moment—in grief and regret, I realized—before he jerked his chin at the body. Hamilton finally lowered his rifle—yet kept it slung over his shoulder—and the two of them went to fetch the body, dragging it between them. I watched them pass by me, then went over to Gita, offering her a supporting arm under her shoulder when I realized it wasn't just shock that kept her rooted in the spot. She was bleeding from a wound in her thigh, but it wasn't life-threatening from what I could tell, just a hell of a painful nuisance.

The woman stepped out of their way as Nate and Hamilton reached the door, yet Nate lingered right in front of her for a second. "Why are you here? I guess I was kind of hoping for it, seeing as you were helping Decker, but—"

She shushed him with a surprisingly gentle sound. "Oh, don't be ridiculous. You know that it makes sense that she tracked me down soon after she killed him, and not just because she likely found our correspondence. She wanted to use me against you, of course. She was pretending to be diplomatic, so I turned the tables on her and accepted her offer to help her. It was too late to warn you, and she didn't give me a chance to contact you once she'd stashed me here. And then there were no phone lines operational anymore, with that nasty apocalypse business. People were disturbed about what was going on, and I very quickly made myself indispensable so she couldn't kill me on the spot. As they say, the rest is history."

Nate remained mute, staring at her as if he was waiting for more. She just looked back, then readjusted her scarf and walked away, the clack of her heels quickly disappearing in the distance. Giving himself a visible shake—that I very much empathized with—Nate started walking again, Hamilton quickly following along.

As we passed, the staff with their flashlights backed away, giving us as wide a berth as they could manage. As soon as we reached the first staircase, we saw a few soldiers standing around, but none of them raised a weapon. In fact, they were very quick to keep their hands where we could see them, turning to equally silent bystanders. From the gallery, I saw the rich and powerful below huddled together in clusters around light sources, murmurs and the odd confused shout ringing out. Faintly, I could hear a man in a trembling voice explain something about a temporary power outage, and that a maintenance crew had already been sent to restart the generators. Everybody, please stay calm.

Fuck calm.

When we reached the long corridor leading to the elevator, we found it as empty as the reception desk we'd just passed. Our jackets were still waiting for us. I grabbed them, not wanting to add to the guys' burden. The elevator was out of commission, frozen here on the lower floor, but there was a door next to it with a staircase behind. It took us several laborious minutes to make it to the top, Nate needing to stop several times but refusing to let Hamilton carry the body alone. I couldn't help but draw what felt like my first unencumbered breath as Hamilton pulled the door of the shed open, warm evening air blasting in our faces. I trotted on for a few more steps before I let Gita slide from my grasp, with her ending up sitting in the grass. Hamilton dumped the body next to her before he turned to Nate.

"Did I get that last part right? She told us to nuke the fucking exit?"

Nate gave the smallest nod possible.

"How the fuck did she know we had the nukes?" Hamilton asked.

He got a slight shrug for his trouble. "No fucking clue. She might not even have known. She probably assumed we wouldn't come here without carrying our weight in explosives."

I waited for anyone to speak up, but all Hamilton did was eye the shed as if to consider whether he should go inside or behind it to drop his pants. At least he was considerate enough that I didn't need to see his junk again. The day had been bad enough as it was.

"What about the radiation?" I asked when nobody said anything. "Not sure how I feel about giving all those assholes cancer."

Nate gave me a look that said plainly that he had no fucks left to give. "They won't be stupid enough to check on the caved-in elevator without taking a Geiger counter along," he finally said. "They built this bunker to withstand a nuclear war. And if they are? Not my problem."

We ended up doing the nuke removal behind the shed, taking turns—and no, this time I didn't refuse Nate's offer for help. My hands were shaking with more than just exhaustion, and I figured that was the least he could do, considering this had been his idea. We ended up letting Gita cut the triggers out of our palms, with her glaring at us balefully, which all three of us ignored. Nate taped them to the—thankfully still intact—tubes, and then dropped all four into the empty elevator shaft. I cringed as I heard them clank down the walls and land on the elevator cabin, but no explosion followed, so I figured, we'd jumped off that sinking ship alive. Twenty minutes to go.

Just as we reached the Rover—still dragging Red's body along with us, but Gita now managing on her own—a convoy of cars came racing along the trail we'd followed here, the Ice Queen jumping out of the Jeep before it had come to a halt. I remained standing where I was as someone pulled the rifle from my hands and exchanged it for a bottle of water, telling me to drink. It was only when Martinez started to prod me that I realized my arm was in worse shape than I'd thought, but at least the wound wasn't beyond what could be sewn back together. It would go well with the scars on my hip—for what little time I had left to enjoy them.

I saw Cole sauntering over to Gita once Sonia let her get up, a bandage on her leg wound. A look from me was all he needed, declaring with a grin, "I presume the trick with the lights-out worked?

I'd love to claim that one for me, but all I needed to do was connect my laptop to their central power grid and enter the password she left for me. Damn fine work." The last was obviously meant for Gita, who even managed a bright smile in return.

"I knew you'd figure it out," she offered.

"Please. That was child's play compared to France. You wound me."

They continued to joke for a little longer. I ignored them, instead watching as Burns and Pia were both working on cutting Nate's clothes off him so they could get to digging out the bullets. "Uh, shouldn't we, I don't know, leave?" I suggested. "There's a nuke going off in less than five minutes."

Concerned looks turned to me—and just as I opened my mouth to explain, I felt a dull thud underneath me. Oops. So much for keeping track of time. Pia's more than slightly concerned look zoomed to Nate but he shook his head. "Airlock on the shed door is tight," he said. "And I'm sure that now it's locked forever. But yeah, maybe we shouldn't linger."

"Where to?"

It was a valid question that the Ice Queen posed, but none I could answer. We all stared at each other, or mostly the rest of us stared at Nate, who continued to just stand there and bleed.

Gita cleared her throat, looking slightly off. "Aren't you going to Canada now?"

I couldn't quite quell the irritation in my tone. "Why the fuck would we go to Canada?"

"Emily Raynor's base," she offered, then trailed off, confusion slowly morphing into realization. "Fuck, you don't know."

"Don't know what?" I asked. "There's no cure. We know that."

Gita started to laugh, but cut herself off when I must have glared too hard. "No, she doesn't have a cure for the zombie virus, or for the braindead scavengers. But she's found a way to stop the deterioration, as she calls it." A snort followed. "She thinks it's not enough because she's a perfectionist and this is not a perfect solution, but not turning into a walking menace was more than enough for me."

It took me a moment to puzzle out what she was saying. "You already got it?"

Gita nodded with a grin. "Before I let myself be found and brought here. We debated whether that was smart, but since I can't fight for shit, I figured that if I died, at least I wouldn't turn into a nuisance. I still can't catch the virus anymore since it's inactive all over my body, but it can't activate, even if I catch it anew. Ask her about the details. She told me twice but it went way over my head." She offered me another grin. "You'd understand. It might even be something from your notes. She kept muttering about them even two years after she got them. I think she's jealous of your brain. She really doesn't handle the fact well that you're smarter than she is."

That... was about the last thing on my mind right now. I found myself staring at Nate just as he was staring at me, a flicker of hope starting up in my chest.

A second later, he was already rounding on Pia. "Plot us a course to Esterhazy, Saskatchewan. You can sew me up later when we camp for the night."

And, just like that, we were off, desperate to leave not just this place but all our troubles behind.

Chapter 24

We ended up driving well into the night, silently agreeing that it simply made the most sense to camp in the same spot as yesterday, even if that meant we only got there as the sky was already starting to brighten, and I was getting seriously concerned about both the Rover's batteries, and the way the entire car was reeking of blood. Nate had refused to waste any time on getting patched up, which was fine with me at the time, but damn, it would take a long while to get those stains out of his seat.

Wound cleaning and sewing had to wait another hour while we established our camp, and Burns and Hill took turns digging a deep-enough hole so we could bury Richards. We all just stood there, silent, bleary-eyed, and swaying with exhaustion, nobody in the right mind to find words that could only be wrong. Gita had filled us in on the few gaps that still existed—that I had been right in guessing that Marleen forced Richards to come along and he reasoned he might be more use to us as accidental infiltrator than dead. From the first day he got there, the two of them had been working together, him mostly standing watch or running interference so she could sneak off and hack into the bunker grid. How Gita had ended up there included a little more subterfuge. Gabriel Greene hadn't been lying, exactly, but had actually not quite known where she'd been at the time I had turned back up in California. Nobody had known, except for Emily Raynor and a few of her staff, it turned out. After returning to New Angeles when Burns dropped her off there after France, Gita had soon gotten approached by an interested party, as she put it—one of the many spies reporting back to the doomsday bunker. She'd resisted for a while, then hitched a ride back to Canada when Raynor contacted her about what she hoped might be a solution for the serum issues. Gita had agreed to play guinea pig; the reason behind her being ideal was that she had received what was very close to a perfect version of the serum when I'd shot her up with it in France, trying to keep the infection she'd caught at bay, but hadn't been inoculated for more than a year. It grated on my nerves to have to realize that several people could have been saved from instant conversion for months already, but doubted any of us would have gone for it before the danger that we thought had been Decker was dealt with. The Ice Queen herself was quick to voice that—and include that Andrej would have agreed.

The sun was casting its first rays on the lake as we crawled back into the Rover, the solar panels set up to charge the battery while we slept—or dozed, or simply stared at the roof of the car, trying not to move to keep pain at a minimum. We were well into the second hour of doing that when Nate uttered a low groan before he grabbed me and pulled me close, giving me a somewhat awkward kiss over my shoulder before folding his body around mine, one hand splayed in an almost possessive gesture over my lower stomach. I couldn't help but smile as I nestled against him, twining my fingers with his. Neither of us said anything, but then nothing needed to be said. We were both still standing—and nothing else mattered.

We were well into the second hour of driving the following day—after checking all wounds again, and Martinez chewing us out for having bullets lodged in body parts that should have needed to be dug out the night before already—when I finally asked the one question I still had no answer to. "Who was that woman? I know you must have met before, judging how familiar you both were with each other."

Nate grimaced, spending a good ten seconds staring at the road in front of us before he answered. "That was my mother."

I almost slammed my foot down on the brakes, which might have been smart since I had to swerve hard not to crash into the next tree. "Your what?!"

He looked faintly amused as he cast me a sidelong glance. "My mother," he repeated. "Contrary to what you may sometimes fling in my face, I didn't hatch from an egg, or crawl out of some primordial slime."

My mind was still reeling, incapable of processing this. "But—"

When nothing more made it over my lips, he finished the question for me. "Why didn't we take her along? She chose to stay. Don't ask me why. Since she didn't offer an explanation, she wanted her reasoning to remain her own. I think she was too proud to admit that she was scared of roughing it out on the road. Much more likely, she found the idea of observing the end of what we once called civilization from a seat in the first row appealing. I've long ago given up trying to make sense of her. If you think I'm hard to read sometimes, I have nothing on her."

My mind still refused to catch up with that. "Why didn't you tell me? I could have at least, I don't know. Said hi."

His smile turned wry. "I'm sure she knew exactly who you are. If she'd wanted to talk to you, she would have said something. Don't tell me you're eager to get her approval. Trust me, that's not a journey you want to embark on. I didn't so much give up as accept defeat." And still, he was smiling, as if his mind was filled with fond memories.

"What was that part about her working with Decker?" I hadn't missed that, either.

Nate's smile dipped a little but didn't disappear. "She was consulting with him on how to handle me." He looked at me again, that smile turning into a smirk, likely at the look of horror on my face. "It's a long story."

"Well, we have a long ride in front of us. And if what Raynor cooked up actually works, much more time after that, as well."

"I'll tell you one day," he promised. "Maybe."

"For sure."

He shrugged, which, knowing him, was not a "yes." I gritted my teeth and started coming up with plans for how I could force him to tell me—but then dropped the point. If he wanted to share with me, he would. If not? Then I would hopefully live a very long life, constantly wondering, but ultimately feeling like it didn't matter. Somewhere along the way, I'd learned to let things go... and I had zero intention to go back on that. Sometimes, it just wasn't worth it.

We ran into minimal obstacles on our way northwest into Canada, trying very hard to fly under the radar. Of course we could have swung by Dispatch, if only to let Rita know that we'd taken care of things. We did plug one of our radios in for an hour to sign back in with our people in Utah and California, if only to let them know that we were still alive, and intending to stay that way for as long as possible. Most of the detours required were because of ruined roads and bridges, and the odd shamblers to dispose of. We let the scavengers do most of that since they felt short-changed, not having gotten to kill anyone at the doomsday bunker.

I was still musing about how weird it was that they'd simply escorted us in and then let us walk out again, when Nate finally deigned to offer up his opinion on that.

"She may have been good about hatching out revenge plans that ultimately drove her insane, but the rest? Random acts of anarchy that kept spiraling out of her control, and none of that was her doing. She had been lucky to have found extremely competent henchmen. She didn't plot the apocalypse, she bumbled into it. I didn't see the blueprints, but the only reason that bunker wasn't busted was because nobody knew about it who wasn't invested in keeping it going. If we'd had to break in, we could likely have managed within a week." When I just stared at him, he shrugged. "I'm not going to say it's a scam, but whoever built it paid a lot of attention to turning it into a luxury resort, and little to setting it up as a permanent solution for survival. Maybe they'll hold out for another five years. Maybe they have already suffocated. I don't care. As far as I'm concerned, I'm trying very hard to forget it ever existed."

"What about the staff?" I asked. "Everyone who wasn't loaded and got their special VIP ticket, and who hasn't even fully realized that we've been bashing each others' heads in out here."

Nate seemed unperturbed by my concern. "They had several years to make contact with anyone on the outside. They chose to stay in their cozy hideout. Let them rot with the rest."

"You are mighty cheerful, even for you," I remarked—kind of agreeing with him. Yeah, maybe that made us both assholes, but really, we'd bled enough for this country. And what for?

Nate gave me a fake grin that made me roll my eyes at him. "Better?"

"Forget I said anything," I shot back... and couldn't help but smile. In a sense, life was better. And maybe with enough time passing, it would one day feel good again when that pervasive sense of it all having been for naught would recede into the very back of my mind where I could ignore it forever.

We finally reached the Canadian base a week after burying Richards by the lake. Nothing looked familiar until we reached the gate where, a long time ago, I'd barely been able to stand on my own and was spitting up blood. Finding everything not covered in several feet of snow did make a difference. The fact that I'd been hallucinating and not really able to think straight anymore didn't help, either. I felt a lot less desperate as I sauntered up to the camera above the gate, waved, and told Emily Raynor to get her British-bitch ass out here, stat. Nate was running out of jerky and I was certainly at the end of my patience. I doubted much about either would change, but it was worth a shot.

It took a good hour of soldiers coming, soldiers leaving again after getting yelled at, more soldiers coming with backup and two tanks, Hamilton getting involved in the yelling as well, and us pretty much threatening to go nuclear on their asses if they didn't send their queen in a white lab coat out here. Then we had to wait another twenty minutes since it took a while for her to get all her gear since we refused to enter the base proper. It was hilarious to watch the procession of five scientists and nurses, looking around them, frightened out of their wits, just because they were walking around topside, with the local soldiers stationed here having made sure that no undead lurked in a thirty-mile radius—and I was sure that all of the scientists were inoculated with the serum to start with. Us they didn't seem to be very afraid of, which just underlined, yet again, that wisdom and intelligence had few things in common.

I was surprised that Emily Raynor did seem to have a touch of compassion and common sense since she went so far as to hug Gita—which weirded me out on so many levels—and seemed to at least try to appear courteous when she stepped up to Nate and me. Curiosity was burning in her eyes, and I knew we were maybe three sentences away from dropping terms like "mystery meat" and "questionable origin." My resentment toward her was bordering on physical, although I was the first to admit that I owed her my life—and soon would again, for the second time. I knew that a lot of it was because, in a sense, I blamed her for all the things I'd lost on that operating room table, since it was easier than being grateful for what I'd gained. I also felt like punching her in the throat for temporarily sterilizing me with that IUD she had planted inside of me, but there was that whole matter with her switching up her notes, which was the only reason why Marleen hadn't ended up killing me. I was more than ready to consider us even if whatever she had come up with worked.

"I presume you have so many questions—" she started to say but I cut her off right there.

"Is it working? That's all I care about."

She frowned, as if my brash demeanor had insulted her, but I figured it was simply her not understanding how I couldn't be burning with curiosity.

"Yes, it is working," she offered. "To a point. Your notes have helped me solve that riddle. But I'm still working on expanding that research with what you shared from the laboratory in Dallas and the compounds that—"

This time it wasn't me who cut her off but the low-level growl that came from Nate, making it very clear that neither of us was interested in getting yet another reminder of what had transpired.

"We don't need you to reverse all the effects of the serum," I pointed out. "All we want is to not die. It's not too much to ask, right?"

Surprisingly, she was quick to incline her head. "Very well. But I have to warn you. We haven't had the time nor opportunity to thoroughly test this. There is still a chance that the injection can make you convert instantly."

"All the better we do this out here then," I pointed out. "Promise we'll take care of putting anyone down who happens to go full-on zombie on you." A few of the scavengers found that incredibly funny.

Raynor didn't look very impressed but was ready to move on. "Good. Then, if you would please let us take a blood sample pre- and post-injection. Fifteen minutes of waiting should be fine."

I didn't need Nate's sidelong glance to stiffen and immediately shake my head. "Fuck, no. You've already collected more than enough data from me, for several lifetimes. All you get is the outside observation of how many of us instantly convert. You don't need more."

She looked ready to protest, but then her expression went blank, followed by a look of surprise. "You're pregnant again," she muttered. "That's why you won't let me draw your blood. You're afraid that will somehow change our minds and not let you walk away from here."

I hated being that transparent, but at least I had a good answer to the last part. "Oh, I am walking away from here, and don't even think for a moment that you—or anyone else here—will stop me." And I really didn't mind having Nate right next to me, in his growling, hulking glory. I knew that he was laying it on thick, but that didn't take away from my diabolical glee.

Raynor looked as if she'd bitten into a particularly sour lemon but then motioned for one of her underlings to hand her gloves. "As you wish. I cannot predict how the antagonist will affect the fetus, but it should be fine. The mechanism is dialed to interact with the activator which keeps pushing the serum—which should be inert—toward conversion, and it stands to reason that…"

Giving up on shutting her up, I let her drone on as she swabbed the crease of my left elbow with alcohol, and without missing a beat, injected me with what looked like the most inconspicuous liquid ever. I hardly felt the needle prick my skin, and there was no burning sensation or anything. I'd gotten flu shots that had been more painful. There still was a latent sense of unease in my stomach, but I didn't feel much different immediately after the injection, and also not at the fifteen-minute mark when Raynor was done with the last of the scavengers, leaving only Hamilton, Cole, and Hill.

I was surprised to see all three of them refuse the shot, but maybe shouldn't have been.

Cole turned to me, grinning. "I'm not quite done playing superhero just yet. If anything changes, we know where to go. Until then, I don't mind playing Russian Roulette a little longer." He cast a sidelong glance at Hill, including him in his next statement. "It's been less than five years since we got inoculated. We're showing minimal signs, and likely have another five years to go, if not more." I gave him a shrug, letting him know I didn't really care either way. In fact, I was a little surprised they'd even come here with us.

Hamilton was a different topic altogether.

Since the bunker, he had been broody and quiet, which hadn't disturbed me in the least. It still wasn't exactly pleasant to have him along, but he was much easier to ignore now. What had changed, though, was how Nate was acting around him. I wasn't completely sure, but I would have been astonished if they'd exchanged more than ten words between them. I kind of understood why. Hamilton hadn't voiced a note of protest concerning why his sister had to die, but I likely wouldn't have wanted to chat with her murderer, either. As for Nate? He was squinting at Hamilton now as if he was considering what to do, and the hard set of his jaw didn't look like he was in favor of burying the hatchet.

Hamilton looked up, holding his gaze for a second before a wry twist came to his lips. "I guess this is goodbye."

Nate inclined his head, but it was a rather stiff nod. "If I ever see you again, I will tear you fucking limb from limb, and without hesitation. You know that's not an empty threat."

In the back, one of the scavengers gave a whoop. It stood to reason they were hoping for that death match to start any moment now. I was a little taken aback by the vehemence of Nate's promise, but also very pleased. Look at that, my husband finally—irrevocably—standing behind me... and just when I didn't feel the need for it anymore. Typical. So very much like him to make me give up my last hint of neediness before he turned a protective leaf.

Hamilton snorted and glanced over to me. I half expected to be called "diseased cunt" to my face one last time but all he did was nod before turning to Cole and Hill. "Mind if I hitch a ride with you for a while longer? I have a lot on my mind, and graveyard shifts are great for deep contemplation."

"We'd be honored to have you along," Hill enthused. I visibly shook myself, still not getting how they could remain loyal to him.

Cole noticed, laughing under his breath.

"Are you even still in the army? Won't they miss you?" I asked.

He shook his head. "We both got our discharge after dropping you off on the coast with your people, before coming along for the raid on the slaver camp. All of us who showed up there, actually. We'll let the others know about getting the shot, if they want it. Besides that, I presume they've split up by now, half of them slumming it in Dispatch, the others getting cozy at the Silo. Not sure where we'll end up. Not being chased around—or doing any chasing—sounds good for now." He held out his hand for me to shake. "If you ever need us, send word. If we feel like it, we might as well drop by." His eyes narrowed in Nate's direction. "The offer stands for you. Not him. You're hilarious to be around. He gets us killed. Just saying. Nothing personal, just an observation."

Shaking his hand—and trying hard not to wince as he got a really good squeeze in—I accepted his offer for what it was. Hill followed up with his own goodbye, and then the three of them were back in their Humvee, turning it back around the way we had come.

Nobody else made a move to drop away, and since the fifteen minutes had passed for Amos—having received the shot last—it was time to go.

I hadn't really planned on saying something, but as I watched Raynor put away her things, I felt the need to speak up. "I'm sorry about Richards. He was a friend to me, and a valuable ally. But I know he meant way more to you. I'm sorry for your loss."

I hadn't expected her to ask many questions, but the look of dejection on her face spoke volumes. That she already knew about his demise—and not just from his absence here—also told me a thing or two. "He was a good man," she finally said. "If one with a few too many secrets. I warned him that this would be the death of him. I've never hated being right more."

I waited for more to come, but she turned away, fussing over something that didn't need fussing over. Her obvious dismissal hurt, but maybe shouldn't have. We all dealt with our personal grief in different ways. Before I could come up with something snarky to insult Raynor with, Gita suddenly spoke up, looking mighty guilty. "Do you mind if I stay here?" she asked me of all people. When she caught my frown, she shrugged. "I made some friends while I was up here. And they are one of the last places on earth with a satellite connection, computers, and what remains of the internet."

"What about New Angeles?" I asked.

She shrugged. "It hasn't felt like home since Tanner is gone. And I have all their remote access codes. Plus, it's too hot in the summer."

"And what about coming with us?"

She almost winced as she replied. "A little too cold, you know? And I'm really not sure about all the last-minute building you need to do. I'm not that much of a survivalist. But maybe I'll drop by in a year or two, once you've got everything set up and cozy. If you'll still have me, then."

No question about that. Even without her setting up the back door that had allowed us to survive—and told us about how to literally not die—she would always be welcome. I told her as much as I hugged her goodbye.

"I'll spread the news about the cure," she promised me as she stepped away. "Or anti-serum, or whatever it is. Not sure how many people are around who can benefit from it, but I'll make sure they know where to get it."

I nodded my thanks. I was glad that was out of my hands. "There are likely a few hundred infected scavengers still out and about. You may want to tell them to behave first," I suggested.

Gita allowed herself a smirk. "Don't worry. I'll make sure they know they need to play nice, at least for as long as they intend to stay here. I wouldn't be surprised if you set an example with dropping in on the fly."

"Good."

Then it was time to leave, and Emily Raynor one-upped my petty attempt to insult her by already having everything stashed away again and simply walking back onto the base proper without another word to me—or letting me get one in edgewise. I should have been glad, but of course that left me feeling slightly annoyed. I was sure she was counting on the fact that I would eventually get curious, and likely planned on selling me any information I wanted for blood samples of me—and my baby.

Well, hell would freeze over before I let that happen. If I'd proven one thing, then it was that I could be petty to my very last breath.

"No second thoughts?" I asked as I turned to Nate, already knowing his answer.

His lips curved into a smile, but rather than berate me, as usual, for asking questions like that in the first place, he leaned back, looking tired for a second—tired of the world. "I'm more than done playing the hero," he professed. "Or villain, or avenger, or whatnot. I don't think I've ever believed in the innate good in people, but if the past five years have taught me anything, it's that humans aren't built to follow grand ideals. We do much better if it's every dog out for his own good. I get it—when resources are tight, everyone is out for themselves only. I think it's about time that includes us, as well."

Wise words, although until recently, I would have debated them. Somehow, learning who had been behind it all—in a sense, because most of the shit we'd had to deal with was really consequence based on consequence based on random actions—had doused the flame of wanting to matter deep inside of me. Or maybe that was simply the first tendrils of my onsetting nesting urge. I'd given so much for this world—no, we all had given so much; it was time we let people fuck up their own lives.

Turning from scrutinizing the base one last time to Nate, I couldn't help but smile brightly at him. "Ready?"

"Ready!" he called to the others, shooing the lot of them back to the cars.

Climbing into the Rover, I made sure to run through my usual pre-check list before starting the engine. It still annoyed the living fuck out of me that it barely gave a whine, but I was slowly getting used to it. "To Alaska?"

"To Alaska," Nate confirmed.

And off into the sunset we drove.

Epilogue

As rumors went, the exodus of the group formerly known as the Lucky Thirteen was rife with them. Part of it was due to the reputation they had built. But more so, it was people's morbid curiosity that kept the gossip mills churning. Tales ran from their utter defeat and consequent annihilation to chosen exile right to plans to build up a new civilization in the far north of the continent. Little actual details were known, not even by those who had personally known them somewhere along their journey to notoriety. Fact was that way more people than the surviving seven members disappeared; several of the settlements along the West Coast in particular saw a few of their people leave over the last weeks of that summer. Some claimed it was just a few old friends and acquaintances, bringing a few provisions along. Others swore that entire trains of scavengers and traders loaded everything from basic survival gear to furniture onto trucks to make the long and dangerous journey north.

None of that mattered to the residents of the forests and tundras of Alaska. Life for them hadn't much changed over the past years, few enough people had died in the outbreak and barely a shambler making it that far north without becoming grizzly chow first. Theirs had always been a life of hardship and few luxuries, and they didn't much care about who was bashing in whose heads in the lower forty-nine states.

Some of them were surprised to, one morning, find a group of strangers at their doorstep, asking about where they might possibly find a place to settle down. More because he was a jerk than concerned with their business, Old Tom sent them to one of the logging camps near the Canadian border. He knew that the camp was infested, and even dropped a few hints about that. Stupid as outsiders were, they thanked him and went on their merry way to their death.

He almost swallowed the tobacco he'd been chewing for the past hour when, a week later, they were back, thanking everyone in town for the tip about the camp—which they'd cleaned out, as they explained. They'd even brought some things from the camp with them that they didn't need but might come in handy in town. They also asked about where best to hunt game, and some other things like when winter usually started, and how long until they would thaw out again. With the first flurries of snow already starting to chase across the frozen ground, Old Tom didn't give them much chance to survive.

He was happy to have been wrong when their new neighbors kept dropping in every few weeks, trading furs for tools and hammers, and where needed, know-how about how to keep things running up here throughout the cold seasons. They weren't all bad, for southerners. Better than most of the kids who had been working in the tourism industry most summers. They at least knew how to make themselves useful, and from what some of the younger men said who had dropped by to visit the camp a few times, they were hard-working people. Old Tom could respect that.

Of course, half of them would freeze to death or starve, and the rest would likely get picked off by wolves. They'd had quite some trouble with wolves in the winter. A shame, really, because they seemed hearty folks.

But they kept coming back, week after week. Some got sick; a few died from accidents, but with close to two hundred people, that was no rarity around here. They also sent people when the town needed help, like when one night, Marge Bugle's house caught on fire. They also had a doctor, and a nurse, although that young lady had a tongue on her to cure most mysterious illnesses before they had a chance to break out. They also had a handful of kids around, and one of their village council members was pregnant—a pesky woman, some of the younger men in town claimed, but only where she couldn't hear it. Old Tom quite liked her; she was a feisty one. Always quick to offer up a smile and greeting. Not many of the young people had proper manners to do that. Only sometimes, her light-blue eyes turned distant, but he'd seen that before, too. Old Tom had fought in 'Nam himself, and he knew not to ask questions when someone clearly didn't want to give you an answer. Like that husband of hers—but he didn't much come to town. Old Tom could understand that, too. Maybe come spring, he would go up into his attic and look if he still had some of the kids' toys around. Or maybe a blanket. She would smile at him, that fiery-haired spitfire of a woman. He'd very much like that.

A FEW MONTHS LATER…

Vernon had known it was a bad idea to drive north to Alaska. Who in their right mind would do such a thing? But Peter hadn't shut up, raving about the idea for months. He'd barely listened when Vernon had told him to wait until the snow had had a chance to thaw. And that said nothing about the reception they likely had waiting for them.

But none of that was on Vernon's mind right now as he screamed at Gunter to floor it, another round of bullets pinging against the side of the beat-up car they were in. Gunter was a good driver, but they'd been up for going on two entire days, half the tires of the car were shot, and the gravel, interspersed with holes filled with mud, didn't make for easy going. It had been over an hour since they'd last seen any of the other cars. Vernon didn't want to consider it, but they were likely all dead.

Gunter wrenched the wheel hard as he sent the car careening around yet another bend in the road, the left rear wheel losing traction and spinning them into more of a whirl than expected. For a moment, he was convinced that they would end up in the gorge below the cliff, but Gunter somehow managed to regain control of the car again and floored it. The decline was a steep one, and to Vernon it felt more like they were sliding down in an avalanche of mud and small rocks than going down the road. There were trees everywhere, interspersed with streams and boulders. Maybe they should leave the car and try to get lost in there somewhere?

The next shots biting into the chassis of the car convinced him otherwise. Gunter kept cursing to himself as he tried to get the car to go faster. They more flew than drove over a bump in the road, the suspension screaming as they came down hard on the other side. The rear broke away again, spinning the car sideways, giving Vernon a better view of their pursuers than he'd ever wanted to get. Three cars were left, but he could hear more coming in the distance. And all for what? The sacks of grain and seeds they were carrying were hardly worth anything. He'd even told Peter that, saying it was more insult than bribe. But Peter had insisted that it was the perfect ticket to get them into the camp, at least to get a look around while they unloaded. Now they'd die over what people would trade you for a TV and two generators. Fucking asshole.

The car stalled, and that was when Vernon knew that it was over. Gunter kept trying to get it started, but after three failures it was obvious—they had run out of juice. That's what you get for driving through the night in the fucking Canadian forests!

"We need to leave," Vernon shouted, grabbing his kit and a rifle. Maybe the bandits would be happy with the car and leave two assholes running into the woods alone.

"You're insane!" Gunter muttered, but abandoned his undertaking in favor of grabbing his own pack from the back. "Gimme five seconds, and we're out of here."

Because he didn't want to look at the bandit cars chasing down the mountainside now, he stared into the deep greens and browns of the forest—and drew up short when his attention snagged on something. Had that been a flash of red in the underbrush? Probably just his imagination. Or what was left of some unlucky bastard's gear who had been mauled by a bear ten feet away from the road. A million bears could be hiding in that wood, and he wouldn't be the wiser until he was about to be eaten. Fucking perfect!

Just as Vernon scrambled out of the car and hitched his backpack high, he again saw something, behind a tree—and this time he was damn sure that it was a pair of eyes, bright blue, staring out of a face streaked with camouflage paint. Fucking perfect! So either the bandits shot them, some weird forest cannibals ate them, or the bears got them.

He heard the bandits screech to a halt behind their car, shots chewing into a tree right next to him. Forgetting all about cursing the world, Vernon ran, his only concern not to fall to make it any easier on any of the predators than he had to.

A howl rose in the distance. Perfect—why not add wolves to the mix as well? A second answered, from much closer, and then several more, until Vernon realized: those weren't ordinary wolves. At least not the kind of wolves he'd been dealing with since his early childhood on the farm in Montana. Sure, it was still spring here, with the odd patches of snow compacted in hollows, but there must have been food aplenty for them everywhere. Either they were rabid—or they weren't wolves at all.

Shots followed him and Gunter, almost at a casual pace—until that changed, too. He heard shouting, followed by frantic firing, then a single ear-piercing scream—and then nothing. Gunter skidded to a halt next to him, turning around to look, but Vernon kept going, ignoring the branches lashing at his face and body, on and on—until he broke out of the woods and onto a small clearing, where three cars were waiting for him, a single armed woman standing guard.

At first, all he could do was stare. The woman regarded him calmly, her rifle lowered but she clearly knew how to use it. He was afraid she'd have those same eerie blue eyes as well, but of course hers were a dark brown, intense but friendly. "Hello, stranger," she called out in a clear voice.

He found himself nodding, unsure what else to do. "Are you out here alone?" he asked.

She gave him a look that told him she'd expected better. "And how would I have driven three cars on my own?" she joked. "I'm here with my friends. They will be back any minute now."

Vernon startled at a squawk, but it was only her radio going off. She listened to words that were too low for him to catch, then told whoever was on the other end that she'd found him. Fear gripped his heart anew, but the woman was quick to smile. "They found your friend," she told him. "He's back at your car."

"We ran out of battery," Vernon mumbled. "And the bandits—"

"They've been taken care of," the woman assured him, signaling him to join her at the car closest to her. "Why don't you hitch a ride with me?" He felt he had no other choice, even though gratitude to still be alive made it easy to follow along. "I'm Sonia, by the way," she told him as she eased the car back onto the road.

"Vernon Grant," he quickly replied when the silence became too long. "Have you maybe found my brother Peter?"

"He should be back with us at the camp," she offered—and that was all the answers he got.

The drive was longer than he expected, a good hour until they reached a larger clearing around what one of the dilapidated signs in the woods stated had been a logging camp. He could see that, but there were a lot more buildings now, an entire town having sprung up. He knew what this place was—the town that Peter had wanted to visit. An outpost, they called it, although he had no idea whether there were others like it. They had to drive through sturdy defenses after several rows of trenches and barb-wire fences, and even a moat. Vernon wondered what they thought they needed all those for. He doubted there were many zombies roaming the near-arctic forests.

Sonia dropped him off inside the gate and told him to wait there. A few minutes later, five cars followed—among them his and Gunter's, being towed by a large truck. The other three he thought were those of the bandits. There was blood on some of the shot windows. He quickly averted his eyes. The truck halted, and Gunter came scrambling out the passenger side, his eyes huge with wonder but also a little fear. The cars drove deeper into the settlement before Vernon got a good look at the drivers. He had an inkling what he would see if he looked into their faces.

He and Gunter quickly stepped aside when two more trucks followed, the heavy tarps covering their beds bulging with what was stashed underneath. They both stopped at two squat buildings, standing side by side, not far from the gates. People came out to help unload the cargo. Three deer and a moose were quickly brought down steps into the cellar of the warehouse—as close to a natural freezer as it got these days, Vernon guessed. The cargo of the second truck was unloaded by the drivers themselves, the bundles, wrapped in blankets, not something Vernon wanted to investigate further. They disappeared into the cellar of the other warehouse. Because it was easier to focus on the people, that's what he did. His eyes kept snagging to the tall, blond man with the wind-beaten hair and grizzled beard. Why, he couldn't say, until he realized what made his beard look distinctly red—blood. Vernon was sure that he hadn't made a sound of recognition or dread, but in that exact moment the man halted and stared straight at him, those bright blue eyes promising death and violence. Vernon blinked, and a moment later, the man was gone. Likely to do whatever tasks needed to be done since it was impossible that he could have simply disappeared like a specter. He watched the other hunters—because that's what they were—return from the cellar, one by one. Of course he couldn't see clearly at the distance, but he was certain all of them had those eerie blue eyes. It made sense on the tall man, or on the woman he saw following him, her red hair in a braid appearing when she pulled off a black cap. It looked wrong on the burly black guy who came last, laughing loudly at a joke someone must have cracked. Yet when he paused for a moment and looked toward Vernon and Gunter, those eyes were just as hard and cold as the others'.

"Welcome to our little town here," a friendly female voice said right next to him, making Vernon jump. As he turned, he found a young woman standing there, not much shorter than him. She also had blue eyes, but hers were a natural blue; normal. He was about to relax but then a small whirlwind of a child came running toward her, screeching, and the woman turned to pick her up and swing her around before sending her toward the hunters—and just as the girl gargled with glee, he saw her eyes, and they were that same unnatural blue as well.

Of course he'd heard the stories, but he'd always known they must be nonsense. Now he wasn't so sure anymore. Glancing at Gunter, he realized his friend was unconcerned. Maybe he hadn't noticed.

Vernon couldn't help but stare back at that second warehouse. No, he hadn't made that up, he was sure of it.

When he looked back to the woman, he saw her watching him, and while she seemed amused, he could tell that the look she gave him was a warning. Not that he needed one, for sure. He wasn't stupid. After all, they had let him ride in the car, rather than dead on the bed of that truck.

"You're part of Peter's group?" the woman asked.

Vernon was quick to nod, giving their names. She nodded as she crossed something out on the notepad she was carrying. "Good. You're the last of your group," she observed, then turned somber. "I'm sorry that Larry and Mos didn't make it. We were able to recover their bodies. They are over there in the chapel"—she pointed at a squat building set aside from the others. "We'll help you bury them, if you'd like. Or erect a funeral pyre. I'm so sorry for your loss. If we'd known about the bandits earlier, we would have sent a party south sooner." A smile started playing around her lips. "You should have called ahead."

Gunter blinked. "But your town has no permanent transponder code."

"Exactly," she offered. "If you will please follow me? I'll show you to the guest barracks where the rest of your people are staying. I presume you'll want to head to the town by the coast next? That's what your brother said was your destination."

Vernon was ready to blow that bull but then thought better of it. "Yes. We have a contract for some fur deliveries," he prattled on. "There should be some grain in the cars. And seeds, if you want them? As a thank you for rescuing us."

"That won't be necessary," the woman explained. "But thank you for the offer. I'll check with our greenhouse, but I think we have everything we need for the coming year." Her smile turned wry. "We don't really need many vegetables up here. Lots of hunters, eating lots of meat, you see?"

Oh, did he ever, and he had a certain feeling that she was laughing at him, inside. "Yeah," he muttered.

They were halfway across the square when he heard a shout coming from somewhere behind them. When he searched for where it might have come from, he saw a woman with a fussy baby in her arms step out of one of the houses. Her voice was sharp and held a tone of annoyance as she called, "Lewis, get your lazy ass over here! I don't have all day to look after your spawn!" Yet, the way she looked down at the little bundle, securely swaddled in her arms, it was full of love and adoration.

The red-haired woman from before came hurrying out from behind the cars, as soon as she was out in the open slowing down to a brisk walk, as if she was trying hard to pretend she hadn't been running at first. She passed by Vernon with only a few feet between them. When she glanced at him and winked, he realized that it must have been her he'd seen in the woods, the flash of red not his imagination but her hair disappearing underneath her cap. He was sure that she could tell, a smirk on her lips just as she faced back forward. It was only as she took the baby out of the other woman's arms, cooing to the bundle, that he realized that her dark jacket and pants were sitting rather tightly on her—a trim body, no question, but still soft in places after giving birth not too long ago. He had no idea how old that child was, but it couldn't have been older than a few weeks. As to underline his guess, he heard her continue to talk to the baby, still cooing, but the words not quite that appropriate for a child. "Such a little trooper you already are! Being all well-behaved and silent. And so intent on staying an only child, not giving your Mommy and Daddy a moment alone the second you realize you can monopolize my tits again!"

On second thought, maybe he should stop listening in.

That turned into a "definitely" when he caught the blond-haired brute glaring at him as he walked past them and over to the women, the group disappearing back into the house. That was one dude he definitely didn't want to antagonize.

The unease he felt lessened when he saw the others waiting for them in the barracks. Peter was over the moon with excitement, of course, barely reacting to Vernon giving him an update on how they had survived. "This is so freaking cool, man," his brother muttered, standing by a window and glancing outside. "Did you see them take down the bandits? They didn't even carry any guns! It was all 'run them down, pounce on them, slash their throats, or cave in their skulls'! Man, this was so worth it."

Vernon couldn't suppress a shudder. What kind of people would do that?

This kind, of course. He'd heard the stories—of how they'd been the first to organize after the undead turned the world into one endless wasteland. How they had risen up to fight for their freedom when civil war had been about to break out. Vernon and Peter had seen very little of that, still busy keeping their livestock safe and bringing in two harvests by hand, enough to feed their families and then some. They'd done the same for the next two years as well, what little contact they had with traders bringing messages of worsening conditions—bandits, raiders, crazy cannibals on the roads, getting worse and worse with each year…

Until last summer, when it had suddenly stopped, or so the word spread. And when this spring there had been the first official census after the end of the world, Peter had been all over himself, needing to find out what had happened to the heroes that had saved what was left. Their sister had been sure that it was all propaganda—just like the supposed civil war and unrest that followed. But their homestead was running out of everyday things, and a trader group had been happy to hand over a few contracts they'd picked up, one of them about getting furs from the north.

Vernon couldn't wait to be back with his nieces and nephews. Whatever these people did up here, it was none of his business. From what he could tell, their exodus must have been by choice. Good for them, if it was this that they wanted—to be on their own up here where nobody else wanted to settle except for the people who had been living off the land for generations. And he was damn glad they'd kept the bandits from killing him and his brother. It was none of his business how they'd gone about it, or what they did with the corpses. But he very much hoped that was moose or deer in the stew that he got served before they got ready to reach the town the next day.

He remained silent throughout the long hours of the drive and was glad when they reached their final destination. They'd been asked to take a few boxes from the camp to the town, and he was happy to be rid of them. The townspeople were delighted about the early delivery, and Vernon felt bad when he saw that the boxes were full of wool, pelts, and eggs.

"They are good folks, you know?" one of the women who was counting eggs and distributing them told him with a twinkle in her eye. "Not the kind on whose bad side you want to end up on, but they are quite handy to have around. We haven't had a single bear or wolf attack all winter long, after losing a handful of people every winter before that. And I've heard they are planning on building a few more outposts, so they can migrate with the herds, if need be." She laughed briefly and made a throw-away gesture. "Don't mind an old woman. I know you southerners don't understand why we love to live up here, where life is harsh, hard, and lonely. They get it, and they love it just as we do. Go back to your warm, green fields, country boy. This life up here is not for you."

Vernon couldn't have agreed more.

THE END

Acknowledgements

My editor, Marti, and my trusty beta readers, deserve a round of applause. You are the best! Couldn't do this without you.

My amazing readers, thank you so much for reading this series. To say that it changed my life is an understatement. I started writing the first book—Incubation—in 2013, and when I published it in August 2015, I never, not in a million years, would have dared dream that this would become a twelve-book series loved by thousands of readers all over the world. The series also made my dream come true of being a full-time writer. If I'll have my way, I'll never go back to a traditional day job—and you made this possible. I can't express how much that means to me. And, good news! It's great for you as well since it allows me to continue to write books that (hopefully) tear out your heart and eat it. Ah, that pun never gets old.

I won't lie. Finishing a series is always hard. I've been living with these characters for half a decade now, day in, day out. To say I felt lost when I finished writing the first draft of the book in September 2019 and suddenly Bree's voice was gone from my head from one day to the next, is an understatement. I've been living in her head and skin for far too long to simply shake off that loss within a week, or even a month. If you were wondering why there's no epilogue from her point of view, the explanation is simple: she's done telling me her story, and I won't get another word from her. There's a very good chance that Nate still has something to say and you might get one more short story set after the end of the last book, but that's it. It's bittersweet for me, too. I love this world and its characters, and I hate to let them ride off into the sunset. But at the same time I am happy I could give them this ending as it is. For me, it's the perfect ending for them. I hope you agree.

And there are also the other Green Fields short stories on Patreon, and some of them soon coming to Amazon. I still have more of them to write, so if you're not ready to say goodbye, there's no need to do so quite yet!

All this begs the question, what is next? More end-of-the-world goodness, hurrah! In the very end of the editing stage of GF#12: Annihilation, I woke up, and the vast emptiness in my mind, left by Bree's silence, was suddenly starting to fill up once more. New characters, new world, new zombies, new apocalypse! I can't tell you much about it yet, except that I am very excited, and I've already started writing on the first book. It's very different than the Green Fields series, but it's just as raw and gritty where it counts. I hope I'll see you again in 2020 when the first books of this insane ride come out!

Until then, thank you again for being the best audience imaginable, and don't let the zombies bite you!

About the Author

Adrienne Lecter has a background in Biochemistry and Molecular Biology, loves ranting at inaccuracies in movies, and spends increasingly more time on the shooting range. She lives with the man and two cats of her life in Vienna, and is working on the next post-apocalyptic books.

You can sign up for Adrienne's newsletter to never miss a release and be the first to know what other shenanigans she gets up to: http://www.adriennelecter.com

Thank you

Hey, you! Yes, you, who just spent a helluva lot of time reading this book! You just made my day! Thanks!

Want to be notified of new releases, giveaways and updates? Sign up for my newsletter:
www.adriennelecter.com

If you enjoyed reading the book and have a moment to spare, I would really appreciate a short, honest review on the site you purchased it from and on goodreads. Reviews make a huge difference in helping new readers find the series.

Or if you'd like to drop me a note, or chat a but, feel free to email me or hit me up on social media. I'll try to respond as quickly as possible! If you'd like to report an error or wrong detail, I've set up a separate space on my website for that, too.

Email: adrienne@adriennelecter.com
Website: adriennelecter.com
Twitter: @adriennelecter
Facebook: facebook.com/adriennelecter

Books published

Green Fields
#1: Incubation
#2: Outbreak
#3: Escalation
#4: Extinction
#5: Resurgence
#6: Unity
#7: Affliction
#8: Catharsis
#9: Exodus
#10: Uprising
#11: Retribution
#12: Annihilation

Beyond Green Fields
short story collections
Omnibus #1
Ombinus #2

World of Anthrax
new series coming 2022

Made in United States
North Haven, CT
22 July 2023

39384156R00226